WORLD AT WAR

Book 3 in The Curtain Series

DAVID T. MADDOX

Made for Grace Publishing
P.O. Box 1775 Issaquah, WA 98027

World at War (Book 3 in *The Curtain* Series)

Copyright © 2018 by David T. Maddox. All rights reserved.

Designed by DeeDee Heathman

Scripture taken from the New American Standard Bible, © 1960, 1963, 1968, 1971, 1972, 1973, 1975, 1977 by the Lockman Foundation. Used by permission.

This novel is a work of fiction. Names, characters, places, and incidents either are a product of the author's imagination or are used fictitiously. Any resemblance to actual events, locales, organizations, or persons, living or dead, is entirely coincidental and beyond the intent of either the author or publisher.

Library of Congress Cataloging-in-Publication data Maddox, David T., date,
World at War / David T. Maddox.
p. cm.

ISBN-13: 978-1-64146-367-6 (pbk.)
ISBN: 978-1-64146-371-3 (eBook)
LCCN: 2018961959

To contact the publisher please email service@MadeforSuccess.net
or call +1 425 657 0300.

Made for Grace Publishing is an imprint of Made for Success, inc.

Printed in the United States of America

DEDICATION

THE CURTAIN IS dedicated to four people who have most influenced my life and ministry over these many decades. There have obviously been many others that God has used, but these people have changed my life and I want to acknowledge them and affirm how God has used them.

RICHARD OWEN ROBERTS—In my life Mr. Roberts has been like "the Bookseller" in this story—the one who opened God's word and revealed hidden truth. He taught me about revival and awakening and showed me what it means to walk without compromise at a high cost.

DR. HENRY BLACKABY—Henry (as he prefers to be called) opened my eyes to what it means to walk intimately with the Lord—to hear Him speak, to discern what He has said, to see Him working around me. He has encouraged me in the way of obedience, made me aware of the cost of my obedience to those I love, and so much more.

KYLE & LAURA MARTIN—This couple opened my eyes to what we are called to in the Great Commission, what it means to put no limits on the Holy Spirit, the importance of the Jewish people in end times, what it means to be prepared for the return of Jesus, what it means to walk in faith in total dependence on God, and so much more. Time to Revive, the ministry they began, is the only revival ministry I have encountered that David T. Maddox doesn't' just study revival or pray for revival, but actively seeks to gather churches together in revival. I have been privileged to be a small part of this ministry for the last five years. Here God is mightily at work.

JANET WHITEHEAD MADDOX—My bride, my completion, the one God uses to keep my focus and to confront me when I get off the path.

No man was ever more blessed than I have been in sharing my life with her, our kids and grandkids—sharing our relationship with God. To minister together with the same heart has been the joy of my life.

ACKNOWLEDGMENTS

WRITING A BOOK is a long journey which for me began in 2007 when the Lord inspired me to try and take the truth of Scripture about the invisible conflict that goes on around us and picture it in such a way that people could have a better understanding of this reality which affects their daily life. My attempt has in some cases been futile, but hopefully what is shared within the pages of the book is Biblically accurate and will open eyes to help answer the why questions for much of what we face today.

Many people have encouraged and helped me along the way. In 2007, Matt and Kim Clark read each chapter as the book progressed giving me valuable input and perspective as the story and characters developed. As a trial lawyer, I was used to telling stories and being sure that the stories matched the evidence, but as this book continued the characters took over the story and drove it in surprising directions. Later others including Mel Sauder and Jerry Jagoda would read revisions, there were seven in all, and similarly gave input and encouragement.

For me, the "hero" in this process has been my editor, Catherine Barrack whose insight and discernment was invaluable. Her maturity as a Believer enabled her to ask the right questions to be sure that the story did not go beyond what was Biblically possible as have others who attempted to write similar stories. Her skill and sensitivity gave new life to some of the characters at critical points in the story and gave me insight that only a third person reading the story can give. It is a much-improved story because of her partnership in the process.

Special thanks must also go to Buzz Leonard, who introduced me to Bryan Heathman and Made for Success Publishing. They quickly understood what I am trying to do and have been helpful at each stage of the process working patiently with a first-time author.

Ultimate thanks go to the Lord, who despite me having stage four cancer has enabled me to finish the book in between this past year of chemo treatments. I am hopeful that the book will bless the reader even as writing it has blessed and taught me. If it does bless you, please share it with others.

INTRODUCTION

"We look not to the things that are seen but to the things that are unseen. For the things that are seen are transient, but the things that are unseen are eternal."
—2 Corinthians 4:18

"WHY ME?" OR "why not me?" are questions which seem to pervade life for all of us. Much of what we face at times seems unfair and totally beyond our control. Often our best efforts are not enough, or we succeed when we know we should have failed. Is there some purpose at work in our lives beyond mere chance? Could there be something beyond our control, something of which we may be completely unaware that influences the decisions we make and arranges the circumstances we face? If there were, that would provide the answer to much that cannot be explained in our lives.

The Bible speaks of parallel worlds—one visible, the other invisible. They are said to exist separately, but not independently. We are told that in our lifetime we occupy the physical world, the place of flesh and blood. The other world is described as being spiritual and is inhabited by eternal beings invisible to us who are in constant conflict over control of the physical world and those who live there. The frightening thing for us who live in the physical world is that if the Bible is true, the invisible can influence us and the events that affect our lives without us even being aware of their activities. When we die, we leave the physical world and occupy our place in the spiritual world, having become one of the invisible. The answer to the question "what happens then" is beyond the subject of this book, although our story will picture some who make the transfer from one world to the next. For them, the answer will be obvious, as will the reason for their future placement.

The author asks that as you read this book, you be willing to assume that the Bible is true and that what it says about the visible and invisible is, in fact, the reality in which we live. You are invited to consider what you would see if the curtain which separates the visible from the invisible were suddenly opened, revealing the conflict, tactics and methods of the opposing forces—and how they actually impact your life.

The reader is cautioned that although this is a work of fiction, it often crosses the line to truth if what the Bible teaches is true—not in personalities or in the events described, but in how those events would be viewed if we could actually see everything that happened as it happened in both the visible and invisible worlds simultaneously. For those willing to search for the truth about what really affects their life, this book will be an adventure.

As a reader, you will also no doubt find descriptions that may be personal as your eyes are opened to the forces said to be daily contesting over you. It is the author's hope that the events detailed herein, and the characters' response to those events, will help you to better understand the biblical view of the reality of the world in which we live, so that if it is true, you can live in response to what is and not be a victim of what it only seems to be.

Draw your own conclusions, but be open-minded to the reality of the invisible. It unquestionably exists and impacts everything we do.

CHAPTER 1

The Fight for Friday

Wednesday, February 13—MD minus 26 days

EVERYTHING ACCELERATED IN the visible and invisible worlds as America careened toward the fast approaching MD date. Powers wrestled over events they could see coming, from the planning for the Thursday attack on Kingdom Daycare to MD now scheduled for March 11th. As important as these events would be, the only day of true significance was Friday when America and Americans would be required to consciously choose whose side they were on. It was D-Day, "Decision Day," and America's future depended on those decisions. Unfortunately, few truly understood what was at stake.

Some had already decided. The president had made his choice and issued the call for America to follow him in prayer and humbly choose God. The Senate majority leadership had made their decision; they would ignore the president's call and continue with business as usual. For them, religion was a "private matter" that should not interfere with their politics. At that moment in history, they saw what they perceived to be a vulnerable president and were circling in for the kill.

Businesses had to decide whether they would allow their employees a day off on Friday—the day for national prayer. Workers had to determine what they were willing to do and at what cost. Churches had to decide whether they wanted to have services on Friday where people were to gather and confess sins. The word "sin" had become the most unpopular word in modern American Christianity. Who could lead such a service since those who called themselves Christians were not in agreement on what was sin? But then again, many of them weren't born again, so how could they know? Those without the guidance of the light inside argued over what was acceptable, ignoring what the Bible called sin. For them, confession would be impossible because they didn't consider their conduct to be wrong.

The battle in the invisible world centered in America, for the forces of darkness recognized the opportunity to turn America further away from God. The hoard of Keepers and Tempters were released in all directions in an attempt to influence every person in America to reject the president's call as unimportant and inconvenient. He was pictured as a "good man" who was becoming a little fanatical about his religion. After all, hadn't the so-called leader of the enemy offered to meet and discuss peace? There was really no need to call out to God to help America. He was obviously already helping.

Likewise, Guardians and Providers acted to draw every person in America to join with the president, or at least make a reasonable choice whether to stand before the Lord with some understanding of its importance. The battle raged person by person; dividing homes, families, and friends. It was like oil and water as the two views found no place to compromise. Either it was important to stand before God and seek forgiveness for offenses to God, or it was neither important nor necessary. There was no middle ground.

Turning to Barnabas as they had gathered over Williams with others of the forces of light, Lucius observed, "This is one of those moments of choice which Jesus warned would come when He walked the earth. Do you remember?"

"Yes," Barnabas answered, "these people—although made in His image—have never really understood the reality of choice. They have fallen for the Dark Master's deception that Jesus was a man of tolerance, peace, and love and thus they should expect to be able to live as they wish in complete harmony with others who live as they wish, all under the blessing of God. And when they die, so the fable goes, they will all go to 'a better place.'

"They think they don't have to make a choice; that God accepts them where they are and as they are. I have difficulty understanding how they can be so foolish. God would not be God if that were true. The people would be God because they could dictate what was is right and wrong."

"There is nothing worse than the result of people not reading the Bible," Lucius answered. "The deception and half-truths are more dangerous than the lies. The teachings of Jesus are taken out of context, and thus He is pictured falsely. Jesus didn't call Himself a man of peace, although in Him is peace. What He actually said was that He was God[1] and therefore you must choose who you will follow and obey. He warned that the wrong choice would bring conflict into every part of the life of those who made the wrong choice. He said:

Do not suppose that I have come to bring peace to the earth. I did not come to bring peace but a sword. For I have come to turn a man against his father, a daughter against her mother, a daughter-in-law against her mother-in-law—a man's enemies will be the members of his own household.[2]

"For centuries, nations and societies have sought to hide the sword—the division of choice—in secrecy and increasingly in the modern idea of tolerance and compromise, to maintain 'peace and unity' at any price," Lucius continued soberly. "It is sad what that deception has produced as God's word is ignored and people are encouraged to live their lives in direct rebellion to God's teachings. They have had their way these past decades, but the choice now hangs over America, and this time they will not escape making that choice."

Below the celestial gathering in the city proper, a small group met in Chaplain Forrest's office. It was the chaplain, Pastor Wilson, Pastor Scribes, the Bookseller, and Paul Phillips. As they prayed together, the light within each of them burned brightly as the Holy Spirit sought to unite them with the will of the Father. Their eyes had been opened to the significance of Friday's call, and they sought God's wisdom to know what they were to do in order to share what they had been shown.

This little band had not been spared the Dark Master's attacks. God had placed limits, but within those limits, every possible means had been used by the forces of darkness to discourage, tempt, divide, and deceive. The Bookseller had been approached by other networks and publishing companies that offered him a quick fortune for a signature that would have made him their exclusive property and enabled them to control his access to the world stage. The forces of darkness had orchestrated this effort, and they followed up by flooding his mind with the deception of all "the good" that could be accomplished for God's service with the millions he was being offered. Fortunately for America, the Bookseller responded even as Jesus did when tempted by Satan and rejected the lie as a lie.[3]

"Mr. White," Pastor Wilson spoke quietly when there was a pause in their prayers. "I sense that God wants to use you further to open people's eyes to the importance of Friday and to draw people to Him. We have this website that is available worldwide and through which God has been working amazingly.[4] We have reports from numerous nations that when believers go to this website, they have been able to understand it even though it's not in their own language. God is working mightily! Perhaps posting a message from you is what God would have us do. After all, from the first day, you understood that the issue is for believers to decide. The question is whether they will return to the Lord so that He may bless and protect America. He has made communication with believers possible through this website, and has called you to be His spokesman."

"Why me?" the Bookseller asked, sincerely humbled, much like Moses.[5] "I am nothing, just an old man who has struggled with his faith at times just like other people. I have no great following, and for the most part, I have been rejected throughout my ministry. There are so many others who appear much more capable than I to be out-front calling the people back to the Lord. No one on earth wants to be used by God more than me, but I am not special."

"That is true," Pastor Scribes observed, "it is true for all of us, but the Lord does not look on a man as we do. God looks at the heart, and as He took David as a simple shepherd from the hills of Judea to become the great king,[6] He has obviously called you. The key is for you to keep the heart of David. Remember what God said about David's heart? 'I have found David son of Jesse a man after My own heart; he will do everything I want him to do.'[7] He knows your heart, and thus He can and will use you.

"I agree that God wants us to put something out on the website. Let me pray, and then I will write. Perhaps God will provide me another opportunity on ITN to speak to the nation before Friday. I sense that is a possibility. Whatever He wants."

"Then call them, Mr. White. They have made it very clear that they would be glad to have you on again anytime," Paul said excitedly.

"No, no. It is not for me to seek an opportunity to speak," the Bookseller responded quickly. "That is God's providence. If he wants me to have that opportunity, He will provide it. My place is to be ready to speak what He gives me to say boldly if He gives me the opportunity."

"I am confused by how God works and how I am to work for Him," Paul answered.

"Good, welcome to the crowd," Chaplain Forrest answered. "I am fifty-two years old, and I don't know either. He acts as He will simply because He is God and we are not."

"Listen, Paul, often the most active place for us is not in doing something, but in waiting for God to show us what He would have us do and how He wants it done. His work is too important to simply do something that seems logical or reasonable based on our knowledge and experience. God is not limited by logic, reason or our experience, and what we may do 'for Him' because it seems right to us could mean we miss what He really wants us to do. We could actually be in rebellion against God while thinking we were doing something for Him. That verse where Jesus says, 'My sheep listen to My voice; I know them, and they follow Me'[8] means just what it says. Listen, and then follow. We never lead in any way other than by following Him."

"Wow," Paul responded, "that is a head full. I have so much to learn."

The Game Begins

In Washington, the majority party reacted with glee when they heard the newly broadcast tape recording of the Sheik acknowledging their acceptance of his invitation to meet and discuss the causes of hate. Former President Cox was instructed to check into the Cham Palace Hotel in Damascus,

Syria, by March 7th, at which time he would be given instructions on the location of the meeting. Their apparent good fortune encouraged the majority party to step up their hearings on the amendment to the Hate Crimes Act and the investigation of the administration's interference with Harkins College. Only one fly in the ointment appeared. The Together Tomorrow crowd was insistent that the open roads proposal had to be effective by March 7th or they were through funding campaign activities.

"I don't get those folks," Senate Majority Leader Howard said, expressing his frustration. "Who really gives a flip about trucks coming into and out of Mexico and Canada? Why does it have to be by March 7th? If these people didn't have real money, I'd investigate them."

"Yes, but they do have real money, and a lot of it has ended up in this party's coffers," Chairman Crow responded. "We need their money, so they get to make the rules. That's politics in America."

"Fine, call the secretary of transportation and see if he is prepared to issue regulations that would effectively open the roads on March 7th," the majority leader agreed reluctantly. "I am not sure it is 100% legal, but who cares if it works. We would never be able to accomplish that legislatively. We cannot get a bill passed in time, and if we did, it would only get vetoed. He can go public on the 7th after the trucks are rolling, and then it will be hard for the president to undo that which is already done. Even if he does, we will have demonstrated our willingness to comply, and his actions would prove we need the cash to get the White House and a super majority in Congress. If they are serious about their agenda, the cash will flow."

"Life is sure going to be different when that boy in the president's office has to retire. No more vetoes and no more of this religion crammed down everybody's throats."

"It can't come soon enough," Crow agreed, "but we have to defeat his protégé, this vice president."

"That should be no problem since he has publicly aligned himself with religious excess and against peace," Howard replied.

Elsewhere in Washington, Baqir Dawood arrived from Saudi Arabia with the envelope for Ahmad Habid from the Sheik. He had a flight already set up to take him to Phoenix, where he would arrive Thursday afternoon. For now, he had a few days to enjoy Washington in all its glory in the final days before MD.

The Search for Targets and Weapons Continues

Officially, Washington was a hub of activity as the Joint Chiefs, the Survival Commission, Senator Lieberman, Attorney General Rodriquez, David Barnes, Darrell Reed, Kayla Walker and others raced to find answers and prepare a response to the MD threat. It was non-stop activity after Darrell Reed's interpretation of the meaning of the video message was heard. The window for preemptive action was rapidly closing. Time was short.

"Do you know how many refineries, power plants, dams and water and electric systems there are in the United States?" General Hedge asked with great frustration.

"How are we to know the specific targets? We can't defend them all."

"There are over 75,000 reservoirs and dams in the United States alone," Barnes answered.

"Someone has been doing their research," Tom Knight commented.

"I have, and I've learned a lot about the possible target list the Joint Chiefs have suggested," Barnes continued. "I agree it is an impossible job without more intelligence on specific targets."

"Don't lose your focus," the president interrupted. "Obviously, we prepare first for the largest and most critical of the possible targets, and we must have a national strategy. If their goal is to cripple the country, they have to hit us everywhere. Divide the country into manageable sections and prepare for the most damaging targets in each."

"What about the weapons? How are they going to do that much damage?"

"I got a report this morning from Darrell Reed on the truck issue," Barnes began again. "The terrorist training camp was an oil terminal operation; they were training on gasoline delivery trucks. I know from a source that some of the many calls to report suspicious activities involve large trucks being used to transport people throughout the US who have gotten across the Mexican border. Something is definitely going on with the trucks, and I am sure that is not all. Lest we forget, gasoline explosions and fires brought down the World Trade Center and also caused significant damage to the Pentagon. One cup of gasoline has the explosive power of two sticks of dynamite, and then it burns. Trucks, I believe, are one of the weapons."

"You could be right," General Hedge agreed. "We have been testing that possibility and the capacity of fuel trucks to do substantial damage if positioned properly. But how could they get that many trucks filled with gasoline, and what kind of explosive mechanism could be used for maximum effectiveness?"

"I don't care how you divide this up," the president said, "but I want answers to those questions and a way to protect the major possible targets from a gasoline bomb—whether driven over land or launched from the air." Pausing in frustration, he said, "Look, we have to be missing something here. These people cannot possibly hijack enough aircraft and gasoline delivery trucks to do this. They have to have access to the vehicles and airplanes, but how? Also, have you looked into the ammonia bombs like the one that brought down the federal building in Oklahoma City?"

"Mr. President, we are looking at everything," General Hedge assured him. "Can we have a minute to discuss troop deployments here and abroad? We have to reposition our forces to address what may happen here and in the Middle East on MD."

"Absolutely, General," the president said. "We want maximum flexibility to deal with the danger here and in the Middle East."

"Eric, you need to be at this meeting to coordinate with Israel. The vice president will be called in when we have our plan in place."

"Mr. President, before you leave, I want you to know that we have moved quickly to impanel a grand jury to investigate the Harkins student or faculty terrorist. Subpoenas have been issued. We have also noticed the deposition of Harkins' president on an emergency basis for tomorrow, and have issued subpoenas for the records they will not give us. These records may disclose not only the identity of the J-14 leader but perhaps the whole gang if the plot really was hatched at Harkins.

"One more thing, we have found some unusual business activities in the US trucking and aircraft industry as well as in Mexico. We may be onto something about how they will get the weapons of choice without having to hijack them."

"Great, everyone, stay with it," the president said excitedly. "We have to find out before they can strike."

"General, Eric, let's retire to my office and discuss troop redeployment. After we are through, I would like a little time with you two," he said, pointing at Tom Knight and David Barnes. Then he rose and excused himself for the next meeting.

Varvel Returns to Williams

Back in Williams on Wednesday, Carl Varvel was again on the move looking for the Bookseller. He had another message from Iran, and as he walked to the warehouse, he still wondered what this could possibly have to do with the National Security of the United States.

Opening the envelope, the Bookseller's whole countenance changed. He understood immediately what was meant by the message from the Iranian brothers. "Margaret, come here and look at this," he said, walking into his study away from the ears and eyes of the waiting Varvel.

"Every message is more intense and more direct. Whether this threat is against America, clearly it is increasing in urgency, and the battle for the hearts and minds of the people is where it will be won. There has never been a comparable period in our lifetime where the spiritual issue has so clearly been drawn. These messages from the Iranian brothers seem to affirm what God has been showing so directly that it almost appears to be from the hand of God Himself."

"I think, you're right, Samuel. This note seems to be clear guidance from God," Margaret said as she read again:

> *Brother, the days are now much shorter, and God's protection is essential to prevent disaster and open eyes to deception. Don't believe what you see. Ezekiel 3:17, Jeremiah 8:11, 15.*

"When I read this, I almost want to turn off all the news channels and throw away the newspaper," the Bookseller responded.

"Don't be silly," she answered tenderly but forcefully as only a wife can. "You must hear and read what the public is hearing and reading to know how to pray and how God would have you respond when He gives you the opportunity to speak. How can you identify the deception if you hide in a cave? Clearly, this message refers to the false video offer of peace which some have already foolishly embraced, and the verses are instructions to you. Please don't start the 'why me' stuff. It is you because God has called you."

"I surrender to you and to God," he responded. "The verses are clear. I am accountable to God as a watchman appointed to warn the people, and I am not to be out there like others saying 'Peace, peace,' when there is no peace.

"The one that really troubles me is that last one, Jeremiah 8:15." He read, "'We hoped for peace but no good has come, for a time of healing but there was only terror.' Hope is not going to get us through this time. God will protect us, or we are finished just like biblical Israel and Judah. Whose side is America on? That remains the question."

Taking the paper, the Bookseller paused to pray as he prepared his response for return delivery to the unknown brothers in Iran. He marveled at how God used them to encourage him and hoped that the day would come when he would meet them in this life.

The note read:

My dear brothers, please pray as Epaphras in Colossians 4:12 that I be as the man described in Jeremiah 23:22.

Once again, Carl Varvel was off for the return trip to Iran.

Preparations for the Morrow

In the physical world, those under the influence of the competing powers moved for good or ill accordingly. What was seen in the Bookseller and others with the light inside was contested by the actions of those whose minds were directed by Keepers for the forces of darkness. From Cambridge, Massachusetts and major US cities, the leadership coordinators for MD made their way to Phoenix, Arizona. They traveled under the cover of the American Teachers Society's annual convention which was being held at the Kierland Resort in Scottsdale. There, in a secret gathering, final plans would be made for the March 11th attacks.

In Washington, the president had made his final plans for the secret trip to Williams for the memorial service. The Secret Service had objected with all the authority and influence they could muster, but the president had reminded them who was president, and that was the end of the discussion. Covertly, David Barnes and Tom Knight were to travel with the president and Janet under the cover of darkness. The president was strangely at peace as the journey began, looking forward to an opportunity to finally meet the Bookseller, yet still unsure what he was to say at the memorial service.

In Williams, another kind of final plan was being made. The three surviving terrorists from the original group of eleven were preparing themselves for what they hoped would be a series of attacks beginning in the morning at Kingdom Daycare. As they readied themselves to kill and die, darkness descended upon them, and anger and hate flooded their hearts. Their motivation was no longer their reward—they wanted only to hurt and kill and cause pain. Had they known of the president's plans to attend the memorial service, they would have shifted their target, but they were ignorant even as the rest of America. Pastor Scribes, the Bookseller, and Paul Phillips had felt a strong compulsion from the light inside to guard their knowledge that the president was coming to Williams. The secret had been kept, and that alone would preserve the president's life in the coming day.

Elsewhere, Susan Stafford still could not sleep. It was that sound again, the crying of the children. She could not shut it off. She had heard it before and knew what it meant, for The Curtain again had opened briefly, and she heard the sound of the children's angels crying out to the Father for their protection. In her compulsion, she had called the office of the Citizen's Militia and begged to be assigned to guard Kingdom Daycare. She sensed the risk was there, and that was her assignment from above. After much argument, Sam Will gave in and authorized her to be a part of a two-person team in the morning assigned to Kingdom Daycare. Knowing the physical limitations that resulted from her wounds, he assigned himself as the second member of the team and arranged to pick her up so they could travel together.

Susan had finished her letter. She sealed it in a plastic bag, then placed it carefully in an inside pocket of the new red jacket she had been given to replace the one in which she had been shot. She felt a sense of peace that was absurd when she considered her circumstances. She was a woman with no hope; a killer who now understood the full measure of the evil that had so dominated her existence in those months of the shooting spree. She deserved nothing but a slow and cruel death for all the pain she had caused. That she knew, but she no longer feared the second death, for she had come to believe that even she could be forgiven and be born again—and she did—the light glowed brightly in her heart.

In the invisible, there had been great rejoicing among the forces of light when God did that which only He could do and changed Susan's heart by the new birth. "These humans do not understand God's holiness or God's love," Barnabas began. "Because God is holy, all sin merits the second death, but when Jesus died, it was to offer the opportunity of forgiveness even to the vilest of all sinners.[9] Remember Saul of Tarsus who became Paul. He was a lot like Susan. He killed and imprisoned innocents simply because they were believers, and yet God forgave and used him.[10] God did the same for Susan because she, like Paul, came to the place of understanding her sin and God's choice.[11] She chose wisely."

"Glory," Lucius replied. "Even now I am still overwhelmed at God's mercy which is available to all."

"Yes," Manaen replied, "but she still faces the earthly consequences of her sin. I wonder how God will allow that to play out?"

"We may see tomorrow," Barnabas answered.

Another post had been completed earlier that day and was uploaded to the Together We Pray website. It had taken some time, but the Bookseller finally completed a short piece to send to the believers of the world. As he prayed and wrote, he was mindful of everything the Iranian brothers had said and the verses they had directed him to. He felt insufficient because he was insufficient, but he knew God was more than sufficient and that if he had been called, he would be enabled. So he released what he had done, and had peace resting in that knowledge.

The Defining Question

There was great activity in Heaven this night as the great cloud of witnesses joined with brothers and sisters on earth in bringing America in prayer before God. Their prayers were directed by the light within and paralleled the prayer offered by Daniel, who while living in captivity in Babylon had stood before the Lord and prayed for himself and for his nation. The prayer in the 9th chapter of the Book of Daniel had been the subject of the Bookseller's posting. Daniel had prayed:

O Lord, the great and awesome God, who keeps His covenant of love with all who love Him and obey His commands, we have sinned and done wrong. We have been wicked and have rebelled; we have turned away from Your commands and laws. We have not listened to Your servants the prophets, who spoke in Your name… [12]

Daniel's conclusion is the reason God was able to answer the prayer, for Daniel's request reflected the truth that they were not worthy of an answer. He closed by praying,

Now, our God, hear the prayers and petitions of Your servant… We do not make requests of You because we are righteous but because of Your great mercy. O Lord, listen! O Lord, forgive! O Lord, hear and act! For Your sake, O my God, do not delay, because Your city and Your people bear Your Name. [13]

America, the "Christian" nation, whose people had proclaimed to the world to be "one nation under God," desperately needed to repent. The only question was, would they? America's future hung on the balance just like the Jewish nation living in the Babylonian captivity, dependent upon their answer to that single question.

CHAPTER 2

KILL THE CHILDREN NOW

Thursday, February 14—MD minus 25 days

It was a very straightforward plan. All they were to do was steal a car and drive to Kingdom Daycare, arriving around 7:45 AM after most of the parents would have dropped off their kids on their way to work. Two would storm the front door, and one would go around to the backyard to eliminate the teachers and kids in the playground area. They had five minutes to kill as many as possible, then race back to the car. Then they would drive to the designated drop zone—where it would be abandoned—so they could escape on the hiking trail. This path surrounded the city, and ultimately went all the way to Chicago. Returning to the house, they could rest in preparation for Saturday's attack on the Jews.

There were no second thoughts that day. The second thoughts had come earlier as the forces of light attempted to open their eyes and draw each of the terrorists away from the evil that dominated their hearts. But free choice reigns in human hearts because God allows it to be so. Thus, they knowingly chose hate and death.

Ackmid Hasine spoke with cold dedication, "If you see any of those red-coated fools who partnered with Farsi, kill them quickly, so we don't have another disaster like the church attack. There are only three of us left. The five cowards who would not fight with us have received their 'reward.'

We must seek to survive as long as possible so that we can complete our mission, but do not be deceived—you will die today, Saturday, Sunday or soon thereafter. But before you are taken, we will have struck a blow these American infidels will never forget. Those cowards who claim our faith but will not stand with us will know the meaning of terror when they find the remains of the five, just like Farsi."

In the invisible, Legion smiled approvingly. "They have learned well," he thought. He watched with anticipation as their Keepers poured the Dark Master's influence into their hearts and minds. "Death to the children of these infidels" was their mantra; "kill them now before they can grow to be enemies" was their mission.

Already present at Kingdom Daycare were Susan Stafford and Sam Will. They had arrived before 7:00 AM to be visible as the children were dropped off by the parents. At 7:30 AM, they separated, with Susan remaining at the front for any late arrivals and Sam at the back to be visible to the children playing there before formal activities began at 8:00 AM. Susan watched carefully for what she sensed was coming, yet she was strangely at peace.

The forces of light had been active early on this cold Thursday morning. They had awakened believers throughout the world with a compulsion to pray for children. Their prayers moved the Spirit to inspire Susan's awareness and peace. Those called to pray wondered for whom the prayers had been solicited. Soon, everyone would know.

Air Force One landed right after Susan and Sam arrived at Kingdom Daycare. The president had been successful in slipping out of Washington without notice. As the plane taxied to a secured location under the protection of the Alpha Force, he too found himself strangely burdened to pray for children. So he did.

Back in Williams, an unmarked military vehicle had just picked up the Bookseller

and Paul Phillips at the warehouse to take them to meet with the president. As they left the city limits of Williams, the stolen vehicle driven by Ackmid Hasine arrived at Kingdom Daycare. The three in black hoods rushed from the car to their assigned positions, with automatic weapons raised. Janice Foster screamed and grabbed her child as she saw the three figures, pulling little Todd back into her car and falling on him in a single motion as he cried. Bullets pierced the glass flying over her now prone body and striking the other door. Hasine ran toward the car to finish his kill as the other two momentarily froze to watch.

Susan had seen the men as soon as they left the car and immediately ran from the front door toward them. She fired at Hasine, hitting him twice in the back as he had turned to kill the mother. He fell, hitting the car as the remaining two opened fire, striking Susan numerous times in the chest and legs. As she fell, Sam Will raced around the corner, firing at the terrorist who had been heading toward the backyard hitting him in the chest and face. The remaining terrorist quickly spun and returned fire, hitting Will in the arm, side, and leg. As he fell, the terrorist ran toward the door seeking to complete the job they had come to do. Up from the ground, another shot was heard that dropped the terrorist before he could reach the porch. Writhing in pain and cursing, he was immediately paralyzed as his spinal column was severed and his weapon slid out of reach.

Across the tracks, the gunshots had been heard by the Alpha Force team members assigned to secure College Church for the memorial service, and a strike force was immediately dispatched to address the threat. They arrived moments later, followed by the ITN camera crew who had been setting up for the service. Sam Will had crawled to Susan Stafford, holding her as she whispered, "Sam, there is a letter inside my jacket. Please read the letter. Forgive me. I'm so sorry," and just like that, she was gone. But the end for Susan Stafford was very different from the two who came to kill the children, for as evil as she had been, she had been made a new creation in which 'the old was gone.'[14] She faced death and judgment as a sinner forgiven.

Sally Johnson and Pete Samson arrived soon after. Medical personnel were working with the critically injured terrorist and trying to stabilize Sam Will's injuries—which although numerous, were not life-threatening. One medic observed to Sam, "Either you are the luckiest man on earth this morning, or God doesn't want you dead yet."

Before they separated him from Susan Stafford's body, Sam had reached into the inside pocket of her jacket for the plastic bag containing the letter, now covered with her blood. He quickly breathed out the story of Susan's last moments and gave the unopened plastic bag to Sally Johnson. She wiped the blood off and placed it in her coat pocket to read later.

Emerging from her car frightened and traumatized, but with only superficial wounds caused by the breaking glass, Janice Foster held Todd close while thanking God for protecting them both. Ambulances arrived to remove the two injured men as the ITN camera crew brought the whole scene live into homes across the world. The president had been notified and was watching as the television crew tried to reconstruct during a live broadcast what had just happened. They interviewed anyone who would talk with them and showed the children safe inside the house. America breathed a collective sigh of relief. Those who had been called to pray now knew why and paused to thank God for His gracious protection of the children and for the joy of being called to be a part of what He was doing that morning.

The Secret Service insisted that the president leave for Washington immediately, as they could no longer guarantee his safety in Williams. The president responded firmly and ordered them to stick to the schedule. "I am going nowhere until after the service, and I will speak at the service. You do the best you can, but don't interrupt the service and don't unnecessarily inconvenience the mourners. I am not afraid. Don't be afraid."

"But, Mr. President," the chief insisted.

"But nothing," the president responded. "You go do your job, and if I get killed, blame me. There will be no further discussion on this," he said insistently.

Janet added gently, "Jeff, it's alright. We really need to do this."

"Yes, Mr. President," the chief responded in surrender and left to organize the impossible.

Still Blind

Across the city behind a small family grocery store, Gloria Morning screamed hysterically as she dropped her garbage bags and ran from the grisly sight which confronted her. There in the large trash receptacle were five headless bodies and five heads. The Williams College students who had sought to house the terrorists but not be involved in the killings had paid the price for fence-sitting.

In Washington, still unaware of events in Williams, Chairman Crow was making his opening statement for the hearings on the dangers of religion and the need to amend the Hate Crimes Act to address the threat caused by religious intolerance. Present and prepared to testify was Williams College professor, Dr. Daniel Thompson, who had been waiting for a stage from which to declare publicly the need to change what he called, "America's religion-based foreign policy toward Israel" and accept political reality.

Former President Leonard Cox had earlier inked a deal with one of the major networks for an exclusive on his upcoming trip to Syria to discuss the causes of hate with the Sheik in response to his invitation. Majority Leader Howard had called in Harkins constitutional law professor, Dr. Trice, to prepare for the beginning of tomorrow's judiciary committee hearings on alleged abuses of the government in launching a racially motivated attack on Arab students and faculty members at Harkins.

As aides rushed to pass notes to the participants, decisions were uniformly made to ignore the events in Williams and continue with the hearings. "Don't be concerned," Chairman Crow told the majority party members after his introductory comments. "This will be turned to our advantage, but now is not the time to address it and change the focus. The events in Williams this morning are really nothing more than further evidence of the danger of religious fanaticism gone wild. Had the president responded positively to the Sheik's invitation, this would never have happened. It's the president's fault. We have to deal with these people, or the violence will never end."

Back in Williams, word of the discovery of the five bodies was passed by police radio and picked up by Sally Johnson and Pete Samson at Kingdom Daycare. "That has to be the five we were tipped about," Samson said. "Let's go now and search the place. Perhaps we can find evidence to end the threat."

"We have no search warrant," Sally reminded him, "but I think we can get one quickly."

"Who gives a damn!" Samson answered. "We're not trying to find evidence to prosecute anyone. We are trying to find leads to end the terrorist threat here and now. Look around you. Remember Sunday morning? I am not going to worry about some legal technicality and possibly lose the chance to stop an even greater threat to the memorial service later this afternoon.

"You can come or stay. I'm going now. You cannot fight terrorists with law books."

And with that, they ran together to a black and white, racing off with the siren blazing.

The President and the Bookseller

Aboard Air Force One, Paul Phillips and the Bookseller were ushered into the traveling office of President Strong. They were greeted by the president, Janet, David Barnes, and Tom Knight, who all stood out of respect for the Bookseller. "Mr. White," the president said, "thank you for coming."

"It is my privilege, sir."

"Have you seen this?" the president asked, pointing to the television set carrying the live ITN broadcast from Kingdom Daycare. "These people will stop at nothing. Thank God those two from the Citizens Militia were there, or all the kids would have been killed. As it was, none of the children were killed, but it was at a high price. One of the Citizens Militia members was killed, and the other seriously wounded. This time at least we have one of the terrorists alive. Perhaps we will be able to learn more about their plans when he is questioned."

"Who died?" the Bookseller asked.

"It was that woman who was wounded at the Security Fair," David Barnes answered.

"I guess God answered her prayer," the Bookseller thought out loud, "and that explains why I was awakened and burdened to pray for the children."

"I was also awakened," the president responded. "God was clearly at work in this for His purposes."

"What did you mean that the woman who was killed had her prayer answered?" Janet asked.

"I really cannot answer that, but it seemed she had some things burdening her heart in my time talking with her in the hospital, and I hope she found peace. I'm sure that we will learn more about that woman in the coming days," the Bookseller answered. "I watched her fight some great spiritual battles that she ultimately overcame, but I could sense there was some really dark history in her past. When I took her home from the hospital earlier this week, I had the sense she expected to die soon—maybe even *wanted* to die."

"I guess we shall see, but I am thankful for her sacrifice," the president said. "Mr. White, the reason I asked you here was first to thank you on behalf of the country for your faithfulness to share the truth when you had the opportunity. Your statements have been used by the Lord to pierce my heart, and I know they have affected many other hearts both here and around the world."

"It is not me, it is the Lord," the Bookseller responded.

"I know that, but you have been available to the Lord so that He could use you, and for that, I thank you. I wish I could tell you all that we face and how right you are to say what you did about the need for God's protection. I cannot, however, because it would make you even more of a target for the terrorists than before."

"Mr. President, I may know more than you think," he said pulling out the last message from the Iranian brothers. "I know that the government is working in Iran through two men who are believers. We have been carrying on an exchange of messages through a CIA carrier that I am sure you must have approved for that purpose. I need to show you their last message." He handed it to the president, who read for all to hear:

Brother, the days are now much shorter, and God's protection is essential to prevent disaster and open eyes to deception. Don't believe what you see. Ezekiel 3:17, Jeremiah 8:11, 15.

"Mr. President, I feel compelled to give you my understanding of this message. I believe it means that whatever you are facing is coming much sooner, and the video message from the Sheik is a mere deception to get your eyes off what must be done. Whatever it is, it cannot be done apart from God.

"I am so thankful that you have called our country to stand before the Lord tomorrow to confess wrongs and seek forgiveness. I believe that the response of the people to your call will determine the ultimate outcome of what you face. America must choose whose side it is on."

"You are correct on all points," the president agreed. "It is much worse than you know. We are learning more daily, but without God's intervention we cannot possibly be prepared to confront the coming attack with any real hope of eliminating the threat."

"How do the verses fit into the message?"

"The first passage is addressed to me," the Bookseller answered. "They are saying that I am God's watchman and must warn the people and dissuade them from their evil ways. If I don't warn them, their blood will be on my hands. Obviously, I have not yet said or done all that the Lord intends, and the peoples' response clearly indicates that they have not yet heard and understood. I believe the other two verses are for you."

"What do they mean?" the president asked.

"They are warnings God gave through the prophet Jeremiah regarding those who proclaimed not the truth, but what they wanted to be the truth. The first is directed against those who falsely declare peace; peace when there is no peace. The second is chilling. It recognizes that we all want peace, but what we face is terror. It reads, "We hoped for peace but no good has come, for a time of healing but there was only terror.""

"I could have gone all day without hearing that one," the president answered. "I know it's true, but oh, how I wish it weren't." Pausing to consider the magnitude of what he had just heard, the president shook his head. Janet got up and walked behind him, placing her hands on his shoulders.

"Mr. White," he said, looking up, "tomorrow we will be holding our service in the East Room of the White House. Would you please come back with us to Washington and lead that time? You could fly back with us after this afternoon's service, and we will make arrangements for your return. You can bring your wife and your young friend. I strongly believe that this is what God intends."

"Give me a little time to pray about it, Mr. President. I certainly don't feel that I am needed, as you are the one God has used to call for this time, but if that is His plan I will certainly come.

"Would it be possible for us to travel separately if we go? I don't want to become a political character, and I don't want you to be saddled with me as you stand to address the threat to the country," the Bookseller replied.

"You don't understand, Mr. White. I don't care about politics anymore. There is no time for that. Unless God reveals the intimate details of the plans for the attack against America, there very well may not be another election. I am trying to walk in obedience to God for the good of this nation and to honor Him. Frankly, I would covet some time with you on the flight to let you know where we are and what we need you and others to pray for specifically. We have room for all of you at the White House for tonight. Please come."

"Mr. President, we will," he responded. "I know that it is God's will that I learn how to intentionally pray for what we face so I can be effective and tell others. Had you said anything else, I don't believe I would have agreed to come, but prayer is the only weapon we have that can overcome this enemy.

"I assume you know about the Together We Pray website and the miracle of tongues that we have heard is occurring throughout the world?"

"No, tell me!" the president responded. With great excitement, the Bookseller shared how God had provided a vehicle to communicate with believers around the world.

"Can believers respond to the website?" the president asked, equally excited.

"We don't really know how to do that," the Bookseller answered. "We are actually really primitive in computer skills. This website is solely a work of the Lord."

"I know who can do that," David Barnes jumped in. "Darrell Reed. He could do that in his sleep."

"Well, wake him up," the president directed, "and get him to whoever is in charge of this website. If believers who have been praying were also to pray for God to reveal activities or people connected with the plan, God might open their eyes and use this as a means to reveal the danger and enable us to overcome."

"Yes, but be very careful," the Bookseller warned with unusual bluntness. "God has been using this website to unite believers around the world in the call for America to make a decision to repent and be on the Lord's side. It is not an intelligence effort, and if it is misused or even used for the wrong purpose, we will lose even what we have. Please don't change your focus. Tomorrow remains the key to having God provide the answer, however it is to be provided."

"I do understand," the president responded respectfully, "but I believe that God may have made this website available for many reasons beyond what we now know, and that when He has accomplished what He desires, it will no longer be available. This may be part of His plan."

"You may be right," the Bookseller answered. "God always moves in ways that man cannot duplicate and take credit for themselves. It is always something that only He can do or can enable a person to do."

"Mr. White, David, and Darrell are real believers. You can trust them. I will put David in charge from the government side, and he will coordinate with Darrell to get the site changed so that communication can be both ways if the others agree."

"I need to get back, sir, and pack and prepare for today's service," the Bookseller said. "I will need some way to communicate with you or whoever you want me to communicate with."

The president took a card and wrote down the number of the secured phone that never left his presence. "Here, Mr. White," he said, handing the card to the Bookseller. "You can reach me on that number any time of the day or night. Use it. I will always take your call."

"If you don't mind, I am going to have David go back with you to meet with your friends about the website so that he can coordinate with Darrell and get that up and running as soon as possible—that is, if they agree it is what God would have them do."

"That is a good idea, Mr. President. It is imperative that someone who knows what would be involved comes and explains it to the group."

"I have one last request before you leave," the president said. "May we pray together?" Without question, everyone stood, took hands and formed a circle, and began to pray.

Susan's Note

Arriving at the rent house, Sally Johnson and Pete Samson forced open the door and entered what was obviously another crime scene. What they saw was reminiscent of what Special Agent Andy Samuels and his FBI strike force had encountered when they stepped into Farsi's house, only five times worse. It appeared to be a slaughterhouse that had been stripped of anything that could provide knowledge of who lived there or what they had been doing.

"I'm calling forensics," Samson said. "There is nothing obvious here. Maybe they can find something."

"While you do that, I am going outside for a minute," Sally said. "I can't take any more of this. I have seen too much blood this week. What kinds of people are capable of such inhuman conduct? What could possibly motivate this?"

"I think you know the answer to that," Samson replied. "You of all people should know. You encountered them at the Security Fair, College Church, and this morning at the daycare. Their hatred is beyond belief. It's certainly not human."

Leaving the house and finding a seemingly peaceful place among some trees in the front yard, Sally sat and cried. The impact of the past days had taken an tremendous toll on her. The killings, her friend Tom Campy's injuries, and now Susan Stafford's death had left her emotionally exhausted. On top of that, they were nowhere close to finding out about the larger risk of which the president had warned. She mixed her tears with prayer and was suddenly reminded of the note taken from Susan Stafford after she died. She opened the plastic bag to uncover the envelope which contained the note and began to read.

> *If you have found this note, then hopefully by God's grace I am dead, and hopefully, I died better than I lived. My life was a waste. I was evil and cruel beyond human imagination; cold and uncaring until my eyes were opened to the truth of what I had become and I screamed in horror at myself.*
>
> *I <u>WAS</u> the one you called the Williams' shooter. I am solely responsible for all the hurt, injury and death, and am without excuse. I deserve the cruelest punishment and death ever devised for what I did, and I know what that is. It is crucifixion. I deserve to die that way.*
>
> *I cannot change what I did, or I would. I am so sorry now for the pain and anguish I have caused. I am unworthy of anyone's forgiveness, so I will not even ask.*
>
> *I have one request. In the upper left drawer of my desk, you will*

find a journal written by two very different authors. It chronicles the horror story as a daily diary from the day my evil plans were conceived to the day before you find this note. In it, you will learn of pure evil confronted and hopefully changed forever. It is a story that those who have suffered at my hand need to hear, and those who have been evil like me need to read. I said that there were two authors; I believe the journal will make clear how that could be.

I ask that my journal be given to the Bookseller, to whom I surrender all rights so that it can someday be published. I wish for every dime made to be distributed to care for those I have injured, for the spouses of those I killed, and for their children through some kind of entity headed by Sally Johnson, who held out her hand to me in friendship. It does not in any way resolve what I have done, but it is all I can do. Again—I am so sorry.

Susan Stafford

The tears became a torrent as Sally held the note and wondered how this could be. After taking a moment to collect herself, she placed the note securely back in the plastic bag and returned to the house. "Pete, we have to leave here right now and get to Susan Stafford's house as soon as we can. There is something there we have to get—now."

"What are you talking about? This is a crime scene; the place where the terrorists lived. The forensic team hasn't even gotten here yet!" Samson responded in disbelief.

"Pete, shut up and give me the keys to the car. I'll drive, and you read this," she said handing him the note. "Then you will understand."

Grumbling under his breath, he threw Sally the keys and followed her into the car. Just as the forensic team arrived, they were on their way, siren blazing.

CHAPTER 3

A TRULY LASTING MEMORIAL

Thursday, February 14—MD minus 25 days

OBLIVIOUS TO WHAT was going on beneath the surface, Dr. Janice Girds continued with final preparations for a special posthumous presentation. They were to honor Abdul Farsi as the teacher hero of the Security Fair at Thursday night's American Teachers Society's opening banquet. The conference would be dedicated to his memory in honor of his sacrifice.

"What a significant opportunity we have been given to raise the public's perception of a teacher's love for his students. We must also see this as an opportunity to attack the president's insane perception that we are at war with all Arabs and Muslims," Girds declared to the executive committee gathered to review the final program. "We have a message to send to the American people, and for once we should have an audience to hear. Two of the major networks have agreed to cover the presentation. Tonight is our night."

"Be careful not to make this overtly political," Sandra Freeman cautioned. "Let the public draw their own conclusions. The contrast should be obvious from the program. This award, along with inviting former President Cox to be the keynote speaker, should be enough. Not every American teacher sees the issues as we do. Speaking of that, what do we do tomorrow about the president's call for people to gather to pray and seek forgiveness? There are Christians here among our membership."

"Look, religious fanaticism is what has generated this nightmare of terrorism," Girds answered. "I say we simply have a moment of silence and get on with the agenda."

"That will not be enough for some," George Cook pointed out, "and frankly, I am one of them. I have never objected to the political direction of this organization, and I am not a Christian, but when you choose to ignore the president's call to stand before God, I have to draw a line. Whether you like him or not, he is the leader of our country and what he asked has a historical basis. We should honor that."

"You do what you want on your own time, but we have too full an agenda to give up an afternoon," Girds answered. "We only meet once a year."

Ignoring Dr. Girds, Cook went on, "I propose that we change the agenda and dedicate tomorrow afternoon as a time when those who attend have the opportunity to follow the president's request if that is what they desire to do. Those who don't would enjoy some free time to golf or shop, but those who want to do as the president requested should have the opportunity."

Debates like this were occurring all across the United States as decisions were made about the president's call. Many ended as this one did—with nothing more than a moment of silence set aside. But this was not the case for all, as some people truly understood the significance of the choice.

In the invisible, every entity, event, and person was a spiritual battlefield as people were making their choice about tomorrow.

Events Accelerate

Even as the ATS executive committee had debated their choice, a Saudi diplomatic aircraft landed at Sky Harbor Airport carrying Baqir Dawood and the envelope containing the Sheik's instructions for Ahmad Habid. Moving quickly through the airport with no luggage other than a locked diplomatic briefcase, Dawood entered a limousine for the drive to the Westin Kierland Resort. There, Habid waited with Phygelus Aladr.

Together, J-10 and J-14 waited for the arrival of this message and the other teacher coordinators from across the country.

Further South, Seth Wilson was an hour away from Carmen, Arizona. He had been sent by Homeland Security to follow up on the conversation Kayla Walker had with the kid, Juan Martinez, regarding suspicious activities at the old Craig place.

In Washington, Darrell Reed had been scrambling; working quickly with Pastor Wilson, long-distance, to set up the Together We Pray website so it could receive messages as well as send out messages. "God must be working in this," he thought as he heard the test results. He had called the archbishop of Rwanda, who had responded and sent a message from Rwanda in the Igikiga dialect, which Pastor Wilson reported was viewed by Christians in Williams clearly in English. "Believers anywhere in the world can communicate with each other," thought Pastor Wilson as he quickly prepared a message to post which advised the readership around the world.

Through the wisdom of Darrell, a computer link was set in Washington so that believers in the CIA and Homeland Security would be able to read messages instantly with those in Williams as they came into the website. An urgent message was posted, calling for believers around the world to ask God to open their eyes to anything suspicious around them that pointed toward terrorist activity or military movement within the next thirty days. Believers were asked to share anything God revealed, regardless of the perceived importance. The request ended with these instructions, "Whatever God may show you as an answer to your prayers, please share by return email. Trust God that you will be protected. Together let us seek God to end the violence and protect the innocent, and to change hearts and open eyes to Him."

The little group in Williams stopped to pray even as the request was posted, asking that it might be seen by those who could be used to reveal the plan and the participants. They prayed not knowing what they were standing against, but they were sure in their hearts that only God could provide the way to overcome.

Elsewhere in Williams, Sally Johnson sat stunned, having completed her initial reading of Susan Stafford's journal. "I can't believe this," she said. "The first three-fourths reads like it was written by a demon from hell, and then everything changes. It is as if a different person entirely is writing another story, looking back on the nightmare. She chronicles every shooting. There is no doubt she was the shooter, and it appears she acted alone."

"What now?" Samson asked. "We need to make her letter public as soon as we can. We don't want people at the memorial service making comments about her without knowing the truth, but the journal is a whole different issue."

"I agree," Sally added. "I would like to respect her wishes and keep the journal away from the press if Chief Thompson agrees. It needs to be published, and if that can be done in a way to help the injured and the families of the victims, that would be a good thing."

"Let's make some copies and take them to the chief and see how he wants to handle disclosure," Samson suggested. They left quickly for police headquarters, calling forensics to comb Susan Stafford's apartment for further evidence to be absolutely certain no one else was involved.

Besserman's Explosion

Back in Washington, the recess had ended, and Professor Daniel Thompson had commenced his testimony on the dangers of a religion-based foreign policy before the Senate committee looking to amend the Hate Crimes Act. His focus was on separating biblical Israel from the political state of Israel, which he contended are not the same.

> *For generations we have dealt with the political entity Israel as fiction, causing us to skew our policy to every other nation in the Middle East at a terrible cost. America's hands are covered with the blood of innocent Arabs killed in the on-going conflict which we fund and support unconditionally. Generations of Arab men, women, and children have endured poverty and desperation, lives without hope so that America could maintain the fiction that Israel exists on the Promised Land given to them by their God. You need to go no further than this to see the dangers of unbridled religious fervor.*
>
> *The hate and violence we face in these terrorist attacks, even the attempted killing of the children in Williams this morning, although*

terrible, is nothing other than payback for the deaths America has caused by allowing religious fervor to control our foreign policy. That same danger flows over into individual relationships, which is why I am here today to urge this committee to support the proposed amendment to the Hate Crimes Act to stop religiously motivated hate speech and conduct.

America must first police itself on the home front and then practice what it preaches by devising a new foreign policy which has as its goal as fairness and the ultimate good of the United States. Religion is a private matter and must not be allowed to motive individual conduct at the expense of another or the nation's foreign policy at the expense of the country. Thank you, Mr. Chairman.

Senator Besserman rose before his microphone, finger pointed at the witness, shaking with anger and said, "So what you're telling us, Professor Thompson, is that we should sacrifice the only true democracy in the Middle East, a trusted friend and ally of America, to appease those who kill us in the name of their religion, people who refuse to care for their own and who have condemned generations of their own to refugee camps? You need to change your name to Daniel Brutus; you already have the knife in the back."

Chairman Crow pounded his gavel shouting, "You are out of order! Sit down, Senator."

"No, you are out of order, Mr. Chairman," Besserman responded loudly. "The whole committee is out of order, and I for one will have nothing further to do with this circus! Mr. Secretary, you be sure to let my office know when the vote comes up on this amendment so I can come back and vote NO. I am out of here." And with that, he stomped out of the hearing room, the whole event carefully captured and broadcasted live to living rooms across America.

Act III—Not Exactly According to Script

In Cambridge, Massachusetts, the day was not so bright for Dr. Harold Bristol as the Justice Department lawyers zeroed in on their subpoena as part of his deposition in the "civil rights" lawsuit he had filed. Things just weren't going according to the script.

"Dr. Bristol, where are the documents which you were subpoenaed to bring today?" asked Larry Jordan, an assistant United States attorney. "You must understand that both individually and as the representative of Harkins College, you have not simply been asked to produce documents, you have been *commanded* to produce them."

"Hold on a minute, we object to the overbroad nature of the requests," responded Professor Trice, who was acting as his counsel. "These records are covered by privacy rights of students."

"I am going to have fun if you make that objection to the grand jury subpoena," Jordan responded. "That objection is trash, and you of all people know that. I am prepared to call the judge this very minute, and you can make that argument. We want those records now. It is a matter of national security, life, and death. I suppose the next thing you will tell me is that this morning's attempted killings of the children in Williams were really only the accidental discharge of a firearm."

"Wait a minute," Dr. Bristol insisted. "The terrorist attacks in Williams have nothing to do with Harkins students or faculty."

"Dr. Bristol, I am not going to argue with you, but what do you think the president was trying to tell you confidentially? One of your students or faculty members was coordinating a major terrorist attack against the United States from your campus and was using your Graduate School of Education computer lab to communicate with conspirators. The whole plan appears to have been launched on your campus and is being carried out under the leadership of your graduates. You are the ones who chose to try and make this a political issue. It's not. It's a criminal issue—a national security emergency. We will not allow you to delay disclosure and make this a political circus."

"You are way out of line," Trice responded angrily. "You fools think you see a terrorist under every bed. This is nothing more than an attack on our Constitution and this institution, and you will not succeed. The American people won't allow it."

"Enough," Jordan replied, equally angry. Turning to a staff lawyer, he said, "Jim, see if you can get the judge on the line. Tell him we have a significant documents issue in the middle of a deposition relating to national security.

"While we are waiting for the court to schedule us, let's continue with the deposition. Dr. Bristol, other than Professor Trice, with whom did you discuss the possibility of filing this lawsuit?"

The question was met with silence. "In particular, I want to know with whom in Washington you discussed the possibility of filing this lawsuit before it was filed."

"I am going to instruct you not to answer that question," Trice stated with authority.

"Are you going to refuse to answer?" Jordan directed his response to Dr. Bristol, looking him directly in the eyes.

"I have to follow my lawyer's advice," Dr. Bristol coldly responded. "I decline to answer."

"Fine, if that is the way you want it. Jim, advise the court that we want to discuss contempt and sanctions too. Dr. Trice, you know those instructions are a violation of the rules of civil procedure, which specifically prohibit such conduct unless the question seeks communications between an attorney and his client. Are you sure you don't want to withdraw that instruction?"

Before Trice could answer, Jim announced, "The court is on the line. The judge will hear us now."

"Great, put the phone in the middle of the table and set it on speaker," Jordan responded.

"Good morning, your honor, sorry to interrupt your day," Jordan began.

"No problem, Mr. Jordan," Judge Hightower responded. "This is what I get paid to do. What is this about, a national security issue?"

A Different Way to Overcome

Chief Thompson agreed; the journal would remain private for some time, and Susan Stafford's note would not be released until after the memorial service was completed.

"Thank you," Sally Johnson said. "As important as this is, it shouldn't divert attention from the memorial service. Those hurting people need this special time, and the national press is already all over it."

"Someone needs to help me understand this," Chief Thompson replied. "All that cold-blooded, calculated evil in every word, and then those experiences with supposed angels of light and darkness? I don't get it. Suddenly, this killer is risking her life to protect others and claims to have found God. If it weren't for the way she died and her refusal to blame anyone else or destroy the journal, I would write her off as another fraud trying to escape the consequences of what she did. But this letter and journal are not fake, that's for sure, and she didn't have to die this morning."

"I'm with you, Chief," Samson added. "There are a lot of people that are going to be asking those questions when this all becomes public."

"Pete, we need to go. We have got to get a copy of this note to Pastor Scribes so that he and anyone else speaking this afternoon is informed about the shooter and don't simply paint her as a hero."

"Agreed… but in the end, wasn't she a hero?"

As they left for College Church, the president had already been taken secretly to the church's educational facility, where he surprised the waiting relatives of those injured and killed, along with many of the wounded who had been gathered in a large assembly room. He too was surprised when he encountered the smiling Tom Campy, still in a wheelchair, but miraculously recovering quickly. He was humbled by this man who had stood alone against the assault, and thankful that the millions of prayers for this courageous man had been answered. The Bookseller had told him of Tom's invitation to the press conference that really launched the whole prayer movement—which was now greatly impacting the nation. "It is a wonder," he thought, "how God uses simple acts of obedience which seem at the time to have no relevance to anything going on in the world. We have no concept of the plans of God or how He wants to use us."

One by one, the president and Janet went to each person and family group, listening intently to their stories, seeking to comfort and encourage. There were tears and hugs, prayers and deep sighs. The president felt helpless seeking to fill the void, wishing he could somehow end the hurt and eliminate the pain. It was the hardest thing he had ever had to do.

There was, however, a wonderful moment of joy in the midst of the tears as he got to thank both Tom Campy and Sally Johnson, who had joined the group after giving a copy of the note to Pastor Scribes. He paused to thank Campy for his vision and courage, and Sally for her state of mind to react to the danger and preserve lives. Campy responded, "Oh no, Mr. President, it is you that God has given both vision and courage. I am praying for you."

Humbled, the president thanked him and was then interrupted briefly by Pastor Scribes. "Mr. President, I apologize, but there is something I have to show you before the service," and taking him aside, Pastor Scribes handed the president a copy of Susan's note. The president was immediately stunned, but then asked, "Pastor, may I have this? I may want to refer to it in my comments."

"Mr. President, this has not even been released to the press," Pastor Scribes responded. "The police were going to hold it until after the service."

"I don't want to steal their thunder," the president answered, "but this is really important to what we are doing today. Don't you see? Even a serial killer can be changed by God."

"I understand. It's yours."

After a pause, "Mr. President, it is about time to go in and begin the service."

"Thank you." Turning to the crowd of survivors, relatives, and loved ones, the president said, "Before we go into the service, will you join with Janet and I in a time of prayer?" Reaching for her hand and Tom Campy's, the whole group spontaneously joined hands to pray. "Any of you who wishes, please pray out loud, and when you are finished, I will close."

The time came for the service to begin as the waiting audience wondered at what was about to happen. In the invisible, there was great rejoicing among the forces of light as the music of the collective prayers was lifted to Heaven. The Father listened intently, and His response to each prayer was immediate as he dispatched what each of the praying people needed. He answered whether they had known to ask for it or not and whether their prayer had been out loud or simply in their hearts. The two remaining archangels, Michael and Gabriel, were dispatched to confront the forces of darkness—which always sought to hinder and delay the answers to prayers—for on that day, in that place and at that time, no delays would be tolerated. A peace fell upon those assembled in prayer.

They were experiencing the joy of the Lord. The light within burned brightly in every committed heart.

The delay was almost thirty minutes, and the waiting crowd was shocked as the president and Janet came in with the families, led by Tom Campy being pushed in his wheelchair by Sally Johnson. The people rose to their feet as strings of loud curses were heard in the White House press room as the Press Corp saw on TV that the president was in Williams for the service. Once again, ITN had streamed the broadcast on its website for the world to see, but this time they had also made it available on the Together We Pray website at the request of Pastor Scribes. The Senate committee hearings in Washington were preempted, and their television audience was transferred electronically to the Williams service, even as Pastor Scribes stepped to the podium to pray.

"Lord," he began, "we come before you this day to ask that Your hand of healing rest on the injured, Your presence be among the grieving and for You to change our hearts that we might forgive even as You forgave those who crucified You.[15] Give us joy as we celebrate the lives of those who are now home with You. Be honored in all that we do this day. In Jesus' name, Amen."

The large screen at the front of the auditorium was filled with a compilation of home videos and still photographs interspersed with tributes to those killed and injured in the attacks. At Pastor Scribes' request, they also included tributes for soldiers killed anywhere in service around the world that week. Behind the visual presentation was music with a message including Ray Boltz's moving song, "Thank You for Giving to the Lord." Soon there was not a dry eye in the building, and few among those watching as people came to realize the tragedy of the lives cut short by unbridled hate.

There were solos and old-time congressional singing of familiar songs including, "In the Garden," "It Is Well with My Soul," and "Amazing Grace." It was like a family sing-along with words that comforted and refreshed the soul. "What a contrast," thought Paul Phillips as he held Samantha's hand, remembering the funeral for her dad that had started his journey. "If the Curtain opened now, I am sure I would not see so many of those dark things."

What Paul thought was absolutely true, for that service was under

| 35

God's protection. The forces of darkness had abandoned the fight in the building and now sought to draw the television audience away.

After Pastor Scribes completed his message, which once again focused on forgiveness, the president stood and walked to the podium.

"I stand before you today not as the president of the United States, but as a grieving friend who has been privileged to spend the past several hours with these precious hurting people," he said, opening his hands to indicate the families and relatives present before him. "I wish all Americans could have joined with Janet and me to hear their stories and share their tears. I am thankful for the beautiful video we were able to watch together; in a small way, it painted a picture of the loss they have suffered individually and the loss we have suffered together as a nation. These were not people who can be easily replaced, for they were men and women of character, faithful to their spouses and children and their faith in the Creator and giver of all life. They truly represent the foundation upon which this nation was built, and the only hope it has for the future.

"We live in perilous times, as this morning again evidences. Hateful people seek only to kill, steal, and destroy all that we hold dear. These are times which require courage and sacrifice, character, and forgiveness; the very best there is in people. It is what we expect from those who are men and women of faith. It is what has been found in this city, and in this place.

"We are gathered today among heroes. Two of these heroes stood and fought. One of them is a pastor who literally ran to the terrorists and offered his life, diverting the attention of the terrorist long enough for Officer Sally Johnson to find the gun which had been lost. Tom Campy fell to the ground from the wounds he suffered while defending the innocents whose only 'crime' was a desire to attend a church service. The horror of the possible mass destruction was eliminated, and God was gracious, but we have before us the remnants of the pain, hurt and death launched here only a week ago.

"My friends watching across America and around the world, there are lessons here in Williams we need to learn quickly. Had you been with me in our time with the families and friends of those needlessly and indiscriminately struck down by the killers, you would have seen the difference between a religion of hate where self-appointed judges carry out what they perceive to be the wrath of their god without mercy, and the God of these suffering men and women of faith who motivates them with love to reach out to share their faith and leave judgment and wrath in the hands of God. There were many words of anguish and many questions, but there was no hate or desire to strike back apart from self-defense or preventing future attacks.

"Some in America—and around the world—seek to equate passion for the Christian God with the passionate religious hate which motivated the killers. That thought would never enter the mind of one who walked with those who are suffering and grieving here in Williams. Their passion is expressed by reaching out even as Jesus did when He walked the earth and gave Himself up for all who would put down their wants and desires to serve Him. They will tell you of their faith and pray that you become a believer, but no one fears that they will kill you if you choose not to believe or decide to believe something different. I am thankful to be one of them. And just like them, I have made my choice to be on God's side. Tomorrow I will join with fellow brothers and sisters to stand before God in repentance for the things we have done and are doing in this nation that offends Him, and things we have not done that we know we should have. Many will gather in this place, and I hope you will find a place or make your home a place for others to gather and make their choice.

"As we grieve, we must not lose hope, for the God of love is also the God of the impossible. He is the only one who can change hearts and turn a soul dominated by hate and evil into one filled with love and light. Yes, we must forgive, even as Pastor Scribes just said, and we must fight to defend ourselves against those who seek to kill us. We must pray for changed hearts; both our own and those who have chosen to be our enemies.

"Can God change a heart filled with hate and evil into a heart of compassion?" He paused to let the question sink in as he spread the copy of Susan Stafford's note before him.

"I want to read a portion of something to you which is indisputable proof that we must not respond in hate but in prayer that a people of hate be changed, for they can be changed. Listen carefully," and he began to read.

If you have found this note, hopefully, by God's grace I am dead and died better than I lived. My life was a waste. I was evil and cruel beyond human imagination, cold and uncaring until my eyes were opened to the truth of what I had become and I screamed in horror at myself.

I WAS the one you called the Williams' shooter.

There were audible gasps from the crowd as they realized what the president had just read. He continued slowly and deliberately so that every word would be heard and understood.

I am solely responsible for all the hurt, injury and death, and am without excuse. I deserve the cruelest punishment and death ever devised for what I did, and I know what that is. It is crucifixion. I deserve to die that way.

I cannot change what I did or I would. I am so sorry now for the pain and anguish I have caused. I am unworthy of anyone's forgiveness, so I will not even ask.

"This is only a portion of a note that was taken from the body of Susan Stafford this morning after she was killed by terrorists. She was taken as she stood and confronted them when they sought to kill the children at Kingdom Daycare, less than a mile from where I now stand.

"Think about that carefully—the shooter who killed and hurt so many in this city, dying in one of those red jackets as she stood to defend children against those who were doing exactly what she herself had done. How can this be?

"The answer is right here," he said as he picked up Pastor Scribes' Bible that had been left on the podium at the president's request. "Let me read 2 Corinthians 5:17. It says, 'Therefore, if anyone is in Christ, he is a new creation; the old is gone, the new has come!'

"There it is. God removed the old in Susan Stafford's heart and replaced it with a new heart of love; His heart. Now, if God can do that with a serial killer who terrorized this city for months, He can surely do that with anyone whose life is dominated by hate.

"Some believe that hate can be removed by legislation or compromise, or a change in foreign or military policy. They are well intended but ignore the lessons of history and the intricacies of the human heart. Hate can only be removed by God, and only then by the gift of a new heart.

"As we seek this day to remember those who are hurting and grieving, let us honor their memory and those who have died at the hands of terrorist attacks. Let's honor them by committing to join together to pray without ceasing that hearts be changed so that hate is exorcised that we all may live without fear. That would be the real living memorial to the victims of all these attacks—a world without fear of terrorism."

The president stepped back as the Bookseller walked to the podium and closed the service in prayer.

Nothing but Ashes

"He has lost it! There's no one at home—it's lights out at the White House," former President Cox yelled at the television as the memorial service ended. "The man is a terminal fool, a religious nut! How will we ever survive the next twenty-two months?" he declared loudly to no one other than himself.

Located high above everyone in the Presidential Suite of the Westin Kierland Resort, Leonard Cox had been watching the service less than a hundred feet from Demas Assad and Phygelus Aldar's suite, four floors below, as they opened the envelope delivered by Baqir Dawood. The message read simply, "MD March 11—execution teams cease all current activities and become part of MD." The message was in English, and not encoded. No signature or indication of where it originated was included or necessary. They knew.

"Good," said Assad shaking his head up and down in approval. "Now we know when and we can tell our people. There is enough time to prepare and to escape."

"Yes," Aldar agreed, "and the addition of the execution teams on MD will further confuse and strike terror into the hearts of the Americans."

"I am glad for another reason," Assad continued. "It was clear we needed to do something. The Williams experiment failed miserably. We lost everyone, and the enemy only got better organized. They are looking for us everywhere, and it is obvious from the Harkins lawsuit that they are close. We have to get the word out tonight after the opening session and appoint new leadership. We won't last until MD. My flight leaves from here tomorrow morning. I will travel under a new name with new identification. I suggest you do likewise. I'm not even going back to pack."

"Agreed," Aldar added. "I hadn't planned on leaving this early, but it makes sense. I have several remaining alternative identities and papers. We can work from the Mexican side until March 11th, and then we move to Europe to prepare for life after the United States."

"Did you get the room list from conference management?" Assad asked.

"I did," Aldar responded.

"Good. We can move quickly room to room tonight and go through the new instructions."

"Who will be your replacement?"

"I will use Walid Ghazi, and I suggest you use Tariq Qusay. They are both based in California, which is a long way from Cambridge. We have had little contact with them over the years, and they are not Harkins graduates. The Americans will have difficulty tracing them from us. They work well together, and remember, they were with us that summer when we did the initial planning."

"Good choice; they can be trusted," Aldar replied. "Qusay had to dispose of one of his operatives earlier. He didn't flinch. They will do whatever it takes to succeed."

Lighting a match, Assad set the note on fire, dropping it in an empty trashcan as the flame rose. Smiling he said, "That is how America will end; in fire, nothing but ashes on the trash pit of history."

CHAPTER 4

IN THE AFTERMATH OF TRUTH

Thursday, February 14—MD minus 25 days

THE SECRET SERVICE had quite a time trying to hustle the president out of Williams before the large crowd left the memorial service. He was not in the mood to be hustled.

The president walked with Janet to the pews where the families of the victims lost in the terrorist shooting had been sitting. He wanted to spend some more time with them, seeking to comfort and encourage them one by one. He changed the return plans when a spokesman for the family group asked if they would stay and join the families on site for lunch. Janet smiled, for that was what she had wanted to do all along. The Secret Service was beside themselves, but understood that this president had a different agenda—and unfortunately, his personal safety was not part of it.

As they began to move through the tunnel to the educational facility where they had initially gathered, David Barnes was on his cell phone talking to Darrell Reed. Suddenly, it was as if a light switched on and Tom Campy remembered something. He turned abruptly to Sally Johnson, who was pushing his wheelchair, and asked, "Sally, did you remember my cell phone? Did you get Farsi's cell number off it?"

"We checked out all the cell phone companies in the Williams and Chicago area, and no one had an account in Farsi's name," she replied.

"He had a cell phone," Tom insisted. "I spoke with him on it. He must have had it in another name. Where is my cell phone?"

"It must still be at the hospital," Sally answered. "We'll look when I take you back."

The president had avoided the press completely, with the exception of George Murphy, the writer for the *Times Daily* who had been invited to join the presidential party for the trip back to Washington. "Mr. President," Tom Knight said, taking the president off to the side for a private conversation. "You cannot offend the Washington Press and ignore the national press and not pay a steep price. They are the ones who have the eyes and ears of the people. They're going to paint you as a dangerous religious nut. You cannot lead if the people will not follow, and they must follow, or you cannot confront MD successfully."

"Tom, I understand your concern, but these are not normal times, and 'the normal rules' don't apply. What is important is not to worry about who the people follow. It is who I follow. Success against MD is dependent on God's protection only, and I sincerely believe that if I follow Him, the people will be led by Him to follow me.

"The media does not concern me. Have you noticed the rise of ITN as a broadcast alternative? The people want more facts, and they want it presented in such a way that they can make a choice. ITN has filled that void and profited greatly by their different approach. And then there is this prayer website, seen all over the world. We have an audience now that we have never been able to communicate with before. Even George Murphy is giving us a fair hearing, and he will have the opportunity to watch for himself and report what he sees. The Creator of the universe even controls the media. The White House press corps need to understand that their position is a privilege, not a right. A good dose of humility might help them even if it is forced."

"I hope you know what you are doing," Knight replied.

"Don't worry, Tom. I am not hiding from the press. I simply want to be careful how and when information gets out. I have offered Diane Conway an interview before we leave for the plane. She writes for the local paper. The Washington crowd can follow her lead. It is refreshing to converse with someone outside the Washington bubble. She listens without an ideological agenda.

"Enough business for now," the president said firmly, but kindly. "I want to spend this time with the families." Taking Janet's hand, they walked to the group of waiting relatives and friends and joined them at a table for lunch.

An Unanticipated Result

The call between David Barnes and Darrell Reed was a report on Dr. Bristol's bad day that had just gotten worse. The hearing with Judge Hightower had not gone as Professor Trice expected. One minute into the hearing, as Larry Jordan explained the government's position and the immediate national security need for the documents and answers to relevant questions, the judge interrupted.

"Wait a minute, Mr. Jordan. Do I understand you to be telling me that the CIA has traced communications through a known terrorist website—one that is actually being used to communicate with American operatives in preparation for an attack within the continental United States—to the Harkins Graduate School of Education computer lab, and they are refusing to provide the government relevant information?"

"Yes sir, communications were forwarded through that website and had been used by others in the United States in connection with the recent attacks in Williams. Plans for others which are under investigation," Jordon replied.

Turning his attention to Professor Trice, the judge said, "Your reputation surely precedes you here, but you better have a real argument on why your client is refusing to produce documents and answer questions. I am setting an evidentiary hearing on this matter in fifteen minutes. Mr. Jordan, I want the government to set up a conference line to my office, and in fifteen minutes I will expect a call. I want evidence that what you are telling me is correct. Dr. Trice, you produce whomever you want on that same call to provide evidence that the government is wrong—or whatever your client's legal justification is for ignoring the subpoena—and for you instructing a witness not to answer questions. Fifteen minutes," and he hung up.

"Jim, set up the conference line while I get a hold of Darrell Reed," Jordan yelled.

Trice turned to Dr. Bristol, and out of the earshot of Jordan quietly said, "You are our only witness. You will have to testify about what the president said in the call. Be careful not to conflict with your affidavit. Here, I have a copy. Read it quickly."

"I don't like this," Dr. Bristol responded. "This is getting out of hand. It is one thing to play the media, but the media isn't here."

"Just leave it to me," Trice answered. "You can't win if you don't fight."

The Hearing

Before the hearing commenced, Jordan asked the court to seal the proceeding because of the national security disclosures that would be required. "Absolutely," the judge responded. "This hearing is sealed, and the parties and their lawyers are instructed that nothing communicated in the hearing may be repeated to anyone without advance authorization by order of the court."

"Mr. Jordan, call your first witness."

The hearing was candid and chilling as Darrell Reed answered questions from Jordan and the court. The cross-examination was ineffective as there was no government effort to do anything beyond attempting to stop the planned attacks. The testimony of the connection between the communications from Cambridge and what was happening in Williams was particularly useful. The judge had taken a recess from pending matters to watch the memorial service, and it was during that service that Jordan's call had come in.

Darrell was as careful as he was smart and disclosed nothing of substance about MD or Iran. No one from the government side trusted Professor Trice to honor the court's confidentiality order.

After Reed's testimony was completed, the judge turned to Professor Trice and said, "I have heard enough from the government. What is your response? Call your first witness."

An unexcited and uncomfortable Dr. Harold Bristol then sought to explain how the president was after Arabs as a racial group. He shared that the disclosure of the alleged use of the Harkins Graduate School of Education computer lab by a possible terrorist student or faculty member would cause the university irreparable harm. Professor Trice then made his student record confidentiality argument, along with violating the civil rights of unknown Arabs argument, finally throwing in the danger of profiling argument as his conclusion.

"I don't need to hear anything further from you, Mr. Jordan. I am ready to announce my ruling.

"I find that there is clear and convincing evidence of a threat to the security of the United States, and probable cause that a crime has been committed by use of the Harkins Graduate School of Education computer lab. Because of restricted access to the lab, I further find that the perpetrator was most likely either a Harkins employee, faculty member or student and that the government has an immediate need for information regarding those who would have had access and could be the perpetrator. I find that the call from the president was an attempt to obtain the needed information in a confidential manner in order to protect the university and speed the process so that the perpetrator could be identified and apprehended. Finally, I find no legal justification for the refusal of Dr. Bristol to produce the subpoenaed documents or for Professor Trice to violate the rules of civil procedure by instructing the witness not to answer questions from the government.

"I order that the deposition of Dr. Bristol be continued until 1:00 PM tomorrow, at which time it will commence in my chambers. I am to be present until it is concluded. The plaintiffs have until 1:00 PM tomorrow to produce all documents requested by the government. Dr. Trice is sanctioned by this court for his knowing and willful violation of the rules of civil procedure and is fined $1,000, which shall be paid to the government by 1:00 PM tomorrow for their cost and expense required to reschedule this proceeding and force compliance. The $1,000 is to be paid from the personal funds of Professor Trice, and not be reimbursed by his client or any third party. This is a personal sanction against him."

Speaking slowly and deliberately, Judge Hightower continued, "Dr. Bristol, Professor Trice, listen closely. If this order is not fully complied with by 1:00 PM tomorrow, or if during the continuation of his deposition Dr. Bristol evades a question or is instructed not to answer a legitimate question, I will hold the violating party in contempt and send them immediately to jail. There will be no further delay. Am I clearly understood?"

"Yes, your honor," all parties responded.

Disappointment in Carmen

In Carmen, Arizona, Seth Wilson had completed his interview with Juan Martinez, the High School Junior who had observed and reported suspicious activity at the old Craig place involving over the road trucks. Juan had given a sworn statement on what he saw, which Wilson took to the local police station as a basis for further investigation.

"Sergeant Thomas," Wilson began, "I need for you and some of your men to accompany me to the Craig place to interview the occupants. Based on what Juan Martinez observed, and upon our continuing investigation, Homeland Security believes that the Craig place may be where terrorists sent over the border have come to be transported to their assigned places in the US for future attacks; perhaps like we have seen in Williams, perhaps part of something much larger. We simply don't know for sure right now. Our real concern is that all Juan ever saw was Arab men. The men in the house, the drivers and the passengers were all Arabs. That is really suspicious in this day of terrorism on our shores."

"Listen, you have more than enough evidence to get a search warrant from Judge O'Connor," Sergeant Thomas answered. "Let's go there first. If your suspicions are correct, we need to be prepared to move immediately."

It didn't take long to get the warrant, and soon two Carmen police cars raced to the old Craig place, one approaching from the front while the other came up the street behind the house to cover any attempted escape out the back. With guns drawn, Sergeant Thomas knocked on the front door, announcing, "Carmen police. We have a search warrant. Open the front door now!"

When there was no answer, the door was forced open, and the police entered as trained, setting up fields of fire and making sure they were ready for a fight. They immediately dispersed throughout the house, quickly doing a visual search for anyone remaining inside. They saw plenty of evidence that people had been there, but no current occupants. The refrigerator contained spoiled food, and there was trash strewn everywhere.

"We'll watch it," Sergeant Thomas said, "but it looks like we're a little late. This place has been abandoned."

"Jeff, you and Steve tear this place apart and see if you can find any evidence of who was here or what they were doing. Make sure you give whatever you find out to Mr. Wilson to help with the national investigation."

Unknown to the frustrated crowd of lawmen present in Carmen that day, the decision had been made some time ago to abandon the house. No more drivers for MD were being brought into the country. The required number were already positioned and prepared for the attack. The men that had been coordinating the distribution activities had returned to Mexico to help with the truck invasion, which would commence immediately before MD was launched.

The Answer to the Question Not Asked

After lunch, the Bookseller stood and turned to the friends and families and said, "Before you leave, I'd like us to share in the Lord's Supper together. But first, I need to answer the questions I know all of you are secretly asking—why did God allow this, and why did it happen to my loved one?"

Every eye in the room was attentive to the Bookseller, and there was absolute silence as people strained to hear the answers.

Speaking slowly and deliberately, the Bookseller continued. "There are no accidents in God's economy, particularly when it involves His children. This tragedy is not a case of good people being in the right place at the wrong time. This is a case of people being exactly where God wanted them to be, at the exact time He wanted them to be there, for His purposes.

"The first question is actually easy. Jesus Himself provided the answer immediately before He served what we have come to call the Lord's Supper. Do you remember what He shared with the disciples in those moments? John wrote about it in great detail starting with the thirteenth chapter of his book, continuing all the way through Jesus' prayer in the seventeenth chapter.

"Jesus spoke words of warning and hope. They were what we as believers must expect because of our association with Him. Do you remember?"

Searching their memories or grabbing for their Bibles, the group sought diligently to find the answer. They somehow knew that it was important—not just to them in their difficult circumstances, but to the greater family of God around the world. It was a subject that they had never heard any pastor address.

"Not once, but on three separate occasions during those moments, Jesus warned of suffering simply because a believer was associated with

Him. It was even one of the subjects He specifically addressed in His closing prayer after serving the Lord's Supper. Let me read those three passages.

> *If the world hates you, keep in mind that it hated Me first. If you belonged to the world, it would love you as its own. As it is, you do not belong to the world, but I have chosen you out of the world. That is why the world hates you. Remember the words I spoke to you: "no servant is greater than his master." If they persecuted Me, they will persecute you also. If they obeyed My teaching, they will obey yours also.* **They will treat you in this way because of My name, for they do not know the One who sent Me.**[16]

> *... a time is coming when anyone who kills you will think he is offering a service to God. They do such things because they have not known the Father or Me.* ***I have told you this, so that when the time comes you will remember that I warned you.*** *I did not tell you this at the beginning because I was with you.*[17]

"And in His prayer,

> *I have given them Your Word and the world has hated them, for they are not of the world any more than I am of the world... As You sent Me into the world, I have sent them into the world.*[18]

"The Father allows believers to share in the sufferings of Christ. The answer to the second question tells us why these particular brothers and sisters were chosen to suffer in this way.

"Shortly before he was to be killed by the Romans, Paul answered the second question in a letter to his young student Timothy. You may not like the answer, because it speaks of the future of which Jesus warned. Paul wrote, 'In fact, **everyone who wants to live a godly life in Christ Jesus will be persecuted.**'[19]

"The real question we should be asking today is not 'why them' or 'why was this allowed,' but rather, 'why not us' and 'why not more often,' for we too are part of the 'everyone' Paul referred to. It applies to us if we truly want to live a godly life in Christ Jesus.

"In the Book of the Revelation, there is a repeat of the warnings of Christ. There, Satan is pictured as a dragon, defeated in his attempts to destroy Jesus. The twelfth chapter describing that event ends with this chilling reality."

> *Then the dragon was enraged at the woman and went off to make war against the rest of her offspring—those who obey God's commandments and hold to the testimony of Jesus.*[20]

"Have you thought about those who were killed or wounded last Sunday? Every one of them fits within the warnings of Jesus, the statement of Paul and the conclusion in the Revelation. These men and women were selected by God because of the purity of their faith to suffer as a witness to the rest of us. They were not Christians by name only; they were men and women whose lives were identified fully with Jesus Christ."

Pausing at the sound of weeping, the Bookseller cleared his throat, wiped tears from his eyes and continued. "Now beloved, as we turn to celebrate the Lord's Supper, I want you to remember something else Jesus said before He served the first such supper.

> *Do not let your hearts be troubled. Trust in God; trust also in Me. In My Father's house are many rooms; if it were not so, I would have told you. I am going there to prepare a place for you. And if I go and prepare a place for you, I will come back and take you to be with Me that you may be where I am.*[21]

"Last Sunday, the Lord Himself came and fulfilled that promise for your loved ones. It was sealed by His blood on the cross for them—and for us—and for all who will ever be born again. It is the sacrifice we remember as we share the cup and the bread together."[22]

CHAPTER 5

SEEKING ANSWERS

Thursday, February 14—MD minus 25 days

AS AIR FORCE One went wheels up and arched its way toward Washington, Williams' Police Chief Thompson was concluding a press conference regarding the Kingdom Daycare attack and Susan Stafford's note and journal. He had waited patiently for Officer Sally Johnson to be able to participate after the Memorial Service. The effect of her standing in describing the attack and Susan's death was only enhanced by Tom Campy's presence in his wheelchair, and the news that Sam Will was out of surgery and resting in ICU with a good prognosis.

"I frankly cannot explain the note or the journal," Chief Thompson responded to reporters' questions. "It is beyond my understanding how anyone who was such a cold-blooded killer could completely change, but she obviously did. I will have to leave that analysis to others. All I know is that the Williams shooter is dead, and that threat is removed forever."

"I know how," Barnabas smiled in the invisible, turning to the gathered Lucius, Niger and Manaen. "It is just as Gabriel said to Mary so long ago, 'nothing is impossible with God.'"[23]

"Yes," Lucius responded, "and did you see the light inside burning brightly as Samantha prayed for Paul before he left with the presidential party? Her search has been answered."

"I did see," Barnabas answered excitedly. "It is a great victory, but such a large war. Tomorrow is the key. How goes the fight?"

"How can we really know?" Niger replied. "God does not give us that knowledge. I can tell you what I see, but that is only a small part of the whole. Only God knows for sure."

Pausing to reflect on the enormity of the question, he continued. "I see that the battle is on everywhere around the world because of the prominence God has given to what the Bookseller shared. The worldwide network broadcasts and the protected prayer website all combine together to declare that no one will have an excuse for they have all heard the Truth, and now they must choose."

"At least the president has chosen. Will that alone be enough?" Barnabas asked Lucius.

"It could be that God spares America during Joshua Strong's service as president like He did for King Josiah when Josiah responded to the discovery of the Book of the Law and heard its Truth for the first time,"[24] Lucius answered.

"Yes," Manaen added, "but remember, even Josiah's faithfulness was not enough to ultimately save the nation. Even under a righteous leader, the people did not choose in their hearts to follow God, and they were eventually destroyed.[25] I don't know, I am only an angel, but I cannot believe that God will save America even temporarily if the people ignore the president's call to stand before God tomorrow and allow Him to reveal what He considers to be their sin. Especially for them to then agree that it is sin because God said it was sin, and for them to be changed and turn away from that sin. To do so is the essence of bowing before a holy God to worship and serve Him.

"I fear that America has become too proud and arrogant to bow down before anyone. It has become its own god. It makes its own rules. The darkness over America has become too great, and its negative influence around the world has become too high a price for God to allow its survival for long as it is," Lucius responded soberly. "People across the earth are being deceived by America and are being led as fools into the eternity of the second death, separated from God forever. America cannot be allowed to continue unchanged, or God will no longer be God. Either it will change when God's people change, or God will allow its destruction as a nation, and it will fade into history as has every great world power before it."

The families and friends of those who died or were injured at the hands of the terrorists had made their choice. They would return to College Church tomorrow morning to join with others to stand before the Lord as the president had requested. They now had a much greater understanding of its significance and wanted to be changed.

Cox's Assault from Phoenix

Demas Assad and Phygelus Aldar were visibly uncomfortable with the posthumous presentation for Abdul Farsi as the new purported Arab hero who rescued Christians and sacrificed his life. They knew it was a total lie and feared that the more it was publicized, the more likely it would be that the whole house of cards would fall. Somewhere out there was evidence of their involvement together over all these years. They needed to complete the update and transfer leadership so they could assume other identities and get out of the country as quickly as possible, but they could not run until this event ended and the information was passed later tonight to the gathered coordinators.

Former President Cox was almost through his comments when he turned ugly. For decades, he had been one living under the influence of many Tempters including lust, pride, jealousy, hate, and anger. In him, they became a "full house" of evil to which he often willingly surrendered, in their time manipulated his thoughts and actions. Working together with his Keeper, the Tempters were able to make Cox an instrument of the Dark Master's agenda when needed, and he was needed now to attack the President's call for tomorrow.

"I must close with a warning and with thanksgiving," Cox continued, pausing for effect. "Our military forces have attacked Mosques in the Middle East, and we express surprise when a church is attacked here. The book on which so many rely would call a person expressing surprise at such an attack in light of what we have done in the Middle East, a 'hypocrite.' Can we truly be surprised or angered when we receive back 'an eye for an eye'?[26] Perhaps it is time for us to look at the log in our own eye before we attack one with a speck in theirs.[27]

"Listen closely. The public tone of our nation has changed the past few weeks. We now hear much about God and how we must change because He is somehow angry at the way we live. I might pay more attention if those who used His name were addressing how He views the way our government treats others around the world, or even our own people here at home.

"Remember that you heard it from me first—tyranny will come in this nation disguised as a cross wrapped in a flag." It will look good, even religious and patriotic, but it will be nothing more than a slick, deceptive political scheme to grab your emotions and control your life. It will steal your freedom and make you a puppet.

"We face one of those manufactured moments tomorrow. Our president has called us to stand before God because God is displeased with you—but not with him. I suggest that you comply with the president's request to spend a few moments before God tomorrow, but spend those moments asking God to open the president's eyes to his sin and evil before his policies turn the whole world against us.

"We don't have to be a victim of terrorism. We can be a friend rather than an enemy. We can address the causes of hate rather than giving others a reason to hate. It is there that America has sinned, and that sin is not yours or mine. That sin rests on the president. Don't allow his call to divert attention from the real sinner. He is the guilty one with blood on his hands.

"Lastly, parents, as the keeper of our children, yours is a sacred trust; it is truly a responsibility before God. Continue to teach and open eyes to the reality of what we have become as a nation. Expose them to the lies of history so that we will move forward in our evolution into a society which protects the rights of all men and women to pursue happiness however they may choose without being subject to the hypocrite's hate or the Pharisees' legislation.

"Thank you, and good night."

"Finally, he is finished," thought Assad as he left the auditorium with Aldar to begin their room to room gatherings to pass on the Sheik's message and transfer leadership. Then they could escape while the plan moved forward.

The President's Return to Washington

Watching the Cox speech aboard Air Force One, the president shook his head as he turned the television set off. "Hard to believe that man was once the president of the United States," he said to Janet. "It is frightening, frankly. How did we make it through that time in history?"

"We made it the same way we will make through your's—if we do. It will be by God's grace and nothing else," Janet responded.

"You sure have a way of taking a few inches of a man's height," the president said, smiling. "Thanks."

"No charge," was the response. "A First Lady's most difficult assignment is always to manage her husband's hat size."

"Mr. President," Tom Knight said seizing an opportunity to get his full attention.

"Yes, Tom," the president answered turning for the moment from Janet to give him his full attention.

"David and I need a minute."

"Sure, what do you have?"

"I want to leave this communication from General Hedges with you for your review," Knight began. "This is the Joint Chiefs' recommendation on troop redeployment, both in the States and overseas. We will need to move whole units almost immediately from Europe and elsewhere to bases here, as well as redeploy naval taskforces near our coast to be prepared for MD on whatever accelerated schedule we face. Time is short, and the obvious problem is that it takes time to redeploy, and redeployment cannot be done in secret. As soon as major troop and ship movements begin, the Russians will pick it up and not far behind them the press will get a report from somewhere."

"We have to have a strategy for dealing with the Russians sooner rather than later," the president responded thoughtfully. "I think I have come to know President Sorboth well enough that I have difficulty believing he understands what Vandenburg and Krenski have been planning with the Iranians. I think I need to deal with him one on one. I am not yet sure how, but I am working on an idea."

"Is the vice president coming tomorrow for sure?"

"Yes, Mr. President. He will be in Washington before we arrive and will attend the services in the East Room tomorrow."

"Good. No business tomorrow. I want to devote that day to exactly what I ask the people to do unless there is an absolute national security emergency. Be sure that word is put out, no appointments, no phone calls. I need that whole day. Cancel everything."

"On Saturday morning, I want to address all of this, and I need the vice president. He has to be involved from now on in case something happens to me."

"Tom, get with Troy Steed and Eric Besserman. I want to be in a position to make decisions Saturday on our military preparation both here and abroad, how we bring our European allies in, and how we deal with individual nations in the Middle East. I want to know who we can trust and involve and who we must confront. We have to be on board with Israel on all of this, particularly on how we deal with Iran. I will need to meet with the Attorney General, the Joint Chiefs and with the Survival Commission. Keep it all as confidential as possible. Make sure everyone understands this is national security 'eyes only' stuff."

"Yes, Mr. President," Knight responded. "That will be an ambitious agenda."

"It will, but we don't have time to wait. It may be an interesting day for another reason as God answers the prayers raised tomorrow," the president replied with obvious excitement in his voice. "If the people really take this seriously, I know in my heart that God will move and we will be able to see that movement."

"Speaking of tomorrow, Mr. President, how do you want to deal with the ITN request to broadcast the Whitehouse service?"

"Have you asked the Bookseller?"

"I have not," Knight answered.

"Well, then let's go ask," the president said, leaving his office for the passenger quarters to find where he was seated.

As he approached, he saw the Bookseller in serious conversation with George Murphy and heard Murphy ask, "Do you believe we are living in what the Bible describes as the last days?"

The group stood as the president approached, and he quickly said, "No, no, please stay seated, and if you don't mind I would really like to hear the answer to that question Mr. White. Please continue," the president said, sitting and listening intently.

Ignoring the president's presence and focusing on George Murphy, the Bookseller continued. "Mr. Murphy, how could I know what Jesus said He didn't know, and what difference would it make anyway?"

"You are going to have to help me on that one," Murphy answered.

"Well, Jesus said that no one knows the day or hour, not the angels or even Himself, only the Father.[28] If He doesn't know, then I certainly don't. One thing you can be sure of is that when any of those self-appointed prophets tell us the end is coming on a date that is certain, it won't. They don't know either, but why should it matter if you knew for certain that the end was coming tomorrow and Jesus would be returning at 4:30 in the afternoon?"

"I can tell you how it matters," Murphy responded quickly. "If I knew Jesus was coming back at 4:30 tomorrow afternoon, I would address things in my life and get ready to face Him."

"I am sure you would if that were possible, which is precisely why you won't know the day or time," the Bookseller responded. "If you knew, you would believe that you could live any way you wanted until near the end, and then decide to change your life. Think about that. If you were God, would you want people to know your schedule so they could ignore you until the end? How foolish. God is not like that, and He isn't looking for a bunch of last minute 'conversions' where people live like hell and then grab for the 'golden ring' of fire insurance at the last minute. Do you really believe that Jesus suffered all He did on the cross for a bunch of last minute 'me too' commitments?"

Pausing to give Murphy time to find the answer, he continued. "Jesus' answer to your question is to live every day like He would return. He said you 'must be ready because the Son of Man will come at a time when you do not expect Him.'[29] He said we must 'keep watch and pray,'[30] and that when He returns we are expected to be found actively involved in His business.[31] I often think of the character in one of the old religious novels written about those involved in the crucifixion. It tells the story of a follower of Jesus who was always looking up wherever he went. Finally, the main character in the book asks in frustration, 'why are you always looking up?' The answer? 'Because He may return today.' That is how Christians are told to live. We are to live every day expecting His return that day."

"But Jesus gave us signs of the end times, and we should not ignore them," the president interjected.

"He did, but do you honestly believe that as president there is anything you as a man could do to speed those days or change God's plan? If you do, you are a fool."

The group became quiet waiting for the president's response, astounded that the Bookseller would dare to say something like that to him.

"You are obviously correct," the president responded humbly in a low tone. "I am so thankful that God has given us someone in these difficult days who will speak for Him without fear of the audience. For me, that affirms your words can be trusted."

"If I ever consider my audience, I am no longer God's servant," the Bookseller responded.

"Mr. President, you must be like any other Believer and seek God and obey, leaving the consequences to Him. The fact that you are the president does not change that. You have no different assignment than any other Believer on this plane. We all are to listen for God's voice and when we hear we are to obey."[32] For you as president, however, there will be a higher standard for to whom much is given, much is required."[33]

There was more silence as the little assembled group took in what they had just heard. George Murphy wrote furiously, making notes knowing that what he had just witnessed was important and wanted to be prepared to report it accurately someday when the mysterious crisis passed—if it passed.

"Mr. White, I came out here to ask you a question about tomorrow," the president said breaking the silence. "ITN has asked to broadcast live the Whitehouse service. Should we do that?"

"Have you prayed?" the Bookseller responded.

"Well, no. I was simply going to ask you your opinion."

"Nothing without prayer, Mr. President, if you truly want God's leadership and blessing,[34] Let's take some time to pray and discuss this later. I don't know how to answer you without asking God for guidance." And so they stopped and prayed.

"I don't have a definite direction yet, Mr. President," the Bookseller said when the prayers ended. "I am sorry, but that decision will have to wait."

"Of course, I understand. I don't either."

"I have a question," Murphy said, changing the subject. "What miracle do you expect in answer to tomorrow's prayer? I know that there have been miracles in Williams as people who should not recover do and quickly, but what is the miracle you are all going to be praying for tomorrow?"

"I am not praying for miracles tomorrow," the Bookseller answered. "You have this all wrong. An answer to prayer is never a miracle. An answer to a prayer in God's will is what we should expect because that is what is promised.[35] If it takes what the world defines as a miracle for the prayer to be answered, that will happen, but it is wrong to call it a miracle. Nothing is impossible for God, so nothing is a miracle to God.[36] They are only miracles to man."

"Have I confused you?"

"You have," Murphy responded.

"Tomorrow as we pray, I am expecting God to answer our prayers within His will; whatever it takes, because He is God. You can label the answer anything you want, but when a prayer raised within God's will is answered, that is the norm. It is what we should expect. That is why we pray. Those who don't pray simply don't believe that prayer is heard and answered. They are the fools who live by choice outside of the power of God."

"I am going to have to work with that one for a while," Murphy said.

The Search for J-14

Returning to the president's office aboard Air Force One, David Barnes took the opportunity to report on recent developments.

"Mr. President, I have been on the phone with Stephen Hollister, Attorney General Rodriquez, and Darrell Reed. We are close to J-14."

"I don't like 'close,' I like caught," the president responded.

"Sorry Sir, I don't make the news, I just report it."

"So report, please."

"Homeland Security got to Carmen, Arizona late by a few days. A group had been using a house as a place for individuals crossing the border illegally to hide and then be transported to their assigned location by over the road trucks. The young man who reported the incident said that the people in the house were Arabs, as were the people who left the house and the drivers of the trucks. Apparently, they abandoned the site. Our best guess is that they left because adequate operatives are already in place for MD. We have a lead on the trucking company, but nothing more at this point.

"After we left Williams, Sally Johnson took Tom Campy back to the hospital, and they got his cell phone. It had a number on it in the directory that Abdul Farsi had given him as a contact number when he joined the Citizen's Militia. The number had a 617 area code—Cambridge, Massachusetts again, same as Harkins College. The FBI is checking with cell phone companies to get the records for the number. Again, no contract with anyone by the name Abdul Farsi, but the number remains active, and the records are being retrieved. We should have them later tonight and will check for other 617 numbers he called. The physical address is not helpful, a post office box in Boston. It is being watched."

"And the good news is?" the president asked.

"Actually, there are two pieces of good news. The first is that the return email on the prayer website works, and we have great hope that it will be something that will provide us desperately needed intelligence. The other good news is that the Justice Department lawyers clobbered the Harkins' President in court today. The Judge has ordered the documents to be produced at 1:00 PM tomorrow and has already sanctioned the lawyer for instructing his witness not to answer a question. The deposition is going to be completed in the Judges' chambers, and he has threatened them with jail if they disobey any of his orders. We should find out what they know tomorrow and ought to get the lists we have been looking for. There is a good chance we will have the probable identity of J-14 by early afternoon."

"That is good news," the president responded. "I only hope it will not be too late."

But it already was too late, as Demas Assad and Phygelus Aldar had completed their series of one on one meetings with the coordinators and had left the Phoenix Westin Kierland Resort under new identities. They would spend the night in the Embassy Suites Phoenix Airport hotel and catch a 6:00 AM flight to Mexico. By the time the deposition convened tomorrow in Cambridge, they would have been in Mexico for hours to help with final preparations at Oaxaca for the great border crossing.

CHAPTER 6

THE TWO QUESTIONS

Friday, February 15—MD minus 24 days

THE FINAL DECISION was made on the helicopter ride from Andrews Air Force Base to the White House. The beginning of the East Room service would be broadcast so that people who did not have a place to go could participate in their homes or offices; those who did not understand what the president had called them to do would be able to see exactly what this day was to be about. After a call from Tom Knight, ITN quickly agreed. Their feed would again be made available to the other networks, on their website as well as the Together We Pray website.

Throughout the world, millions of Christians were awakened in their sleep to pray for America and the coming day of decision. The burden was heavy and carried with it a call to pray for their own countries and governments, to confront their sin as God views sin, and to turn from that sin and be changed. It overcame the desire to sleep or eat or focus on anything else. Believers were being invited to unite and share these moments with the Lord, even as Peter, James, and John had been invited to do in Gethsemane.[37] Those three slept, but this wasn't the case for many believers that night. Guardians protected them while the light within opened their understanding that this was not about what God wanted them to do, but rather what God wanted to do in them. They were being invited to share

His heart and passion and stand against the forces of darkness—and stand they did.

If the earth could have been viewed in those hours as seen from behind the Curtain, individual bright lights would have been apparent in every city and nation. The sound of millions of voices raised at once, united in purpose in many languages would have been heard. It was an amazing moment; one not witnessed often since the day Adam was given life and placed in the garden.[38] The power of the prayer muted the efforts of the forces of darkness. People would be free to choose.

As dawn cascaded across America, people began to gather in sunrise services and private moments together in their homes. There was an awareness throughout the land that an opportunity to participate together as a nation was being offered when the East Room service would begin. All night long the announcements had appeared on radio and television, and headlines regarding the East Room service greeted those who picked up their morning papers or who listened to early morning newscasts. Even nonbelievers had a sense that the televised service was a way to resolve what they saw as a problem by providing something for believing employees without "wasting" the day or insulting their faith. The East Room service was set to begin at 11:00 AM, which would allow for it to be broadcast at a convenient hour throughout the country. Schedules were adjusted to make that time available for any who desired to participate. Churches that had scheduled their services at that hour hustled to make arrangements to have televisions available to join in the East Room service.

Sleep had not come to the Bookseller that night. The burden was heavy on him to be careful to say only what God wanted him to say. He remembered God's cry of frustration and anger to Jeremiah against self-appointed "prophets" who ran with a message that He had not given them, leading God's people further away. "But which of them," God questioned, "has stood in the counsel of the Lord to see or hear His Word?" The Bookseller wanted to be such a man; a man who stood in the counsel of the Lord to hear His word because of how God said He would use such a man. God had declared, "But if they had stood in My counsel, they would have proclaimed My words to My people and would have turned them from their evil ways and from their evil deeds."[39] He knew that God's declaration must be his purpose for this day and the few moments he would have to open the East Room service. His words must be God's words to God's people.

A peace came over the Bookseller as he dressed. He passed on breakfast, for this was not to be a day to focus on himself, even in the simple act of eating. This was a day to deny himself, even that small pleasure, so that he could focus fully on God. Taking Margaret's hand, he smiled. "I must admit, I never thought I would live to see a time when a modern president would have the courage to call the nation to repentance. God has done an amazing thing. He must have a clear purpose for a changed America."

"Yes, if America will allow itself to be changed," Margaret replied.

"It is not America as a whole that is at issue this morning," the Bookseller responded. "It is we who call ourselves Christians, but who live in active rebellion against the teachings of the Bible. Many Christians' lives effectively declare that we can be our own god and live any way we want. By our lives, we have said to a watching world that the Bible is a lie and Jesus is not God. Who in their right mind would want to become what they see of Christians today? The only argument for being a Christian is the 'happy church good time hour' or the theology of 'grabbing fire insurance before it is too late.' Church has become a club in which you don't even have to pay dues if you don't want."

They were silent as they were led to a small room near the East Room to await the time to begin. The little group of three from Williams held hands and prayed. The Bookseller had been given no program, no time limitations, nothing. What would happen in these next few public moments had been left completely in his hands. Those were the president's instructions, again over the objections of many advisors who warned of possible adverse political consequences. The president, even as the Bookseller had passed on food, was passing on political consequences. Nothing must get in the way of hearing from God.

The battle in the invisible had gone on throughout the night. Unbeknownst to those now gathering in the East Room, Professor Trice had been awakened by a representative of an organization called Government Without God, better known as GWG, to immediately file suit to block the broadcast. He had moved quickly, understanding the importance of standing against what he saw as an attempt by the religious forces to take their message to the public without restraint. He truly feared what could happen if the American people heard the message of the Bible without restraint and without "clarification." His Keeper dug his fingers deep into Trice's brain to plant the passion and influence necessary to fight this last-minute battle in the midst of the Harkins setback.

Suit was filed by 2:00 AM, claiming the broadcast was a violation of the First Amendment prohibition against the establishment of religion. A pre-selected favorable United States District Judge who had been appointed by former President Cox was then awakened. Judge Hightower had been carefully avoided since he had demonstrated that he could not be trusted on a matter of this importance. An injunction was issued without the government having the opportunity to appear and oppose the request. The order would allow the service to go forward, but not be broadcast. Professor Trice notified the White House and ITN demanding that the broadcast be canceled.

But Professor Trice was not the only legal mind awake at that hour. Attorney General Rodriquez had been up all night preparing for such a battle. He had been directed by the light within to expect a challenge, and the appeal papers to seek reversal of an expected injunction were ready. The United States Court of Appeals for the 1st circuit had been notified of the possibility, and a panel was on call if needed. The appeal was filed quickly, and the matter was fully briefed and argued by both sides as the sun rose over Washington. By the time most in the Capitol had finished their breakfast, a decision had been rendered.

The court's opinion was direct and simple.

We reverse the District Court. No evidence was presented to demonstrate compulsion by the president or this administration to force the broadcast or to force anyone to watch. No government funds are being expended, and thus there is no state action to establish any particular religion.

The president is also a private citizen with the right to the free exercise of his religion as he may wish. There is historical precedent for political leaders in this nation, including presidents, to call the country to voluntary prayer and repentance. If the media wishes to cover the event, that is their First Amendment right. The injunction was issued in error and is hereby dissolved.

There was no time for a Supreme Court appeal. Professor Trice was tied up with Dr. Bristol, making sure they would have all the documents together for the 1:00 PM showdown with Judge Hightower. Dr. Bristol was willing to stand for what he believed in as long as he did not have to stand behind bars. Trice shared that opinion. The appeal would not have been heard anyway as the Supreme Court was in recess this morning. The majority of the members of the court were now sitting in the East Room awaiting the start of the service.

By 10:30 AM, the East Room was full, with an overflow of people standing in the back. The president's invitation to members of his administration had been almost uniformly accepted. Present in the room were the vice president, cabinet secretaries, heads of departments, advisors, the Joint Chiefs, members of the Survival Commission, and as mentioned above, most members of the United States Supreme Court. Although no one knew what to expect, there was a sense of history and anticipation in the room. Some prayed while others simply waited and wondered what was about to happen.

The nation paused at 11:00 AM, some from deep commitment, others from curiosity to hear what the old man from Williams was going to say. People throughout the earth had been drawn together for this moment, and it began simply with a plainly dressed little old man with white hair and a white beard walking to a podium at the front of the room carrying a Bible and a single sheet of white paper.

Taking his Bible, the Bookseller turned to the 28th chapter of Deuteronomy and said by way of introduction, "To his people, to those who publicly had declared that they would follow Him as their God, the Lord through Moses laid out consequences of their future choices, for God is a God of the moment, and the consequences we face individually and as a nation are not the result of history—they are dependent on the choices we make now—the choices we make today. Listen to the Word of God.

If you fully obey the Lord your God and carefully follow all His commands I give you today, the Lord your God will set you high above all the nations on earth. All these blessings will come upon you and accompany you if you obey the Lord your God:[40]

"Consider this one blessing out of the many:

The Lord will grant that the enemies who rise up against you will be defeated before you. They will come at you from one direction but flee from you in seven.[41]

"And now consider the consequences of a different choice:

However, if you do not obey the Lord your God and do not carefully follow all His commands and decrees I am giving you today, all these curses will come upon you and overtake you:[42]

"Consider this one curse out of the many:

You will live in constant suspense, filled with dread both night and day, never sure of your life... because of the terror that will fill your hearts and the sights that your eyes will see.[43]

"Is God really serious about the consequences of the choices that would be made, whether to obey or go their own way?

"Looking back from Babylon, Daniel knew the answer, for the nation of Israel had been completely destroyed by a foreign enemy and many of those who survived were taken away into captivity. It was a moment like today that changed history when Daniel chose to stand before God for his now non-existent nation. He chose to pray for forgiveness of their sin of rebellion against God, which had brought about their defeat. He confessed that, 'We have not obeyed the Lord our God or kept the laws he gave us through his servants the prophets,' and that as a result, the curses I just quoted and the others in that passage had been poured out upon the nation and it had been destroyed by its enemies.[44] He acknowledged that 'The Lord did not hesitate to bring the disaster upon us, for the Lord our God is righteous in everything He does; yet we have not obeyed Him… we have sinned we have done wrong.'[45]

"God heard and answered, and a decree was issued by a foreign king who ruled over them that ultimately allowed the temple to be rebuilt,[46] and then the city of Jerusalem.[47] In time, Israel was once again a nation until its people again made wrong choices, they rebelled against God, and the process repeated itself.

"This truth is not limited to Israel, for no great world power has yet survived throughout all of history. America has no reason to believe we will be treated any differently if we make wrong choices.

"What then needs to happen to assure that we are aligned with God; that we are on his side individually and as a nation?

"The answer is found in the experience of Isaiah the prophet in the 6th chapter of the book that bears his name, when he encountered God. That is the purpose of today: to encounter God. What happens when you encounter God? Well, what happened to Isaiah?

"The Bible gives an elaborate description of what he saw, but what is important for us is not how God appeared to him, but how it affected him and what he did about it. When Isaiah realized that it was God Himself, he cried out, 'Woe to me… I am ruined! For I am a man of unclean lips, and I live among a people of unclean lips, and my eyes have seen the King, the Lord almighty.'[48]

"A real encounter with God will reveal what in us is considered sin. For Isaiah, it was his mouth. In you, and for America, it may include your mouth, or it may be something completely different. Let no one tell you what they believe your (or America's) sin is. Don't decide for yourself; you can't know for sure. Just like Isaiah, let God reveal your sin, then confess it and allow God to change both you and our nation.

"In the passage, after Isaiah confesses his sin, he sees an angel come with a piece of coal taken from the altar before the throne. His lips are touched, and he hears these words, 'See, this has touched your lips; your guilt is taken away and your sin atoned for.' Suddenly Isaiah could hear God speak and quickly found himself being used by God, living under His enablement and protection.[49] That cleansing and change and empowerment is what we seek today for ourselves and for our nation. We desire to live under the blessings and protection of God, which means we must desire to obey Him fully and repudiate anything He calls sin.

"Please repeat with me the Lord's Prayer," he asked. Both in the East Room and throughout the world, voices were raised together repeating the familiar lines.

Our Father in Heaven, hallowed be Your name, Your kingdom come, Your will be done on earth as it is in Heaven. Give us today our daily bread. Forgive us our debts, as we also have forgiven our debtors. And lead us not into temptation, but deliver us from the evil one, for Yours is the kingdom and the power and the glory forever. Amen.[50]

"As you approach God today, let me suggest that you begin by asking Him two questions from the prayer we just raised together. I believe that in His answer you will discover your sin and America's sin as God views it. The first question: what in my life or our nation dishonors the holiness of God's name? By name, scripture means everything that is God—His character, His power, His righteousness, His sovereignty; even His Word. The second question: what in my life or our nation is not God's will being done as it is in Heaven?"

The sound of pens quickly writing notes filled the East Room as the Bookseller continued.

"God has given us some very specific promises in the Bible for anyone seriously searching for Him this day. It says, come near to God and He will come near to you.[51] Jesus says, seek me and you will find me.[52] In the last book of the Bible, the Book of Revelation, Jesus reveals another truth about this day. He affirms that it is He who is knocking, and we who must open so that He may come into our hearts and dwell with us.[53] Seek God. Open your heart and mind to Him. Then ask the questions and listen, for He will come with the answers even as He has promised.

"What will this look like, and how should we respond? Let me read the prayer of one man who sought God and then confessed before the Kansas House of Representatives what he believed God had revealed to him as America's sin." Taking the single sheet of paper, he read:

Heavenly Father,

We come before you today to ask Your forgiveness and to seek Your direction and guidance.

We know Your Word says, "Woe to those who call evil good," but that is exactly what we have done.

We have lost our spiritual equilibrium and reversed our values. We confess that.

We have ridiculed the absolute truth of Your Word and called it pluralism; we have worshipped other gods and called it multiculturalism; we have endorsed perversion and called it an alternative lifestyle.

We have exploited the poor and called it the lottery; we have rewarded laziness and called it welfare.

We have killed our unborn and called it choice; we have shot abortionists and called it justifiable.

We have neglected to discipline our children and called it building self-esteem.

We have abused power and called it politics.

We have coveted our neighbor's possessions and called it ambition.

We have polluted the air with profanity and pornography and called it freedom of expression; we have ridiculed the time-honored values of our forefathers and called it enlightenment.

Search us, Oh God, and know our hearts today; cleanse us from every sin and set us free.

Guide and bless these men and women who have been sent to direct us to the center of Your will, to open their hearts and their minds to receive your guidance.

I ask this prayer in the name of Your Son, the living Savior, Jesus Christ.

Amen

There were audible gasps in the room as the prayer was read. Throughout America, some were angered and offended by what they heard. The Bookseller placed the paper down and spoke slowly with authority.

"Some of you were obviously offended by this prayer. That is of no concern to me. What is of concern is how God feels about the subjects mentioned in the prayer, and whatever else is on His heart. I read this only to make a point. It does not matter what you think or feel about what you hear. It matters only what God thinks and feels. You may disagree among yourselves, forming competing political parties with different platforms and agendas. But, hear me well: you do not have the right or privilege to disagree with God if you want to live under His blessings and protection, and avoid His curses.

"Now, choose—but choose wisely." He walked away from the podium and knelt beside his chair, closing out everything and everyone around him to continue his time before God in prayer.

The ITN broadcast pictured the kneeling Bookseller as it faded to a series of photographs of America while playing quiet background music. It was as if the television was showing the world what it was they were standing for as the scenes changed each morphing into the next. ITN had set aside a full hour of silence during which the pictures of America would be shown as the people prayed.

The Iranian Surprise

In Iran, as elsewhere around the world, millions had watched either on television or through the ITN feed on its website or the protected prayer website. The six gathered to pray at Hiram Urbay's home in Teheran turned off the computer as the picture faded from the Bookseller kneeling to the scenes of America.

"What in my life or our nation dishonors the holiness of God's name? What in my life or our nation is not God's will being done as it is in Heaven?" Hushai repeated. "Those are the questions." And the sounds of multiple prayers were heard as they sought God's answers. There were tears of conviction and shouts of rejoicing, confession of individual sin and the collective sin of their nation of Iran as the night moved on quickly as though only a moment had passed.

Shortly before the sun would begin to rise across the Eastern sky, Ittai stood and turned to the still kneeling little band and said, "Brothers and sister, we must not forget America this night, for they are in great peril. Without God's help, they will certainly be destroyed—and soon. We must not forget the Bookseller, who only recently sent us this message, 'My dear brothers, please pray as Epaphras in Colossians 4:12 that I be as the man described in Jeremiah 23:22.' The first passage reads, 'Epaphras, who is one of you and a servant of Christ sends greetings. He is always wrestling in prayer for you, that you may stand firm in all the will of God, mature and fully assured.' The second reads, 'But if they had stood in My council, they would have proclaimed My words to My people and would have turned them from their evil deeds.' I think he was asking us to wrestle in prayer that he stand before God and hear what God would have him share, and then be enabled to do so.

"We should pray for him now," Hushai said. And so they did; praying together out loud.

After their time of prayer came to a close, Hiram asked, "What is this about America being in great danger? Is that what the American president has been talking about?"

"It is much worse than what he has shared," Hushai spoke with passion, "and our nation is in the middle of it. We too are in great danger, having chosen to cooperate with terrorists against America and to use the opportunity to strike against Israel. We have searched for information and have found shadows of what is planned, but not sufficient details to allow the Americans to stand against the planned attacks. We know that a group from America gathered here not long ago to work through their plan in a terrorist training camp in the North. We have learned that our government has the plan having taken it from one of the American operatives as he passed through the airport, but we cannot get details. The Bookseller sent us a message, which indicated that God would provide. But it hasn't happened yet. We need to pray that we find out so we can advise the Americans."

As they prayed, conviction fell hard on Hiram. He remembered the airport search and knew that he might have what they were looking for. "Does the term 'Final Solution' mean anything in what you are looking for?" he asked.

"It could, I don't know for sure," Ittai answered. "The term 'Final Solution' is what Germany called the attempted extermination of all Jews during the second World War. Why do you ask?"

"I work for the SSF, as you know. One of my assignments was to copy the hard drive of some Arabs who were working in America while they were detained for questioning in the airport. I copied one in particular that the SSF had a real interest in. I felt a strange compulsion to copy a file labeled, 'Final Solution,' which I did secretly on a flash drive. I have it here. Could we send it to the Bookseller? Maybe that is what you are looking for."

"Can we have it and take a look at it now?" Hushai asked.

Hiram paused and then said, "I am not trying to be a problem, but all I feel confident to do is to send it to the Bookseller. He will know what to do with it. God will show him and open the way. Can you get it to him?"

"We can do that," Ittai answered. "If you have it, we will compose a message for the Bookseller, which I can have delivered to him in America by Sunday."

As Hiram left the room to recover the hidden flash drive, Ittai turned to Hushai and said, "I don't care what he says, we have to copy the flash drive at least. That is the only known copy outside of the terrorists or the Iranian government. We cannot risk it being lost or intercepted."

"My brother, stop thinking like an agent and start walking like a believer," Hushai said. "Let's pray about what to do. I am not going to deceive my brother here and copy it if he doesn't agree. We have to trust God and send it on to the Bookseller immediately, unless God changes his heart or directs us otherwise."

As they began to pray, Hiram returned with an envelope and joined them. They prayed passionately against the terrorists and their own government's plans. They asked that God protect America and grant President Strong discernment to prepare for the planned attacks. For themselves, they sought God's wisdom to understand clearly what He wanted them to do. They understood the significance of what may be in Hiram's possession, but as they prayed, the reality became clear that what mattered most was to do exactly what God wanted, exactly the way He wanted it done. To do one or the other, but not both, would be disobedience—which would take them outside the blessings and protection of the Lord. The consequences could be catastrophic.

After a pause during a time of silence, Ittai said, "While we were praying, the Lord made real in my heart the answer He gave to King Jehoshaphat's prayer which effectively started this journey. Do you remember? It is 2 Chronicles 20:15, 'Do not be afraid or discouraged because of this vast army. For the battle is not yours, but God's.' Let's send the flash drive to the Bookseller. It makes no sense to me to send it to him, but I agree that is what God wants us to do and He doesn't have to make sense. That is why He is God, and I am not."

Together they composed a short note to the Bookseller as follows:

My brother: the enclosed flash drive is for President Strong. We believe that this is God's answer to our prayers for wisdom and discernment into what the terrorists have planned.
—Your Iranian Brothers

Ittai left quickly as the sun rose to send the unknown treasure on its way to Williams.

CHAPTER 7

THE FALLOUT BEGINS

Friday, February 15—MD minus 24 days

JIM HUNT'S PHONE rang as the hour of quiet neared its end. Despite the work before him, Hunt had been stricken by the two questions and had struggled in prayer seeking the answers for himself as well as the country. His heart and mind were flooded with the importance of the moment, and he did not want to miss whatever part he was to play in God's plan for this day.

"Jim, this is Carl Stern. Look, we can't just drop this prayer emphasis at the end of the hour. I found myself struggling with those two questions, and I know most of the rest of America is wrestling too. What about taking several minutes at the top of the hour—for as long as the East Room prayer time continues and go live—showing people still praying and putting the two questions on the screen to keep the focus on what the Bookseller said?"

"I agree, but understand what that would mean to the network," Hunt answered. "The only way we could do that would be to drop commercials at the top of the hour, which would reduce the day's revenue by half and risk angering all the affiliates. They might not be willing to waive their end of the hour commercials, which would mean it would not be broadcast anyway. We have already had some negative reaction from the hour we set aside for quiet reflection."

"Well… I may be unemployed at the end of the day, but let's do it," Stern responded. "I will send something out to the affiliates, and they can book the time as public service. This is important."

As the hour of reflection ended, the ITN broadcast went to a live picture of the president in prayer, overlaid by the two questions. "What in my life or the nation dishonors the holiness of God's name?" and "What in my life or our nation is not God's will being done as it is in Heaven?"

The effect of the questions had been startling, as most people had never seriously considered how God viewed their lives or the nation. The assumption had always been that God founded America, and thus would always bless America. All we had to do was ask. The possibility that God could be displeased with their lives or with America was a new concept, introduced initially by the Bookseller at the press conference in Williams. Now, however, as they actually prayed about the questions, the answers began to come, and people understood how God viewed their lives and their country. The response was either an outpouring of grief or anger. Grief was experienced by those who truly wanted to be on God's side, and anger by those who refused to bow their knee to anyone or anything.

The sword of division, which Jesus said He had brought,[54] cut deeply throughout America and the world. People had to choose when they asked the questions and got answers. Would they agree with God and turn from what God identified as sin? What had been previously accepted as the norm was suddenly not.

The sword of division cut most deeply in churches and ministries which had turned to follow the will of the people or their leader and away from the teaching of the Bible. The leaders who had been directing this parade suddenly found their leadership questioned by people who were no longer willing to ignore what the Bible said on any subject.

There was anger and fear among those of the nation's politicians who were without the light inside, and those with the light who had ignored it to maintain their positions. If the two questions were applied to politics, platforms would have to change, and programs that were long in place would have to be eliminated. The focus of government as the "all-powerful provider god" would have to be dropped, and people would have to held accountable for their actions inside and outside of government. Political statements made over the years could assure defeat unless this movement could be stopped quickly. Because of the flood of calls and email that descended on state and federal politicians' office, there was a quiet panic.

Senate Majority Leader Howard was livid. He had been unable to even muster a quorum to proceed with the majority party agenda because so many members were in their offices or in caucus rooms praying. Chairman Crow couldn't get a committee majority together to continue the hearings on the amendment to the Hate Crimes bill. In Phoenix, the ATS convention found its afternoon sessions sparsely attended while former President Cox, now back in Washington, sat dumbfounded, wondering what had happened to America. He was confused and struggling with the whole concept of the two questions. Could there really be a God to whom he was accountable for every action and thought? He cringed at the idea and quickly rejected it. "That cannot be true," he thought, as his Keeper dug deeper into his skull to maintain control of his thoughts.

Back in Williams, the families and relatives of the victims of last Sunday's shootings had joined with many of those who had been victims of Susan Stafford's reign of terror. College Church was full, as was the campus chapel and other community churches. The bond of those who had suffered was deep. There were tears and hugs as people cried out to the Lord together for the answers to the two questions. Something very unusual was being done in College Church as Pastor Scribes stood before those assembled with a whiteboard after the East Room broadcast had ended.

"As you seek God for the answer to the two questions, if God reveals to you public sin or sin you have committed against this body of believers, we have an open mic here for you to come and share and ask the body for forgiveness. When anyone shares and asks for forgiveness, I ask that those of you who feel led by the Spirit come surround them and pray with them. If the sin God reveals is private, or against a person present, go to that person privately and ask them for forgiveness and pray with them. If the sin revealed is the sin of this church or of America, but not necessarily your sin, please share with us. As God brings us to unity on what is the answer to the two questions, I will write them down for all of us. When we believe that God is finished, we will seek God together for what He would have us do in response to what He shows us.

"As you pray, remember to pray for America and for the president. Pray that God will give our leaders wisdom and direction to address the threat to this nation from the terrorists among us. Pray for protection, and that God will reveal the plans of those who would spread the terror throughout America they have already shown here."

Among the crowds assembled throughout Williams were armed red jacketed members of the Citizen's Militia who were taking no chances. Elsewhere in America, police were visible in every public gathering; their presence discouraging any possible violence against those assembled praying or any attempt to forcibly interrupt the assemblies.

Around the world, the two questions were producing similar results as the light within revealed the answer to those who prayed—always individual to the questioner and their nation. The results were uniform throughout the earth as those who had taken the time to seek God had found Him, for He was waiting.[55] There was increasing awe at what was happening and a growing desire for God to rule in individual lives which would result in His rule over nations. Long held opinions changed in light of the revelation of God. Suddenly the darkness was revealed as darkness and evil as evil.

"It is time," Molech said, and multiple masses of Tempters were released throughout the earth to draw people into emotional responses and away from seeking God in prayer. Keepers filled the minds of those still blind to the truth with a desire to share in the emotional excitement of a spiritual experience; people began to shout, falling to the floor writhing or in uncontrollable laughter. Some shook violently all over, while others simply passed out as if struck by an invisible sword. People began to speak in gibberish, a counterfeit of the gift of tongues,[56] and some declared that they had a message from God which sounded strangely like those laced in darkness. Because so many in churches were not truly Christian, the forces of darkness had no difficulty launching this attack there.

Among their committed servants, the forces of darkness unleashed a response of hate and anger. The desire to strike out against any Christian circled the earth, and a campaign of individual violence commenced against anyone found praying. The terrorist leadership sought a way to strike America now, even before MD, to show the world that this God to whom the Christians prayed would not be able to protect them. The importance of MD increased, and the focus changed to include a final attack on the Christian God. "The infidels must be shown for what they are," the angry Sheik roared in anger. "They must never again be able to challenge our faith."

But throughout the day, the ITN minutes at the top of the hour repeated the two questions and the live pictures of those still praying in the East Room, drawing the audience back to the purpose for which they had gathered. Leaders of church groups and others were given wisdom to understand what was happening as the attack of the forces of darkness was launched, and many of those involved were confronted and removed from the prayer gatherings. God would not allow sincere searchers to be stopped on this day.

Truth Compelled… and Consequences

In Cambridge, the whole ugly truth began to come out as the afternoon progressed and Dr. Bristol's deposition continued. Documents had been produced as ordered, and they revealed a long list of Arab nationals who had been granted admittance to Harkins Graduate School and others as part of a secret bequest from a distant member of the Saudi royal family five years ago. Harkins had accepted a $50 million gift as part of an agreement to admit students nominated by a committee of Saudis for study in the Graduate School of Education. Pursuant to the agreement, at least one graduate would be placed on the Harkins faculty, and the others would be helped with placement in high schools across the United States after graduation. Harkins' list was incomplete since it only included the group which had been admitted there. The total numbers were much larger. The program had ended after three years, and all of the students had been placed and assisted in obtaining the necessary immigration status to remain in the country at their teaching jobs.

The faculty member was revealed to be Professor Demas Assad. He had been on an excused absence the past few days in attendance at a teachers' conference in Phoenix, Arizona. Larry Jordan asked for and received a break in the deposition, which he used to place a call to the attorney general's office for authority to get a search warrant to search Assad's condominium in Cambridge and to get a warrant for his arrest in Phoenix. Part of the records produced revealed Assad's cell phone number was included on the cell phone bill of one Abdul Farsi in Phoenix, AZ. This man was clearly J-14, and if they moved quickly, they should be able to search his apartment in Cambridge while arresting him in Phoenix.

The authority was granted immediately, although the attorney general was not present. He remained in the East Room praying with other leaders of the administration. Judge Hightower was more than willing to issue the search warrant on the basis of what he had heard in the deposition, and the warrant was turned over to the local FBI bureau chief who assembled a team and left immediately to conduct the search.

The arrest warrant was a little more difficult because of the need to involve the grand jury, so the judge issued a warrant which authorized Assad to be held as a material witness. After a call to be sure they understood its significance, the warrant was faxed to the Phoenix FBI offices, and they raced to the Westin Kierland Resort to arrest Assad and search his suite.

The deposition resumed, and the truth about the political involvement of the Senate majority leader in the decision to file the suit and hold hearings came out. Judge Hightower was livid and issued an ex parte order that Majority Leader Howard appears to show cause for why he should not be sanctioned for abuse of judicial process. It helped that Senator Howard was a lawyer licensed in certain federal courts. Professor Trice sighed deeply, seeing his future Supreme Court nomination floating away.

"You can't do that, Judge Hightower. You are talking about a United States senator who is the majority leader. He is immune for what he does in Congress."

"That may be true regarding the hearing, but there was nothing legislative about encouraging the filing of this totally bogus lawsuit. That is nothing more than abuse of legal process by a member of a coequal branch of government," Judge Hightower responded. "You might remember that former presidents have been held in contempt and even had their license to practice in the Supreme Court revoked for what they did to abuse the legal process while in office. I don't put Howard above a president."

"I move to dismiss the suit right now," Professor Trice said. "It was a mistake to file and we admit that."

"Nice try," the judge answered, "But until the issue of sanctions against you, your client and the Senate majority leader are fully heard, I will not dismiss the case. I am, however, going to issue an order publicly exposing this farce and compelling the attendance of all I deem subject to possible sanctions. After that hearing, I will consider dismissing this suit."

"You can't be serious?!" Professor Trice said in disbelief.

"I'm as serious as a heart attack," Judge Hightower responded. "Mr. Jordan, do you have anything else you want to ask Dr. Bristol?"

"No sir, I am through for now," Jordan answered. "I will ask them the remainder of my questions before the grand jury already impaneled to investigate them and the criminal activity of the Harkins faculty member."

"What do you mean by 'them?'" Professor Trice asked.

"Professor Trice, consider this formal notice which will follow in writing that you and your client are now targets of a grand jury investigation on possible obstruction of justice."

"Wait a minute!" Dr. Bristol jumped in, now frightened. "I didn't do anything but what Professor Trice recommended and Senator Howard requested. How can that be criminal?"

"Let me give you some free legal advice," Jordan interrupted quickly. "Anything you say can and will be used against you in a court of law."

"There is no way you can make this stick," Professor Trice responded incredulously. "All you are doing is trying to make a political statement. No court in the country would uphold an indictment for simply filing a civil lawsuit, even if it is found to be a frivolous lawsuit."

"Maybe yes, maybe no," Jordan answered. "The evidence will determine that, and you know the drill. If a decision is made to seek an indictment, you get your chance to talk the head of the criminal section or the attorney general out of it."

"This is unreal," Professor Trice said, shaking his head. The blood drained from Dr. Bristol's face and he sagged in his chair.

Completion

By late afternoon, the search of Demas Assad's condo was completed in Cambridge, and the attempt to arrest him in Phoenix had been made. Both had failed. There was nothing of value remaining in the condo and Assad—now with a new identity—was already at work in Oaxaca, Mexico preparing for the great border crossing planned to precede MD.

Justice had the FBI working through the list provided by Dr. Bristol in response to Judge Hightower's order. Contacts were being made at other universities, and the education department was now involved in trying to locate the graduates. For all their work, the FBI missed the obvious reality that nearly all of them were in Phoenix attending the ATS conference. For some reason, no one connected the dots. The obvious is always more difficult to see.

In Washington, the service in the East Room continued uninterrupted. Many had left as the day proceeded, but the Bookseller remained, and it seemed that the president and others were not going to leave until the Bookseller left. The consensus was that if he wasn't through, God wasn't through… and they weren't leaving until God was through.

Following their lead, ITN continued every hour on the hour, pausing to go live and show someone praying in the East Room. The two questions were prominently displayed in the background. Many in America—and around the world—followed the lead of those in the East Room and remained in prayer.

Back in Williams, as the sun went down, Pastor Scribes again went to the podium to speak to those that remained in prayer. "I need to finish for you what the Bookseller began," he said. "The passage in Isaiah is our model, but Isaiah's encounter with God did not end when he recognized his sin, confessed it, turned from it and was cleansed and forgiven. It actually only began there, for only after he was cleansed and forgiven could he hear God speak. If we stop now, having been convicted of sin, having confessed that sin, even with tears, and having been cleansed, we will have failed in what God desires to do this day. God is preparing us to be useful, and when that has been done, then He is ready to use us.

"When Isaiah was finally able to hear God speak, he heard God talking amongst Himself—that is, the Father, Son and Holy Spirit. God's question was, 'Whom shall I send? And who will go for us?' Isaiah's response must be your response. He said, 'Here am I. Send me!'[57]

"Do not leave this place until two things have occurred. First, that God has given you the answer to the two questions and you have responded in confession and repentance to anything He reveals as sin. Second, that you have listened for God to speak and answered as Isaiah, 'Here am I. Send me!' Hardness of heart is produced by hearing the Word of God and doing nothing in response. Everything accomplished here thus far will be for naught if we do not hear the voice of God and respond in obedience to whatever God asks.

"The final lesson from Isaiah's example is to understand that Isaiah was ready to obey before he knew what it was that God wanted him to do. That must be us, and frankly, that must be America."

The View from the Invisible

In the invisible, there was evidence of great rejoicing, but it was not what would be expected on earth. It was not just the angels or the great crowd of witnesses who rejoiced, but it was God Himself in His glory celebrating the return of many of His people. It was that joy of the Lord which the Bible says is the strength of Christians.[58]

Back in Washington, high above the East Room, Barnabas, Lucius, and Niger had gathered to watch the continuing work of the light below. "Do you remember when this house was occupied by Abraham Lincoln during those dark days that the evil of slavery was being excised from America by force?" Lucius asked.

"I do," Niger said. "I can picture even now the nights when Mr. Lincoln, unable to sleep, walked throughout this house crying out to God, often all night long. The anguish and suffering never left him until his time was finished and he was called home."

"Yes, but he was changed and grew enormously once he accepted that the fact that the Civil War was God's judgment for the evil of slavery," Barnabas added. "One of my two favorite places in Washington is the memorial they built to remember him—not the statute or the words above his head, but the words on the wall to the right as you stand facing him. They are excerpts from his second Inaugural Address, which evidence his growth and understanding of what was happening to America. It is why God was able to use him to bring America out of that tragic war as one nation. Remember?

> *The Almighty has his own purposes. "Woe unto the world because of offences! For it must needs be that offences come; but woe to that man by whom the offence cometh!" If we shall suppose that American Slavery is one of those offences which, in the providence of God, must needs*

come, but which, having continued through His appointed time, He now wills to remove, and that He gives to both North and South, this terrible war, as the woe due to those by whom the offence came, shall we discern therein any departure from those divine attributes which the believers in a Living God always ascribe to Him? Fondly do we hope—fervently do we pray—that this mighty scourge of war may speedily pass away. Yet, if God wills that it continue, until all the wealth piled by the bond-man's two hundred and fifty years of unrequited toil shall be sunk, and until every drop of blood drawn with the lash, shall be paid by another drawn with the sword, as was said three thousand years ago, so still it must be said "the judgments of the Lord, are true and righteous altogether."

"When the need is desperate, the Father has always raised up a leader for America that He grows into the man needed for the times at hand," Lucius declared. "This house has seen all kinds of inhabitants, great evil and weakness, but in the most difficult days of darkness, God has walked here with men who sought Him out of the midst of their desperation. Lincoln was one, and so is the man kneeling there, I believe," he said, indicating Joshua Strong.

In the darkness, the emphasis had changed. "We cannot defeat this movement of prayer," Legion spat out in frustration. "We must move quickly to change the subject, or we will lose again. Enough of this foolishness. How can we kill this man and speed the attack?" he shouted into the darkness. He turned around and quickly left in search of someone to fulfill the need.

CHAPTER 8

UNEXPECTED BLESSINGS

Saturday, February 16—MD minus 23 days

AT MIDNIGHT, THE ITN moment at the top of the hour continued as it had throughout the day—a live shot of people still praying in the East Room with the two questions superimposed over the kneeling figures. Suddenly, the Bookseller stood and walked somewhat shakily to the front of the room. To all who were gathered, he said, "This day has ended, and God has answered those who sincerely sought Him both here and around the world. Go now, even as Isaiah left the presence of God, cleansed and in perfect obedience to what you have been shown."

The Bookseller was unaware that what he had just shared had been broadcast throughout the world. He had directed his comments to the small, but faithful cadre that had remained throughout the day and into the night. Still present were the president and Janet, the vice president, Tom Knight, Troy Steed, Darrell Reed, David Barnes, General Hedge, George Murphy, Margaret, and Paul Phillips, along with some thirty others. Excited, but very tired and feeling all of his years, the Bookseller was ready to sleep and await God's activity in the morning.

But not all slept, for God was not finished with many. So they remained in prayer, despite the Bookseller's declaration. At public locations and homes throughout the world, the Holy Spirit continued to deal with the hearts of those who remained before the Father for as long as they would remain. There was no norm or consistent pattern. God dealt with each person individually.

The movement of God was not, however, limited to those with the light inside, as Keepers throughout the earth found themselves in battles to retain control over the hearts and minds of those they had dominated for years. Many people had seen and heard enough to light a fire to want to know more. As the desire to become a searcher rose within, a Guardian would initiate a struggle to free that individual from their Keeper so they could search, even as Paul Phillips had been freed to search. Many spiritual journeys were begun this night.

For Darrell Reed, the end of the East Room service had meant checking in at his office to obtain an update on the prayer website. He called on his cell phone as he drove away from the White House. In his heart, he expected an explosion of new information as a result of the prayer raised throughout the day for America, and he was not to be disappointed.

"Darrell, you have to get over here immediately," his co-worker Trace Anderson advised. "That prayer website has been taken down three times by sheer traffic volume around the world. We have so much information we don't know where to start evaluating it. We need more people. Grab any believer you can. Please, hurry!"

Reed was paralyzed for the moment by the importance of what was before them this night. Information regarding MD had been so restricted, he didn't immediately know what to do or who could be trusted. "OK, give me a minute, and I will get some help." He drew a blank until suddenly he had a thought and clapped his hands together, declaring "Yes!" to no one in particular.

He pulled over and made the obvious first call to David Barnes. "Look, David. Help. Call Kayla Walker and any other Christians you know and trust and get them over to my office as fast as you can. The prayer website has exploded with information, and we need help. This can't wait. We have to do this now, or we could lose it forever because of the volume," Darrell said, speaking so quickly it was hard to understand him.

"I got it, geek," Barnes responded. "Let me see what I can do from this end. You get to your office and get this thing organized. Don't forget—lots of coffee. It's going to be a long night." Suddenly an idea invaded his mind.

"Darrell, wait a minute. Do we have someone in Williams who could set up a computer network immediately where people with home computers could get involved?"

"What in the world are you talking about?"

"Listen to me. The prayer website is initiated from Williams, and those people are solid. I believe they could get lots of Christians together on short order to help us go through the emails, and at least separate them by subjects. If I can get clearance from the president, can we turn College Church's education facility into a computer center within the hour?"

"I don't know, but we can try," Reed responded. "You leave the technical part to me. I know who to wake up that can do this, and he has the equipment in his house if you can get clearance from the president and put security on the facility."

The president was interrupted as he sat eating a bowl of soup with Janet, George Murphy, the Bookseller, Paul, and Margaret. It was their first meal since Thursday night.

"Mr. President, I apologize," Barnes began, "but this is important. I need your clearance to do something really radical and somewhat dangerous. It concerns MD," he said, noting the people around and indicating that confidentiality was needed.

"I have no secrets from this group after what we have shared today," he responded. "George, this is still background for now. You can use it later." Murphy nodded, acknowledging the request. He was undoubtedly excited about the stories he would be able to share with the world when this was over.

"David, what is it you need?" the president asked.

As Barnes raced through an explanation of what had happened with the website and his "wild" idea of how to deal with the crisis presented by the volume of responses, the president just smiled. "That sounds like God, doesn't it?" he said as he picked up the phone and asked for the White House operator to get him Pastor Scribes, Tom Knight, and General Hedge—in that order.

Within minutes, the calls had been completed, and Tom Knight had set about getting Christians who had been involved with the MD investigation over to Darrell Reeds' office. Pastor Scribes was calling the family and friends of victims of the violence in Williams who had been with the president at the memorial service, asking them to come to the church and bring their home computers. General Hedges did his part, and security was on the way. At the president's suggestion, the East Room was quickly transformed into an intelligence lab where other known Christians in the administration were woken up and asked to come in with their home computers. Every email would have to be reviewed and categorized.

"Joshua," Janet said, taking the president's hand, "you have all those meetings in a few hours relating to MD. As exciting as this is, and as important as it may be, the best thing you can do for America the remainder of this night is sleep so you can be clear-headed in the morning. There are significant decisions you must make. Come," she said, standing and leading the president to the family quarters.

"Can I help?" Paul asked David Barnes. "I can use a computer. There has to be a spare computer somewhere in the White House."

"Wait a minute, what about me?" George Murphy asked. "This is national security from the inside. I want to help."

"Absolutely," David responded. "Both of you, come with me." They left for Darrell Reed's office, where George Murphy would work this night with Kayla Walker. Paul would return to the East Room later with David to help organize the effort there, based on what he had learned watching efforts at Reed's office.

The Bookseller smiled and looked at Margaret, knowing in his heart that God was mightily at work in all of this, wishing he was thirty years younger and computer literate. Margaret took his hand and said, "Janet had some good advice. Come on, old man; let's leave this to the young ones." They followed a White House steward to the Lincoln Bedroom where they would sleep that night, overwhelmed by all that was happening but totally at peace and filled with a joy that they knew was a gift from God.

Organizing the Effort

As the sun came up in Washington, much had already been accomplished. Barnes and Reed had quickly organized the effort to categorize the emails and had working teams in Reed's office, the White House and in Williams.

The effort had expanded in Williams to include members of Pastor Wilson's church. It took a few late-night calls, but the high school auditorium was opened and made available for their use. Security was quickly organized by Sally Johnson, and the people kept coming to help throughout the night.

The instructions had been simple. All they were to do was read through enough of each email to be able to make a decision to put them into one of several files on the network. The same basic speech had been given by David Barnes to all the groups, either in person or by phone. It went something like this: "Listen up carefully please," he had begun, understanding that his audience was Christians who had gathered to review the emails that had come into the prayer website during or after the day of prayer.

"We believe that what we are doing tonight and tomorrow is the fruit of the prayers of many people across the earth. We believe that in this mass of emails, God may have provided the answer to what we must know of the plans of our enemies if we are to protect America from the attack the president has been warning of these past few days. The threat is certain, and without God's help, we simply cannot be prepared. That is the reality which the president has already acknowledged.

"This night you are God's instrument to review what He has provided. Approach your task with that understanding. Please, before you begin and as you continue, pray for wisdom to be able to discern what is important and how each email should be categorized and into which of the subject files it should be placed. You are being assigned a set number of emails to review, which are being placed in a file identified by your name. You can access that file by using the password which was given to you. Here are the categories.

"If it refers to foreign activity anywhere other than the Middle East or Mexico, put it in the file labeled 'Foreign General.' If it relates to activity in the Middle East, put it in the file by that name. If it relates to activity in Mexico, put it in the file by that name. If it relates to activities in the United States or Canada, put it in the file labeled 'Continental US.' If it relates to military activity anywhere, put it in the file labeled 'Military Threat.'

"If the emails relate to prayer issues, please be very careful to put them in the file labeled 'Ministry Follow-up.' We want to be sure none of those are lost and that they are all provided to the coordinators for the prayer website.

"The categorization of these emails will put them where they can be reviewed together by subject and the information provided combined to get a better picture of what is happening in all of these areas. The system has been backed up and will automatically continue to back up as you work. If you have a question or a problem, let the on-site coordinator know, and they will provide you with whatever guidance you need. Don't be afraid to make the decision on which file to place an email. Just follow your heart, and it will be fine. If you make a mistake, it will be caught later.

"Let me pray for you briefly, and then we'll begin. Lord, before us now is the work of Your hand. We seek Your wisdom and discernment to take what You have given and use it for the purpose provided. Guide and bless those who have come to categorize the information You have provided by subject, and those who will follow after them to dig deeply into what has been revealed to find our enemies' plans and to prepare a response. We thank you in Jesus' name. Amen."

Each of the subject files had been assigned to groups of Christian intelligence officers who began the review work even as the categorization work was in process. It was clear that this effort would take more than one night, and would be continuous as additional emails would be sent. By dawn, Barnes already had been briefed by the intelligence teams on the extent of the information being provided. Prayers were being answered. He could not wait to tell the president.

The Morning After

As the Bookseller read the copy of Susan Stafford's journal, he realized there were real tears covering the pages. The copy had been given to him by Sally Johnson in accordance with Susan's last wishes immediately before they had left College Church for Air Force One. The first opportunity the Bookseller had to read the journal was in the brisk hours of a Washington DC morning, just as the sun came up.

"What an unbelievable waste of a life," he said in the direction of the still sleeping Margaret, who began to stir when she heard him speak.

"You are going to have to try that one again," Margaret said, sitting up and wiping the sleep from her eyes. "I only heard about half of what you said."

"Sorry, I really didn't mean to wake you, but we need to get home," he responded. "This journal needs to be in print immediately, and we must have some kind of memorial service for Susan Stafford. She was evil for so much of her life, but she died a believer. We should honor what God did to change her life. Do you have Pastor Scribes' number?"

"I do somewhere. Let me look," she responded and reached for her purse.

The Bookseller picked up the phone and was greeted with an immediate cheerful, "Good morning, Mr. White. This is the White House operator. How may I help you?"

"I don't really know how any of this works, but can you tell me what I need to do to see the president about going home?" he asked nervously.

"Certainly, sir, the president asked that you be connected to him as soon as you were up."

"I really don't want to bother him," he protested, even as the phone connected and the president answered. "Good morning, Mr. White. I am going to send a steward down who will show you and Margaret the way to join us for breakfast." And with that, he hung up, not giving the Bookseller the opportunity for any response.

Turning to Margaret, he said, "Well, you better get ready quick. The president is sending someone right now to take us to join him for breakfast." Just as the words were out of his mouth, the knock came on the door. "Just a minute, please," and they raced to get dressed.

Already at breakfast with the president were Wilburn Marshall, the vice president, along with a tired but excited David Barnes and Tom Knight. Before breakfast, the vice president had been thoroughly briefed on MD by Tom Knight and had just finished asking a myriad of questions.

"Wilburn," the president interrupted. "Let me tell you how I want to go forward to address this. Your specific area of responsibility will be Europe. You know most of the leaders personally, and they trust you. As soon as we are ready to move, I want you to fly to Europe for a prearranged secret meeting with our allies. Until then, in order not to raise suspicion, I want you to continue on the campaign trail, but with a reduced schedule so we can conference you in on what is going on. I want your input, and

I want you ready to lead the country through this if something should happen to me."

"Whatever you want, Mr. President; I am available," he replied.

"Thank you. I knew that would be your response," the president said with sincere gratitude. "Now for the rest of today, I want you to sit in on all the meetings regarding MD. I have a full schedule of every major group involved in intelligence and preparation for the attacks. By the end of the day, you should be able to get your arms around this and can add your views to the mix. Time is short. Hopefully, we will have a better understanding of when the attack is planned shortly, but I don't intend to wait. I want to be ready to move in less than three weeks."

"That's impossible!" Tom Knight declared.

"I really don't care what is possible," the president immediately responded. "That is what we are going to do. I will not take the chance of waiting until it is too late. We will strike with what we have at what we know," the president said, surprising even himself with the conviction he felt.

"At least," he thought, "we have National Guard units in every state slated to be present at synagogues today and churches tomorrow. No more College Church attacks."

"Sorry to interrupt, Mr. President," a White House steward said as he escorted Margaret and the Bookseller into the room. Again, everyone stood, and the Bookseller was embarrassed.

"Mr. President, please excuse us, we don't want to interrupt your business today. We just need to find out how to make a long-distance call back to Pastor Scribes and make plans to go home."

"We will do both, but come, take a moment and eat with us," the president responded. "You will want to hear how God is answering the peoples' prayers. It is nothing short of amazing."

"No, Mr. President, it is not amazing," the Bookseller answered matter-of-factly. "What is amazing is that it took America so long to get around to allowing God to deal with our sin and then to pray. That is not only amazing; it was foolish and almost fatal."

A loud "Amen" was heard in the invisible from the chorus of the great cloud of witnesses.

Change Everywhere

As businesses opened on Saturday morning, there were lines of people waiting, but not to shop. Crowds greeted most owners with tears and apologies for past thefts and times when they had cheated or been the beneficiary of a mistake made by the business. There were many others who awoke compelled to write letters and send checks or make arrangements with the IRS or their city and state taxing authorities to correct past false tax filings. Letters were also being written regarding dishonest business dealings, some decades old and forgotten by the victim—but not by God, who had reminded the one praying yesterday of that sin. There were even some who went to police stations to confess past crimes. It was as if some portion of America had been awakened to their need to be clean, and they anxiously sought to remove past stains which they now saw dirtied their lives.

Phones rang, and emails were sent throughout America as people who had not even spoken for years sought to heal fractured relationships. The move impacted families and friends, work associates and competitors, and even past enemies. It seemed like healing flowed everywhere throughout the nation as past wounds were addressed and people were freed of anger and hate that had dominated their lives for decades. There was a strange sense of joy which came upon each individual who confessed what they had done and sought to make it right.

Groups gathered spontaneously outside churches and places where they had prayed yesterday. They wanted more time together before the Lord to ask the two questions which had become a national passion for those who had the light within.

What in my life or this nation dishonors the holiness of God's name?

What in my life or our nation is not God's will being done as it is in Heaven?

Pastors knew the topic for their sermons tomorrow. They expected full churches of searchers who had been freed to seek God and who desperately wanted to know the answer to those questions in their lives. They also knew that there were many things they must make right now before their congregations and in private relationships. They too had been shown their sin from God's perspective. Many felt no longer worthy to be a pastor, which in reality made them truly worthy for the first time.

Those without the light within were astounded and frightened by what was happening. They could not simply dismiss it as an isolated occurrence, for it seemed to touch everyone in some way. They watched in amazement as people confessed past wrongs and sought to make them right. They wondered at what could cause a people to be so foolish as to drag up the past and try and deal with it now. Isn't it better to let it alone?

ITN had been searching for the Bookseller since midmorning, trying to find someone to explain what was happening across America. Their calls to the White House had been late. Margaret and the Bookseller were already on a plane for Williams, accompanied by a sleeping Paul. Their flight had been personally paid for by the president himself, who did not want to give any opportunity for GWG or others to claim wrongdoing in connection with funding for the East Room service.

As he sat looking out the window at the scene passing before him, the Bookseller again asked the two questions and listened carefully to hear God's response. He knew that if those with the light inside continued to ask, God would continue to answer and America would be changed. It would be a land that God could bless, but if not, it would be a land left to the terrorists' desires.

CHAPTER 9

A SIGNIFICANT DISCOVERY

Saturday, February 16—MD minus 23 days

BECAUSE OF WHAT was occurring in the invisible, things began to happen quickly in the visible as prayers were answered and the forces of darkness moved to counter any new passion for God with hatred and anger.

It was not difficult for Legion to find many who were easily inspired to kill the president. The country was full of operatives waiting for MD, any of whom would rejoice at the chance to kill this one who was leading the infidels. The problem was an opportunity, and that is where Legion's focus centered now. He knew that there were willing instruments in every major city, including Washington. He had to find the opportunity somewhere to rid the earth of this Christian scourge before he could further interrupt their plans.

Unknown to the forces of darkness, this change in focus from MD preparations to finding a way to kill the president had not been born in the heart of the Dark Master, but rather in the heart of God. It was God who had suggested this new agenda by merely feeding Legion's heart of hate. It quickly became his single passion, and thus his influence over those who sought to carry out MD lessened.

In the Williams Hospital

In Williams, Sam Will was out of ICU and in a private room. He had watched the East Room service broadcast and joined in asking the two questions. Sober and hurting from the surgery as the pain medication had been reduced, he was greeted with, "Hey you old dog. Get out of that bed and let's hit the road!"

"Jason Wilson, you sure know how to bring a little light in a dark place. This hospital stuff is for the birds." Jason was Sam's old trucker friend. It was always good to see him.

"Agreed," Wilson responded. "I have done a serious study and found that more people die in hospitals than anywhere else. You need to get your body out of here while you're still breathing."

"Thanks for the encouragement. What takes you off the road this morning?"

"Well, I wanted to see a certified hero that I'm proud to call a friend."

"Thanks, Jason, but the hero died. I just came around the corner and played clean up. Susan Stafford—as evil as she may have been—was the real hero on that day. She went directly after them knowing she would be killed. She didn't have to do that."

"OK, then there were two heroes. But listen, I need to tell you something," Jason said, with an obvious sense of urgency as he moved to the real reason for his visit. "Remember when I told you there were strange things going on at Brothers Trucking?"

"I do. What now?" Sam responded, grimacing in pain as he sought to sit up in the bed.

"You are not going to believe this one," Jason continued. "Brothers has moved the date again and has just told the drivers of its fuel trucks that the company is giving them paid vacation starting Friday, March 7th through March 12th. They aren't doing this for the drivers of any other kind of trucks; just fuel trucks."

"What is the explanation this time?" Sam asked.

"They say it's part of a full fleet maintenance program to outfit the trucks with some new gizmo to make them more efficient, and that as they finish trucks, they will call the drivers back—but not before the 12th."

"That makes no sense. How can they meet delivery requirements if they shut the whole fleet down for five days?" Sam responded.

"I don't know. The instructions to the drivers are to go to their assigned supply point, fill the trucks, and bring them into the depots and leave them until the 12th. It gets me thinking, how in the world can you install something on a full truck without blowing the thing up?"

"Jason, you have to help me right now. This may be a big deal," he said, pressing the button on his bed to call a nurse. The response was quick because Sam Will was only hours out of ICU.

"Nurse, please, you need to help my friend Jason get my wallet. It has a phone number in it. I have to make a call right now. This is an emergency."

"Slow down, Mr. Will," she responded as she checked the monitors. "You have elevated blood pressure. Your request can wait. Your friend needs to leave now, and I need to give you something so you can rest."

"Young woman," Will responded, his voice now trembling with passion, "either you help my friend get that wallet right now, or we are going to test the doctor's sutures cause I'm getting out of this bed and going myself. You don't understand. This is a matter of national security. I have to call Washington right now, and I have to have that phone number in my wallet!" He was already moving to try to disconnect himself from the tubes and machines.

"Alright, alright, Mr. Will!" she responded quickly. "If you stop trying to get up, I will go with your friend, but you must understand if you try anything else, I am going to get an army of orderlies in here, and we will forcibly sedate you."

"You better make that an army and one," said Jason. "I don't know what this is about, but I know this man, and if that phone number is this important to him, we'd better get it right away."

The situation was tense, but suddenly the nurse, Paula Christianson, understood that something different was at work here. She broke a stack of hospital rules in taking Jason to find that phone number, leaving her patient alone for the moment.

Seizing the Prayer Initiative

The activity around the White House on this Saturday was anything but normal. A rotating group of tired Christians continued to work diligently in the East Room, seeking to categorize the massive volume of messages that had flooded into the prayer website. Members of the cabinet, the Survival Commission and the Joint Chiefs were gathering for a series of meetings with the president. The public cover for all of this activity was that the vice president was being briefed on the status of the investigation of the potential attacks, while others were being allowed to continue the prayer service in the East Room. The White House Press Corps were not fooled, but they could strangely find no one who would enlighten them on what was really happening. Security was unusually intense and openly visible.

Up the street, a different crowd had gathered in Senate Majority Leader Howard's office, reeling from the events of the past twenty-four hours as one coming out from a drinking binge. "What the hell just happened?" Majority Leader Howard asked, confused and angry. "Can anyone explain to me the asinine change that has come over our membership? We can't even get a quorum from our own party to advance the agenda they approved, and we publicly declared only days ago!"

"Who cares about our membership!" Chairman Crow yelled with passion and anger. "What about the rest of the country? In just twenty-four hours, we have lost initiative and direction. We are sitting here trying to find out where the country is going so we can get in front and lead. This is a disaster! We have an election in some twenty months. This is our chance to control. We must find a way to attack that religious idiot in the White House and turn the country back to our plan."

"Do you have the votes to get a bill of impeachment through the House?" asked former president Leonard Cox, remembering what the minority party had done to him when they were in control.

"Bill of impeachment? We can't even get a quorum on the judiciary committee to investigate the Harkins College situation!" Crow responded. "Dr. Bristol and Professor Trice have both refused to testify. We haven't got anything to investigate, even if we could get a quorum."

"How could that be?" asked Majority Leader Howard.

"Somehow those two got a federal judge mad, and now they are the object of a criminal investigation," Chairman Crow revealed, shaking his head in disbelief. "How can this be happening to us? We're the majority!"

"Slow down; we still have the peace conference. I will be leaving for Syria in three weeks," Cox reminded the group. "Let's make that the focus and turn the people to hoping for an end to the violence by a negotiated settlement."

"Yes, that might work. Let's add a new wrinkle which will return us to the 'white hat' category: we'll call a press conference and ask the American people to pray for the peace conference. Let's organize prayer meetings for the peace conference, and not eat like the president did. What's that thing called?"

"Fasting, I think," Cox replied.

"Let's get smart and use this religion thing to our advantage," Crow said excitedly. "We will use his own tactics to take his followers away from him. All we need is an offset to the old man from Williams. Anyone have an idea of who we could use?"

"I know just the guy," Cox smiled cunningly. "He is the pastor of one of those super-sized churches with a radio and TV program and has sold tons of books. Everyone knows his name, and he has been against the Bookseller from day one—purely jealousy."

"And who is this 'miracle worker?'" Howard asked, somewhat cynically.

"Pastor Roy Elkhorn of Faith Church of Joy in that same town, Williams. Everyone in America has seen his face and knows his name. He's our man."

"Call him and see if you can get him on a plane tomorrow after he finishes his church service," Howard responded. "If you, a former president, ask him to lead a prayer effort for peace, he will wet his pants to get in front of the camera before a national audience."

As the Senate majority leadership celebrated their new inspiration and former President Cox made his phone call, Molech smiled in the invisible. "Crow's Keeper is really good," he thought to himself as he left the gathered conspirators to complete their plans. Well, it was actually his plan to hijack the new religious movement. He moved on to coordinate the inspiration needed to push the terrorist operators toward execution of MD. "We are close. We must not fail," he said to the gathered darkness. Dark wisps were quickly sent throughout America with instructions for the hoard of Keepers and Tempters.

White House Moves on News

In the White House Cabinet Room, the president had just finished an opening prayer as the cabinet gathered with the vice president, members of the Survival Commission, the Joint Chiefs and others to address the threat.

"Many of you on the cabinet have been unaware of the magnitude of the threat we face from an imminent terrorist attack, which our intercepts reveal has been labeled simply 'MD' by our enemies," the president began. "We believe that the name was originally tied to the initial date planned for the attack: Memorial Day. Now, however, because of our efforts to discover and prevent the attack, it has been moved up significantly, and we must be prepared to move against it within three weeks." There was a collective gasp in the room as the president paused to let that thought sink in.

"You have been brought here to be briefed on the threat and given your assignments. This is not a drill. The nation is at serious risk. The enemy's plans are for a single swift series of attacks, that if successful, would cripple the nation for at least a decade during which terrorist leaders with sympathetic nations would crush Israel and eliminate us as a military threat. For obvious reasons, all of this is top secret—for your knowledge only. There can be no discussion of any of this with anyone outside this room without specific clearance from Troy Steed, my national security advisor. That includes your staff, your spouse and the leadership of the opposing party.

When we are ready to go public, we will go public, but until then, our enemy must know nothing of our response plans or our level of knowledge. We don't want them to know we are even remotely concerned. Absolutely no one may speak to any member of the media, on or off the record, with no exceptions. Any disclosure risks our ability to complete our investigation and respond. If you have a problem with that, submit your resignation and leave now."

The mood in the room was stone cold sober as the president had intended. Everyone who was learning of this for the first time literally leaned forward in their chairs, waiting for what was next.

"I have asked Tom Knight to review for you in detail what we know of the threat. Listen closely, because many of you may have information that has crossed your desk which could be critical to the final formulation of our response. At my request, Tom has chaired a working group we labeled the Survival Commission to coordinate the investigation of the threat and plan a response. The Joint Chiefs have been on this from the beginning of its discovery, and military forces are being redeployed both here and abroad even as we speak. Senator Besserman has joined the team to coordinate our response and intelligence effort with Israel. As expected, they have proven invaluable, and their designated representatives are with us this morning as part of the team. Tom, you have the floor now."

"Thank you, Mr. President."

For the next hour, Tom Knight used maps, photographs, and a PowerPoint presentation to walk everyone in the room through a summary of what was known of possible weapons, operatives in the country, targets, foreign involvement and anticipated timing. He also presented a horror show depicting what computer models revealed of the damage that could be inflicted if the attacks were successful.

A sense of panic filled the room as the reality of the threat fell upon those who had not been involved until now.

"My God, Tom," the secretary of the treasury said, expressing what many others felt. "We have a hidden enemy already here, possible targets throughout the nation, an attack within thirty days or earlier and we don't even know for sure the weapons they intend to use other than trucks, possibly. How can we defend against that?"

As the discussion deteriorated further into frustration and helplessness, the secured cell phone in David Barnes' pocket began to vibrate. Few people had this number, so Barnes pulled it out to see who was calling. It was Darrell.

"Mr. President, I have to take this; it's Darrell Reed."

"Sure, please step out. If it's something I need to know, just call me out," the president responded.

Leaving the room, Barnes said, "Darrell, what do you have?"

"I think we know when or close to when," Reed responded in a no-nonsense tone. "Kayla got a call from the injured Citizen's Militia guy in Williams; the one who was shot defending the kids at the daycare. If you remember, he was a truck driver. One of his friends came by again to see him in the hospital and shared the news that Brothers Trucking is giving all the drivers of its fuel trucks paid vacation from Friday, March 7th through Wednesday, March 12th. They have been instructed to fill their trucks at refineries or fuel distribution depots and drive them to their assigned Brothers' yard by midnight on the 7th and park them. There is your window, and there are some of the weapons at least.

"I did a quick internet search, and Brothers has yards in nearly every major city in the country. The operatives must be drivers. That is what they were trained for in the camp in Iran, and probably elsewhere. They are going to equip those trucks with some kind of explosive device and drive them into the targets."

"And that's not all; the emails from the prayer website are providing real information on other activities here and abroad that appear connected to the planned attacks. You would not believe it. We will need some time to put it all together, but we have thousands of leads which are being fed into a central data computer once they have been categorized, reviewed and culled. We should have tons of useful information by Monday at the latest. The information keeps coming in by the minute. It's nothing short of a miracle."

"Well, the Bookseller says answered prayer is not a miracle," Barnes responded, "but this sounds pretty miraculous to me. Go for it all. We are close once again. I have to go and get this information to the president. Oh hey, give Kayla a hug and my thanks—but not too much of a hug, alright?"

"I got you, brother," and the geek was off on the run as Barnes stepped into the room and motioned that he needed a minute with the president.

The president immediately excused himself and walked out into the hall. They were gone only a few minutes when both returned and the president interrupted the discussion. "You all need to hear this. I think we have a date, and at least assurance on some of the intended weapons."

Barnes detailed the conversation and then deferred to the president.

"Alright, the date is clearly within the March 7-12th window. I would expect what they plan is intended to be over by the 12th. It will take some time to equip the trucks with an explosive device. Most likely dates for the attack are the 9th through the 11th. Anyone know how many fuel trucks Brothers Trucking has and where their depots are located?"

"I don't know now," Tom Knight replied, "but we can find out fairly quickly."

"What about our union friends in the trucking industry?" Senator

Besserman added. "I can make some calls and find out if there are other companies involved."

"I don't know how many friends I have among the unions, but you can make that call," the president responded, when suddenly an embarrassed and trouble secretary of commerce spoke.

"Mr. President, I don't know whether this is part of what is planned, but the overlap is too close. I am embarrassed to say that the Senate majority leadership has been pressing me to institute an open roads policy for both Mexico and Canada. It is part of that Together Tomorrow push. That organization is the major funding group for the majority party in the coming elections, and they have demanded that open roads be in place by March 7th."

"What would that mean in practice?" General Hedges asked.

"That would mean fuel trucks could cross the Mexican and Canadian borders without inspection at will," he answered.

"That can't happen," General Hedges answered. "You can't issue that order. What you would be doing is giving an invitation to our enemies for a legal invasion of some of the very weapons they intend to use to destroy us."

"That explains activity we have been monitoring in Mexico for some time now," CIA Director Crenshaw added. "We located a camp-like facility in southern Mexico, much like what we found in Iran. It appears to be an oil terminal of some nature with lots of trucks and drivers. They have been training operatives right under our very nose for years."

"It's too late," the secretary of commerce said, appearing distraught. "I issued the order secretly to help my party, and if I withdraw it now, the terrorists will know we have discovered their plan. I'm so sorry. How can I be so stupid?"

"That's OK," the president jumped in. "Leave it alone for now and let their preparations continue. General Hedges, I want military units with whatever it takes to stop those trucks secretly deployed near all major highways into this country from Mexico and Canada by March 6th, awaiting my orders to block those roads and stop all—and I mean *all*—incoming truck traffic."

"Shouldn't we move against the Brothers' truck terminals now?" the vice president asked.

"Not yet," the president answered. "We need to continue to dig for more information. Brothers Trucking cannot possibly be the only company involved. We don't want to send any messages that we know what is coming, or we will lose the chance to deal with the operatives already here. We can't leave them in the country, or my last year and a half will be spent fighting against terror units like those that caused so much havoc in Williams. We need a plan to strike first, but not until we have more information.

"Tom, can we get surveillance on those depots so we know what is happening and can move quickly if required?"

"Yes, Mr. President, the FBI can do that," Knight replied.

"General Hedge, I want you to get back to me later today with information on those depots and what it is going to take to be prepared to secure them in a single strike and stop the trucks from leaving. Can we use local law enforcement, or do we need a military response? Do we need to get the governors involved? My concern is that everyone who knows is another possible leak."

"Yes, Mr. President," General Hedge responded.

"What about former President Cox's so-called peace mission?" Senator Besserman asked. "He frustrates me, but I hate for my party to be used by our enemies."

"Cox has been my greatest political enemy," the president answered, "but on this occasion, he and the rest of that crowd are simply blind to what is really happening. They're not bad people," he paused silently, seeking guidance on what he should do. "That being said, the reality is that their blindness and greed for power is an asset to us right now. Let them go on with their efforts as it lulls our enemy into believing we are still asleep and divided. It is a perfect cover for us while we are preparing to strike first. It diverts the terrorists' attention from what we are doing. Let him go with all the fanfare they can muster. Just ignore it. We cannot tell them and keep our response secret."

"Let's break for a minute and then change the subject. I need to make a phone call. When I get back, we need to address finding the leaders and the operatives. We need to talk about defending known targets and bringing our foreign friends and enemies into this mix. Everything has to happen at once if we are to be successful. Anything we miss will be lost."

CHAPTER 10

MORE, BUT NOT NEARLY ALL

Saturday, February 16—MD minus 23 days

AS HE ENTERED the Oval Office and sat at his desk, the president picked up the phone and asked the always pleasant voice of the operator to find Leonard Cox. As he waited, there was a knock at the door, and he stood to receive Attorney General Rodriguez.

"Mr. President, I apologize for intruding, but what we just learned about the timing for the trucks fits with what we have discovered from the Harkins College investigation as well as inquiries at the airlines. I didn't know how much you wanted to discuss in the larger group."

"Please come in, Felix," the president answered. "I appreciate your discernment. Only a very small group needs to know everything." He came around, and they sat on couches facing each other, joined by the vice president, David Barnes, and Tom Knight.

"The list we finally got from Harkins of Arab graduate students in education included Abdul Farsi and two others who worked at schools in Cambridge, and were probably J-10 and J-14," the Attorney General continued. "One was a professor at Harkins, as we thought, and the other was a civics teacher at a local junior high. The names under which they lived and received their degrees were Demas Assad and Phygelus Aldar. Those two are AWOL. There is no record that they left the country and no evidence of their current location. Their apartments appear as if they left without taking anything other than clothes to travel. Our forensic teams are conducting searches as we speak, but I don't expect to find anything of value. They must have known we were close after all the publicity surrounding the Harkins suit.

"We were able to trace them both to a teachers' convention in Phoenix that ends today. They were there the first day, Thursday, but vanished that night. We assume they have left the country under phony identifications."

"What about the others?" the president asked.

"Most are probably still at the convention, but we can't be sure. We are in dispute with the leadership over their attendance list and have had to go for a grand jury subpoena to force production. It never ceases to amaze me how these people justify protecting those who may be planning their destruction."

"You have the Harkins names now; can you get the list from the hotel and arrest them?" the vice president asked.

"We probably could if we wanted to go that way," the Attorney General answered, "but there is a risk we will miss some that may not be there, and we will still have all those operatives loose in the country to wreak havoc. I think we are better off to identify them and then put full intelligence on each one to try and identify everyone involved in the plan before we strike."

"Agreed," the president said. "We can't do this a little at a time. We have to have a plan to respond once to all of it. We will only get one chance to stop this."

"And I think we now know more about when the attack is coming," the attorney general continued. "The airlines' information indicates that a large number of reservations out of the country were changed starting Thursday night to a window of Saturday, March 8th to Sunday, March 9th. None of the names of those who made changes are the same as on the Harkins list, but we wouldn't expect them to be. These people have as many different identities as cats have lives.

"Now, on the attack date. Assuming that J-10 and J-14 were at the Phoenix convention Thursday night, and when they disappeared and the reservations changed, they must have delivered the message, changing the date for the attack to the coordinators before they left the country. Based on what we just heard about the Brothers Trucking driver vacations, the final date must now be either March 10th or 11th."

"If that is true, then the operatives don't yet know the correct date, and we could create confusion by moving against the coordinators immediately," Tom Knight responded with excitement. "They wouldn't know when to attack, and some parts of the plan would be scheduled for different times. We would destroy their ability for a united movement against us."

"Tom, that simply doesn't work," the president said firmly. "We are going to have to exercise some patience and faith here. I have already said this before. We have to move in one united strike against everything, both here and abroad, or we fail. I cannot leave 1,000 plus operatives—and who knows how many assassination squads—loose in America to organize their own strikes after we eliminate the coordinators. I know I am taking a chance letting them go for now, but I believe that is the right thing to do to address the whole threat. The responsibility is mine alone. Write that up somewhere if you want. That is my decision.

"Felix, you cover every one of those coordinators like a blanket. Tap their landlines. Set up intercepts for their cell phones. Have them followed and keep them under constant observation. Hack into their computers if possible. Whatever we can do under either the national security intelligence laws or as part of the criminal investigation, do it. We have to find the operatives, identify the weapons and locate all the targets—and we have to do that in the next couple of weeks."

"Mr. President," David Barnes began, just as the phone rang.

"Excuse me for a moment, gentlemen," the president said, picking up the phone. "I placed a call I need to take. You don't have to leave."

"Mr. President," the White House operator advised, "we have located former President Cox. He is with the Senate majority leadership in Leader Howard's office."

"Fine, put him through."

"Leonard, this is President Strong. Sorry to interrupt your meeting. I just need a moment of your time."

Every mouth in the room dropped in unison as they realize who the president was talking with.

"I have called to apologize and ask for your forgiveness. As I prayed yesterday, one of my sins that God made very real to me was the way I treated you with disrespect, even threatening your eviction when you were last here with the Senate leadership. I was way out of line, and ask that you would forgive me."

There was silence on the other end of the line as the former president didn't know what to say or how to react. Finally, after a long, uncomfortable pause, Cox said, "Mr. President, politics is war, and you certainly didn't do anything I would not have done and more. You don't owe me an apology."

"Leonard, you are correct, but my standards and your standards are not at issue here. God was not pleased with me, and He made that very clear yesterday. I violated His standards, and that is not right because God says it is sin. For that, I must apologize and ask for your forgiveness. I have already asked God's forgiveness."

"I don't get this God thing, but sure, I accept your apology if that is what you want me to say. Understand though, I am still your political enemy, and it is my goal to bring your party down and reclaim the White House," Cox replied.

"Thank you, Leonard, you have brightened my day. Perhaps you and your wife will join us here for a private dinner sometime after you get back from Syria?"

"Sure," he answered uncomfortably. "I have to go now," Cox said, quickly hanging up the phone and shaking his head in confusion and disbelief.

Samantha's Answer

As the plane landed at O'Hare International Airport, Samantha was already waiting just past security. When Paul and the others came into view, she rushed to greet him warmly, for she was learning that times apart were becoming increasingly empty.

After a few moments together, she exclaimed, "I have to tell you what we have been doing at the church!" She excitedly explained the work being done to categorize the prayer website emails. "You would not believe what we have learned with just a quick read through the messages. There are believers all over the earth that God has placed in critical places to observe things that have to be related to the planned attacks. It is as if the prayer time before the Lord broke a dam and released a flood of information that could have been obtained nowhere else."

In her excitement, she was saying too much too publicly, so Paul quickly interrupted. "Let's hold off until we get in the car." She immediately understood but found it difficult to contain herself until they began to share their experiences at the White House. Later as they drove toward Williams, the Bookseller asked, "Samantha, your dad was one of those killed by Susan Stafford when she was the sniper, wasn't he?"

"Yes, he was," she responded, and her countenance immediately changed for this was an area of continuing conflict in her heart.

"I read her journal while we were on this trip. She describes that killing and all of the others coldly and indifferently until she is touched and ultimately changed by God. She describes the struggle and the efforts of the evil one to keep her as his servant by deception. She was told that the killings were actually the will of God; that it was His judgment on people who deserved to die. That belief continued until God opened her eyes and showed her the second death. After that, she began her search for truth and was ultimately led to God.

"Did you know that she set out to kill Paul and ended up shooting a terrorist sent to kill me right in front of the warehouse? That is what all the activity that day was about," he paused. "If it weren't for God's intervention, she would have succeeded."

"I think Heaven will be a little like that," Margaret added. "We are going to learn so many things about times God intervened in our lives that we never knew. I wish we could always see His activity, but none of us would be able to handle that in the flesh."

"Samantha, I have to ask you a question," the Bookseller said, returning to his original subject. "After reading her journal and considering the way she lived after she encountered Jesus, I know she was born again and became one of us. I feel burdened to organize a memorial service for her, not as a time to honor her, but as a memorial service should be; a time to honor what God did in and through her. How would you, a victim of her evil past, react to that?"

Another dam broke as Samantha released her guilt over her feelings for the dad who abandoned their family and the reality of what God does through the new birth. She knew because she had also been changed.

"Please, I want to be a part of that service. I want to share. I know what happened to Susan and I know that when she died, she was new; she was a totally different person."

There was silence in the car the remainder of the way back to Williams, as everyone paused to take in what they had seen and heard these past days. Paul's arm went around Samantha, and she leaned her head on his shoulder. The Bookseller had his answer and knew what he needed to do as soon as they got home. Now that he had an answer to the "should he" question, he prayed silently for the answer to how.

Once Again, the Flag is Up

The sun was setting in Iran, and the flag was up. Ittai had seen the flag earlier in the day and made for the agreed rendezvous point at dusk. Hushai was waiting, and they sped to their protected place of prayer, both tired from the earlier night's activity.

"Ittai, you may tell the Americans that God must have been listening to their most recent request. Suddenly we have both people in the government and even a person in leadership with Ahmad Habid willing to provide information and assistance. Their eyes have been opened to what the success of the terrorist plan would mean for the future of the people in Iran. They want a different future."

"How could that have happened in just twelve hours?" Ittai asked.

"All I can tell you is that God created everything you see and what you can't in just six days. Twelve hours is nothing to Him," Hushai replied. "Within a couple of weeks, I expect to know the location of the main nuclear assembly and research facilities, how it can be destroyed from the air, and when and where the leadership of Habid's group will meet for final coordination before the attacks are launched against the Americans in the Middle East. We should also know the orders for the military action against Israel and the identity of all nations who have signed on."

"How can you be sure this is good information?"

"I can't be sure," Hushai answered. "Who can? But what we have is more than what we had before. I am assuming the information will be good because of various sources, but the Americans will need to do everything they can to confirm that the information is correct. Some of it will be easy with satellite intelligence. The rest will hopefully be confirmed by messages posted on the prayer website."

"Hushai, I need whatever you can get by Monday the 3rd. The American response will be launched sometime between the 7th and 9th. They believe the date for the attacks is between March 10th and the 12th. They have to launch first and need specific target information. Having the greatest military in the world is nice, but it is useless unless you know what to attack."

"Perhaps the flash drive Hiram sent to the Bookseller will help."

"Perhaps," Ittai responded hopefully. "I am confident it will help, but we have to stay with it to find out anything additionally we can and get that information to the Americans. Do you know anything more about the Russians?"

"General Vandenburg and Joseph Krenski have been seen again in Teheran. They returned from Russia with instructions. We don't know what, but the Iranian government is still coordinating with them to some extent," Hushai answered.

"I don't know how the Americans can stop the Russians if they are willing to risk a nuclear exchange," Ittai said. "They must think the move by the American president to seek God shows weakness, and that he would back down rather than confront a nuclear threat. I fear they misread him, which is dangerous in itself."

"Well, now that you have thoroughly depressed me with all the impossibility of the circumstances that will be played out over these next weeks; how about laying that at the feet of the only one who can do something about it?" Hushai responded.

"You wouldn't be suggesting something radical like praying, would you?" Ittai answered with mock seriousness. "I amaze myself at how quickly I slip back into looking to myself for the answers. Sorry."

"Apology accepted, but you better begin by taking it up with the One you turned from and offended."

"Yes, you're right," and he opened his prayer with a cry for forgiveness as the two settled into laying before the Lord the responsibilities of the moment.

Still to Learn

Equally as active as those in Washington were the forces of darkness as they prepared for the attacks. Legion was diverted for the moment, inspiring multiple attempts to kill President Strong, but Molech and others maintained focus. Through their inspiration, cell phone calls had been made Thursday night to seconds in command by all coordinators, which meant if Tom Knight's advice had been taken, it would have had no effect on the attacks.

The operators knew the new date for the attack and were in preparation accordingly. Others throughout the world that had committed to be involved were readying themselves for March 11th. Had President Strong fully understood the magnitude of the threat, it could have overwhelmed him. To overcome this threat, he had to trust God for what he knew and what he did not know. That is always true for the followers of God.

What he did not yet know was massive. In America, the weapons of choice were being gathered. The fuel trucks, heavy-duty equipment, and chartered aircraft had been obtained through the purchase of Brothers Trucking (of which they knew), but also of Kingdom Charters and Terminal Equipment Leasing. In Mexico, the purchase of Access Mexico provided a second fleet of fuel trucks being readied to cross the border and move to their targets when the secretary of commerce's open highways order became final.

In the Middle East, Syria and Hezbollah had signed on to join Iran in an attack on Israel. Russia was on board if the America attacks were successful, and the Palestinians could be used as they were always used—good cannon fodder. Ahmad Habid was preparing to finalize attacks on American forces in the Middle East. Iran had committed missiles to the attacks if needed. Coup attempts and assassination plots were in place to be launched from terrorist cells in Saudi Arabia, Egypt, Pakistan, Kuwait, Jordan, and Iraq. By the end of the day March 11th, the hope was to have installed terrorist-friendly governments in each of those nations and to have available the Pakistan nuclear weapons for the continued fight with Israel. The plan included grabbing former President Cox as a hostage in Syria in case leverage was needed.

To divert the Europeans, terrorist cells had been assigned rush-hour attacks on trains. That would turn the European forces inward as the attacks proceeded elsewhere, and then there was always the fallback. No matter what may be discovered and stopped, there were assassination squads like that in Williams in every major American city who would be turned loose on the 11th in coordinated attacks on elementary schools. "That would strike terror into the hearts of the surviving Americans," thought the Sheik, who issued the order. It was, of course, Legion's idea before altered compulsion seeking the president's death.

Looking over the visible preparations from both sides, Molech turned to Chemosh and said, "This time I think we may have them. Even that prayer thing will not be enough. Americans never stay with anything long enough for it to be effective. The microwave approach will not satisfy the Enemy. A day of prayer will never make up for a lifetime of prayerlessness and rebellion. We will win. They will go back to being just like before. They have not really changed."

Observing was Barnabas, who had a different view. "Real revival produces God-changed people, and I believe this revival was real." He thought, "It's not over. It has only begun. These people made real choices. They chose God."

As the day progressed, further evidence of change came from the most unusual of places. Throughout the country, prison wardens were receiving calls from death row guards reporting that some inmates wanted to go public with the details of their crimes and withdraw all pending appeals. They were prepared to die and faced the prospects of their execution with peace. In some prisons, there was even singing among those condemned to die.

CHAPTER 11

AN UNEXPECTED DELIVERY

Sunday, February 17—MD minus 22 days

AS MORNING INTRODUCED another Sunday in America, it was strangely different. Long lines appeared early at the doors of many churches to greet pastors and staff members who came expecting a time alone to make final preparations for morning services. The two questions continued to burn in the hearts of people, and they had come this morning for answers. "What in my life or the nation dishonors the holiness of God's name? What in my life or our nation is not God's will being done as it is in Heaven?" The light within would not release God's people from that search, and it drew others to an awareness of the presence of God and their accountability before Him for conduct He defined as sin. The transformation was radical.

There was a general wonder at what had taken place across the nation, for multitudes had obviously been changed. They thought differently and lived with a new awareness of the presence of God. Life seemed to have a different meaning for them as their focus became less about self and more on others. They saw the suffering and hurt around them through new eyes and spontaneously began to reach out to help. Within affected families, there was a new tenderness and desire to meet needs rather than have their needs met. It was as if overnight, millions received new husbands, wives, dads, moms, children, brothers, sisters and friends who, for the first time in their lives, truly cared more about each other than they cared about themselves.

Those who were untouched within saw the evidence without and wondered. Most would have agreed with Molech, had they heard his thoughts. "This so-called change cannot last, whatever it is." Keepers continued to pour the message that this new passion for religion was dangerous to all who were not involved in the movement into the minds of those still held captive. "It must not be tolerated. It must be ended quickly, or it will hurt you. Soon they will want to take away your freedom to live as you wish." These thoughts were planted with effect. Division was unavoidable.

Within those sent into the country to carry out MD, the new movement generated scorn and hatred. They believed it was a sign of weakness to apologize and ask forgiveness for anything. Their god demanded vengeance and would not tolerate disobedience or sniveling infidels. They were here as his hand to carry out that vengeance, not to whine and moan and ask for forgiveness. Let the weak seek forgiveness. They would seek glory in martyrdom and in destruction, but not on this day as churches were protected by armed private security, police or National Guard. There would be no repeat of College Church this Sunday.

Legion had done his work well in his prior preparations for MD. The forces of darkness had changed their tactics, ignoring those with the light inside to focus carefully on the available instruments in their hand. Any sign of influence from the forces of light was met with an immediate response of total deception to hold their servants to the agenda of darkness. When the accepted language is lies,[59] anything goes, and anything can be made believable.

"We are fortunate to also have many of our instruments in the pulpits," Baal reminded Molech and Chemosh who had gathered to consider how best to use this day. The Dark Master has prepared his alternative message on the two questions, and it has been poured into the minds of pastors and teachers under our influence. And so this day, a different message was also to be shared. Rather than asking the two questions as posed by the Bookseller, the message was twisted to confuse and change the questions, turning the focus away from sin and repentance and distorting the definition of sin itself. Rather than asking "what is wrong in my life that dishonors God," the first question was rewritten to ask "what is wrong with others?" And when the nation was under consideration, what was wrong was surely pure politics. What was wrong with the nation that dishonored God was said to be anything that did not follow the particular political or social agenda of the speaker, and it was always against the president.

The second question was likewise altered. The definition of God's will was changed from the answer a person might find searching the Bible to whatever the one in the pulpit advocated under the influence of the Dark Master. Again, by turning the question into attacks on others and on the nation's policies, the questioner was turned away from an evaluation of self to blaming others. Neither God or His Word had any part in this process. It was purely the opinion of the speaker, which was the opinion of their Keeper.

"Can you believe that it is happening again?" Barnabas exclaimed to those of the forces of light who gathered high above America to observe what was being done in buildings labeled "church" throughout the land. "The truth is being twisted, and the purpose of the Father directly assaulted by these false messengers of Hell."

"Calm down, Barnabas," Lucius answered. "God has not abandoned His throne. He remains sovereign. Nothing new is happening today in the way that the forces of darkness twist the truth. Remember, Satan himself used scripture to attempt to deceive Jesus into disobedience.[60] It did not work then, and it will not work now among those who made their choice for God. Look closely, and you will see."

Below them, in many of the so-called churches under the influence of the forces of darkness, something different was happening today. They saw multitudes of people suddenly walking out in the middle of sermons. Those with the light within who had made their choice for God were no longer blinded by the deception of these false messengers or burdened with their own sin. They could see clearly and understood what was being done. They could no longer be convinced by the deception, so they left to search for a place where the Bible was taught truthfully and completely, wondering how they could have been so blind for so long.

It was also true for searchers without the light inside whose eyes were opened to how the two questions were being twisted. They were looking for answers, not new questions. They had no interest in being shown a way to avoid confronting themselves with what God called sin. They wanted to learn about this God whom they must choose to serve, and so they too left with the Christians, hoping to find a place where real answers would be given. Their search continued as Keepers and Guardians fought over which kingdom would influence each person drawn to church on this Sunday morning as well as those who had not come to church, but knew they should have.

At College Church and others where the light within ruled, the agenda that morning was very different from other Sundays. By the time they reached the church and stood in line to enter, they were already filled with a sense of awe and reverence. The buildings were silent except for the beautiful sound of voices mixed in prayers collectively raised by those awaiting the start of the service.

When Pastor Scribes entered the sanctuary and encountered the prayers, he sat quietly down on the front row and directed the minister of music to do the same. The choir and those who played the instruments were prepared to begin, but sat silently and bowed to pray. The service had already been started by the One who they had come to worship, and they were not needed. In the back sat Margaret and the Bookseller with Samantha and Paul. No one noticed the man who was with the president just yesterday, and who on Friday had set the nation to consider the two questions. He was just another voice in prayer.

Soon it became obvious to Pastor Scribes what was happening as people began to cry out, asking for forgiveness. There was a desperate need felt by those who had been changed to share what God had done in their lives and to publicly confess that God had not truly been their Lord before Friday. Although it was a risk, and the forces of darkness immediately saw it as an opportunity, Pastor Scribes sensed that he should set aside his sermon and open the floor to a time when those compelled to share could do so publicly.

Rising and walking to the podium, Pastor Scribes said, "This day is a day to continue what God began on Friday and to share what God has done. If God leads, the podium is open for you to share what God did in your life Friday and how you have been changed. If God leads you to publicly confess sin against this body, the way is open for you to do so, but this is not about secret sin or sin against an individual. This is about sin against all of us. If you ask, God will lead. By coming, you are declaring that God has something to say through you. If you don't have that compulsion, don't come. If you are looking at your watch because of other plans or commitments, please leave now, for there will be no clock this day to limit what God wants to do here."

Suddenly the aisles were filled, and in a steady stream, people came to the front forming a line that soon reached to the back of the church and into the entry area. Person after person, adults and children, old and young, male and female publicly poured out their hearts in tears over the sin that God had revealed dominated their lives, dishonored Him and kept them from living within His will. There were gasps and sighs, loud agreement and much silent prayer as those gathered joined in each testimony and confession.

People came to the front to embrace a friend who shared and to pray with them. God used each testimony to pierce the heart of others present that had hidden their eyes from similar sin in their own lives. The whole service was out of man's control, but completely under God's. No one present escaped being touched by the hand of God.

Unseen, but quietly entering to stand in the back of College Church was Carl Varvel who had come looking for the Bookseller with another package from Iran. He felt that he was an alien in a foreign place as he watched and listened until he found his heart strangely touched by the witness before him. The battle was on for another searcher who began to see that God must be real.

Once again, a Keeper was defeated as a Guardian lifted the great yellow hands from Varvel's head. As the exclusive influence by the forces of darkness was lost, his heart and mind were suddenly opened to search. His mind began to focus on the two questions which were being shown on an overhead projection system as testimonies were being shared up front.

Long after noon, Pastor Scribes sensed a pause. He took the walking microphone, turned to those still gathered, and said, "The church will remain open as long as people remain here. Staff will be present 24/7 to counsel and pray with anyone who wishes, but there is one thing I want to share before some of you leave as I know you must.

"A mere three days ago, there was another terrorist attack in our city. You will remember. It was just down the street. Three terrorists sought to kill the children and teachers at Kingdom Daycare. God was gracious, and the only one to die that day was a member of our own Citizen's Militia; a woman we would later learn had been the shooter we feared all those months. She died, unlike her life, in defense of others. That was Thursday.

"On Friday, as we sought God in prayer, we learned again that we ALL are sinners and that sin is whatever God defines as sin. There are no exceptions. The Bible tells us not only that we are all sinners, but that 'the wages of sin is death, but the gift of God is eternal life in Christ Jesus our Lord' in Romans 3:23. Susan Stafford was a sinner that deserved to die. Truthfully, so are you and I. We too will eventually die—at least physically. The issue is never physical death, for that will come to us all in God's time. The issue is eternal life in Christ Jesus our Lord.

"The note and journal Susan Stafford left clearly evidence an encounter with God after which her life demonstrated that she had been born again and was a new creation in Christ Jesus who had become her Lord. As such, she is a member of God's family, and to us, she is a sister. We will spend eternity with her; she too cleansed from all sin even as we are by the blood of Jesus shed on the cross.

"Some of you may struggle with this, but just think of the thief on the cross and how Jesus dealt with him. On Thursday, March 6th, we are going to celebrate a memorial service for Susan Stafford to honor what God did in her life. A family member of one she killed and the parent of one of the children she saved has already asked to speak. Mark that date on the calendar and come and join with us at noon as we celebrate the enormity of what God can do in any surrendered life.

"Now let me pray." The formal service closed, though many remained as the testimonies continued.

Earlier in the afternoon, Pastor Roy Elkhorn had boarded a flight for Washington D.C., anxious to get there and begin as the spokesman of the prayer for peace effort leading up to former President Cox's departure for the meeting in Syria. He was still somewhat shaken that the services at Faith Church of Joy had been interrupted when a large crowd walked out as he attempted to discuss the two questions. "Why didn't the people listen to me?" he wondered. "They always did before."

Gift from Iran

Carl Varvel stopped the Bookseller on the sidewalk outside College Church as he and Margaret were walking back to the warehouse. "Mr. White, I have another message for you from Iran. Can we go somewhere private?" he asked.

"Certainly, let's go back to my study," the Bookseller answered. "It's just down the street, as you remember. Can you stay for lunch? I hate for you to always be running back and forth. We have never even had the chance to sit and talk for a few minutes."

"Mr. White, my job is national security; the survival of the nation. I don't know what is going on with this private citizen exchange with our intelligence people in Iran, but my instructions come from the highest level in the CIA. I am not to delay. All I am to do is deliver this package and then wait for your response. I don't think you appreciate how unusual all of this is."

"It is no more unusual than what you just witnessed," the Bookseller responded, "and there is more of a connection between the two than anyone on earth understands."

For some unknown reason, Carl Varvel knew that the statement the Bookseller made was true, although he did not understand it at all. Suddenly there descended upon him a sense of the importance of what he was about to hear, and he was glad to know he was carrying a loaded 357 along with the Iranian package.

As they entered the Bookseller's study, Varvel handed him the package and waited while it was opened. There was the note and Hiram Urbay's flash drive. The Bookseller had never seen a flash drive and had no idea what was now in his hand. Picking up the note, he read:

> *My brother: the enclosed flash drive is for President Strong. We believe that this is God's answer to our prayers for wisdom and discernment into what the terrorists have planned.*
> *–Your Iranian Brothers*

Pausing, the Bookseller immediately fell to the floor on his knees to thank God for what he held in his hand, and to pray for wisdom on what to do now. Carl Varvel was shocked at what he had just witnessed, but that shock was nothing compared to his reaction when the Bookseller handed him the note and then reached for his wallet to get the paper on which the president's secure cell phone number was written. Reaching for the phone, the Bookseller dialed the number, and almost immediately a voice on the other side announced firmly, "This is Joshua Strong."

"Mr. President, this is Samuel White. Please know I would never bother you if it weren't of high importance. The brothers in Iran have sent me some kind of computer something that I am holding in my hand. Their note says it is a flash drive for you, and that they believe it contains God's answer to the prayers for wisdom and discernment into what the terrorists have planned. What do you want me to do?"

"Who is there with you?" the president asked.

"Just Margaret and Mr. Varvel, the man who has carried the exchanges between the Iranian brothers and me," he answered.

"Let me speak to Mr. Varvel, please."

The Bookseller handed the phone to Mr. Varvel, who immediately stood at attention as he said, "Yes, Mr. President."

"The flash drive Mr. White has received may be the key to our defense against a planned massive terrorist attack. Guard that flash drive and the Whites with your life. I assume you are armed."

"Yes, Mr. President."

"We will have someone there within thirty minutes to pick up the flash drive and send the information on it to Washington. When they get there, they will use the password 'life.' If they don't say 'life' and ask for the flash drive, shoot them. They are our enemies."

"Yes, Mr. President," and the line went dead.

A Revelation

Two hours later, an excited Darrell Reed interrupted the president's continuing meetings relating to MD defense. It was the geek's first time in the White House; he had come with David Barnes.

"Mr. President," Barnes opened, "you need to see this." The meeting stopped as Darrell hooked up his laptop to an overhead projector in the conference room and began walking through Demas Assad's 'Final Solution' presentation. It was taken from the flash drive, and it showed the major targets in each state, how they would be attacked and the anticipated damage which would be inflicted. There were audible gasps as the vice president, the chairman of the joint chiefs, Tom Knight and others watched with the president how MD was intended to attack major oil refineries, dams, power plants and associated distribution networks, exposed pipelines, water purification plants, and distribution systems.

"Good God, Mr. President," General Hedge exclaimed. "If this actually happened, America would be set back a hundred years!"

"General, it is because God is good that we have this," the president admonished the chairman. "Now the question is not 'if' this happens, but how can we stop it? We have the targets, and we know the weapons and the approximate date. Is that enough? It has to be enough."

"I will get a team on this immediately," General Hedge responded matter-of-factly. "Sorry about the God comment, Mr. President. The magnitude of this caught me by surprise, and it's a sinful habit. This is more complicated than we could have ever imaged. We have to focus on fuel trucks, large equipment, and aircraft as potential weapons. From the presentation, it is also obvious they expect to be able to use truck explosives like were used in the Oklahoma City bombing. I will have an outline of a defense tomorrow morning. Somehow we have to stop the trucks and planes before they can attack and be prepared to defend against those we can't stop," he was heard mumbling as he left for the Pentagon with a box of copies of Hiram's flash drive.

"Tom," the president instructed, "get Commerce and Justice chasing down foreign purchases of aircraft companies or fleets and large equipment companies in the past five years here and in Mexico or Canada. Look for common ownership or common sources of money for the purchases. If we can find the fleets, we can stop their use."

"Yes, Mr. President," he said, leaving to make the calls.

"Another front to consider, Mr. President," Stephen Hollister, the director of Homeland Security inserted. "Remember the execution squads like the one in Williams?"

"I do. What have we learned?"

"The FBI station chief in Chicago reported to Homeland Security that the questioning of the surviving terrorist of the daycare attack has confirmed that groups like theirs are distributed throughout the country, and have been for months. The wounded terrorist did not know details, but there were ten in his group, and they were ultimately responsible to Abdul Farsi, the teacher. If that is true, and he could be lying, the execution squads are probably located in the cities where the operatives are working, but they are not living in the same physical place, and they have very limited contact. The Williams group was staying with Palestinian students who were legally attending Williams College on student visas. They will be difficult to find unless the coordinators make a mistake."

"Not likely this late in the game," Attorney General Rodriquez added. "These people already have their plans and schedules. They won't need to be contacted more than once to confirm the new date, and that was probably done from the Phoenix convention by phone. The coordinators have to know they are being watched. They're cowards, but they are not stupid."

"I wouldn't worry about it, Governor," Darrell responded, not being sure who had been speaking. "You haven't seen the detail we have received on that prayer website. It will be tomorrow before we can give you the first summary, but I would say that if one of those fellows drops a quarter on his bedroom floor, we will know which side is up. That is true both here and abroad for those planning moves against American forces there and against Israel. The level of detail in these emails is beyond belief."

"I hope you're right, Darrell," the president said. "Without God providing us with exact detail on where these people are, we will never be able to prevent a reoccurrence of Williams' style attacks all across the country. As soon as we are sure, we have to bring law enforcement in on this. The military can deal with the physical targets, but we need law enforcement ready to deal with the execution squads."

"What about foreign issues?" the vice president asked. "How are we going to deal with the threats to our troops and the potential attack on Israel?"

"There is news on that front too," reported CIA Director Crenshaw. "The same guys who sent us the flash drive have been able to identify moderates within the Iranian leadership, and even one among the leadership of the group that has been organizing attacks on our troops in Iraq who understand the consequences of MD and wants to help stop it. We expect to have information soon, which may include the location of the main nuclear weapons research facility and when and where leaders of MD are meeting for final coordination. If we get that information, we will be ready to move on it as ordered, Mr. President."

"Wilburn, for now, you have to leave and stay with your campaign commitments to avoid attracting unnecessary suspicion by our enemies," the president continued. "We will stay in contact by secure phones so you will be totally up to speed on what is happening. On Thursday the 6th, you will be traveling along with many in the cabinet to advise our friends and warn our enemies. We will move with what we have after midnight D.C. time on Friday the 7th—everywhere at once. If some of the operatives leave for hotels near airports before that date, it could be earlier."

"That is a lot of days to maintain security on a response plan," the vice president responded. "How are you going to complete what has to be done to prepare without tipping off the enemy and causing them to change the schedule again?"

"We are going dark—absolute silence," the president answered. "I don't want friend or foe to know what we are doing or how close we are to a response. I will clear my schedule and stay here and work through the plan until the last ten days or so. At that point, I will go to Camp David under the guise of a working vacation. I expect our 'friends' down in the Senate majority leader's office will continue to be a useful diversion in my absence from the public arena. They will most likely continue with their 'peace is at hand' campaign, which should lull our enemies into a sense of safety as they continue to prepare for their attack. That should give us the time and cover we need to be ready to launch first."

Above them all, unseen and there by a convoluted combination of permission and rebellion, sat Argon, a mere tiny wisp who had heard only the end of the president's conversation—but that was enough. "Going to Camp David," he thought. "That means a flight in and out of the White House grounds; just the opportunity the Dark Master needs." Smiling, believing that now he knew his way back into power, he departed quickly in search of Legion, the one member of the Counsel of Darkness who he believed shared his level of hatred of this president and who might be willing to give him a second chance.

Then, as if a light went on inside—which it had—the president paused for a moment and turned to address David Barnes. "David, make a note and remind me to instruct General Hedge tomorrow that I want a covert military unit to provide hidden security on Leonard Cox while he is in Syria. They are going to have to be prepared to extricate him by force if an attempt to take him is made. He is a fool to go, but he is a former president, and we are not going to let him be taken and then have to deal with a hostage situation."

Down the street at that same moment, there was a different kind of meeting going on in Senator Howard's office. They had their man; Pastor Roy Elkhorn was totally on board and would announce the creation of the National Committee to Pray for Peace tomorrow. A Senate resolution would be offered, calling for the nation to pray for former President Cox's peace mission. "That ought to turn the tide away from this 'preacher' president," Senator Howard gloated after Elkhorn had left. "We'll even ask him to be a part of the prayer effort and hold a public prayer meeting in the Capitol. He has to attend."

"Perhaps," Cox agreed, "but don't underestimate that guy. He's scary."

CHAPTER 12

INSPIRATION

Monday, February 18—MD minus 21 days

IT WAS NOW exactly three weeks until the rescheduled MD date. Having been cooped up for months hiding in apartments and rent houses waiting for that day, there was a sense of relief in these final weeks of preparation, although most knew they would soon die in the attacks. They were the chosen ones, privileged to strike the mortal blow against the Great Satan of the West, and their time was finally near.

What to a Western mind would seem unthinkable was all they lived for. From childhood, it had been poured into them that martyrdom was their purpose in being born. Some had even played with suicide dolls when they were little. All had been taught and believed in the great reward awaiting those who were faithful to death in killing their enemies. What they would now deny themselves in this life, they were convinced they would receive many thousands of times over in their death. Legion had done his job well.

These days were filled with rehearsals on laptops practicing manipulation of the large vehicles and driving over the exact route they would take to their targets. The special programs each of them used enabled them to memorize the route and practice detonation at the precise location within the target for maximum effect. The simulations would reveal whether they had been successful or merely caused minor damage to their target. Soon it would be real, and their passions flamed in excitement.

The organizers of this feast of death and destruction were also hard at work making sure all the parts were functioning properly to enable MD to succeed. Their efforts were business-like as they coldly supervised the gathering of the materials and equipment and personnel needed to carry out the attacks in which others would die.

Large shipments of specially manufactured devices were being delivered on schedule to the yards owned by Brothers Trucking for the final weekend's modification of the fuel trucks to enable the timing of the explosion to be under the control of the drivers so that it would have the maximum possible destructive radius in the target's most vulnerable location. The prepackaged kits had been manufactured in a specialty facility in Oaxaca, Mexico, where the training on that side of the border continued. They would be delivered in the trucks of Specialty Disbursement Solutions, a Mexican company ultimately owned through a series of shell companies by the same Saudi group that had purchased Brothers Trucking and funded Together Tomorrow. After their deliveries, the trucks would return to Mexico to be outfitted as rolling bombs to return after the commerce secretary's order opened the roads so their cargo would not be inspected.

Over the weekend, carefully selected sites in Mexico had been raided to obtain additional thousands of pounds of ammonium nitrate fertilizer, along with other ingredients including liquid nitromethane, Touex, and ANFO to replicate an Oklahoma City-style truck bomb. This effort had been ongoing in Mexico for a year. The material would be loaded into these same Specialty Disbursement Solutions trucks upon completion of their initial mission and wired for use in the MD attacks. Present in Oaxaca to help with the final coordination were Demas Assad and Phygelus Aldar, J-10 and J-14, glad to be safely out of the United States and waiting excitedly for the post-America world which would arise on March 12th.

Some of the selected targets would be too difficult to access directly with fuel trucks, which was the reason the plan had called for the oil monies to be used to purchase the fleet of aircraft owned by Kingdom Charters. No need to hijack airlines this time. They owned the planes and had trained pilots smuggled across the Mexican border waiting throughout the United States, who were currently practicing on laptop simulators.

To help access the difficult sites, which were not targeted for aircraft attacks, the heavy equipment of Terminal Equipment Leasing would be used to break down barriers and clear a path for the fuel trucks. Where the explosive power of the fuel truck was not adequate to destroy the target, the Oklahoma City-style truck bomb would be used. The assassination squads were just a bonus to create confusion, terror and divert authorities. They had been given their instructions, and they too waited and prepared in these final days. However, the wait was more difficult with nothing left to really practice.

In Iran, preparations and coordination for the March 11th attacks were proceeding. Sealed orders had been distributed to military commanders in Iran and Syria for the attacks against Israel to follow the attacks in America. Hezbollah was ready. Russia was apparently on board to hold off nuclear strikes by the United States or Israel, and to destroy the United States military satellites. Ahmad Habid had set a final coordination meeting of the leaders of the forces who would attack US troops in the Middle East on Saturday morning, March 8th at the training camp in the Kerman Province. The terrorist cells in the Middle East were preparing for the assassination attempts on pro-Western leaders and the attempt to gain control of Pakistan's nuclear weapons on the 11th. The cells in Western Europe were readying attacks on transportation centers to tie down those governments and keep their focus on protecting their homeland as attacks proceeded elsewhere. It was a good plan, which had thus far only been partially discovered.

Another Message and a Test

The president was in bed late and up early as these final weeks began. His heart was heavy as he prayed for guidance and asked that the hidden things be revealed. "There is so much we know, but so much is still hidden," he thought. "We cannot defend comprehensively with what we have now."

Quickly getting dressed, he made his way downstairs to the Oval Office, where he found Carl Varvel sitting outside waiting to deliver a message from the Bookseller. He stood as the president approached, and said, "Mr. President, I have an 'eyes only' message for you from Mr. White."

"Thank you. I was unaware he had sent one other than the flash drive."

"Well, Mr. President," Varvel continued, "it is strange, but after I took the flash drive to Homeland Security in Chicago, I had a compulsion to go back to Williams and see if Mr. White had a message for the Iranians. He didn't. He had a message for you. So here it is," he said, handing the sealed envelope to the president.

"Thank you," the president answered, opening the envelope and taking out the note which read:

Mr. President,

I believe that I am to share with you the remainder of the passage describing the time when Joshua was considering how to take the city of Jericho and encountered the Commander of the Army of the Lord who we know from the Book of the Revelation to be Jesus. Joshua was required first to decide whether he was on the Lord's side. Then he was required to acknowledge the holiness of God. I believe you have led the country to do both.

Now, you must do as Joshua did next and ask, "What message does my Lord have for His servant?" and then you must do exactly what God leads you to do, exactly as He leads you to do it, exactly when He commands it be done. Only when Joshua did that was he successful. Only if you do that will America be preserved. The complete passage is Joshua 5:13-6:7.

Praying for you, brother,

Samuel Evans White

Soberly, the president reached for the Bible that always sat on his desk and looked up the passage. As he completed reading, he immediately knelt to pray. Feeling very uncomfortable but not knowing what to do, Varvel also knelt as the president prayed silently.

Later he returned to his feet and said, "Sit for a minute, I think I know something I am to do right now." Taking a piece of White House stationery, the president wrote a short message, folded it and placed it in a White House envelope on which he wrote, "Personal: 'Eyes Only' President Sorboth from Joshua Strong."

"I want you to hold onto this for a week and then go to Moscow and deliver this into the hands of President Sorboth. Do not give the message to anyone else. If he does not accept the message, you are to leave with the message in hand and unopened. If he takes the message, wait for a reply and bring that back immediately. Talk to no one about where you are going or why. Say nothing about what happens. Your mission is to be cloaked in absolute secrecy. Do you understand?"

"Yes, Mr. President," he answered and left wondering what he could possibly be carrying. On his way out, he passed David Barnes and Tom Knight, who were coming to begin a long day with the president. They were soon joined by an excited Darrell Reed, who came bearing news.

"Mr. President, you just have to see this. It's the coolest thing on the planet. Only God could do this," Reed said as he started to set up his laptop.

"Slow down, guys," the president responded. "First we pray." And they did, for wisdom and guidance, that what God had begun He would complete, and that they not be allowed to make a mistake or miss a message He sent.

Invisible but present were Lucius, Niger, and Barnabas, who watched in amazement and thanksgiving as these four men sought to open their minds and hearts to hear from God. "I never thought I would see this again here," Lucius spoke with quiet reverence, listening and joining in their prayers. The Father had covered this office with protection, and thus they had been sent to defend against anything the forces of darkness might bring. They watched and listened for instructions carefully, not wanting to do or allow anything that might affect what the Holy Spirit sought to do in these men. They could see all the way to the throne from which Gabriel was even now being sent, with the answer to these men's' prayers not yet finished. The Father was at work, and it was a wonder to see. The light within burned brightly in all four, and their prayers were beautiful music before the Lord.

"Alright, Darrell, you can start now," the president invited.

"Let me give you the short-hand version," Reed said, excited and frustrated all at the same time. "The volume of information coming in over that prayer website is simply unbelievable. I am going to try and break it down into the categories we had the messages divided into. Understand that they continue to come in, and I am not going to give you all the detail we have, or we will still be talking next Thursday."

"Don't have till next Thursday," the president responded somewhat impatiently.

"Just a figure of speech," Reed replied. "I sometimes forget that nothing about this can be made light of—it's just all so unreal.

"Let me start with Mexico. Over the weekend, and apparently for some time now, there have been thefts of large quantities of ammonium nitrate fertilizer and other chemicals. Those are the makings of a bomb like the one used in Oklahoma City. At that training facility in Oaxaca, apparently the same thing is going on that is happening at the Brothers Trucking yards. Fuel trucks are going to be brought in for modifications. Employee and contract drivers are to be being given paid days off by the company which owns the trucks. The company is named Specialty Disbursement Solutions. Their trucks are making deliveries to Brothers' Trucking yards here in the United States as we speak.

"In the Middle East, we got crazy reports concerning bragging being done by known terrorist connections regarding changes in governments at basically every nation over there, which is favorable to the West. The messages speak of acquiring control of a nation and its nuclear weapons, which has to be India or Pakistan. They speak of the end of Israel. There are emails from people working at missile facilities in Syria and Iran that have been put on stand-by for March 10th through the 12th. One Palestinian Christian reports that Hezbollah is preparing for action against Israel.

"In Europe, there appears to be excitement among those with known terrorist connections regarding plans there for the same time period. Here in the United States, we have hundreds of reports on the locations of Arabs living in groups; many near college campuses. Another report says that charter aircraft pilots for a company called Kingdom Charters have been furloughed with pay for all of the week of March 10th. We have the same report for a heavy equipment company with rental and salespeople. The company is called Terminal Equipment Leasing.

"That's it in a nutshell now, Mr. President."

"That's plenty enough for now. How do you read what this means?"

"I think we clearly have the weapons and the date now, Mr. President," David Barnes answered. "It's definitely March 11th, and the weapons include fuel trucks, charter aircraft, and truck bombs. It looks like we also have the names of some of the companies involved."

"Tom, get the FBI all over the locations of that equipment company and charter aircraft company right now. We need real-time intelligence on what is happening and a better idea of what they have and how it could be used in MD."

"Yes, Mr. President."

"And call General Hedge and brief him on all this information. Darrell, you help Tom and be sure that General Hedge gets all of this on what we have learned that is happening here and in the Middle East. Tell him to get satellite intelligence on that Mexican training facility. I need his conclusions and recommendations as quickly as possible.

"Wait, don't leave yet," the president stopped Tom Knight and Darrell Reed as they made for the door. "Tell the FBI that it will also be their responsibility to cover every lead about Arabs living in groups near college campuses. If they don't have the manpower, use local police or even the CIA. Coordinate with the Attorney General to use grand jury subpoenas to get any additional information necessary to help identify whether these people are involved with MD or those killing squads. We have to find them to stop them."

"Yes, Mr. President. May we leave now? Sorry, there is just so much to do."

Ignoring the question, the president turned to David Barnes and asked all of them, "What could it possibly mean that there are going to be changes in friendly governments? What about the nuclear weapons issue? They can't possibly launch that kind of military strike. They don't have the forces."

"It must be a military coup or assassinations—or both," Barnes answered.

"That makes sense, but they can't possibly believe they can kill them all and seize Pakistan's nuclear weapons in a day," the president responded incredulously.

"Respectfully, Mr. President," Reed jumped in, "they believe they can take out the United States and Israel in a day. Why not take out friendly

Arab governments and obtain nuclear weapons too? Remember the Tet Offensive? Those attacks were desperation attempts to win in a single blow. They suffered massive defeats, but their loss produced victory because it appeared they won and the American public demanded surrender. They are not desperate, but the tactics are very similar, and our risk is similar if they can cause substantial harm to our friends and us all at the same time. Once again, the sheer scale of the attacks would make it appear we have been defeated everywhere, and no one would want to stand with us against them."

"I am afraid you are right, Darrell," the president said. "That is why something is also planned against Western Europe at the same time. They will appear to be unbeatable when the world views a massive coordinated series of attacks launched simultaneously on three continents. Who would be willing to stand and fight against that? The pressure to negotiate surrender would be overwhelming, and this time it would be worldwide. The terrorists would have won."

Shaking his head and gritting his teeth, the president continued. "Tom, you and Darrell can go now, but I want something back by early afternoon. David, I am appointing you to be my special assistant on terrorist threats from now on. I will have a place for you to sleep here in the White House, and you will travel and be with me until it's over. I don't want the regular staff passing on information or making calls. We need to hold the circle with knowledge as small as possible. You will be responsible for coordination. Tell Kayla I'm sorry, but your country needs you."

"She will understand, sir. What do you want me to do?"

"Call Senator Besserman and get him over here as soon as possible. Call the secretary of state and director of the CIA. I need them here to help me work through how to deal with the foreign threat. Get the head of Homeland Security over. We have to have a plan to deal with those killing squads."

Now alone for the moment, the president's fist struck his desk repeatedly as he cried out, "Impossible, impossible, impossible! I can't do this!" With that, he fell to the floor to seek strength and answers from the only One who could.

When he rose this time, he was changed. Nothing in the circumstances was different, but now he had peace, for he understood even as

Jehoshaphat did when facing that vast army he could not defeat. The battle was not his own, but the Lord's. He rested in the reality that God was sovereign, and the outcome had already been declared. Win or lose; it was for him to remain on God's side. He simply had to walk in obedience to what he was shown, and leave the results to God.

A Different America

The change which was so apparent on Sunday across America continued as the work week progressed. In Hollywood, there was puzzlement and frustration over the weekend numbers from theaters. Movies that had been declared hits and were just beginning their theater runs suddenly had half the audience. Overnight television ratings were similarly confusing to network executives. It was as if the desires of a large portion of the population suddenly changed, and that change was reflected in what they were willing to watch.

Car sales were also affected as some people no longer wanted a car that "turned them on" or was what they "deserved." They simply wanted reasonable transportation. Other businesses had similar weekend experiences; either positive or negative depending on the nature of the business. Unknown to confused business owners was the reality that those who had truly chosen God now asked the question whether their purchase or participation would dishonor the holiness of God's name and whether the purchase was God's will for them. When the focus turned from self to God, conduct changed immediately. Life was no longer dominated by "wants" and desires. It was, at least for the moment, a different America.

In businesses, there were respectful requests for places to gather and pray over lunch breaks. Groups of employees focused on their work with a new dedication, and production increased immediately; however, that focus did not necessarily translate to profits for these same individuals had different goals than before. They were no longer willing to cut corners to make a sale or misrepresent a product. The new business ethic that some now carried conflicted with business as usual, and immediately created problems for owners who did not have the light inside. How to deal with these "over-righteous" workers was an issue that could not long be ignored.

What had been acceptable business practices a few days ago were no longer tolerated by some. Frustration was quickly turning to anger.

Darkness never surrenders to light, and thus the change so apparent in some was not assumed to be permanent. "We've been here before," Molech reminded the gathered Counsel of Darkness. "Remember those difficult days they call the Great Awakening and the Second Great Awakening? They were national, even international movements of the Enemy, but they never last. The change is permanent in a few, but for the majority, attention can never be kept off themselves. By nature, these humans are a selfish mob seeking only what they want. Conflict is inevitable. This movement will not last. Ignore it and go for our instruments. They remain untouched. When pressure or persecution begins, these so-called changed ones will again run for safety from conflict intolerance, and we will rule all the more. Just watch. It's nothing new," he said with contempt.

Keepers and Tempters set to work following that agenda, and even before the day would end, workers who had been changed would be threatened or fired by those under the influence of the Dark Master. Divided families would face conflict and churches would encounter the wrath of those who were on the membership rolls, but were not born again. The counterattack had begun while efforts toward advancing MD continued.

Politically, it was easy. The deception track was proceeding as planned with the press conference launch of the Prayer for Peace campaign by Pastor Elkhorn. Also present for the announcement were former President Cox and Senate Majority Leader Howard. The call for prayer as the former president went to Syria was carefully staged in the Capitol, and was accompanied by the announcement that the Senate would consider a resolution to make Friday the 7th a National Day of Prayer for Peace. The president was publicly invited to join with the Senate leadership in a prayer meeting that would be held in the National Cathedral.

Legion, however, was absent from this effort as he continued searching for a means to kill the president. "Destroy the leadership of this movement, and it dies," he screamed to a gathering crowd of the forces of darkness who had joined him in this effort. "There must be a way and an opportunity. Keep looking and keep impressing on those under your influence the importance of destroying this man. He and that Bookseller are the human enemies we must overcome. America has followed them. We have been prohibited by the Enemy from killing the Bookseller, but I have heard no such prohibition regarding the president."

Again, there was wonder among the forces of light watching all of this. What would God allow, and what would He stop? They waited, listening closely for even a whisper from the Holy Spirit, ready to respond immediately in obedience.

CHAPTER 13

FOR AND AGAINST

Wednesday, February 27—MD minus 13 days

IT WAS NOW less than two weeks until the rescheduled MD. Ignoring the politics of the moment, President Strong had secretly left the White House on Monday for Camp David, where he intended to remain until it was time to launch the response. There was a cover story leaked yesterday that shared he needed a break from the stress and was still struggling with the two questions. America was confused by his action in the face of the threat but took comfort that the information being provided must have somehow helped him know there was time. The opposition was livid but rejoiced over the seeming foolishness of this man. Cox remained skeptical. There must be something more.

In Iran, the flag had been up for a long time with no response. It had been there for a full day, and Hushai was not at the regular place of meeting. Praying quickly for Hushai's safety, Ittai raced to Hiram Urbay's safe house to find out what he might know. "Since he works for the SSF," Ittai thought, "he might know something." Ittai could not shake a sense that Hushai was in great danger.

Hushai had spent the last twenty-four hours in a house that was anything but safe. His last charge had been to solidify the information from the new contacts in leadership with Ahmad Habid and the Iranian government.

One wrong step and he was dead; not simply killed, but tortured for information and then cruelly murdered on film to warn others of the consequences of their treachery. He was strangely at peace in a place of real darkness.

He had been taken from the hotel violently—in the middle of the night, a sack over his head, driven to who knows where and left tied up in a room. He slept as he waited. Knowing that God was truly sovereign left him simply wondering whether he would survive. He was not afraid. He knew the risk, and he was prepared to pay the price. He didn't want to dishonor God in the way he died if this was his time.

The sack was pulled from his head, and he faced a heavily armed, dark-skinned man who spoke in whispers. "Listen carefully and do not speak. Next Saturday morning, the 8th—at the camp in Kerman Province, in the large underground meeting room—it will happen there. I am placing a device in your pocket that has a 25-mile range vertically and horizontally. I will send a signal to this device at the precise moment when the Americans can strike that target and kill Habid and the other terrorist leadership coordinating the 11th assaults against their forces in the Middle East. Do not fail." And with that, the sack was back on his head, and Hushai was forcefully taken back to a car and driven into the city. There he was surrendered to another group of men waiting in a car on a street within a mile of the hotel.

He was driven again to an unknown destination, this time out of the city for several hours. The men dragged Hushai out of the car and delivered him to a shed, forcing him into a chair with a sack still over his head. He heard a deep, raspy voice speaking and was certain this was the end until he heard, "Our future is not in war and death. Our people must not be forced to live in fear, governed without mercy in god's name. It ends here. I am placing in your pocket a flash drive with the location and plans for the single nuclear facility where the weapons are to be assembled. It must be destroyed, or the hell of a nuclear nightmare will engulf us all."

Hushai sat in amazement as he heard a door swing open and a car start. He was left seated in silence as the car departed, wondering how he would be able to get the precious information back to the Americans. He waited, afraid to move for he also heard other activity and knew that those who had brought him remained. He waited for their instructions for what seemed like hours. Now hungry, thirsty and needing to relieve himself, he struggled with his body. "Please, may I use the toilet?" he said to whoever was there. Not a very memorable comment in the midst of what had just occurred, but it was either ask for help or make a mess.

"Come, it is time," a voice offered. He was taken to a place to relieve himself, then placed in a car for the long trip—hopefully back to the city. The sack remained over his face, and he could see nothing. No one spoke. Later he was pushed down on the seat, and he heard the sounds of the city as the car sped on toward its destination.

"We are going to untie you and release you, but you must not remove the sack for two minutes to allow us to leave. Do you understand?"

"I do," Hushai responded, "but how will I know where I am and how to get back to the hotel?"

"You will, man of little faith." The comment pierced his heart, and he sat in silence, asking God for forgiveness that his faith had failed in the moment.

The car stopped. He was untied and led out of the car to a place to sit, and the car sped off. He waited as instructed; his heart filled with excitement and wonder which only increased when he removed the sack and found that he had been dropped in the secret place of prayer where he and Ittai had encountered Gabriel. "This has to be the hand of God," he thought.

Unseen, but present, a circle of protection surrounded him so he would not be visible and could not be harmed by the forces of darkness in that place. The whole time he had been on his journey, he was shielded from their sight. So much so that they were totally unaware of what he carried in his pockets. Rushing to the nearest busy street, Hushai flagged down a cab and returned to the hotel where he saw the flag was still up.

The Knockout

Meanwhile, two men sat outside the grand jury room, waiting their turn to testify at the federal courthouse in Cambridge, Massachusetts. The men were Harkins College president, Dr. Harold Bristol, and Harkins constitutional law professor, Dr. Larry Trice. They were under a grand jury subpoena to appear and testify, having been notified they were subjects of an obstruction of justice investigation. It was anything but an academic moment.

"Listen to me and do exactly what I tell you to do, and you will walk away from this," Professor Trice repeated; he had already said the same statement at least three previous times before arriving. "Take out your driver's license. You can answer questions on whatever information is on that, but when they ask anything else, tell them you want to consult with your lawyer and come out and tell me what they asked. I will give you instructions on how to respond. If I tell you not to answer, you will tell them that on the advice of counsel you cannot answer that question because it might incriminate you."

"Wait a minute; I'm no criminal. Why can't I just tell them what they want to know?" Dr. Bristol complained bitterly.

"What is considered criminal is in the eyes of those people sitting in that room. Furthermore, what that over-zealous prosecutor Larry Jordan thinks," Trice answered angrily and soberly, "is what matters. A federal prosecutor can get a grand jury to indict a bowl of Jell-O if he wants. They honestly believe you and I acted to keep information away from them regarding a terrorist leader at Harkins. Don't you see that? It is the 9/11 threat mentality that has dominated this country this past decade, justifying everything from subversion to spying on its own citizens and torture. These people are dangerous. Don't take this lightly or you will be defending your indictment before the Harkins board as well as in front of a jury of your peers."

"This cannot be real. This is not happening to me," Dr. Bristol mumbled.

A federal marshal came out of the room announcing, "They are ready for you, Dr. Bristol."

"One minute, please," Trice replied. He took the frightened college president aside for one final instruction. "There is a trick in all of this which you must avoid," Trice cautioned. "As you refuse to answer questions because they might incriminate you, at some point, they are going to ask you if you are refusing to answer all questions on the grounds that they might incriminate you. That is the trick question. If you say you are not going to answer any questions, you waive your right to use the Fifth Amendment. You must respond that you cannot say what you will answer until you hear the question. Do you understand?"

"Yes, I am not stupid, but why do I have to play this game?" a frustrated Bristol repeated.

"You play because you don't want to be another victim of the so-called American justice system."

Entering the grand jury room was like entering a whole different world. As he sat in the witness chair, Dr. Bristol looked around at the plainly-dressed common people who held his future in their hands. "How could it come to this?" he thought as he repeated the oath and swore to tell the truth so help him God. "There it was again," he said to himself, "this God thing. Will we survive the Christians?"

It didn't take long. Fifteen minutes and two trips out to see Professor Trice, only to return and take the Fifth Amendment. Then came the expected trick question, "Are you going to refuse to answer every question because they might incriminate you?" He gave the right answer, and Larry Jordan excused himself to step outside to confront his lawyer.

"What can I do for you, Mr. Jordan?" Professor Trice asked with a tinge of glee.

"You know, Professor Trice, you are the best in the nation at the academic exercise of constitutional law. You can take a set of facts and argue before the Supreme Court for your ongoing anti-law enforcement agenda with great success, and have for years. But you are out of your element now. This is where that set of facts is made, and the problem you have is that both you and Dr. Bristol gave a civil deposition. You waived the Fifth Amendment by not taking it when questioned previously on the same subject. I am going to seek contempt against Dr. Bristol, and you too after we play this game again. If that is not successful, I will give him immunity and force his testimony, then indict you for obstruction of justice. See what that will do to your Supreme Court license to practice." And with that, he walked away back into the grand jury room.

For the first time in his legal career, Trice panicked. His heart raced, and he began to sweat, for he knew what Jordan had said was true. Now came the conflict: how to save himself and not sacrifice his client. He had to think fast because the door opened and out came Dr. Bristol who had been excused in the presence of the federal marshal who was calling for him to now enter and testify.

"Tell Mr. Jordan I want to talk with him first," he responded.

As the federal marshal went back into the grand jury room, Professor Trice turned to Dr. Bristol and shared his prior conversation with Larry

Jordan. "Great, nothing is working, but at least it will be your head on the chopping block," he responded, less than enthusiastic.

When Jordan stepped out, Trice asked, "What do you really want to know? Isn't there a way we can resolve this?"

"Let me make it simple," Jordan responded with cold bluntness. "I want two things. I want to know the names of everyone who was involved in the decision to block the inquiry into the terrorists at Harkins, and I want Dr. Bristol's total cooperation to find and identify all potential terrorists that went through his school and the other Ivy League colleges within the next forty-eight hours."

"That list of people goes up pretty high in government circles. Are you sure you want that list?" Trice responded with unusual sincerity.

"Mr. Trice, I don't care if the list includes the president's wife, the law applies equally to all people regardless of position. Give me the names and Dr. Bristol's immediate full-time cooperation, and I will not seek to indict either of you. Decide now."

Dr. Bristol, who had been listening intently, responded loudly, "You've got it from me. I'm yours the next forty-eight hours, and I will give you a complete list of names and details."

"Fine," Jordan said to Dr. Bristol, ignoring Professor Trice. "I want you to go back in with me, and I will advise the grand jury that your appearance is now as a cooperating witness, not a target of the investigation. But I must warn you, if I find out that your testimony is not truthful either in what you say or don't say, I will seek a perjury indictment. Is that perfectly clear?"

"Perfectly," Dr. Bristol answered with obvious relief.

"Wait a minute," Professor Trice objected. "I'm his lawyer; we get to confer about this for a minute first."

"Wrong," Dr. Bristol interrupted. "You *were* my lawyer. You're fired. Dismiss that civil suit and get out of my way," he said, pushing Trice aside and following Larry Jordan quickly into the grand jury room.

Before closing the door, Jordan turned and said to Professor Trice, "You're excused for today. I will be in touch with you later once we decide how we want to deal with you." The door closed, leaving the vaunted professor to ponder his fate and who he should call to represent him.

A Second Chance

Somewhere over Washington, a brooding Legion pondered how they could kill the president to end his interference in the plans for MD and stop this prayer movement in America. Help came from an unexpected source as one of those irritating dark wisps flew up to him and got right in his face, calling his name.

"Who do you think you are? And how dare you interrupt a member of the counsel at work!" Legion responded as he swatted the irritant away. "I am Argon," the wisp said after gathering himself and returning. "I was not always a wisp. Once I ruled a city for the Dark Master until the Enemy overcame a planned killing and I was reduced to this as a cover for another's failure."

"I know you," Legion responded. "You are the one who sought to kill that old man who is the genesis of this religious explosion that endangers everything. I thought you should have been awarded for your attempt, but it was not my decision. Molech correctly sought to protect himself. That is our means of survival, as you know. All failure is punished, but I like your passion. You and I think alike."

"Exalted one," Argon began carefully. "I know that one such as you have no time for wisps like me, but I have a plan to accomplish what you want and have perhaps found the instrument and means to carry it out."

"Are you prepared to risk again?" Legion responded.

"Yes, for this man has not been granted the protection that the Bookseller had," Argon answered. "The Enemy has not told the Dark Master he cannot be killed, so it remains possible. We must try and shut the mouth of this one who leads many away from darkness and endangers the Dark Master's plan. He cannot be allowed to continue to live. He must be stopped."

"You are my little clone," Legion said, smiling. "What is your plan? How can you kill the most protected man on earth?"

"We overheard that orders have been issued to move military units across from the White House over the weekend of March 7th and 8th to protect against possible attacks. They know something about the timing of MD, but apparently they have missed the targets. The White House is not a target, but the team that was selected offers the opportunity we need. One greatly under the influence of both his Keeper and Tempters will be in command of one battery of air defense weapons. This instrument lives the double life and is under the control of his lust and passions. The humans would say he is addicted to pornography. We would say he is simply being the animal he is with a little help from our side."

"How can we use that to motivate him to kill?" Legion asked.

"Guilt—a guilt so deep he cannot stand himself. Since he cannot satisfy his passion because it only grows, and since his guilt grows with every transition into the deeper darkness, he has to do something to end his pain. The religious movement—the two questions that he confronts everywhere—drives him deeper into despair. He is ready to kill himself even now, but can be influenced to do that while simultaneously taking out the object of his pain, Joshua Strong."

"You have an instrument, but what is your plan?"

"It's simple, really," Argon continued. "The air defense battery also has access to Stinger missiles, which are heat-seeking shoulder fire missiles that an individual can fire at any flying target. You will never get close enough to this president to kill him with guns or bombs, but he flies in and out of the White House on Marine One, the presidential helicopter. We know that Strong is at that presidential retreat, so he has to return to the White House sometime. We may not know when, but if it should occur while our boy is on duty, we could take him out easily at close range."

Staring at the little dark wisp before his face, Legion smiled eagerly and said, "You are truly evil. You deserve better than you have received." Touching him, he commanded, "Be restored," and Argon was indeed restored as his body resumed its previous size and form. "You will be my assistant now with authority over the Keepers and Tempters necessary to complete your plan. Go and kill Strong, and if you succeed, you will again find a city at your feet."

Rejoicing at his good fortune, Argon raced away to coordinate the preparation of the chosen instrument. "I will once again rule a city; perhaps a territory, or even a nation," he said to himself, fully committed to the task at hand. Then remembering, he thought, "I must find little Zaccur. He will share my good fortune."

An Intimate Moment Alone

Seventy miles away, in the Catoctin Mountains of Maryland, the president walked hand in hand with Janet, staring at the stars and taking it all in like a deep breath. "I love this place," the president whispered. Turning to Janet, he continued, "Camp David is the only place I can walk with you just like anyone else. No press, no public—just us. The beauty and peace of this place refresh my soul."

"It feels like God resides here," Janet answered. "Even in the midst of all the ugly events that circle around us now, there is peace here."

The president shook his head in agreement and smiled, quietly reflecting on the events of the day and all that would begin to unfold tomorrow. They walked on in silence, each lifting up silent prayers for the other and for the nation. Later, as they sat out under the stars, the president spoke soberly.

"Janet, I want you to stay here with me until next Friday. It is safe here, and if you are back reasonably early on the 7th, it should be well before things begin to happen. I want you in the White House close to the bunker long before the 11th."

"Well, what about you?" she responded, looking deep into his eyes for the real meaning of what he was saying. She could see everything he felt through his gaze, and as long as she could look him directly in the eyes, she knew what he was saying even without the words.

"I'm not sure yet where I will be, but there is a good chance that I will have to travel next week as part of our response and will not return to Washington until sometime Saturday or Sunday."

"Where will you be going?" she asked.

"Don't ask right now; there are just too many contingents. I promise I'll let you know when those decisions are made. Just pray for wisdom and that God will give us the missing pieces so we can deal with this crisis. We simply don't have enough yet, and time is running so short. I have to confess that some of what is being contemplated troubles me, and I have to make the final decision."

Relief

The flag was down as Ittai drove by in the cab, but as he made the big circle, he saw Hushai working the door and left for the place of meeting to wait for him. "Thank God he is alright," Ittai thought, "there must be news."

CHAPTER 14

DREAMS AND CONSEQUENCES

Wednesday, February 27—MD minus 13 days

PAUL AWOKE FROM the dream instantly and lay in bed contemplating the meaning of what he had been shown. It was very different from the first dream. He was not afraid of anything other than a wrong interpretation. He knew that he had been shown something from God, and prayed for wisdom to understand. Later he rose to wake the Bookseller and share what he had seen. It was important, he sensed. It could not wait until morning.

Now that he lived in the adjoining apartment in the warehouse, it was merely a journey down the hall and a knock on the door to be with the Bookseller. It wasn't long before he was greeted by a sleepy old man who also knew this must be important. "Yes, what is it Paul?" the Bookseller asked.

"I had another dream, and I think I understand most of it, but this is important, and I think it concerns the president," Paul responded.

"Come in, I want to hear too," Margaret said from behind the Bookseller. He entered the house, and they sat in living room, all dressed in robes to shield against the night's cold.

"What I saw was in Washington out on that park across from the White House. I could see the White House and the Washington Monument clearly. Standing there was a figure larger than the Washington Monument with a drawn sword in one hand—his right hand—and he was looking down into his left hand, which held a card with writing on it. Then he raised his head and looked to the White House. That is how I know it has something to do with the president."

"Keep going please; give us more detail on the figure, anything you remember," the Bookseller urged.

"He had a robe that went all the way down to his feet and a golden sash around his chest, his head and hair were white like snow and his eyes stared out at you as if they were blazing fires. I know this sounds crazy, but that is what I saw and the only way I know to explain it," Paul said quickly.

"Keep going, everything you can remember," the Bookseller spoke softly, seeking to encourage and gesturing with his hands.

Paul continued, "His feet looked like they were glowing like metal in a steel furnace, and his face was as if you were looking into the bright sun on a cloudless day. He did not speak. He seemed to be standing there considering what he would do next, and what that would be was dependent on what was being done at the White House in comparison to what was on the card. It was like the card was a standard against which the White House was being measured.

"Should we call and warn the president? That has to be an angel or something that is judging what is going on in the White House right now."

"Slow down and let's work through this. How can we know who you saw in your dream? How can we be sure the dream is of the Lord?" the Bookseller asked, always the teacher.

"All I know is that it cannot be one of those dark things I saw in my first dream. This has to be of God," Paul answered.

"Good use of logic, but logic can be wrong," the Bookseller responded. "Always remember that the forces of darkness have great powers to project themselves to appear as righteous. Scripture says that Satan can even masquerade as an angel of light.[61] Logic is never enough; you must search the scriptures to determine whether your experience is biblical and only then seek to know what that experience means."

"I don't understand," Paul asked.

"The terms are confusing, sorry. By your experience, I mean, did God ever speak in a similar manner to a New Testament believer? Did God speak in dreams as you had a dream?"

"Yes, I remember one in the gospels," Paul answered. "Joseph, Jesus' earthly father, had dreams in which he was directed what to do to protect the baby and his mother."[62]

"You are right, scripture details times when God does speak through dreams," the Bookseller continued, "even as your first dream; and a dream from God always has the purpose of advancing what He is seeking to accomplish. Since the experience could be from God, now we must test whether it was from God or is a counterfeit. Never forget that the forces of darkness counterfeit most of the miracles of Jesus and seek to use deception to mislead and confuse believers to advance their purpose."[63]

"How can I know that for sure?" Paul asked.

"That is not difficult," the Bookseller said with emphasis. "God will never contradict scripture, so your next inquiry is whether the message you believe was given is biblically accurate. The question is, would God stand with a sword over a believer who was either going to go God's way or his own? Can you find anything in scripture that would support that picture?"

"I am not that versed yet. Please, Mr. White, is there anything in scripture like that?"

"Have you have read the story of Balaam's donkey in the Old Testament? When Balaam tried to go against God's instructions, his way was blocked by the Angel of the Lord with a sword drawn in His hand, ready to strike him if Balaam continued. Only the refusal of the donkey to proceed protected Balaam until his eyes were opened and he saw for himself what he had been rescued from."[64]

"I must have seen the Angel of the Lord in my dream," Paul interrupted. "That had to be who it was."

"Or was it the commander of the Lord's army that Joshua saw when he sought the plans for an attack on Jericho,"[65] the Bookseller asked, "the same one who will return with all believers for the final battle described in the Revelation?"[66]

"It must be," Paul exclaimed.

"Yes," the Bookseller said, "I believe you are right. We know that the Commander of the Lord's Army is Jesus, described in the Old Testament as 'the Angel of the Lord.' The picture you saw lines up in many ways with the description the Apostle John gives of the resurrected Jesus in the first chapter of the Book of Revelation when he had the first of his visions of

Heaven. Let me read it to you. I think it will be strangely familiar," he said, taking a Bible from the coffee table and turning to the last book.

I turned around to see the voice that was speaking to me. And when I turned I saw... someone "like a son of man," dressed in a robe reaching down to His feet and with a golden sash around His chest. His head and hair were white like wool, as white as snow, and His eyes were like blazing fire. His feet were like bronze glowing in a furnace... [67]

"John's description goes on, but clearly that is who you saw, and I think you have the message right. God is weighing whether America will act as He has commanded. That decision is still being made individually, but God's focus this minute is on our government's response to the threats. How the president decides to respond will determine whether we are on God's side or we become His enemy.

"Based on what has been happening across America, I think that card had on it those two questions which have been before us since Friday from the Lord's Prayer. Remember? Does anything in the plan dishonor the holiness of God's name, or is not God's will being done here as it is in Heaven? On the answer hangs perhaps the very survival of this nation."

"We have to call the president or do something. He must know. You have his private number," Paul exclaimed excitedly and fearfully.

"Do you really believe that the message God sent in the dream is for the president?"

"Of course it is," Paul answered. "Isn't it obvious?"

"Then why didn't the president have the dream?" the Bookseller asked. "The God who could communicate with you through a dream could certainly communicate with the president through a dream. The message is not for him; it is for us."

"How can you say that? The nation sits in obvious danger, and you are not even going to let the president know?" Paul responded.

"Paul, the message is for believers so we will know how to pray for the president. If we pray and stand together before the Lord, He will put the right answer before the president. It is not His will that the president would make the wrong choice, or you would never have had that dream. We must earnestly pray that he will make the right choice, and we must pray now because you just had the dream. This is what is on God's heart right now, and this is one of those special moments like that in Gethsemane when Jesus asked Peter, James, and John to pray with Him about the coming crucifixion.[68] When the sun comes up, we will have this posted on the prayer website for believers to join together worldwide."

As they prayed, the president was awake, struggling with the plan to respond to MD, still short of the details necessary to deal fully with what they knew was coming and troubled by some of the proposals.

Multiple American Dreams

There were other dreams given that night. Tom Campy, who had just been released from the hospital, awakened at home from a dream which pictured mass attacks on elementary schools similar to the attack on Kingdom Daycare. Senator Besserman was shown nuclear explosions in lands surrounding Israel with the poisonous radiation returning as a plague on Israel for decades. Janet saw a world in flames with no leadership, and she was standing over a fresh grave in tears. It was the nightmare of what could be that had been shown to those God could use to stop it—if they were listening and were available to be used.

Without exception, each of those who had been spoken to in a dream prayed for wisdom to know what to do with what they had been shown. They all recognized the significance of their dream and sought God's purpose. They acted in what they would come later to understand to be "the fear of the Lord," not wanting to do anything outside of God's will or act in a way that would dishonor the holiness of His name.[69] It was the reality of the two questions in practice.

Tom called Sally Johnson to share his dream, only to learn that she too had an overwhelming sense of danger for the children. In her sleep, she had heard the cry of the children's angels for protection and awoke knowing exactly what to do. Across America, police officers with the light inside had similar dreams or felt a similar compulsion to protect school children, and they too knew exactly what to do.

Senator Besserman understood his dream, and in the morning immediately sought to meet with the delegation from Israel to share the dream and warn against using nuclear weapons of any form in the upcoming struggle. He knew that use of tactical nuclear weapons was in the tentative plan to stop the anticipated invasion. He also knew that Israel had a delivery system capable of striking even Russia with a nuclear weapon. The plans had to change. He sought a meeting with the president but learned he was at Camp David with the Joint Chiefs working on the military response. Later he would place a call to the president to share what he had been shown and learned that the president already knew.

Janet interrupted the president's meeting with the Joint Chiefs to share her dream with her husband. They had walked outside to be alone, and he was silent for a time after she spoke. Then, looking deeply into her eyes, and with all the love he had for her, he responded tenderly, but firmly. "Janet, you must understand that I may not survive this, even as you dreamed, but as you said long ago, I have been put in this position for such a time as this—just like Esther.[70] Please do not be afraid. God is sovereign, and He loves us more than we love Him, so when you pray, don't focus on my protection, but rather pray that I do nothing outside His will or which dishonors His name. That is the only hope America has to survive the coming attacks. That is the only hope I have. It will be God who reveals and delivers, or we will fail and be defeated."

Pausing for a moment, he said, "Please know that I love you more than my life and have treasured every moment we have had together. May God grant that there be many more, but if not, and that is what it takes to defeat this evil, His will be done. I will meet with you again in eternity, my love."

He gently embraced her and held her close, and his mind flooded with memories and hopes for their future together after leaving the burden of office. Janet felt a divine sense of peace in whatever was going to happen. "I understand," she said as he held her. "Just know that I love you and am not ready to walk without you."

"Believe me, I'm not either," he responded, "but that's decision is in the hands of one much more capable than we. Thank you for sharing your dream. I have sensed the Lord's direction this morning, and there are things that must change in our plan. Your dream only confirms that.

"I have to go now, beautiful. See you at lunch." And with that, he kissed her and returned to the meeting with a new sense of clarity and purpose, encouraged that though he might not survive, America had a chance. Janet left for a long walk to pray and to remember. There was much to be thankful for.

The President Decides

"General," the president said, addressing General Hedge and the assembled Joint Chiefs as he reentered the conference room, "we need to change a couple of things about the plan."

"Yes, Mr. President. What specifically should we change?"

"Two things—I don't want first strike use of nuclear weapons to be considered as an option, and we are not going to preemptively assassinate political leaders, even our known enemies. I know why those were included in the tentative plan, but we simply cannot do that. I am prepared to use nuclear weapons if necessary to defend against their use by the Russians or others, but we will not use them in our initial response. I am prepared to kill military leaders or terrorist leaders who are involved in the planning for these attacks—even preemptively if we can find them—but no assassinations of political leaders, as much as we might like to be rid of them. By that, I specifically mean Iran and Syria. We will leave them to their people and the opposition in their countries."

"Mr. President, what plan we ultimately use is your decision, but it makes our defense much more difficult if we eliminate the first strike use of nuclear weapons and assassinations," General Hedge argued. "Tactical nuclear weapons used against massed troops or weapons installations gives us the ability to respond anywhere quickly with devastating force. Right now we still don't know where the attacks are coming from or the specific nature of the attacks. We can't take any option off the table, and tactical nuclear weapons must be available to the commanders in the field as first strike weapons."

"No, we are not going to do that. The long-term damage of such a response and the number of innocent deaths is simply not acceptable," the president responded firmly and finally. "General, I understand everything you are saying, but when I put that part of the plan up against the two questions, I cannot say that they honor God's holiness or are within His will. Either I believe that He is God and that He rules, or I rely on myself and ignore Him. I am simply not going to do that. I believe that we are to rely on Him for what is missing and not on assassinations or first strike nuclear weapons.

"Here are your marching orders; if I am killed, the vice president will have the authority to issue orders allowing the use of any nuclear weapon, and that is the final word. I want that in every field order, so there is no possibility of misunderstanding or confusion by the commanders on the ground."

"Killed? How can you be killed?" General Hedge responded. "When this plan goes into effect, you will be so far below the earth in a protected bunker that they could drop a nuclear weapon directly on you and you would survive."

"I won't be there, General, but that is a subject for another day."

An obviously confused and frustrated chairman of the Joint Chiefs dropped that subject and tried to resurrect the prior discussion. "Mr. President, I don't get it, but please reconsider part of your instructions. Can't we kill the leaders of those responsible for these attacks? A headless enemy cannot function and soon dies."

"General, please hear me, a president has to consider the future 100 years from now and not simply what is before us at this moment. What we do in response to this immediate threat will not only determine whether America survives now, but what kind of world there will be in 100 years. The Middle East must change for there to be a world we would want to give to our descendants, and it must change from within. If this malignant militant form of religious hate is allowed to continue to fester, there is no hope for change. If we give an opportunity to those who rule by deceit, their movement will only grow, and there is always another who would be the leader.

We can't force change, militarily or otherwise, for real change is an issue of the heart. People have to want to change, and we need to be careful that what we do reveals evil in others, not displays evil in us. Drop the assassination plans. We will trust God to use the truth about the threat and our response to change hearts against those responsible."

"Mr. President, you have to understand our frustration, "General Hedge continued. "Our charge is to protect America at all cost. We have discovered a wealth of information on the planned attacks, which both encourages and depresses for we do not yet have enough to strike first and that is how we win. If we are left only to respond, this is going to be another Pearl Harbor."

"We will strike first, and I believe that we will have the information we need before we need it. You forget, we have a nation and a world praying for us," the president answered. "Just be patient and prepare for a preemptive strike in the Middle East sometime next Saturday morning the 8th and for our forces stateside to be ready to move as well. I want our defense in place at the same time we strike preemptively. I envision one effort coordinated worldwide simultaneously."

"That is impossible, sir. We simply don't have the information necessary to do that," General Hedge responded respectfully.

"General, you plan based on what we know, and God will provide the missing details."

Rising and turning away from the General, the president continued. "Tom, I want you and David to come with me while the Joint Chiefs continue their work here. We need to begin to move on the diplomatic front."

After they left, General Hedge paused and observed, "I don't pretend to understand this man's religion, but I have to admire his faith."

"True enough," another commented cynically, "but his faith may get us all killed."

How to Do the Impossible Secretly

Entering his Camp David office, the president began issuing instructions even before they were seated. "Tom, get the vice president back early next week. I want him to leave Thursday morning with the others who will advise our European friends of the threat against their transportation systems and our plan to address MD. He will cover the British. They were with us in Iraq and will want to be involved in our plan as it relates to protecting their forces on the ground. He will need to organize people similarly to advise the forces in Afghanistan. I am going to leave their selection totally to his discretion.

"I want our special Middle East envoys to be ready to leave next Thursday the 6th to advise our friends of the assassination plots and our plan to address MD. I agree with you that it was a good idea to use members of the Survival Commission for this assignment. They clearly understand the threat and are totally on board.

"Oh, and get the secretary of state here. I want him to be our representative to Mexico. They need to be on board when we strike that training camp and blockade the border highways. Hopefully, we can do some of this as a joint exercise. Mexico is not our enemy. We have to work together."

"Mr. President," Tom Knight said, interrupting the flow of instructions that seemed to stream from the president's mind as if he were reading from a hidden list, "how much will the people you are sending know about our response to MD when they leave on Thursday morning?"

"They will not know anything when they leave," the president answered. "They will get details and timing on Friday after they have arrived. Calls seeking audiences with foreign leaders will be made from the White House. They are to sit and do nothing until they get additional instructions. No one is to know when they will leave or where they are going. Not even spouses or children. Complete secrecy is required if we are going to be successful."

"What about the Russians?" Knight continued.

"I will take care of the Russians personally," the president responded. "I know President Sorboth well. I believe he will listen to me." There was a pause as he lifted a silent prayer, hoping for a positive response to the note he sent with Carl Varvel, and then he continued.

"Tom, I need your recommendation on three people I can send to confront our enemies."

"Which enemies are you thinking of, Mr. President. Those we face here or those abroad?"

"Come on, Tom. Congress is not the enemy, although they sure aren't on our side at this moment. Let them play their peace game. It is a good diversion and buys us time to complete the plan and have a chance to prevent the attacks. They will be advised when the foreign leaders are advised—not before. By the way, Mr. Chairman of the Survival Commission, that will be your job when the time comes."

"Oh great."

"I am thinking of Iran, Syria, and Hezbollah," the president continued. "They have chosen to be our enemies and take advantage of the attacks. I want to stop them if we can before the Middle East explodes and

Israel is required to move against them with our active support. When we have our plan, confrontation will be part of the simultaneous action."

"That sounds exciting if can work," David Barnes added. "I just wish we knew what the plan was."

"Me too," the president answered, "but then again, God knows, and that is enough. He will let us in on His plan when it is time. We have to be prepared to move based on what we know. The rest is in His hands."

Had The Curtain been opened at that moment, they would have witnessed the Commander of the Lord's Army turning away from the White House. The multiple prayers of the people around the world had been heard and answered.

"The president chose wisely," Lucius observed with joy.

"Indeed," Barnabas answered. "May he continue to choose wisely. America may yet have another chance."

"They are blessed to have him as their leader when they sit so close to judgment," Lucius responded.

"He was chosen for this time," Niger answered. "God gave them what they needed, not what they wanted."

CHAPTER 15

MOVING INTO THE UNKNOWN

Friday, February 29—MD minus 11 days

AS THE DAYS proceeded, there was increasing uneasiness and confusion among those without the light inside. Some continued active opposition to this new movement, while others simply watched and wondered what had happened to people. The economic effects of the sudden change in wants and desires by a significant portion of the population were astounding. It impacted everything from casinos to clothing purchases. Sunday sales had dropped radically, as did attendance at sporting events scheduled to compete with church services.

In the White House press room, angry reporters cornered George Murphy of the *Times Dailey*. "How did you get that inside story on the Williams' shootings?" asked Dan Rutherford, a long-time member of the White House Press Corp. "You couldn't have gotten that information without significant inside help. What do you know that we don't?"

"What is that religious fanatic really up to?" another asked.

"Is this some kind of end-times game for him?" a third reporter added.

"You know, gentlemen, if you would cooperate and try to find the real story and not simply more reasons to attack this man, you might have more success," Murphy responded. "There is a lot here that you are totally missing. I would be careful what you report without facts. In a month, you could look really stupid. This man is real, and what he is seeking to do is important for the nation and frankly for the world. That is all I'm inclined to say."

"Well you certainly have sold out," Rutherford responded. "Are you going to give the 'religious' machinations of the majority party the same attention you gave last Friday's White House event?"

"Do you think for a single moment there is anything sincere in this sudden interest by the majority party in prayer?" Murphy responded. "That is nothing more than a press conference to launch Cox's supposed 'peace' mission."

"And what was the farce President Strong launched with the old man at the White House? None of them are anything but politicians seeking to advance their own agenda," Rutherford continued. "Thank God, if there is a God, we will be finished with that man in a little over a year and a half."

"And do you suppose what is happening out in the country to be a farce?" Murphy answered.

"I don't know what that is, but it won't last. The so-called Christians are suffering from temporary amnesia. They have forgotten who they are," Rutherford answered.

"You missed that one too, Dan," Murphy responded quickly. "They have rediscovered who they are, and I believe that reality will not change."

"Murphy, I like you, and you're a good reporter, but hear me good. You've lost your perspective on this one. I have spoken with your editors, and this insanity could cost you your job. You're talking and acting like one of those religious crazies. Come back to planet earth while you still can."

"I don't want to come back to planet earth. I am exactly what you said. I am one of those religious crazies, and that is not going to change regardless of what my editors may do. If they want to fire me, let them have at it."

At that point, a White House intern came up to them and interrupted, "Excuse me, Mr. Murphy. I have a note for you from the assistant press secretary."

"Thank you," he said, taking the note which read:

Please go home now and pack for eight days. A White House car will be by to pick you up in an hour.

—Pat Jones, Assistant Press Secretary, at the instruction of President Joshua Strong

"I've got to go," he said hurriedly, nearly running to get to his car and home to pack.

An Invitation to the Bookseller

Across the country in Williams, the phone rang in the warehouse. "Mr. White, the president is holding."

"Mr. White, this is President Strong. I am sorry to interrupt your afternoon, but I need you. Can you pack for a week or so and be ready to leave within the hour?"

"Yes, Mr. President, but how can I help you?"

"Just come, please."

"May I bring my young friend, Paul Phillips?" the Bookseller asked. "He is helpful to me."

"Yes, of course you may," the president answered, "but please understand this is not a social event. I cannot tell you where we are going or why right now. Truthfully, I am not sure myself. Please leave word for the prayer website coordinators to request a focus on prayer during this week. Everything is critical right now, and time is very short."

"I will, Mr. President."

"A car will be by to pick you up within the hour. Thank you. I will see you later tonight."

"What is that about?" Margaret asked.

"I'm off to Washington within the hour, then on to an undisclosed location," the Bookseller answered. "Can you help me pack quickly for a week? I have to go find Paul."

"Samuel, call him. He has a cell phone."

"Right, I forgot we had that number. Can you dial it for me?"

"Sure." Margaret dialed the number and handed him the phone.

"Paul, this is Sam. You need to come home now and pack. We leave within the hour for a trip somewhere with the president."

"Mr. White, I'm with Samantha. I can't leave. Susan Stafford's memorial service is next Thursday, and Samantha is one of the speakers. She needs me."

"Paul, this request is a God thing. When you get the call, you go. It's that simple. Samantha might as well learn now that if you two are ever to marry, this is how it will be. She can come and stay with Margaret while we are gone. Don't worry about her. God will provide what she needs to be able to speak on Thursday, and it will be televised so you should be able to watch. Ask her. She may surprise you."

And so she did, and a very surprised Paul was back at the warehouse within fifteen minutes with Samantha, who set to work helping him pack. The Bookseller called Pastor Scribes and asked for the special posting the president requested, explaining everything he now knew—which was admittedly not much.

As soon as the packing was complete, they all prayed together. Then the knock came on the door from the driver to take them to the airport, where a government jet was fueled and waiting for them.

Chairman Crow's Moment

In the Senate majority leader's office, the discussion was heated. "How can you do this to me?" an angry Chairman Crow exclaimed. "You've made me look like an idiot! Here I am holding hearings proclaiming the danger of religion, and you have the Senate scheduling a prayer meeting and calling the nation to pray? How dare you do that to me!"

"Look, I'm sorry we didn't bring you in on this decision," Majority Leader Howard answered. "This was Cox's idea to counter the president, and we made the decision on the spur of the moment. We had to do something to get ahead of this new religious movement. Don't worry about your hearings. That bill is not against prayer. It is against radical religion; the kind that takes away choices and forces opinions. We can easily have it both ways."

"Tell me how you are going to do that," Crow demanded.

"It is really simple if you think about it," Howard continued. "Most who call themselves Christians are no different than you or I. They go to church to get something they want—really they are just using the church. Some for business contacts, some to improve their resume; most because it makes them feel good about themselves. They attend, but it doesn't change anything. There is your constituency. We can snatch them and perhaps grab some of the serious ones if we wrap this in a religious bow. Unless we are stupid, we won't offend those who have no interest in religion. They understand that we have to cater to the religious crowd to stay in power.

As long as we don't advance the so-called religious social issues, our base will have no problem with appearances."

"I don't like it," Chairman Crow said. "It makes my job a lot harder, and playing with religion is always dangerous. You never know what kind of passions you may stir up."

"So what," Howard replied. "Everything political is about passion. The trick is to capture whatever is the current passion and direct it to our purpose. Right now—because of the president and that crazy old man in Williams—religion is the nation's passion. We must ride it and direct it to our purposes. No magic here. If we do it right, we can encourage what we want out of it while attacking the few who actually believe it."

"I hope you are right," Crow responded, having calmed down. "Have you been able to entice the president to be part of this?"

"No, and we got the strangest reply," Howard answered. "He sent a note that said he could not be available on Thursday and that he would be praying for the safety of America. Safety from what? He cannot get over the terrorist threat idea. That is what he lives for."

"I don't know; sounds like a backhanded slap at Cox to me, as if America needed protection from him," Crow opined.

"Well if you're right, that is his mistake. Come next Thursday. We will take this religious movement away from the White House and recast it as a peace movement. The Sheik is no fool. He would not have agreed to meet with Cox if he wasn't going to give something. If Cox can even get a temporary cease-fire, that will take away the terrorist issue, and we will win easily next November. Then we can withdraw from the Middle East, take a chunk out of the military budget, and spend as we wish on programs for our base."

"I could even get 'religion' for that result," Crow laughed, contemplating victory over his White House enemy.

El-Ahab's Assignment

The Senate majority leader's office was not the only place Cox's impending trip was being discussed. The site—while certainly not as glamorous, but altogether more significant to the ultimate outcome of the conflict—was far underground on the Pakistani/Afghan border where the Sheik addressed Ahem El-Ahab. "We are within days now of our glorious strike into the heart of the beast. Nothing can be left to chance, for if we do not kill it this time, its response could kill many of our faithful ones and us.

"I want you to leave now and travel first to Syria to be sure our welcome for that fool Cox is complete. I have a message for you to have delivered to him—this will make him vulnerable. At the first sign of any activity by our enemy against our forces anywhere, he must be seized and held to ransom captured warriors. We will exchange him for our people or mail his head to the American embassy in Iraq in a box."

"I wonder whether this one has the courage to die for his country without fear?" El-Ahab said, thinking out loud.

"Not a chance, but I believe that Strong does, which is why he is so dangerous. He fears his God and not man, and would have been a worthy soldier with us if he worshipped Allah. That Cox cares for nothing but Cox. Right now, he is probably dreaming about the fame of a peace prize. In reality, he will be lucky to keep his head. If we are successful, we will decide what to do with him then. Unless it serves our purposes, he isn't worth killing. I would rather watch him crawl back to the smoke and ash that used to be America." He paused to savor the thought of victory over and destruction of the Great Satan.

"Enough of Cox; he will serve our purposes well regardless. After you complete your meetings in Syria, go to the camp and be sure that all is ready to neutralize the American forces in our lands and that death is ready to be delivered to those traitors who have sold out to our enemies. Our brother, Ahmad Habid, will be gathering the leadership there next Saturday morning for a final time of coordination. Everything must happen at once. The world must see nothing but fire and death in Europe, in America and among those who house our enemies in our lands. I want you back here before the 11th so we can share in our victory together. Here is the note for Cox. Now be gone."

As El-Ahab departed overland for Syria, the USS Kamehameha slipped through the Strait of Gibraltar, passing by Morocco and into the Mediterranean Sea. The Kamehameha was a Benjamin Franklin-class Seawolf submarine modified to support the activities of the Navy Seals. On board was Seal Team 4 under Commander Travis Austin, preparing even now for their mission to extract former President Cox from Damascus if that were to become necessary. Their orders were to be on station off the Lebanon coast and ready to move to Damascus by midnight Friday night.

Seal Team 10 was preparing for a similar mission, but would enter through Israel with the aid of Mossad. Transportation for Seal Team 4 would be waiting when they landed, again courtesy of Israel. A force of this magnitude was deployed at the personal order of President Strong, who had made it clear to the Joint Chiefs that America would not tolerate the capture of a former president by terrorists, even Cox.

Russia Finally Responds

Back in the Catoctin Mountain presidential hideaway, an exhausted Carl Varvel was ushered into the president's office, where he encountered the president, Tom Knight and David Barnes in a heated discussion. Varvel noted that the president appeared tired as well, and had visibly aged even in the time since he had been sent to Moscow with the message for President Sorboth. The president rose and walked out of the office, inviting Varvel to join him. Once outside he asked, "Were you received? What response?"

"I was, Mr. President. Frankly, it was surprising. President Sorboth took me into his office and dismissed all those present before he read the note. Here is his response," Varvel said, handing the president a handwritten note that had already been translated:

Mr. President,

If I had not come to know you personally over the years of your presidency, I would have been insulted by your request. It breaks all the proprieties of diplomatic courtesies, is frankly unreasonable and nearly impossible to accommodate. I have watched the developments in your country these past few weeks and am confused by your actions, but for some unknown reason, I feel compelled to say yes to your request.

I will be there alone and will keep this matter secret between us.

—Sorboth

Smiling and placing the note in his pocket, the president said, "I think I will save this one for history."

"Thank you, Mr. Varvel. In time, you will understand the importance of what you have done." As Carl Varvel left, the president remained outside alone for a time in prayer, thanking God and seeking guidance on how to accomplish what was now before him.

Back in the president's office, David Barnes asked Tom Knight, "What is that about?"

"I have no idea," Knight responded. "The president has so many people working in different ways in different places; only he knows it all at this point. I wouldn't want to be in his shoes."

"You're not," the president inserted as he returned, "and I wished I wasn't either. But enough of that, there is much to do quickly.

"Tom, change of plans. I need to be in Reykjavik, Iceland at the House of Hofoi to meet secretly with President Sorboth at 10:00 AM next Saturday morning—3:00 AM Washington time. I want to leave on Thursday and stay overnight at an Air Force base outside of London where I can meet with Prime Minister Sawyer and bring him up to date on the MD threat and our response. They still have forces in the Middle East that will need to be protected."

"Wait a minute, Mr. President. You're doing what?" Knight interrupted, alarmed by what he was hearing. "You can't leave the country in the midst of this! You can't do that. You have to be safely in the White House bunker in personal command of the whole operation. We need you here."

"Well, you won't be here and neither will David, so just listen up and please do exactly what I tell you."

"Yes, Mr. President," he responded sheepishly, almost sounding fearful.

"I have to stop the Russians from involvement in this without a nuclear confrontation or, God forbid, a nuclear exchange. To do that requires great risks—both personally and to our plans… our incomplete plans. I am aware of the danger, and I believe that I understand every thought racing through your mind. They have been racing through mine since the idea to meet with President Sorboth came to me. I believe this is what I am supposed to do, so that is what I am going to do."

"Why Iceland, sir?" Barnes asked.

"Drawing on a little history for all of us, it was in that exact place in 1986 where President Regan met Mikhail Gorbachev seeking peace through arms reduction. I wanted that symbol and message sent to President Sorboth, though unwritten in the invitation. I wanted him to know it was of critical importance and involves world peace."

"But if he knows and approves of the MD aftermath planned by Vandenburg and Krenski, you have just told him we know," Knight responded.

"That was the risk, and I had to take that risk to stop it," the president continued. "Sorboth is no fool, and he will know that if I am willing to come all the way to Iceland to meet with him secretly, that my intention is to resolve this crisis out of the public's eye so that neither one of us is faced with making wrong decisions because of political pressure or military emergency. He will also know that we will be prepared to respond militarily to whatever they do, even if command and control in the United States is eliminated and I am killed."

"If you are going to be out of the country, can you risk the vice president also traveling?" Barnes asked.

"Good question, David. I had not thought that through when I made the initial assignments. The vice president will be at the White House over the weekend, available to take command if that is required. He is coming back to Washington tonight and will be brought out here immediately. That will give us most of next week to finalize the plan and familiarize him with our options. I trust Wilburn. He is a good man with good judgment who loves America. He will make the right decisions if needed."

"I agree, but if it is OK with you, I would like for you to keep making the decisions," Knight responded quickly with an unexpected sense of fear.

Smiling, the president said, "Thanks, Tom, me too—but then again, that is not our call, is it?"

"No sir, but that will be my prayer."

"David," the president said changing the subject, "call your friend, the geek. I need him up here tomorrow with a full report on what they have learned from the prayer website. Then I need for the two of you to take the flash drive we got out of Iran with the targets and attack modes and prepare a "show and tell" to use as part of a report to the nation for after we've launched our preemptive strike. I also want you to do the first draft of the speech, which I will give next Saturday night during prime time.

The American people have to understand what we have done and why. The speech will have to lay it all out carefully at a time when, if we are successful, our enemies will not have destroyed us."

"Mr. President, I'm no speech writer. How can I do that? This will be the most important speech of your presidency."

"Well, Mr. Barnes," the president answered, "I can't command our response because we still don't know enough of the details to know where and how to respond. So we are in the same boat. I suggest you do like me; pray and then follow your heart. God will enable you just as He is enabling me every day, or we will all fail together."

"Mr. President," Tom Knight asked, "where are you going to be to give this speech Saturday night if you are in Iceland in the morning with the Russian president?"

"Somewhere aboard Air Force One."

"Is that even possible, sir?" Knight continued.

"I don't know, but I know who can set it up if it is possible." Picking up the phone, the president asked the operator to find Carl Stern, the Executive Producer of ITN. Fifteen minutes later the phone rang, and the operator announced, "Mr. Stern is on the line now, Mr. President."

"Mr. Stern, this is President Strong. What I am about to ask is a matter of national security and will require absolute secrecy until I tell you otherwise. Are you on board?"

"Yes, Mr. President," Stern answered. "How can we help you?"

"I need you to do something that may have never been done before. I need for you to put your most trusted production crew aboard Air Force One to travel with me leaving next Thursday to prepare for a broadcast to the nation Saturday night from the plane in flight anywhere in the world."

"Anywhere in the world?" Stern asked. "Could you at least give us a continent so we could set up satellite coverage?"

"I cannot tell you anything about where until next Saturday morning, and we will not officially be asking for broadcast time until midmorning. You will understand why later. Obviously, your feed will be shared with all the other networks, and the broadcast needs to be available worldwide to any who desire to transmit the broadcast.

"Jim Hunt and the same crew that worked the Williams story will be wherever you want them to be, whenever you want them there," Stern said with authority in his voice. "We will do what it takes to make this possible, and we will do it in complete secrecy."

"Good, I like Jim Hunt," the president said sincerely. "Thank you, Mr. Stern. You and ITN are providing your country a great service. Your White House contact will be David Barnes. He will coordinate with you what we need for the broadcast to be successful."

Hanging up, the president announced, "I have one more call to make. Please excuse me.

"Mona," he said to the operator, "please get me the prime minister of Iceland."

"Yes, Mr. President."

CHAPTER 16

FRIENDS AND OTHERS

Monday, March 3—MD minus 8 days

AS THE PRESIDENT continued his late-night meetings seeking the final plan that would address the coming attacks, the sun was rising over the place of prayer in Iran where Ittai and Hushai were ending another night together sharing and praying. They were exhausted but rejoiced as they considered all God had revealed to them over these past few days. The signaling device and flash drive had been transported out of the country and provided to CIA operatives in Bagdad. By now they were in the hands of US military command, who would be seeking instructions from Washington.

Now there was information on another false peace effort that would be coming immediately before the attacks. It seemed that someone in the government had read enough American history to know that even as the attack on Pearl Harbor occurred, America's attention had been diverted by a peace conference being held in Washington DC at that exact moment. Those who don't know history are cursed to repeat it.

"Hushai, have you thought about what you are going to do after the Americans strike preemptively? The SSF is going to know that you must have been involved. They will probably target Hiram too, and they won't miss me. Everyone knows about us. They have simply ignored us because they thought we served their purpose and could be used."

"I don't think about that," Ittai answered. "I have no idea what will happen. You paint an ugly scenario which certainly could be true, but I don't think God is finished with us here yet. I love this nation and its people. The Mullahs stole the country; we cannot surrender it to them. Perhaps these events will be part of God returning the nation to the people and beginning to reveal Himself to them. I cannot run away from that possibility."

The mood had changed, and they were now somber and silent as Hushai drove back to the hotel. There was much to consider. So much was at stake. So much was possible.

Real Change in the Middle East

In Israel, the cabinet was considering Senator Besserman's plea which had been enforced by the president's decision not to use nuclear weapons in America's first strike—and then only if absolutely necessary to defeat a nuclear threat. The president's commitment to intervene militarily with the full force of American military power if necessary to protect Israel's sovereignty ultimately carried the day.

As the meeting concluded, Prime Minister Zimri observed, "This is the first time an American president has gone that far to assure our security. I wonder if this has something to do with the religious movement that has engulfed much of America."

"I do not think so," the minister of foreign affairs, a student of American politics, observed. "This president does believe that the land we occupy is holy land, but that belief is tied to his faith in Jesus and not to our government—or even to this nation. I think what we are witnessing is a fundamental change in the way he wants America to approach the Middle East, and that change may very well have come out of this new religious movement."

"Now you have contradicted yourself," the defense minister said, joining in the debate. "Has this religious movement changed his policy to favor us more or not?"

"Your problem is that you really don't understand what Christians believe. If you are going to deal with this man for the next year and a half, perhaps you need to consider reading what they call the gospels," the minister of foreign affairs continued.

"Ultimately, they say that Jesus reached out to all nations, Israel first, but he didn't end there. He intentionally went to the hated Samaritans and even broke all tradition and practice by speaking to a woman in public. I think this man, like they wrote of Jesus, wants to reach out to all people in the Middle East—Arabs, Jews and Palestinians alike. That is the change we are going to have to acknowledge."

"Help me understand this," the prime minister asked.

"Consider his response to this threat. He is dealing with us as he would deal with the British in a similar situation, like World War II or even the Falkland Islands. It is a special relationship grounded in history, not religion. He cares about all the people in this region, so the American plan includes notifying Arab leaders who are threatened with assassination and provision in Iran and Syria to act in such a way that the people may ultimately be freed from their dictatorial leaders. He has a vision for the future here which is not limited to Israel but includes all the peoples. That is why we were pushed on nuclear weapons use and asked to be restrained regarding the Palestinians. Mark my word, if he survives this threat, the next year and a half will see massive changes pushed in the region to bring us together in a new relationship no longer as enemies."

"Impossible," the prime minister responded emphatically. "For the Americans, peace always means that Israel gives something up to purchase the appearance of peace. That has never worked before, and it never will."

"Mr. Prime Minister, you still have not seen the reality of the changes that are happening in this man. President Strong is not looking for the appearance of peace. He understands that peace is more than simply the absence of active conflict. He is looking for real peace, which means changed hearts. He wants us to live together as friends without a reason for conflict. He wants us to help each other so that all the people of the Middle East can have a life with meaning and purpose."

"That is beyond impossible. He cannot really believe that," the prime minister replied. "We face generations of hate between Arabs and Israelis and hundreds of years of hate between Muslim sects throughout the region. How does he plan on ending that?"

"This man believes that as he prays, his God hears and will answer," the minister of foreign affairs continued. "I think he sincerely believes that is what his God wants here, and he draws that from his studies of the man Jesus who he believes is God. So he prays what he thinks Jesus wants. Remember the two questions he posed to his nation? The second was, "Is this God's will on earth as it is in Heaven?" He believes that it is God's will and that reality will shape his policy going forward. It has to if he is going to serve his God."

"Are we going to be at risk from this change?" Prime Minister Zimri asked, now concerned.

"We are no more at risk from this man than is England," the minister of foreign affairs answered. "The special relationship will not change, but think of it: if he succeeded even one percent in breaking the hatred that dominates lives here, it would be a better place."

"Can you get me a copy of those gospel writings of the Christians? I think I had better at least understand what this Jesus taught if we are going to have to understand a president who believes in him," the prime minister asked.

"You can borrow mine," was the response. "You will find that it is an interesting enough reading," he said as he pulled a well-read copy of the New Testament from his briefcase and handed it to the prime minister.

"What are you, some kind of closet Christian?" the defense minister asked.

"No, not me, I am just a searcher trying to find the truth, and I have become convinced that you cannot find truth until you at least know what Jesus said."

In the invisible, Lucius turned to Niger smiling and said, "Finally, after two thousand years, a crack in the wall."

Vandenburg & Krenski

In Russia, President Sorboth invited General Vandenburg and Joseph Krenski into his private office in the Kremlin. Once alone behind closed doors, he spoke soberly. "I want to rethink this whole Iranian thing. As significant as becoming the sole outside power in the Middle East may be, I am not sure that we want to be a part of their plan to try to bury the United States and crush Israel. There is great risk here.

"This president is not like the others. He is not simply a politician. He is driven by other forces which make him dangerous as an enemy, even if the terrorist strikes are successful. There may be other ways to accomplish what we want without risking a confrontation with the sleeping giant. Do we really want them as an enemy?"

"What do you mean? They are the enemy," Vandenburg responded angrily. "We allowed them to disassemble the empire without firing a shot. They sit back and gloat over what we did to ourselves. I would rather the nation be destroyed in a nuclear exchange than allow them to continue to dominate us and reduce Mother Russia to insignificance.

"President Sorboth, you forget, once we were a great world power, feared and advancing throughout the world. Now we are a minuscule part of what we were. Russia is no longer even consulted on matters of importance. We have been humiliated by the Americans and must strike back or die on the ash pile of history. Is that what you want? If it is, you too are Russia's enemy."

"Do not you threaten me if you want to live beyond the hour," the president responded with power, now equally angry. "You live in an illusion of the past. Russia must seek to regain its rightful place among the world's powers, but the question is, how do we best accomplish that purpose? Fighting the United States may not be the way to get there. That is all I am saying."

"We can kill the man if that is what it takes," Krenski, the former head of the KGP, added coldly. "No one is ever completely out of reach if that is what is required. We still have agents and operatives available in America. It would be a challenge, but it is doable."

"That is always your answer," Sorboth replied in frustration. "Let's assassinate someone or blow something up. That's the KGB way. Look how far it took us when we were the great power. About all that accomplished was killing and imprisoning a good percentage of our population to maintain control through fear. America's Reagan was right. We were the evil empire, and you two would take us right back there again."

"Whatever it takes," Vandenburg answered. "The state is bigger than any man; you included."

"I am going to ignore that for the moment, General, but you two hear me clearly," Sorboth said. "You do nothing until you receive my orders on

Sunday. By then I will know what I want to do. Understand, I am issuing written orders the moment you leave to confirm this, and I want nothing going back to the Iranians. Let them continue to prepare until I decide."

"You cannot do this!" Vandenburg screamed. "We have the chance in a moment to regain what was lost, even more with a new power position in the Middle East. You cannot stop this. We must proceed as planned."

"Silence, General! It is not your decision. Now get out of my sight," and the two left quickly with a new agenda to seek the elimination of President Sorboth if his orders on Sunday were anything but what they wanted.

Picking up the phone, Sorboth asked for Defense Minister Dmitri Petrov, who answered almost immediately. "Dmitri, this is President Sorboth. I need your help. Vandenburg and Krenski are out of control on the Redemption Plan. I am having second thoughts about its wisdom and want everything put on hold until Sunday. Put some people to shadow them and intercept any communications in or out. Let me know immediately if they take any overt action to advance Redemption or to threaten me. They are dangerous."

"Oh thank you, Mr. President," Petrov responded. "I have had a strange sense of foreboding and doom over the Redemption Plan these past few days. I don't know what it is, but I fear the Americans for the first time. Their president does not seem to be one I would want to confront right now. Something is going on out there, and he seems different. We may have chosen the wrong side this time."

Pausing for effect and totally changing the tone of his voice, Petrov continued, "And don't worry about Vandenburg and Krenski. I will put a security team on them that will crawl under their skin. We will know even what they are thinking before they do. I agree they are dangerous, but they can be controlled or killed. They have some following in the army, but less than they think."

"I knew I could count on you, Dmitri. Be sure that there is no unusual movement among our forces that the Americans could pick up by satellite or otherwise. Go ahead with the submarine deployment, but carefully so as not to draw attention. I will be back in touch with further orders on Sunday once I have made a decision on Redemption."

As he hung up, President Sorboth wondered about Petrov's strange sense of foreboding and doom. He had a similar feeling after receiving the American president's message, and it still would not leave him. Suddenly it seems like there was no place to hide, and nothing that could be done in secret. It was as if Joshua Strong was sitting in on all their meetings and taking notes. He knew even now, and if he knew, he would be prepared.

Mexico's Decision

Mexican President Felix Calderon sat dumbfounded at what had just occurred. A late-night call was unusual in itself, but this call came from the North—from the president of the United States. He shook his head in wonder, trying to capture his emotions and decide what to do. His feelings were not his own. As he continued in deep thought, there was a knock at his door, and the Secretary of National Defense Enrique Ramirez was announced.

"Enrique, gracias. I apologize for getting you out of bed, but this discussion needed to be face to face. I don't want anyone aware of this beyond me and you, and that is it for now."

"I understand, Señor Presidente. What is this about?" Ramirez asked.

"You're not going to believe this, but I just got a call from Presidente Strong, who spent the first fifteen minutes apologizing for los Estados Unidos not being a good neighbor to Méjico. He covered everything from border issues to economic issues and even dealt with the way los Estados Unidos has looked down on Méjico as a backward country run by corruption.

"He went on and on, and it got pretty personal. Normally if I had gotten a call like that, my first thought would be, 'What do you want?' But surprisingly, that was not my reaction. He seemed really sincere and even asked for my forgiveness. Can you believe that?"

"No, I don't believe that, and you have no reason to believe that either," Ramirez responded incredulously. "The last time the Americanos came to pay us a visit, it cost us California, Texas, New Mexico and Arizona. They take, they don't ask, and they never apologize."

"Correct historically, but perhaps this man is different," Calderon answered.

"Sí," Ramirez said. "Strong has been el president de los Estados Unidos for how many years? Over six to be exact, and suddenly he 'saw the light?'

Sorry, I will do what you want me to do, but I am from whatever state it is the Americanos call the 'show me' state. Words are cheap, even apologies," he said, pausing to search for a modern example.

"Remember that former president who got caught with his pants down and 'apologized' and 'asked for forgiveness'? All you heard from the media and the 'religious' and 'political' leaders for months was that he had apologized and asked for forgiveness, so you had to forgive him. Had to, as in, you have no choice. Perhaps you have to say the words, but you tell me, would you trust that man alone with your single adult daughter? When I forgive someone, I don't expect to have that reaction if I truly believe they were sorry and have changed."

"I agree, and that is my problem," Calderon responded. "I really believe him, and as for why he has changed, all I can point to is that a lot of crazy things have been happening here and in los Estados Unidos since that prayer thing he did. Something is going on. I think he has been changed and this may be a window to a new relationship."

"I hope you are right, but I'm not holding my breath," the cynic replied. "Enough of the apology, what does he want?"

"He wants our views and help in addressing the terrorist threat he has been talking about these past weeks," President Calderon continued. "Their intelligence service has discovered a training facility of some type in Oaxaca from which they believe attacks will be launched across the border early next week as part of a massive coordinated attack against los Estados Unidos. They have discovered numerous other contemporaneous plans for attacks in Europa and in el Oriente Medio which he wants to share with us, but the focus for us is how to respond to the threat they have identified within our borders."

"Are they asking or telling?" Ramirez answered, now concerned. "Are we looking at a military strike by a foreign power against people in our own country?"

"That will be up to us. Los Estados Unidos will not strike on Méjico soil without our consent and involvement. If it happens, it will be a joint military operation, which is why you are here," the president answered. "Their preferred choice is to take as many of these people as possible alive for their intelligence value, but they are dangerous killers so there could be a lot of casualties if we don't just bomb them."

"We can't just bomb our own people, and we sure can't give the Americanos consent to bomb Mexicanos in Méjico!" Ramirez responded.

"We're not talking about Mexicanos if their intelligence is accurate. We're talking about foreign terrorists that have infiltrated our country from the South," the president responded firmly, now equally frustrated. "Tomorrow afternoon at 4:00 PM, Troy Steed, the president's national security advisor, will be here with los Estados Unidos secretary of state and a military commander to brief us on what they know and to discuss a possible joint response. Between now and then, I need for you to gather everything you can about what is going on in Oaxaca so we can be prepared for that meeting. I want you here with one force commander in whom you have absolute confidence. Say nothing to anyone about this.

"Enrique, I understand how you feel and why you doubt, but let's give these Americanos a chance to 'show me'—to use your words. And let's 'show them' by having a plan to recommend. Be here at 2:00 PM with a plan. Remember, in the 'good old days' they wouldn't even ask. Maybe this is a new day."

"You got me there, Señor," Ramirez said smiling as he left, already aware of some of the strange activity that has been going on in Oaxaca.

Similar calls were being received by America's friends around the world as President Strong asked for personal meetings with his representatives Friday morning regarding urgent matters of mutual defense and active threats within their borders. The reception was universal surprise in that the calls were not simply to advise about something America had done or was about to do, but to set up an opportunity to be personally and confidentially briefed in advance so that they could be part of a coordinated response. Even the most doubtful among the leaders were struck by the sincerity of the president and quickly agreed to the meetings. They all believed and understood the importance of holding the information in absolute confidence.

"Now," thought the tired president as he headed toward the bed, "if we only knew what to tell them on Friday."

As he walked through the lodge on the way to his quarters, the president tripped and almost fell over a man covered in a blanket to shield himself from the cold. "Oh, Mr. White, I am so sorry, I did not know you were here," the president said as he helped the Bookseller up.

"Sorry to be in your way, Mr. President," he responded. "I have been here praying for you. I sensed you were doing important things tonight and I didn't want you doing them apart from God's will. If you are through now, I can go to bed" he said, smiling as he turned and walked slowly to his room.

The president paused for a moment, thankful that he had the prayer support of this old man and so many others. He understood his need for what only God could provide and the power of prayer to help him find the right way to go. Knowing that he was a man richly blessed, he left to get some much-needed sleep. Tomorrow the plan must come together.

From the Invisible

Unknown to the president, it was not only Samuel Evans White who was praying for him that night; the prayer request that had been circulated on the prayer website had been seen by hundreds of thousands around the world who had been compelled by the light within to pray. Looking down from Heaven, the great cloud of witnesses rejoiced as they saw lights emerging from every nation on the face of the earth as those with the light within who had been called actually stopped in obedience and prayed. Soon the whole earth glowed as a single light; something it had not ever done before. And even so, there still remained areas of almost complete darkness.

As they prayed, many were reminded of something they had seen or heard that could be important and they were led to send emails to the address carried on the prayer website. Once again, the computers in Washington and Williams were almost overcome by the flood of information and a call was made to awaken the sleeping Darrell Reed.

"Darrell, you have to get in here. The whole system is almost collapsing from a flood of new emails from all over the earth. Help, we have to get through this and somehow add it to the database for the planners tomorrow."

"Call everyone on the team and get them in there," Darrell responded. "No sleep until this is finished," he said as he grabbed some well and often worn clothes, dressing to race back to the center.

Back at Camp David before he fell asleep, the president suddenly felt compelled to grab the phone and issue one final instruction. "Please find Carl Varvel and get him back up here tomorrow afternoon," he told the operator.

"Yes, Mr. President."

"Now, why did I do that?" he thought as he put his arm around Janet and cuddled close as he fell asleep, exhausted but no longer afraid.

In the invisible, the answer came: "Because you are listening."

CHAPTER 17

Finally, an American Plan

Wednesday, March 3—MD minus 6 days

ON THE DAY before the president's representatives would leave to warn both friends and foes, he was awakened early with good news by Tom Knight and General Hedge. "We have what we need to strike first overseas," General Hedge began excitedly. "Those prayers you spoke about must have been answered. Our Iranian operatives have somehow obtained information on a meeting of the leadership of those who intend to strike our forces in the Middle East and the plans and location of the nuclear facility in Iran where they are attempting to assemble their first nuclear device."

"Hallelujah! Wake the vice president and meet me in my office in fifteen minutes," the president responded as he jumped out of bed to get dressed.

"I just knew something would happen; that somehow we would learn more today," he said to Janet. "This isn't all we need, but what a great beginning. God is faithful. Now I need to be careful to see that our plan remains within His will. Please pray. Today has to be the day. I have to make firm decisions on a plan today. Ask Mr. White to pray," he said as he kissed her and quickly left for his office.

The details on how the information was obtained amazed everyone. "I wonder who these leaders are that are willing to take those risks," the president asked. "I wish we knew their identity so we could work with them in the future."

"That may happen, but for now you have to decide how we use this information to protect our forces and cripple the militarists in Iran," Tom Knight replied.

"What do you recommend, General?" the president asked directly.

"Well, Mr. President, obviously we have to strike their leadership," General Hedge answered. "They are gathering to make final plans for the assault on our forces. This is not an assassination; this is the defense of American and allied forces. We wouldn't be targeting political leaders. This would be military leaders in the process of planning attacks on American forces to be executed within a week. We can't let them get away."

"Agreed," the president responded.

"And what of the nuclear facility shouldn't we take this opportunity to set their program back since we know what they intend to do with it?" the vice president added. "If we don't, can we give the information to Israel and let them strike?"

As the discussion continued, the president just listened, wanting to hear everyone out before making a final decision—although he already knew what he thought they should do. After everyone had their say, he asked, "Do you believe we can count on whoever gave us this information to use the communication device to tell us the exact moment when all the leaders are in the bunker and it is time to strike?"

"Mr. President," General Hedge answered, "whoever this man is, he was willing to risk everything to get this information to us. There is nothing about the way the information was transmitted that questions his credibility. I think we have to trust him."

"I agree," the president responded. "I am willing to risk the whole plan on this timing. We begin with the leadership strike, followed immediately with a coordinated response on the Iranian nuclear facility and hopefully against those using the facility in Mexico. Everything at once is the key.

"General, is there a way to communicate almost instantaneously with both civilian and military strike forces throughout all the theaters where we face a threat?" the president asked deep in thought. "There has to be a way."

"The military would be easy, but civilian forces are much more difficult.

They don't have access to military communications for obvious reasons, and their communications can be monitored by civilians which mean the terrorists can monitor them too. What are you thinking, Mr. President?"

"When we receive the signal to strike the leadership bunker, I want that signal to be relayed instantaneously to all our forces that will be set to strike our enemies wherever we know them to be. First, the Iranian nuclear facility, but also to our commanders in the Middle East and to both military and civilian forces here and hopefully in Mexico so we can move at the same time to eliminate warnings being issued by our enemies once this begins. We want to catch them all unprepared; we want to catch them by surprise, at the same time everywhere," the president responded with a clear picture in his mind of how that would look.

"This has to be seamless, and I know we have to have a backup time if we don't get the signal by a certain time, but can't we figure that based on a Saturday morning meeting in Iran which would be after midnight here Friday night?"

"Certainly, Mr. President," General Hedge answered. "We could use the military communications channels, cell phones, even text messaging. We just need a short, coded message to initiate the attacks after we receive the signal or when the set time passes. The problem is that we still don't have all the locations or the identity of all the people to strike here in the continental United States."

"True enough, General, but I believe we will have that information in time, just like we got the Iranian information. Try this for the coded message to launch the strike: use '9/11'—that will be enough."

"I like it," the vice president added.

"Yes," General Hedge agreed. "By using that simple of a code, we can also access the police bands. No one listening but the intended recipient would know what that means."

"Exactly," the president continued, "and at that moment, those who are the intended recipients will remember exactly what they are up against."

The discussion continued, but General Hedge excused himself to work on an operational plan for the Iranian strikes and communications coordination.

"You haven't seen me do this before," the president said as he walked to a portable whiteboard that had been brought into his office, "but is about the only way I can connect the dots in my mind. I have to see the plan."

"Wilburn, you and I have to understand and agree on all of this, and all of this includes the following," he said while writing.

1. Iran Response
2. Israel/Hezbollah/Syria Response
3. Middle East Leadership Response
4. US Middle East Forces Response
5. Europe Leadership Response
6. US Border Response
7. Trucks/Airplanes/Equipment Response
8. Terrorist Leadership Response
9. Death Squads Response
10. Target Defense
11. People Defense
12. Mexican Response
13. Russian Response

"There it is: our lucky thirteen," the president said, turning around to face the vice president. "That is what we have to be prepared to deal with in less than three days. I am going to take some time and go through our current plan regarding each of these with you in detail, but I am going to start in reverse order because I think that will impact you the most."

"How, Mr. President?" the vice president asked. "What am I to do regarding Russia?"

"Nothing, I hope," the president began, "but because of what I am doing regarding Russia, you are going to be the point person at the White House in my absence. You are going to have to be the man to be sure this plan is executed if I cannot be contacted in time to make a decision."

"Contacted? What do you mean? Where would you be other than in the White House?"

"I going to meet with President Sorboth in Iceland close to the exact moment our strikes begin. The greatest danger we face aside from the attacks at home is a nuclear confrontation with Russia. I intend to tell him face to face what we are doing and try to keep them out of the conflict. I view it as an opportunity to forge a new relationship with Russia and deal a crippling blow to the forces still there which seek to take Russia back to the 'evil empire' days."

There was silence in the room as the small group gathered tried to take in what was just said. Before anyone could speak in response, there was a knock on the office door, "Mr. President, Carl Varvel is here," a steward announced.

"Send him in," the president responded. "Gentlemen, please excuse me for a moment; I need to do something with Mr. Varvel. You don't have to leave."

"Mr. Varvel, I believe you know the vice president and Mr. Knight."

"I know of them, sir," Varvel answered.

"Please have a seat for a moment. I need to write out a couple of notes for you to deliver," he said, suddenly understanding why he had asked for Mr. Varvel to return. Sitting at his desk, he said a quick prayer for wisdom and began to write. Once finished, he addressed three envelopes: one to "The Leadership of Iran," one to "The Leadership of Syria," and the third to "The Leadership of Hezbollah."

"Take these to our boys in Iran—the secret heroes in all of this," he said to Varvel, handing him the envelopes. "They are about to get their most risky assignment. Before you arrive, instructions will have been sent on when these messages are to be delivered and specifically to whom. Timing is everything. Be sure to emphasize that to them, and please tell them that Mr. White has told me of their faith. Tell them I will be praying for them as well and that the time will come, God willing, when we will meet and I can thank them in person."

Varvel left quickly while Tom Knight and the vice president looked at each other, wondering what they had just witnessed. The president was no help as he sat down and penned two additional notes, one to Senator Besserman and one to General Hedge. Stepping to the door, he said, "John, would you mind taking these notes to Senator Besserman and General Hedge? Tell them I will get with them to discuss the details after we finish here."

"Yes, Mr. President," John Thomas, the chief steward answered.

"Thanks, John," the president replied. "Now," he said turning to the vice president and Tom Knight without further comment. "I want to discuss the Mexican response and the meeting later today between President Calderon, the secretary of state and Troy Steed."

"One thing was clear," thought Vice President Marshall, "the only one who will know everything about this plan is the president, and there seems to be something very different about him now. He is not afraid of what is coming even though we are not yet ready and may never be completely ready. He has changed."

"Wrong," commented an ever-present, yet unseen Barnabas. "He has been changed."

Training Exercise

Preparations for implementing the plan were already well underway throughout the continental United States. All military leaves had been cancelled, and military units had been repositioned to temporary quarters near their assigned places to defend known targets and take weapons deployment centers. All of this had been done under the guise of a massive training exercise. The soldiers had left their bases with no knowledge of where they were going or how long they would be gone. Even their field commanders knew nothing more than the location of their temporary quarters. Mission order would not be forthcoming until Thursday night.

Similarly, forces were being redeployed in Europe and the Middle East. Missile defense units had already been positioned and activated to better defend troop installations, and several European units had been alerted and equipped for immediate redeployment to an unspecified location. Air transportation was standing by for orders.

Truckers in the US were discussing the unusual movement of tanks and other military equipment being transported on interstate highways. Behind the obvious was the unseen delivery of equipment by transport aircraft and the repositioning of military attack helicopters and fighters. Nothing was being left to chance. Everything had to be in place by Friday afternoon.

The ships which carried the embryonic "star wars" intercontinental ballistic missile defense system had been repositioned to be prepared to limit the unthinkable. Seal Teams 4 and 10 were now positioned in different locations in Syria ready to respond if required to defend former

President Cox, who was meeting with the Senate majority leader preparing for tomorrow's formal send off. There had been a new development: a peace initiative from Iran. Cox and Howard were giddy as they considered what had happened. The administration had been bypassed by the Iranian government. The invitation had been sent by private channels directly to Cox with an invitation to meet the Iranian president after his meeting with the Sheik.

"This will play well with the press and public," Howard said with glee. "Can you imagine how stupid the president will look with all his talk of terrorist threats when this is revealed? Here the supposed enemy again reaches out his hand of peace. There will be no stopping us next November. We will increase our majorities in the House and Senate and take back the White House. 'Happy days are here again.'"

But they were not happy in the White House press room, and that unhappiness was being televised throughout the country and by satellite to the rest of the world. "Enough of this hermit president hiding at Camp David on a supposed working vacation, religious retreat or whatever. We're no fools," an angry Dan Rutherford said, confronting Pat Jones, the assistant press secretary. "There are troop movements throughout the country, leaves have been cancelled, and families told nothing about where their husbands, wives or children are going or when they will be back. What is happening? We have a right to know. The people have a right to know!" he almost screamed as his voice rose.

"Calm down, Dan," Jones replied. "Don't act so surprised or offended. You have been in this business for a long time, and you know that no president tells you everything happening at the moment it begins."

"Well, he better tell us this if he wants his side reported," Rutherford interrupted. "What is wrong with you people? You cannot ignore the press."

"We are not ignoring anyone," Jones continued, still calm, making the contrast all the more complete. "What you have discovered is part of a military exercise designed to test our ability to respond quickly and effectively to any significant internal terrorist threat. We must be able to move troops and equipment throughout the country quickly to respond or strike preemptively. Because of the threat under which we now live, it is essential to be ready and to test our response capability. You have discovered only a portion of the exercise. There will be a Pentagon briefing at 2:00 PM this afternoon. You just got ahead of yourself.

"Oh, I will tell you one thing for your reports before the briefing—the exercise ends Sunday evening." And with that, Pat Jones excused herself, thinking, "It worked."

"We are blessed. The Americans are stupid. They missed all the clues," Walid Ghazi said to Tariq Qusay. They were watching from their California apartment as final coordination was being completed for the MD attacks next Tuesday. "It could not be better. The American military will be out of position and unprepared because of this exercise. It makes our job that much easier."

"Did you see that fool newsman?" Qusay responded in sincere wonder. "His head would be in the aisle in a millisecond if he had said that about the Sheik near any of his followers. I have lived among these people for years now, and I still don't get it. How did they ever get to be the world's great power?"

"I'll leave that study to you," Ghazi answered. "But after Tuesday, the better question will be, 'How WERE they ever the world's great power?' It will be kind of like looking back at the Roman Empire in ashes," he said, smiling.

"True and tragic, but they have earned that distinction," Qusay answered matter-of-factly. "They had every opportunity for greatness and simply devolved into a filthy pit of selfishness, lust, and greed. The way their women present themselves as objects of pleasure is disgusting. They worship evil. Even the children we teach are sent from their homes dressed like whores. I want out of this cursed place."

"Yes; Mexico looks better every day and Saturday is almost here," Ghazi continued.

After pausing to think for a while, Ghazi asked, "Do you ever feel even the least bit sorry for them?"

"I don't think about that," Qusay replied. "They are fools led by fools who will suffer a fool's fate. There is no place for them in a world led by the Sheik. They must be destroyed and let their filth die with them. They must be exorcised from our lands and crushed everywhere so the world will follow us in fear."

"You are right, Tariq—except for Strong. He is a leader with impressive character as these past days have shown. We cannot underestimate him. He is no fool."

"Yes, but he has no true followers. The fools consider him a fool, and as a result, they will all perish together," Qusay said confidently, even defiantly. "It will be over soon."

Radical Deployment

As the president completed his review of the list that comprised the plan with the vice president, there was solemn silence followed by a knock. "Mr. President, I just got your note," General Hedge said as he entered the office. "Are you sure you want to take this risk? No administration has ever been willing to undertake what you propose, and this is on such short notice."

"General, I understand the risk and wish we didn't have to take it," the president responded, "but I just don't see any other way of stopping this. If you have a better suggestion, then I am all ears."

"The obvious answer to that, sir, is to let Israel deal with Hezbollah. If we step into that breach, we may never come out, and the cost in lives could be really high."

"Pardon me, Mr. President, but what is this about?" the vice president asked. "You didn't cover this."

"If Israel agrees," the president responded, "I am deploying forces from Europe to be placed between where we expect Hezbollah to strike Israel and Israel's strike force, which is prepared to respond. The idea is what we have done for decades in Korea; the American forces will be a 'tripwire.' If they are attacked, we will respond. I am trying to take Israel out of this equation. If that doesn't work, then we will respond together. I want to send a message to the Middle East that it is time for peace and that we will not tolerate the continued conflict and bloodshed on either side—Israel or Palestinian or Arab. These people have to get out of camps and have lives. Children have to have hope for a future on both sides of this conflict. The Arabs have refused to deal with it, and so has Israel. Perhaps we can stop the attack and start a new direction at the same time. I sent Carl Varvel with handwritten notes to be carried to the leaders of Iran, Syria, and Hezbollah announcing this policy."

"Mr. President, you may be sending those men to their death," General

Hedge responded. "No nation has ever been willing to send in a force to act as 'peacekeepers' between Israel and its enemies. No one wants to take that risk."

"I understand all of that, General. I do not propose leaving them there long-term, although we may encourage the UN to take their place and be a more permanent force until the Palestinian issue is addressed by both Israel and the Arabs. Right now, we have to stop this fight before it spins out of control, and I don't have another answer. If Israel crushes Hezbollah with lots of innocent casualties, it only makes matter worse in the long run. The presence of American forces there will also send a message to Russia that we are serious. I only hope Senator Besserman can convince Israel to cooperate. I intend to call Prime Minister Zimri later today."

"Mr. President, respectfully, our focus has to be on defeating MD, not on a future policy move. Until Israel clears this, we can't do anything."

"General, you remember I told you presidents have to think about the world 100 years from now. Do you want that world to be one where everyone has access to nuclear weapons or some worse invention? Do you want the hatred that has bred all this violence to still exist? That is an 'end times' scenario. I know what the Bible says about end times, but that is God's business, and it will happen just as He wishes. I believe that my business is to try and deal with the ugly world we face in a way that brings people the chance to have a real life here. I want them to have an opportunity to hear about God so they may choose for themselves what to believe."

"I am not sure I find that in the Constitution," General Hedge replied.

"Perhaps not, General, but you would find it in the Declaration of Independence and in the Four Freedoms Franklin Roosevelt expressed in his speech to Congress before we entered the war. Do you remember?"

"I am embarrassed to say that my history knowledge does go that far," he answered.

"Well consider these and then judge me on whether I am being radical. Roosevelt said the Four Freedoms were:

> *The first is freedom of speech and expression—everywhere in the world.*

*The second is freedom of every person to worship
God in his own way—everywhere in the world.*

*The third is freedom from want—which, translated
into world terms, means economic understandings
which will secure to every nation a healthy peacetime
life for its inhabitants—everywhere in the world.*

The fourth is freedom from fear...

"I don't think Roosevelt was radical when he made that speech," the president continued. "He was right then, and we should be willing to seek to implement that in our time in the Middle East and elsewhere, and we shall."

"Get the forces in the air, General. I know Israel will agree with this."

CHAPTER 18

TIME TO STAND

Wednesday, March 5—MD minus 6 days

IT WAS A strange crowd that gathered in the president's small private dining room for a late Wednesday afternoon lunch. Some were in the know, while others had no idea why they were there and could only imagine. It was unprecedented—an ITN camera crew with producer Jim Hunt, the Bookseller and Paul Phillips, George Murphy the reporter at the *Times Daily*, the vice president, Darrell Reed, David Barnes, Attorney General Rodriquez, Homeland Security Director Hollister, and of course, Janet—his constant companion.

"Before they serve, I wanted to thank you for being here and set a couple of ground rules for lunch if we can get away with it," the president began, smiling. "Tomorrow we will all divide and depart to our assigned places with specific duties. But for this lunch, I would like it to be a little like the late evenings President Lincoln used to enjoy with William Seward, his secretary of state, when the civil war was in its darkest hours. Often Lincoln would escape the White House and join with Seward's family to share a time of good conversation and stories away from the horrors and criticisms of the moment. In the midst of all we face in the coming days, we can use a few moments like that too. So, the ground rule is that outside of an emergency, this is a time to simply enjoy each other with no conversation about why we are all here. There will be time for that later."

The thoughts in the room were varied in reaction to what the president said. Most who knew why they were there wondered at the seeming peace and confidence with which he faced an uncertain future. Those who didn't know had a moment of panic, wondering how bad it must be. Only Janet dared to speak, "I heartily agree. I want to hear how these past few days have been going in the 'real world' after the day we set aside to stand before God. I know there has been a real change in us, but I wonder about the country as a whole."

"Great topic," the president interrupted, "but first, let's pray. Mr. White, would you pray for us?"

"Well, Father," he began, comfortable in speaking to One he knew well, "we are gathered here in these beautiful mountains which remind us of the wonder of Creation—the one you simply spoke into existence by the power of Your Word. Only You know why we are here or what these next days will bring. We rest in the assurance of your absolute sovereignty over all things, and seek Your wisdom and direction that each of us and this nation may remain in the center of Your will. Give us courage and faith to boldly follow Your direction without fear or compromise.

"We pray for those who have chosen to be our enemies and for their families, that You might open eyes and bring the real peace to all that is only available in You.

"Thank you for the privilege of being gathered here this day, for this time. Give the president the moments of peace and relaxation he needs. Thank You again for Your provision of food this day. In Jesus' name, Amen."

"Amen," the president joined, shaking his head in agreement.

After a pause for the food to be served, the president turned to Jim Hunt and said, "Mr. Hunt, introduce your team. I like to know the people I am going to be traveling with."

"Mr. President, they are the best in the business. Spike Crain and Todd Jones, cameramen extraordinaire, and Alvin Rogers, our electronic wizard. If it can be done, they can do it, and they do it better than anyone else in the industry."

"High marks, gentlemen. Glad to have you with us these next few days," the president replied. "What you will be doing is an important part of our effort."

"What is that, sir?" Rogers asked, stating what the others were wondering.

"See, they already broke the rule," Janet commented, "and so did you," pointing her finger lovingly at her husband.

"Yes, but I am 'pardoning' them by my Constitutional authority. Will you pardon me?" the president replied, laughing. "Sorry, guys, you are going to have to wait like everyone else. We leave tomorrow, and you will learn why and what this is all about when the country does on Saturday evening. God willing, we will have good news to report."

Forty-five minutes later, the relaxed conversation was interrupted by John Thomas with, "I am sorry Mr. President, but General Hedge says this is urgent and asked that I interrupt."

"Thank you, John, I understand. Sorry folks, duty calls," he said, excusing himself to take General Hedge's call in his office.

"Mr. President, we have a problem," General Hedge began sternly. "Several members of the Joint Chiefs are objecting strenuously to the deployment of US forces in Israel. They are threatening to tender their resignations and go public if that part of the plan is not changed."

"Well, General, I want you to listen real close and make sure every word gets back to whoever is objecting," the president said slowly and deliberately. "This deployment is my decision, and lest they have forgotten, I am still the president of the United States—the commander in chief, their superior. If they cannot obey all of my orders, then I want their resignations on my desk within fifteen minutes, and they will be confined to Camp David under guard until the 12th. They are to have no contact with the outside world until the 12th; absolutely no opportunity to blow the secrecy of this mission. Have I made myself clear? I will not tolerate any rebellion among civilian or military leadership at this late hour."

"I got the message, Mr. President. Please, sir, I was only the messenger. I will follow your orders, sir, without objection," he said quickly, somewhat shocked at the harsh tone in the president's voice. General Hedge had no doubt that he meant every word he spoke.

As the president sat waiting to receive copies of the expected resignations, he wondered at the sudden intense level of conflict among his military advisors. He had not expected division only days away from the planned preemptive launch. "The nation is at risk," he thought. "How could they threaten resignation now even if they disagreed?" He was interrupted by a knock at the door, followed by the voice that always had the ability to change the subject and make him smile.

"Sweetheart, Mr. White wants a few moments of your time before you're back buried in meetings if you can spare it."

"Certainly," he responded as he rose to greet them. "I was hoping for some time together before tonight, but events and people seem to have control of my schedule."

Entering in with Paul and Janet, the Bookseller sensed immediately that the president was deeply troubled, angered at what had just occurred. "How quickly his mood had changed," he thought. "The attack on him has already been launched. He cannot falter now."

"I am sorry to interrupt, sir," he began, choosing his words carefully, "but I feel compelled to share a warning my heart will not allow me to dismiss. From what I sense, I may already be a little late."

Smiling, the president responded, "You are a very perceptive man, Mr. White, and that is why you are here. I have come to believe that you do not speak until you have first prayed, and that you do not speak other than what you believe God has given you to say. There are few in America I can say that about. I am all ears."

"Mr. President, you remember Jehoshaphat's prayer that has become your own," the Bookseller began. "In truth, Jehoshaphat almost did not live to have the opportunity to raise that prayer. Earlier in his reign, he allied his nation with enemies of the Lord, who God had judged and intended to destroy. Jehoshaphat found himself surrounded by false counselors who all gave the same wrong advice. Fortunately, Jehoshaphat discerned that he was not hearing the truth and asked to hear from one he knew was a prophet of God. What he heard then contradicted the opinions of all the others, but in his heart, Jehoshaphat knew he had heard the truth. Jehoshaphat was in the wrong place, supporting the wrong side, but God rescued him because he had sought the Lord. He was rebuked by God and the battle was lost, but the nation survived, and he learned a valuable lesson—which led later to the prayer for assistance when he faced an overwhelming enemy alone.[71]

"Please hear me clearly, Mr. President. The message is not that you are on the wrong side or in the wrong place, it is that you must measure the counsel you receive in these final hours by what you know of the counselor's walk with the Lord. Do not be deceived by the words that come from their mouths, even if they are in agreement. This battle is spiritual, not physical. Those who are without the Holy Spirit inside will be used by the evil one to advance his war against God. Your real enemies are those whom Paul described as being not 'flesh and blood,' but rulers, powers and authorities of this dark world and the 'spiritual forces of evil in the heavenly realms.'[72]

"Anyone who has not chosen to be on God's side may be used against you because you have chosen to be on God's side. Select the counselors you listen to carefully, for confusion and division are regular tools used by the forces of darkness to defeat God's agenda. If they can succeed in creating doubts and fear in you, they will be successful in changing the plan away from God's purpose with devastating consequences."

"I believe I have already encountered the confusion and division of which you speak," the president replied. "You would think it is enough that we still struggle against this physical enemy with so little knowledge, and now division begins to appear. What am I to do?"

"You must pray and stand on what you believe in your heart to be right, and if necessary, stand alone. America's survival depends on that. If you are wrong, let it be while trying to do what you believe is right as God shows you," the Bookseller answered. "And then, like Jehoshaphat, you can be used to preserve the nation even if you are wrong."

Preparations Continue Around the World

Elsewhere, other preparations continued. In Iran, the flag was already up to notify Hushai what was coming. They needed to line up Hiram Urbay as the third in the endangered trio who would deliver the president's messages to America's enemies—even as America launched its preemptive strike.

Ahmed El-Ahab continued with his assigned tasks in Syria, preparing the "welcoming" party for former President Cox while Seal Team 4's Commander Austin met with Syrian operatives working on the Cox escape plan now dubbed "Operation Bubba."

In Mexico, mechanics were preparing to begin modifications tomorrow morning at the Oaxaca facility. They were to turn the Specialty Disbursement Solution fuel trucks into controlled weapons of destruction for the beginning of the massive convoy into America immediately after midnight Friday night. At the same time, terrorist explosive experts were completing final preparations to install Oklahoma City-style bombs made of ammonium nitrate fertilizer and liquid nitromethane on cargo trucks to join the convoy into the United States. All was going as planned, with no apparent obstacles.

Throughout America, at the many Brothers Trucking yards, the modification kits had been delivered and practice runs were underway. They had to be sure they could install the explosive controls on the number of trucks required to hit the assigned targets within the time available. The gas tank trucks would begin arriving tomorrow fully fueled, and would be ready for modification over the weekend. Even as the Mexican convoy began to cross the border, the modifications would start so all could be ready by the 10th. Terminal Equipment Leasing would have all required equipment on site by Sunday to be sure that everything was ready for Tuesday. Kingdom Charters would continue with business as usual through Sunday night, but the flights would not be under the control of the terrorist pilots until Tuesday morning.

In Mexico City, the preparatory meeting between President Calderon, Secretary of National Defense Ramirez and General Antonio Lopez Garcia had begun. "I didn't expect what we found," Ramirez reported, "the Americanos are onto something. That facility in Oaxaca is massive and active. Trucks have been going in and out, and there is some kind of training facility there run, but we don't know who or for what purpose. All I have been able to garner overnight is that the land is owned indirectly by some Saudi nationals that also control Specialty Disbursement Solutions, a trucking company. Apparently, they have used their money wisely to buy protection so that no one has a clue what is going on. They have operated here in absolute secrecy for several years using foreign nationals from el Oriente Medio."

"How do you think that may relate to a terrorist attack in los Estados Unidos?" President Calderon asked.

"I assume that is what we will hear from the Americanos," General

Garcia responded, "but I would tell you that it may have something to do with large-scale thefts of ammonium nitrate fertilizer and liquid nitromethane. Those are the essentials to make a truck bomb like the one used in the Oklahoma City bombing. Perhaps they are turning trucks into bombs to be used against the Americanos, and maybe against us here too."

"Wait a minute; I remember reading about the opening of the border for trucks without inspection at midnight on Friday by order of los Estados Unidos Commerce Secretary. Could they be so stupid as to have provided the means for their own destruction?" Ramirez asked.

"Either that, or it is some kind of trap by the Americanos to catch the terrorists before they can attack. If they moved too early, all the operatives would simply escape and prepare for the next attack," President Calderon replied. "Assume the worst; the attacks are aimed at both los Estados Unidos and us. How do we deal with this threat? How can we work with the Americanos?"

"If all you want to do is eliminate the threat, we can hit the facility at will before Friday. We can go in with a ground assault, or we can level the place with air strikes," General Garcia answered. "I don't like air strikes because we don't have sophisticated enough weapons to assure the absence of large numbers of civilian causalities. I really don't want to authorize the Americanos to bomb in our country. That would be a public relations disaster."

"Can we strike together and do it on a timetable that will work for the Americanos?" President Calderon asked.

"Of course, if that is what you want to do, but please remember this is our country, and you are talking about a strike of some nature on Méjico soil," Ramirez responded. "The Americanos should not be involved."

"Enrique, el president de los Estados Unidos is taking a historical risk telling us their plans early and asking for our involvement. I am going to take him at his word and try to work together. This could be the opportunity for a new beginning. His representatives will be here in an hour or so. Map out a suggested joint operation with several alternatives, including destroying the facility, capturing it or simply erecting a blockade of some nature to keep trucks from leaving."

Discovering the Domestic Response

The afternoon sessions had begun in the conference room with a domestic defense agenda. Gathered with the president were the vice president, Tom Knight, David Barnes, Darrell Reed, Attorney General Rodriquez, Homeland Security Director Hollister, and General Hedge.

"I have received no resignations, General," the president began. "What does that mean?"

"It means, sir, they will be good soldiers and obey your order, keeping their opinions to themselves," General Hedge responded. "On reflection, they all admitted that you are doing what you believe to be in the country's best interest, and they recognize that you are the commander in chief."

"Please thank them for me and tell them they may put their opposition in a memo to me and retain a copy. If this thing goes bad, they can blame me," the president responded.

"What is this about?" the vice president asked.

"Wilburn, some things are better left unknown right now. If our plan fails, I want to insulate you—and everyone I can—from blame. You are too important to the future of this nation. If it goes wrong, I take full responsibility," the president answered. "And the rest of you can do the same thing if you feel it is necessary. Write me a memo regarding anything you disagree with to protect yourself in the future. The captain goes down with the ship, but I offer each of you a life raft."

"I can't speak for the rest of them, Mr. President, but if that ship goes down, I will be by your side," General Hedge said, holding back tears. "You have shown courage and bravery in seeking to do what is required to protect this country and our friends. I am proud to serve with you, and I will not second guess you."

"Thank you, General," the president responded. The others also committed to stand together with the president, whether in victory or defeat.

"Enough," the president said, resuming his voice of authority and changing the subject. "This is not the Titanic. We have not struck an iceberg—at least not yet. Let's figure out how to get this ship safely home.

"Felix, where are we on identifying the leadership?"

"Miraculously, President Bristol found his voice before the grand jury and produced the information requested on the location of the Saudi sponsored teachers," the Attorney General responded. "We have obtained intercepts and visual observation that confirms their active involvement with other Arabs here on which we can find no record of legal entry. They all attended the Phoenix American Teachers Society conference, and although the names are different, we can now account for out of the country tickets for the same number of people—all of which were changed from earlier reservations to Saturday or Sunday at the time of that conference. This has to be them, although there is no way to be sure this is all of them."

"What about the actual operatives who would drive the trucks, fly the planes or carry out the killings?" the president asked. "Have we been able to identify them?"

"That, sir," the Attorney General answered, "is impossible. We have some probable locations, but no way of being absolutely certain at this point."

"So, what you are telling me is that we can possibly capture the cowardly leadership who intends to leave before MD begins, but not the operatives who intend to do the killing?" the president said, obviously frustrated.

"It looks that way," the Attorney General shrugged.

"Maybe not, Mr. President," the geek inserted. "My gang and I haven't slept much the past thirty or so hours—as in we haven't slept at all. That prayer website was overwhelmed with extra l emails after you asked for additional prayer. We have lists of locations throughout the United States and overseas where suspicious activities are reported, including concentrations of Arab young men in the cities which the Attorney General has identified as the location of the leadership. Beyond that, we have locations in every Middle Eastern country where we suspect a possible assassination, as well as Europe, where the transportation attacks are planned."

"I have to be honest and say the information is only as good as the source, but I trust this website," Homeland Security Director Hollister added. "Darrell here gave me a couple of the locations, and we sent teams by to observe with sophisticated long-range listening devices and visual aids. There is enough evidence to clearly suspect something illegal is either already occurring in those locations, or contemplated by those residing there."

"Can we get search warrants out of the grand jury and organize a large enough federal effort with the cooperation of the local authorities to move on these locations as part of the plan?" the president asked.

"If they have that kind of evidence, I can get the search warrants tomorrow," the attorney general answered.

"With the FBI's help, we can organize the federal effort. I know the local authorities will join us if asked, but it would have to be done in a way not to endanger the timing or risk early disclosure," Director Hollister added.

"What about the targets of the death squads on the 11th? We may not be able to get all the operatives even with the location information. We can't leave the country at risk," the president continued.

"I may be able to help you there, sir, but this is a little out of 'La La Land,'" Director Hollister said, somewhat timid.

"And just what do you mean by a little out of 'La La Land?'" the president asked.

"Well, sir, I know that we are all way out on a limb if this fails and anyone looks at what we relied on to come up with this plan… but what we have here may be the strangest of all," Hollister answered.

"Stranger than that prayer website that can be read by Christians of every language?" David Barnes asked pointedly.

"Well, maybe not, but plenty strange. This information is coming from dreams. We got calls from well-credentialed police officers in every major city who all claimed to be Christians, and they all had the same dream," Hollister responded.

"And what was the dream?" the president asked.

"They dreamt that there were attacks on elementary schools; indiscriminate killing of children and teachers. You know one of the police officers who had the dream—it was Sally Johnson from Williams," Hollister said.

"I had a dream too that has become part of this plan," the president said thoughtfully. "I assume you got the names of these officers who had the dreams?"

"Yes, Mr. President," Hollister answered.

"Fine, then this is what I want you to do," the president spoke decisively. "The officers who had the dreams are the local contacts I want you to put in charge of the police groups. These groups will cooperate with our move against the terrorist leadership and suspected operatives. I also want them to organize teams to cover the elementary schools in their locale on the 10th and 11th."

"But, Mr. President, you can't just do that," Hollister protested. "These officers are not the heads of their departments, and those departments all have trained swat teams. You are asking police chiefs to ignore their chain of command and those who have been trained for these missions. That is a lot to ask."

"Stephen, not only can we ask it, that is exactly what we are going to do—and it is your specific assignment to do the asking," the president answered. "Before we started this meeting, I had a conversation with a very wise man who warned me about involving people without the vision from God for what must be done. According to you, these people all claim to be Christians and have all been given the same vision of what is at risk from the execution squads. We have been praying for wisdom and direction. I believe this is an answer to that prayer, and those are the people God wants to use. If I am correct, God has already resolved the chain of command issue."

"But, sir, please reconsider…" Hollister began, only to be cut off again.

"Listen, all of you," the president said firmly and finally, "the nation is at risk. We have just a few hours to finish preparation for a preemptive response. This is not about me, and it is not about you or your opinion; it is about our children and their future. I am the president. I have to make these decisions and live with them. I sincerely believe that I have been given a plan by God—which is being clarified as we speak—and I intend to follow what I believe we have been instructed to do. You may not like that, but the time for argument and debate is over. Trust God or trust me, but follow my instructions as if your life depended on it. It does, and so does the country's survival."

"Yes, Mr. President," Hollister replied, knowing the subject was forever closed.

CHAPTER 19

READY FOR ACTION

Wednesday, March 5—MD minus 6 days

WEDNESDAY ENDED WITH the final pieces in place for all the players who would soon be on stage as the competing agendas collided. In Mexico, once the Iranian flash drive presentation was shown and explained by Troy Steed, even Secretary of National Defense Ramirez was on board with a joint response. It was late at night when a joint operating plan and command structure were finally agreed upon, but the American delegation left happy, actually surprised at what had been accomplished.

The remainder of the president's day had been invested in reviewing the detailed orders for domestic military operations, as well as the orders proposed to be issued abroad to be sure they were within the operational limits he had set. Of surprise to General Hedge was the president's insistence on apologizing to the Joint Chiefs for his harsh response when his Israel deployment was questioned and his sincere expression of appreciation for their willingness to follow his direction against their better judgment. "I know," he had said, "that this goes against all tactical reason, but it is the right thing to do, and I believe it will save lives by preventing a larger conflict." He changed no opinions that day, but even the most cynical among them found a sincere new respect for him as commander in chief. They had faith in the fact that he understood his decision and was willing to take sole responsibility for the consequences.

Working with Tom Knight, he had detailed how he wanted presentations made to the various government representatives in the meetings scheduled for Saturday throughout Europe and the Middle East. Darrell Reed had prepared a visual presentation using the Iranian flash drive to explain the planned attacks on America so that foreign governments could grasp the extent of the danger and the need for a bold preemptive response. Other than the British and Israelis, no one would be provided with advance information on the planned preemptive response. The president would make that presentation to the British on Friday during a rest stop outside of London before flying on to Iceland for the Saturday meeting with the Russians.

The Reed flash drive presentation would be inserted in the secret orders to be carried with the government representatives to be opened in their assigned country on Friday. Included in each packed was a personal letter from the president to the government leader, explaining the risk to their nation along with an intelligence report on suspects which had been garnered from believers who sent reports to the prayer website on suspicious activities in that nation. When Reed had compiled the information, it was clear that no nation under threat was excluded. God had provided information for every nation at risk.

The long day ended for the president when the secretary of state returned from Mexico with a report on the planned joint operation to deal with the Oaxaca threat. The president was thrilled with the Mexican response. "Perhaps," he thought, "this can be the beginning of a new day in our relationship with our neighbors. It is way past due."

"Mr. President," the secretary of state asked, changing the subject, "what about the United Nations? Will they be advised before the strikes commence?"

"I wish they could be," the president answered. "If the UN truly was able to live up to its Charter, they could be an instrument to prevent all of this. Unfortunately, they have proven over the years they cannot be trusted with advance notice of anything. It is structurally incapable of action, and has no real public credibility."

"What I want you to do is go to New York on Friday. Then, on

Saturday, you can advise the secretary-general after the preemptive strikes commence. Tom will call you on the secure phone to let you know when to begin the meeting. The secretary-general should be willing to set up a meeting once he learns of the deployment in Israel. That will concern him. Make sure you tell them when setting up the meeting that it is just an exercise. When you meet, you can tell them of the actual peace-keeping nature of the deployment as part of the plan."

"Yes, Mr. President," the secretary responded.

"I will be making calls to reassure Arab allies on the flight to England in a few hours," the president continued. "I pray that the America haters will not be able to organize terrorist attacks on our forces in Israel before we can initiate the plan on Saturday."

"Mr. President, what about Congress?" the secretary asked. "They have been kept completely out of the loop. You might want to think that one through a little more. Public opinion is going to be important on this one; especially moving forward. These are major preemptive attacks on Iran, and a never-before-commenced force deployment in Israel, don't you want to pave the way in Congress? Isn't congressional consent required by the Constitution?"

"I appreciate your concern. I have heard this before," the president replied. "As much as I would like for the UN and Congress to be our partners, I can't trust the current leadership of Congress any more than I can trust the UN. This is about the survival of the nation. If we survive and they want to be angry with me, or even impeach me, who cares. The important thing is to survive, and they have chosen not to be part of our survival. I cannot take the chance that they might do something stupid and go public and leak the plan. We will give them a briefing after we are sure that the crisis is under control, but not before. I have given that 'happy' assignment to Tom Knight."

Noting that the secretary of state was obviously still concerned, the president continued, "We are not going to war, we are simply moving preemptively to stop a war. There is no requirement of congressional consent to defend the nation against a planned attack. If I didn't defend the country with knowledge of the attack, I should be impeached. I absolutely agree with you that in normal circumstances, I would owe Congress the courtesy of some level of advance notice and an opportunity to consult on the plan. But these are not normal circumstances, and they are not the normal leadership of Congress. Look at what they are doing—the congressional leadership has assumed your role as secretary of state and my Constitutional prerogative to handle foreign relations by initiating the so-called Cox peace effort. That is technically criminal conduct. Should I have the attorney general prosecute them? I certainly can't trust them."

"No, sir, that would be political suicide," he replied.

"Perhaps, but again, what difference does it make if we don't survive? This all falls on me if it fails, and it will all be on me with their criticism even if it succeeds. I feel a little like Abraham Lincoln must have felt when he had to take steps before Congress was in session that first year to preserve the Union. He knew he would be criticized and second-guessed, but if he hadn't done that, the Civil War would have been lost before it started. I believe I know what we have to do, and we shall do it. Thank you for the good job in Mexico," he said as he left for his room to get a little sleep before leaving for Air Force One.

Climbing into bed shortly before sunrise, he found Janet awake waiting for him. "So, where are we?" she asked matter-of-factly.

"We are finished," the president answered. "It is in God's hands now. There is really nothing else we can do to prepare," he said, and quickly fell into a peaceful deep sleep.

The Counsel of Darkness Gathers

Somewhere in the outer darkness, those who sought to extend the darkness to the whole of God's Creation met to take stock of their servants' preparation for the great day of destruction. Gathered were Molech, Chemosh, Baal, Asherah, and Ashtoreth—along with Legion, who had brought with him Argon. "What is that useless vapor doing here among the great?" Molech roared in disfavor.

As Argon began to slink away, Legion answered, "I have restored this one, for among all the so-called great only he has come forward with a plan and the means to disrupt the American leadership before they can counter MD."

"And just what is this plan?" Molech demanded. "It better be an improvement on his last failure."

"That was your failure, not his alone," Legion replied. "At least he tried to carry out the Dark Master's orders."

"Let him speak for himself," Chemosh interrupted. "What is your plan, little one?"

Argon spoke fearfully, gaining courage as he continued. "Oh, exalted ones who serve our Dark Master faithfully, the instrument that has been raised up to align himself with the Enemy is the American president. Other than that old man who started all of this, the president is the one who leads people away from the Dark Master's agenda and toward the Enemy's protection. I fear that he has succeeded more than we know, and thus he must be killed quickly."

"Fool, you tell us nothing we don't know. All of us have sought for a way to kill this one and have failed. What plan do you have that can succeed?" Molech responded with obvious contempt.

"I have a willing instrument we control who has both means and an opportunity," Argon began. "It is different from the attempt to kill the old man. That plan was in direct contradiction of the limits the Enemy placed on the Dark Master. We can say what we want and continue to fool ourselves, but we all know that we cannot overcome the Enemy's expressed will or limits. We have to accomplish our purposes within those boundaries."

"Blasphemy," Molech shouted, "even if it is true, it cannot be spoken. Get that imbecile out of our presence."

The response from the others was not as Molech had expected, for there was momentary silence—a clear, unexpressed desire to hear Argon out. Recognizing that he now had their ears, Argon continued with increased confidence. "The Enemy is more powerful than us, and perhaps it is time for us to stop contesting that reality and work within it to negate it. Most of these humans live outside of His will, and we have full run of them. My plan is to deal with what has not been specifically prohibited from advancing the Dark Master's agenda. The Enemy has not expressly prohibited us from trying to kill Strong, so we try to kill Strong. He is the danger here, not so much because of his position, but because of what he says. He is attempting to lead the people back to the Enemy by example."

"Be careful little one. We must obey the Dark Master, even when he is wrong," Chemosh replied. "We all made that decision when we joined in the rebellion and were thrown out of Heaven.[73] We know the reality of the future unless something changes. We are all condemned whenever the end comes.[74] We only have now to fight and draw the humans into the same condemnation we face. The Enemy fooled us and provided a way for them to avoid the second death, but not us.[75] Our sole purpose now is to keep as many of them as possible from finding that way. We have to stick together, and the Dark Master is our leader."

"Do not act like one awaiting their execution. We can hurt the Enemy by our every success," Baal added. "Remember, Jesus cried over Jerusalem.[76] He wants none to perish and all to be saved.[77] They rejoice over their victories but mourn every defeat. He really loves all the miserable human creatures.[78] It's detestable. Let's give them some defeats to mourn now, and leave the future to the future."

"Agreed, we can do that, but don't fool yourselves; the Dark Master doesn't believe that we are defeated for all time," Molech said with passion. "He tried to seduce Jesus into sin and failed,[79] but he has not given up. He still hopes to induce God into some action against His character, which would make it impossible for Him to punish us without being a hypocrite."

"I know that the Dark Master believes that he will one day rule the earth, and is even now preparing to fight all the forces of Heaven again," Chemosh declared. "That is our destiny."

"Perhaps," Argon answered. "I don't pretend to understand anything beyond mutual hatred for these human creatures and a desire to see them all burn forever, but our agenda now has to be to destroy America and the remnant of worshippers of the Enemy who live in America. Other than the Bookseller, Strong is our biggest obstacle. When he returns to the White House, as long as it is after Friday midnight, he dies when his helicopter is shot down. That will cause complete chaos in the plans of America to deal with what they know of MD. His body won't even be cold when destruction falls everywhere."

"You have a heart of evil that is much bigger than your body," Molech finally had to admit. "You are correct about Strong, and even if you fail, the effort must be made."

"Now, if we can get back to the purpose of this meeting," a frustrated Ashtoreth interrupted. "Is the Enemy helping Strong prepare for the attacks? What do we know?"

"It is not what we know that concerns me," Legion answered. "It is what we don't know. I've been getting reports from Keepers and Tempters regarding our instruments that are as we expected. They are ready. They await MD with unexcelled passion and hatred. What we don't know is any details on the efforts of the American government. It is as if a cloud has fallen around the principals the past few days. Strong is trying to use believers for much of this, so we have no Keepers to consult, and the Tempters have thus far failed in their efforts. We have been able to create some division and confusion, but we don't know what we face or how involved the Enemy has chosen to be."

"All of you think too much," Asherah interjected firmly. "Who cares what the Enemy does. Our instruments are in place, and for the first time, we have an opportunity to negate America. We can't lose our focus now. Kill Strong if you can, but if not, he will wish he was dead after the 11th."

"Yes!" they shouted in unity. Suddenly a false sense of confidence fell on them, and they dismissed all their concerns and proceeded to discuss how easy it would soon be without America.

Watching unnoticed had been Lucius, who departed as they rejoiced. He left smiling, as he knew that the sense of confidence they now felt had been sent from the Father to divert their attention from what He was seeking to do. "Truly God was reaching out to answer the prayers of the many raised on behalf of this president," he thought as he eagerly waited for his next assignment.

Terminal Assignments

On the other side of the world, three men gathered in a safe house. They had a different reaction to their assignments, which had been delivered to Ittai by Carl Varvel. "This is a sentence of death," Hiram Urbay said, shaking his head in disbelief. "How can we be expected to do this and live?"

"I think the assignment is to 'do this' without regard to whether we shall live," Hushai answered. "The bottom line is that this is important, and it has to be done. Let me take the delivery to the Iranian government. My only issue is, who should I deliver the message to? If I take it to the president, he may see it as a means to create the chaos necessary to bring on the Hidden Imam and go forward with the attacks as planned regardless. That I know is the exact opposite of the purpose of the message."

"God will have to show us to whom it is to be taken," Ittai responded. "I don't yet know."

"There are those in the State Security Force who might have a way of getting to the real power over this president or to the military leadership," Urbay answered. "Let me see what I can find out tomorrow."

"That sounds like a good plan—pray and ask and listen," Ittai said. "I wonder why the Americans want to use an informal channel rather than a diplomatic channel."

"That answer is easy," Hushai declared. "The American president is using believers for the most critical assignments because he knows they will pray before they do anything. He wants God's involvement in every step. The unspoken reality is that he has no more answers than we do on how to accomplish this. He only knows that it is to be done."

"I will take the message to Hezbollah," Ittai volunteered. "It is not well known, but the CIA has penetrated the leadership. I know I can get the message where it needs to be taken, which leaves Syria to you, Hiram."

"How can I do that? You forget I am only a computer technician with the State Security Forces. I don't know anyone in the Syrian government," Urbay answered.

"That may be true, but don't forget that it was God who used you to obtain a copy of the MD plan in the first place," Hushai replied. "I would imagine that He already has that worked out. You just need to go."

"Easy for you to say," Urbay responded, "I am not a spy or a diplomat... or even a soldier."

"We don't need any of those. What we need is someone who the Syrians believe has the confidence of the president," Ittai answered. "Then they will listen. I will contact the State Department and get a contact for you. The fact that you are carrying a handwritten personal message from the president should give you credibility and access. We can provide transportation."

"You make it difficult to find an excuse," Urbay answered.

"Good, then stop trying," Ittai responded. "We have to do this, and we have to do it on the president's schedule. Did you catch that bit about 9/11?"

"I did," Hushai said. "Sometime Saturday morning we are going to get a call on the secured cell phones we have been given that will simply say,

'9/11.' Then we are to deliver the message. Not before the call or after, but at that exact minute."

"You have it right," Ittai confirmed, "and until that time, we can't say anything about this to anyone."

"I understand, but I'm afraid," Urbay said with real candor and honesty. "I don't mind the losing my head part; it's all that torture before that scares me."

"Well, let me put it to you this way," Hushai said, seeking to conclude the discussion. "Either God protects you, or you have described all of our futures. Whatever it is, we have to do this. Consider the cost if we don't deliver the messages and Iran and Syria attack Israel."

"That is a chilling thought," Urbay responded.

"Enough," Ittai concluded. "Let's go and confirm contacts and get back together at the place of prayer tonight before we leave for our assignments tomorrow. I will be by to pick you up first, and then we will swing by the hotel and pick up Hushai. 10:00 PM here."

CHAPTER 20

THE BELL RINGS

Thursday, March 6—MD minus 5 days

CONTEMPORANEOUS WITH THE rising of the sun, a celestial alarm was sounded, and the instruments of darkness and light awakened and began to move into place for the as yet undetermined conclusion to the holy war. The bell alarm sounded first in the Middle East, where competing armies were being positioned for coming events. In Iran and Syria, members of their armed forces left their families and reported for an unknown deployment. The European contingent of American forces had landed in Israel and was being assisted by their ally in establishing a base between the well-known enemies. Fearful, but determined, the Americans set about securing their perimeter from suicide attacks, hopeful that the cover of a military exercise would deter even the most zealous from striking against them, risking retaliation and a more permanent presence.

Repositioning of US forces continued now that the president's orders had been received. Equipment, including air defense missiles, had been set up to protect against possible missile or aircraft attacks on Middle East forces. The aircraft carrier USS Abraham Lincoln had been deployed in the Gulf. Its pilots and crews were carrying out drills to be prepared to respond quickly to any threat against American forces anywhere in the region.

Suicide squads continued to seek information on where Middle East leaders would be on the 11th so that the assassination plots could be successfully carried out. Even as they had carefully planned and executed the preparation for MD, a focused effort had been made to infiltrate the personal security forces of the targeted leaders over the past four years. Those efforts were bearing fruit as the planners learned where and when a strike was possible.

The two Navy Seals teams were now being finally positioned for response, even as a terrorist cell in Damascus prepared to kidnap or kill former President Cox. Seal Team 4 had a squad already in the hotel where Cox would stay undercover as a touring graduate student group. The remainder of the force was housed nearby in a portion of a warehouse used by the CIA to stage covert activities. Seal Team 10 was positioned in the country equipped with helicopters, ready to respond quickly with massive firepower and transportation wherever needed if abduction occurred.

Hezbollah prepared to initiate what they were calling the "Final Infatida" against Israel with Syria and Iran and hopefully Russia. Finally, the lost land would again be in Arab control, and the hated Jews would be dead or in camps. If any surviving Western power cared, they could open their own nation to the Jews. They were determined that Palestine would never again be home to the Jewish scourge.

El-Ahab had begun his trek from Syria to Iran for the Saturday morning meeting with Ahmad Habid to finalize the plans for attacks on American forces in the Middle East. Habid had learned of the deployment into Israel and was making plans with Hezbollah to include that force as a target in the attacks. "If the Americans are foolish enough to give us more targets, we will not miss the opportunity. They die with the Jewish pigs," he thought with glee.

As the sun rose high above the place of prayer, there was rejoicing over the time of fellowship together. "How I needed this," Hushai exclaimed, "it is life to me. Now I can live or die as the Lord wills."

"Yes," Hiram agreed, surprised at the peace that welled up within. "When I think of believers here who can't safely gather to pray, and of all those others who know nothing of Jesus, my heart breaks."

"It is not your heart breaking, my brother," Ittai replied. "It is God's heart breaking for those who have been blinded to the truth." As they paused to consider what was before them in this place of darkness, they could not hear the universal chorus of "Amen" loudly declared in the invisible.

"If they only knew the extent of the Father's love for those blinded by hatred and false teaching," Niger exclaimed to the gathered forces of light that had been dispatched to protect these men during their time of prayer.

"Yes, and His love for His own people who killed His Son," Barnabas continued. "Perhaps this will be the time when their eyes are opened, and they come to recognize the time of His coming. I know it will happen. The Bible promises."[80]

"Perhaps fulfilling that promise is what this is all about," Niger said. "I have had a strange sense that the events these past years were not really about terrorism, but God asserting His Lordship over His church in the West while seeking to open a way for the light to shine even here."

"How I hope you are right," Barnabas replied, now with tears. "I cannot stand the horror of all these multiple millions living and dying having never heard the truth of the gospel. Even in America, a child can now live and die and never hear the truth of who Jesus is."

Barnabas' candor silenced everyone for the moment, and together they spontaneously began to pray that the Father would not allow these hundreds of millions to perish. "Whatever it takes to open their eyes," they prayed together as they eagerly awaited instructions.

Back in the place of prayer, Ittai interrupted the silence, "It's time. We need to return to the hotel and catch our rides so we can be in place Saturday in time for the calls."

Looking at his new friends, Hiram said, "Please be careful. I have really come to love you, my brothers."

Smiling, Hushai added, "Let's meet here when this is over. God always seems to be here."

Obedience Even in the Unknown

As the celestial alarm rang over the Pacific at a base in the Philippines, Captains Jonathan Adams and Sawyer Yeager, both experienced B-2 Stealth Bomber pilots, received top-secret operation orders that they knew immediately were no drill. Others in their unit had been ordered to fly daily to the Middle East for possible missions early next week, but these orders were mission specific and were for the day after tomorrow. To preserve secrecy, they and their crewmates had been restricted to base and quarantined from their fellows. That had never happened here before. "This must really be big," they thought.

Operational orders had been given earlier for deployment of submarines and surface ships outfitted with cruise missiles both nuclear and non-nuclear. The only mission-specific orders related to when they were to be prepared to fire if ordered. Beyond that, no one on board knew what was coming. The crews had only been advised initially on what had been released publicly during the Pentagon briefing. It was regarding a massive military exercise to test America's ability to respond to a terrorist threat anywhere in the world.

Trident missile submarines and all land and air-based nuclear forces had been notified to be ready for a change in status, which could come at any time within the next forty-eight hours. Leaves had been cancelled, and all vessels were put to sea. Again, the cover for this operation for those with satellite capability who would know of the deployments was the massive military exercise. The Pentagon had notified their Russian and Chinese counterparts of the operation before it commenced.

In Russia, President Sorboth was advised by Defense Minister Petrov of the American deployment. He responded by putting his forces on a higher alert status, cancelling leaves and having all available vessels put to sea. "They know, and are making preparations," President Sorboth declared. "I do not believe that President Strong would ask for a meeting in Iceland, of all places, and then attempt to execute a surprise nuclear first strike against us. It is totally out of character for the man, but to be safe, we will be prepared. They will pick up our deployment by satellite, even as we did theirs. That should deter any possible foolish aggression."

"I agree with your decision," Petrov replied, "but there is no need to fear an American first strike. This is a defensive deployment. If they were seriously contemplating a first strike, they wouldn't notify us in advance and then move their forces so publicly. They know we can track their every move."

"That is logically true, but right now I don't trust anyone and have a real fear of what I don't know," Sorboth answered. "This American is different. He is dangerous because he doesn't play by the rules. What American would dare put forces into Israel to front Hezbollah? And yet, he has done that. What won't he do?"

"I'll tell you what he won't do, Mr. President. He won't invite you to a meeting to declare war on you. There is more risk here from Vandenburg and Krenski than there is from him. That is why I am glad your response was so forceful and will be well known throughout the military shortly. That will put a cap on their accusations that you are not strong enough to lead Russia back to greatness."

"I hope you're right," Sorboth replied. "The internal stuff has to stop. We have decisions to make on how we deal with the West and the lost territories. Division within only makes that more difficult," he said, shaking his head. "In some ways, I am complimented that the US president wants to meet with me before events occur, but I have to wonder how he knows and what he knows. Are these people really our enemies, or can we build a future together?"

"I suppose that is a subject for your meeting Saturday morning," Petrov answered. "Don't worry about the home front. I will keep Vandenburg and Krenski on a short leash. Just don't make commitments, and don't be afraid."

"It is really strange, Dimitri. I am afraid."

Questions in Europe

As the bell sounded in Europe, there were more questions than answers among American's allies. A Saturday morning meeting without a definite time was completely out of the ordinary. Questions circulated among EU Members regarding the massive American military exercise. On the phone with British Prime Minister McDonald, French President George Cresson asked, "What is President Strong doing? The idea of putting troops between the Arabs and Israelis is suicidal. He can't be serious about exposing his military to terrorists like that. It will be Beirut all over again!"

"Perhaps, but there has to be more to all we are seeing than we are being told," the prime minister responded. "The Americans are not playing games, and this cannot be some kind of massive military exercise. Something is in play here. My people have picked up increased terrorist chatter throughout Europe. Maybe the Americans know something."

"I would have more confidence," Cresson responded, "if it wasn't for that religious fanaticism going on in the States. The press reports Strong has been at Camp David on some kind of religious retreat. That man is the leader of the free world? Pardon me for my insensitivity but, God help us."

"Don't write him off, George. If the chips were really down, you would want that man on your side. Just wait, and we will all know soon what this is about," he said being careful not to reveal that he would be meeting with President Strong tomorrow.

North American Preparations Continue

The bell rang in North America as the president had just begun to sleep.

In Oaxaca, trucks continued to arrive. Modifications were being made to have the tanker fleet and truck bombs ready to begin their trek into the United States when the magic hour of midnight Friday had passed, and the roads were open without inspection. In Mexico City, however, a different sort of preparation was underway. Final deployment orders were being prepared for a joint task force consisting of a Mexican Army mechanized infantry brigade and a Company of US Marines to deal with the Oaxaca location.

Throughout the United States, other military units were being positioned for the defense of identified targets, even as offensive units reviewed orders to address the threat from Brothers Trucking yards, Terminal Equipment Leasing installations, and aircraft of Kingdom Charters. Coordination and timing were a nightmare. It seemed like an impossible task.

Filled fuel tank trucks were beginning to be delivered to the Brothers Trucking yards as career drivers began their unexpected vacation wondering what fleet modifications were being made to their units. Those trained in the "how to" of the modification kits would be arriving later in the day to start installation of the triggering devices. It was all proceeding calmly, without incident and seemingly in secret.

The FAA and military air controllers were monitoring the location of every Kingdom Charter aircraft. Flight plans were reviewed to determine where the planes would be on Saturday, and who was included in the crews of each aircraft. Background searches had already been performed on the career crews. Nothing unusual had been found, other than the fact that just like the Brothers Trucking career employees, none of these pilots were yet scheduled for any flights on the 10th or later. Justice scrambled for a legal means to seize the aircraft, while the military focused on how that could be accomplished and how they could be shot down if required.

In New York, several very hung-over Saudis waited for planes out of the country, having celebrated their success at the department of transportation too late and too long. The open roads start to the North American Union farce had succeeded. It was expensive—political favors are always expensive—but it was money well spent, for soon the instruments of destruction would be moving north. "Almost five years," one said with pride. "The Americans have never understood our patience and passion, and now it is too late for them."

"Yes," another answered, "they have no concept that the movement which will soon overcome them began centuries ago. Finally, payback to the West for the barbarism of the crusades. It will be their children without food this time, and our lands will once again be secure and cleansed of the infidels."

The terrorist coordinators had busy days planned to finish up what they must do before catching planes out of the country. They watched reports on the great American military exercise, but discounted it after the Pentagon briefing. It would all be over before it could affect MD. Obviously, the Americans knew something about the plan, but not enough. None of the operatives or leadership had been detained or even discovered. The same air of confidence that had fallen on the forces of darkness gathered with Legion and Molech fell now on the terrorist coordinators. It had the same source.

Attorney General Rodriquez and Assistant US Attorney Larry Jordan were exhausted, as was the grand jury that they had sequestered these past days. Search warrants and subpoenas had been obtained based on the flash drive presentation, affidavits, testimony of Harkins College President Bristol and information provided by Darrell Reed from the prayer website. Now it would be up to Homeland Security Director Hollister to coordinate with the FBI director and the police officers who had the dreams to move in a coordinated fashion throughout the country when the "9/11" signal was given. "That's just nuts," he thought, but those were his orders.

On the Hill, final preparations were underway for the Cox formal send-off. All the news media had been invited, and the "show" would begin promptly at 10:00 AM to catch the maximum audience in all US markets—while beating the lead-in to the Williams funeral.

"I just don't get the curiosity with that killer's funeral," Majority Leader Howard said with obvious frustration. "That woman killed something like 38 people before she did something good, and she killed a terrorist. Why should anyone care?"

"People care for the same reason it frustrates you. The whole thing makes no sense," Chairman Crow responded. "If she was willing to die to protect children, why did she kill children before?"

"It is the fascination with the good that is present in evil people," Cox said authoritatively. "That is what my trip is about. We are going to find some good in the 9/11 mastermind, as well as a way to make peace with him. If you think they like this funeral story, just wait until the cameras roll with the Sheik and me. The peace prize will be mine, and the White House will be yours."

"Well, you sure got a Christmas present with that offer from the Iranian president to meet after your meeting with the Sheik," Howard added. "Keep on, and you might get the public to demand a Constitutional amendment that would allow you a third and fourth term."

"I like that idea," Cox said, smiling. "I have never really been happy since I had to give it up, but if not that, perhaps secretary general of the UN. That has a nice sound to it, particularly as we move toward a one-world government."

"Will you never stop?" Crow replied, knowing the answer.

ITN & Williams Prepare for the Day

In New York at ITN headquarters, Carl Stern scrambled to prepare for the unknown. It was both frustrating and exciting to have his most experienced producer off to who knows where for who knows what with the president. However, knowing what he knew of this president and the level of secrecy required meant something significant was in process… but how could they coordinate a worldwide broadcast from an unknown location with unknown technical requirements in just over two days? It seemed crazy… and near impossible. Jim Hunt and his crew had their cell phones taken and were denied other means of communications. He would find out the time and what was required only hours before the broadcast.

Shaking his head in disbelief, Stern turned his attention to this morning's two events. First, they had to provide coverage of the Cox send-off, and then the Williams funeral. Fortunately, probably intentionally, they had been scheduled so that it was possible to give both complete coverage, and he had assigned quality teams to each site. "How I wish the Bookseller were available to explain all this," he thought, but the Bookseller, like his most experienced producer, had seemingly fallen off the face of the earth.

Meanwhile, in Williams, a small group met in the College Church sanctuary to pray, having been significantly burdened to prepare the way for the funeral and to intercede for President Strong. Gathered were Pastor Scribes, Chaplain Forest and Pastor Wilson, along with Samantha Jones, Margaret White, Sally Johnson, Tom Campy, and Janice Foster—the mom in the car at Kingdom Daycare whose child was saved by Susan Stafford's last act in this world. There was a passion in their prayers, for each of them had become a significant part of the celestial events which were now in play.

In the invisible, an angry and frustrated Alexander raced through the city of Williams, seeking instruments that could be used to interrupt the funeral. Screaming at Keepers and Tempters, he was in a state of disbelief that they could not find a single relative or friend of victims of the shooter who could be influenced to protest and disrupt the funeral. None of the terrorists could be used. It was too close to MD to divert their attention.

Smiling as he observed the frantic activity of the Williams territory leader of the forces of darkness, Manaen rejoiced that the testimony to be given would not be allowed to be perverted. There was a message God wanted to be heard, and thus, it would be heard.

An Intimate Goodbye

Back at Camp David, the brief sleep had ended. "It's time, Mr. President," John Thomas announced as he entered with a strong, black cup of coffee. "There is time for breakfast, and then straight to the helicopters. The rest of the group is waiting in the dining room."

"Thank you, John. Would you ask Janet to join me?"

"Yes, Mr. President."

While drying off from a quick shower, the president heard a pleasant voice, "Two hours—getting lazy in your old age?"

"Thanks, beautiful," he answered, "you know there's lots of free time in this job."

"I have suspected that for some time," she replied as he continued dressing. And then her tone changed, "You have a crowd waiting for you in the dining room. I guess it is time to leave. Joshua, you wouldn't reconsider and let me go with you, would you? I really don't want to be apart right now. Whatever happens, we should be together."

"I feel that way too, but it's not possible. I need you to be at the White House with the vice president. If something goes wrong there, I need to know, and if I can't be reached, you know better than anyone my views on what lies before us."

Pausing as he struggled to find words to communicate what he wanted to say, he looked directly into her eyes and spoke softly. "Janet, I have given John a letter for you should I not come back."

"Stop now, Joshua," Janet replied, firmly walking away and then turning to face him again.

"Take the letter with you. I am not planning any state funerals," she said slowly with emphasis. "You will survive this, or we will both go home. I have no desire to be here without you. Anyway, that would really be unfair to leave me here while you are enjoying life in God's presence. God is gracious. We went into this together, and we will come out together. Please be careful."

"I will," he replied as he walked to her and held her particularly close. "Let's pray before we leave."

Hovering above them in the room as they began to pray, Lucius raised a prayer of his own. "Lord Jesus, if it is within your will, please protect these precious ones and enable them to overcome the plans of the evil one. But not my will; Your will be done."

And he went with them as they departed, still awaiting instructions.

CHAPTER 21

QUESTIONS AND ANSWERS

Thursday, March 6—MD minus 5 days

AS THREE OF the Marine One fleet lifted off from Camp David, they were joined in the air by two others shifting in formation together. The one carrying Janet and the vice president veered toward Washington for a White House arrival, and the other three headed to Andrews Air Force Base to meet Air Force One.

Elsewhere in Washington, another airport trip had begun as the Cox send-off press conference had ended and he headed toward the charter flight that would carry him and a massive press contingency to the purported meeting with the Sheik and the Iranian leader. Most in the White House Press Corps figured that they might as well travel with Cox. They had heard nothing from the president since the public gathering in the East Room almost three weeks ago. The silence was eerie and without precedent. For the Press Corps, the president had become boring, and Cox was old news. Together Tomorrow had provided the funds for Cox to lease the plane, and he was excited to be center stage again with an appreciative audience to carry his message to the world.

Secretly many other military flights were underway, taking members of the Survival Commission and others carefully selected to their designated country to await further instructions. Each flight carried a copy of the Iranian flash drive presentation, detailed information for each of the leaders with whom they would meet, and a personal message from the president. Included in the packet was a secured phone over which a single message would be sent Saturday in a text format when it was time for the meetings to occur. The messengers still had more questions than answers.

In Virginia, another note had been written to be read upon the author's death. It was placed carefully on a table in the bedroom of a small furnished apartment. The author then locked the apartment door and headed for the base to prepare and await transport Friday night to set up air defense positions across from the White House. The whole battery had been restricted to base in preparation for the operation and to ensure secrecy. All cell phones and other means of outside communication had been taken from the buildings where the battery's personnel were being housed for deployment. He didn't care. What he had to say would soon be sealed in blood.

Susan's Memorial Service

Later, as Air Force One went wheels up, the on-board televisions were all tuned to ITN for the follow up on the Cox press conference and the lead-in to the Susan Stafford's memorial service. Off by themselves for the moment in the main cabin, the Bookseller and Paul prayed for Pastor Scribes, Samantha and the others who would participate. They also prayed for the president and for the purpose of this trip, although they did not know what that was. Their prayer was simple: that the Lord's will be done, and that in all things, nothing dishonor the holiness of God's name. They likely understood the significance of the events that surrounded them better than anyone—apart from those directly involved—yet they were strangely at peace.

As their prayers ended, they heard "Amen" from several who had silently joined them as they prayed including George Murphy, the reporter at the *Times Daily*, and the president. Without a word, they turned their attention to the memorial service as Pastor Scribes opened.

> *We have come here today not to celebrate a life well lived, or to ignore the evil and harm done by Susan Stafford in that life, but rather to acknowledge the change which God brought to pass that caused her life*

to end well. It is like the change which God brought to pass when Jesus confronted one who similarly was responsible for the death of many.[81] *Susan Stafford had her own "Damascus road" experience from which she, like Saul, was changed forever. Join with me as we pray.*

The ITN camera crew panned throughout the audience of those in attendance as Pastor Scribes prayed, focusing on those who wore badges with the name of a family member or friend who had been a victim. Strangely there were many tears, but no overt expressions of anger. As he concluded, Officer Sally Johnson rose and walked to the podium. "Let us honor those who were victims of the evil that dominated Susan Stafford for most of her life," she began, and slowly read the list of names. As the names were read, a surviving member of the victim's family stood to answer for their fallen loved one.

"As she neared the end of her life, Susan Stafford was confronted with the monster she had become. I'd like you to hear it in her own words," Sally said as she turned to read portions of the diary Susan Stafford had left. The confession was striking, as was the turn from what she had been to what she became. Finishing the diary entries, Sally Johnson took a seat as Janice Foster rose. She walked slowly to the podium, visibly unable to restrain her tears as she looked down at her husband who was sitting and holding little Todd in his lap. The ITN crew did a close-up on Todd as Janice began to speak, reliving the terror of that day and the heroic, selfless act of Susan Stafford that saved their lives and resulted in her death.

"I know nothing of the monster that killed and injured all those people," Janice concluded. "All I know is that my son sits before me with my husband this day, and I live today because she had the courage to confront the terrorists without thought for her own life. Somehow God changed her and made her a new person. Thank you, God, for doing what only you can do. Thank you, Susan, for allowing God to change you."

As she departed, Samantha Jones stepped to the podium. "My dad, Taylor Jones, was one of the victims of the Williams shooter. He died alone like he lived, leaving two families and a world of hurt. I stand before you today to publicly forgive Susan Stafford for what she did to my dad, and to ask your forgiveness for what I felt toward my dad.

"It is not hard for me to forgive Susan Stafford, for the woman who lies buried in the city cemetery is not the woman who fired the shot that killed my dad and so many others. You have heard the story, so I won't repeat it. What you haven't heard yet is that she is not the only one here today who needs forgiveness. I need forgiveness, and so do many of you.

"When Jesus taught his disciples about anger, he warned them that anger was the equivalent of murder.[82] If you truly hate someone in your heart, you desire to murder them. I felt that about my dad because he abandoned my mother and left us for someone else. Every day was a struggle, and every day the hate within me grew.

"When I stood over his grave at the funeral, my heart was hard, secretly rejoicing that he has finally gotten what he deserved. Yes, I cried and felt the loss, but there was an ugly, dark evil within equivalent to what the murderer Susan Stafford was before she encountered God. I am like her, having also encountered God later and changed. I know what happened to her because it happened to me. The lesson of Susan Stafford's life is not what she was or even what she became; it is what we are now and how we need to allow God to change us."

As she left the stage, a sense of horror fell on those assembled and many watching around the world as the truth of what had just been shared burned deep in hearts where hidden hatred and anger boiled. Suddenly a voice was heard, "Yes, I too am a murderer. Forgive me." They were immediately joined by others, and soon the room was filled with people crying out to be free from the darkness which had been revealed within.

Pastor Scribes understood that God was at work, and dropped his prepared message, praying for wisdom as he walked slowly to the podium. The sound level in the room continued to rise, and tears were present throughout the crowd. Looking down at the blood-stained carpet left from the attack on the church, he could only join in the tears and sit down, for he too had a heart filled with great anger.

The ITN crew was frantic trying to figure out what to show and what to say. Finally, Tom Campy wheeled his wheelchair to the front of the auditorium and was handed the microphone. He began to quietly sing "Amazing Grace" and the audience quickly joined him. Both in Air Force One and across the viewing audience, people watching joined in the familiar tune. It seemed to put into words what they felt.

Amazing grace! How sweet the sound, that saved a wretch like me! I once was lost, but now am found, was blind but now I see.

T'was grace that taught my heart to fear. And grace my fears relieved. How precious did that grace appear the hour I first believed.

Through many dangers, toils and snares I have already come. T'was grace that brought me safe thus far and grace will lead me home.

The Lord has promised good to me, His word my hope secures. He will my shield and portion be as long as life endures.

When we've been there ten thousand years, bright shining as the sun, we've no less days to sing God's praise than when we first begun.

The organist continued to play as the people continued to cry out for forgiveness. Finally, Carl Sterns instructed his crew to go to a commercial break, not knowing what else to do.

The Real Difference

As the service progressed, everyone in the main cabin had gravitated to join with the president, the Bookseller and Paul. During the commercial break, Spike Crain, one of the ITN cameramen, verbalized what most were thinking. "What happened? What did we just see?"

The Bookseller responded, "What do you think you saw?"

"I don't know. I guess the people got carried away in the emotion of the moment."

"What do you feel right now?" the Bookseller asked, as all listened attentively.

"Well, I feel guilty; kind of dirty because there are people I hate," he responded. "Does that really make me, like, a murder?"

"See, what you are experiencing is what they experienced, and I am sure what others on this plane are experiencing. God moved by His Spirit to reveal how He views thoughts, attitudes, and actions. To Him, to hate another is to desire to kill that person."[83]

"But that is against everything I have been taught or seen," Crain argued. "How can that be wrong? You couldn't find five people in ten thousand that thought it was wrong. Certainly killing someone without cause is wrong, but hating them? That can't be wrong."

"It is wrong simply because God says it is wrong," the Bookseller continued. "It does not matter whether 9,995 people disagree or 5 people agree. It doesn't matter what you or I think, or even what the president thinks. All that matters is what God says. You just saw people who have come to understand that reality and are asking God for forgiveness. That is the core truth about the existence of God. If God exists, then He and He alone has the right to determine what is acceptable and what is not. What is not acceptable to God is sin. It is as simple as that, whether you agree or disagree."

"I have never seen Samantha that bold," Paul added astonished. "How could she have done that?"

"She didn't. God opened her eyes to truth in her life and then enabled her to share that truth with others in such a way that it would open their eyes to the same thing existing in their lives. That is what a pastor is supposed to be doing with every sermon—take the truth God has revealed to them, share it with those God sent to hear and be changed even as he has already been changed."[84]

"Help me understand one thing about this," George Murphy asked. "How does this recognition of wrong and correction in a Christian context line up with the Muslim response to conduct they believe to be unacceptable?"

"I think you can answer that from what you have observed in countries they control," the Bookseller answered. "What happens in those countries?"

"Well," Murphy answered, "first they make their religious text law and severely punish any disobedience. The state enforces everything from prayer to dress. The punishment is public and physical, what most in the West would consider cruel and inhuman."

"True, and what about women, how are they treated?"

"Women are property, instruments of pleasure at most—baby factories even," Murphy continued. "They have no value as people in comparison to men and are thus limited in what they can do or become. They cannot vote or drive a car or contest a man at law in many of those countries. They have to dress as instructed, and any variance from the law is punished by a cruel death, usually stoning."

"You are well read on what is happening in the world," the Bookseller responded. "Their religion has no tolerance for unbelievers, and anyone who contests their beliefs publicly will be killed. Their religious leaders rule over their political leaders. Does any of that sound like the Christian religion?"

"Certainly not," the president said, jumping in the discussion.

"Mr. Murphy, when you write negatively about the Christian faith, are you fearful of retaliation or reprisals?" the Bookseller asked.

"Not really; we live in a free country," Murphy answered.

"Yes, and Christians will be the first to fight and die that it remains a free country," the Bookseller answered firmly and with conviction. "The Christian faith is the free man's religion. The Bible commands us to tell you the truth about Jesus—what we call the gospel[85]—but whether you believe and accept Jesus as your Lord and Savior is a choice that you make. The consequence for a wrong choice is left to God. The state is an instrument to punish wrong conduct,[86] but not wrong choices about God. Jesus never advocated a religious state. God reigns in hearts, something no political state can ever control."

"But," Jim Hunt interrupted, "isn't the Muslim god like the God of the Old Testament? That God established a religious nation, Israel, and the Law of Moses in its purest form punishes without mercy."

"That is an excellent question," the Bookseller said, seizing the opportunity. "There are significant distinctions which I am not now going to debate, but think about the key difference today. The Old Testament law demanded punishment of the individual who broke the law, and often his family for generations forward. There were no means to be forgiven, for if you sinned, you must be punished. In that concept, they are arguably similar.

"The difference, however, is in the heart of the God of the Old Testament who is also the God of the New Testament. We learn in the New Testament that even before the first man was created, Jesus, who was always present with the Father, had already offered to come to the earth to accept the punishment due to sinners like you and me.[87] And he did come, and he was punished.[88] That is an indisputable historical fact. After that, the heart of God was satisfied, and sin could be forgiven because

Jesus had been punished for that sin.[89] How the punishment of Jesus can be substituted for the punishment we deserve is what Christians call the gospel. The Bible teaches that those who do not accept the gospel will be punished by God for their sin at the last judgment.[90] Christians are not judges; we merely proclaim the truth of the Bible. No government is required for that."

"Yes, but, shouldn't Christians fight the Muslims who seek to force their religion on the world? Who threaten them as infidels that they must convert or be killed?" Murphy asked.

"You will find your answer in how the Christians dealt with the Jewish leadership and the Roman Empire which did exactly that to them. Christians were being killed because they refused to recant their faith or burn incense and declare that, 'Caesar is Lord.' You read history, what did the Christians do?"

"They continued to proclaim the gospel everywhere and continued to be killed for it," Paul answered.

"You are correct, but note that they did not retaliate or seek to kill those who persecuted them. Rather, they sought to convert them," the Bookseller said, pausing now to find the words he would need to share what was now on his heart.

"When you think of the Muslims, you should probably think of Saul of Tarsus if you want to have a correct biblical perspective."

"Help me with that one," the president asked.

"Saul was a religious zealot. He was passionate about serving God as he understood God and everything he did was intended to honor God, but he was wrong. He actually was fighting God, and in the process, killing or imprisoning the true followers of God.[91] To the Christians who had seen Jesus, Saul was as much of a terrorist as those who seek to kill us today. Yet, God did not strike him dead or raise up an army to destroy him or the chief priests who had authorized his reign of terror. Jesus Himself confronted Saul on the Damascus road, and his heart was changed.[92] He was transformed into the Apostle Paul, the author of the majority of the New Testament and arguably the most effective proclaimer of the gospel in history.

"Think about the passion of the Muslim believers. It is embarrassing to compare their steadfast dedication with that of Christians. Can you imagine what would happen if God opened their eyes to the truth of the gospel and that same passion was exercised for Jesus in accordance with His teachings? The world would be changed overnight into a radically different place. Hate would be replaced with love, but Christians are afraid to share with Muslims for to confront their teaching risks death and most are afraid. The real problem is that we don't love as Jesus did and are not willing as the Apostle Paul to risk everything to share the truth. Please don't misunderstand, that does not mean we do not defend against those who seek to kill us and destroy our nation, but our passion should be to see that their eyes are opened to the truth."

"You are right," the president answered. "One thing I firmly believe is that this government must do more to support freedom of religion in all countries. That is something we can do, which is a legitimate function of government."

"I have a question closer to home," Murphy asked. "If there are Christians in political office, should they make policy and support laws that are consistent with the Bible?"

"You pose what seems to be the key question for this generation of Christian activists, many of whom have assumed politics is the way to advance God's agenda," the Bookseller answered. "They are seeking to change the world without changing hearts. That is impossible. What the Sauls of today need is a new heart; a new attitude that goes far beyond the law. Remember, ultimately the Apostle Paul and the disciples had to be willing to disobey the law when that law contradicted the commands of God.[93] The important thing for a Christian is to be a Christian whether they are in a political office or mow lawns for a living. To God, they are of equal value in what He seeks to accomplish. God wants all believers to listen for His voice and to obey wherever He places them, regardless of the law."[94]

"But the government makes laws and punishes disobedience of those laws," Murphy continued. "Shouldn't Christians in political office push for laws which direct the power of government to enforce God's laws?"

"Do you want a religious government like that in the so-called Muslim nations? There is no biblical authority for that."

"Of course not, but don't Christian politicians have to do something?" Murphy answered in obvious frustration.

"Yes, they have to be Christians, and here I believe is the guideline for Christians, whether in office or simply exercising the right to vote. Our government must never advance something which the Bible condemns. In particular, it should never make laws protecting conduct which the Bible condemns as sin, but at the same time, it should not be used to try and force changed conduct to make people live lives that are consistent with the teaching of the Bible. Again, that requires a change of heart, which no law can accomplish. Similarly, Christians should not vote for those who advocate the government advancing something that the Bible condemns."

"How about an example?" George Murphy asked.

"Well, let's take a really controversial subject—homosexuality," the Bookseller responded. "What should the Christian's attitude be toward homosexuals, and what policy should Christians want their government to advance? What policy should a Christian politician advance?"

"You certainly picked the hot button," the president answered. "Congress is right now trying to advance a bill to amend the hate crimes statute, meaning this discussion might someday soon be illegal."

"Whether it is legal or illegal is irrelevant," the Bookseller declared firmly. "This is a discussion that needs to be had, and the issue is what God would have a believer do either as a politician or as a voter. How do you answer that?"

"Well," Paul began, "homosexual conduct has been illegal for centuries. Only recently was the law changed by the United States Supreme Court."

"Do you believe that God wants homosexual conduct, or for that matter, any sin to be illegal? Would making the conduct illegal stop people from making the choice to be homosexuals? It never did before."

"So what do you believe, Mr. White, is the correct response?" the president asked.

"First, we must cease being hypocrites and remove the plank from our eye before we begin to examine the sin of homosexuality.[95] We Christians are guilty of so much sexual sin that it is almost ludicrous for us to attack anyone else as sinners. There are more divorces in the church than outside of the church. The sins of lust, pride, adultery, and greed are found everywhere among believers. Pastors are caught in adulterous relationships, priests have been found to have molested boys, Christian women intentionally dress themselves and their little girls provocatively, and multitudes of Christian men are addicted to pornography. We have to deal with ourselves before any homosexual will believe that, as a Christian, we have anything to say to them."

"That is, of course, true, but that is not the government," the president noted. "What should the government do?"

"Well, the majority cannot simply lord it over some group because we think we are better than they are," the Bookseller answered. "That changes nothing. If we understand that, then we can step back and consider this from God's perspective, which is what every Christian should do, whether in the government or not. God has declared that homosexual conduct is a sin just as he has declared many other types of conduct are sin.[96] The place of the Christian in government or the citizen who votes for those running for office is to be sure that our government does not advocate or encourage any conduct declared by God to be a sin.[97] We should not have laws that force people to be taught that a particular sin is acceptable conduct when God says that it is not. We should not have laws that elevate a sin or declare it a protected right. People will sin, Jesus said, but woe to the man who causes others to sin.[98] We do not want that woe to apply to our government or to us.

"At the same time, we should not hate those caught in this or any other sin. They, like us, simply need to see the truth and make a different choice. Hopefully, they will choose to be free of this sin, but that is their choice and not the government's, and their accountability is to God who will ultimately hold them accountable."[99]

"I guess the Founding Fathers got it right," the president said. "Two co-equal clauses that relate to religion. One says we cannot establish a state religion, while the other says the government should not act to prohibit the free exercise of religion."

"Yes," the Bookseller agreed, "but America has lost the balance. Just as it is wrong to make all conduct the Bible defines as sin illegal, thus imposing a state religion, it is equally wrong to make calling that conduct sin illegal, which prohibits the free exercise of religion. When our nation goes that far it repudiates its Constitution and aligns itself as an enemy of God. At that point, the American Christian faces the same issue the apostles did when commanded by the Sanhedrin not to speak or teach in the name of

Jesus. Peter said it well, 'We must obey God rather than men,'[100] and so they did—and so they suffered for it. That may soon be America, and it will be up to Christians to decide whom they will obey."

The uncomfortable silence that followed that comment was broken by David Barnes, who entered and reminded the president that there were phone calls he had to make. Excusing himself, the president retired to his onboard office while the others continued considering the exchange they had just witnessed.

CHAPTER 22

FOCUS ON THE FUTURE

Thursday, March 6—MD minus 5 days

THOSE ON THE secured video conference line with the president included Vice President Marshall, the Joint Chiefs, the cabinet, Tom Knight, Senator Besserman, Troy Steed, Darrell Reed, and CIA Director Crenshaw.

After an opening prayer, Troy Steed asked, "Excuse me, Mr. President. I hate to be direct, but why, sir, is George Murphy with you? Do we really want the press to know the details of what we are doing?"

"Yes, actually we do," the president answered just as directly. "I don't know what the outcome will be to all of this, but I want history to know the truth—all the truth—and I have included Mr. Murphy for that purpose. He will not be able to dispatch anything until after I make my report to the nation on Saturday. By then our response will have been fully launched, and the world will already have the broad overview. He has agreed to keep certain matters confidential to protect other leaders."

Although some disagreed, there was an unspoken understanding that the president had made a firm decision and it would not be revisited. Realizing that what was said would one day be public tempered some from speaking rashly, wanting to protect their reputation. On the other hand, the decision encouraged others to speak more for the same reason. What none of them knew was that the president had already ordered tapes of prior meetings and discussions be provided to Murphy.

"Gentlemen," the president began, "I want to revisit what for me is the key to everything—timing. Our response must be launched simultaneously from three continents across at least eleven time zones by my count. We can't have another Bay of Pigs debacle where the Air Force is in the wrong time zone and shows up an hour late, resulting in the ground forces being killed or captured. Are we sure we have that covered since we don't know for sure when the operation is to commence?"

"I believe we have that covered, sir. All timing is initiated by the signal given from the terrorist leadership meeting in Iran," General Hedges answered. "We will have three people on the ground and two air units to pick it up when sent and forward it to the military aircraft over the targets. Because of Mr. Reed's brilliance, we have a secured cell phone network to everyone necessary to coordinate actions here and overseas. Once the signal is received, it will be broadcast in text message format by the simple code '9/11,' and operations commence simultaneously everywhere. We have both military and civilian radio backups."

"I want to change one thing," the president said. "I know we had a firm backup time at which we would begin operations if no signal had been received. I want to change that. Much of what we are doing here is based on faith and is tied to messages from unknown people that came in on the prayer website. I believe we have to be flexible and trust whoever it is that is willing to risk their life to send the signal. Drop the definite time to respond if the signal is not received. Let's have our people in place beginning at 7:00 AM Saturday morning in the time zone for the camp in Iran. However, they are to take no action until we either receive the signal and send the code, or I give an order to commence operations. I want that flexibility in case something we don't know about occurs on the ground, and there is a need for delay."

"Mr. President," General Hedge responded, "we can do that, but it complicates deployment. People are going to be all over the world sitting and waiting for orders with no definite time to commence operations. That significantly increases our risk of discovery since so much of this is tied to civilian operations in the continental US."

"If we are too late, Mr. President," Tom Knight joined in, "we miss the opportunity to capture the stateside leadership and may miss the opportunity to capture many of the operatives in the US waiting to strike on MD."

"Yes," the president replied, "you make legitimate arguments, but if we move too quickly, we could miss the opportunity to get all the terrorist leadership that threatens our forces in the Middle East and kill the one who is willing to risk everything to help us. I sense that he, whoever he may be, is a key to future policy in the Middle East and particularly in Iran. He may be the leader we have been searching for."

"Sir, respectfully," CIA Director Crenshaw added, "there will be no future for America if we miss our opportunity to stop MD."

"Let me jump in here for a minute," Vice President Marshall replied. "I heard a wise man once say that we who lead must make decisions looking 100 years down the road to consider how they will affect the kind of future we are leaving for our children. President Strong will be leaving office in a year and a half. I am one of several candidates who is seeking to inherit his responsibilities, and I cast my vote for the future. We wait and retain flexibility. I want to have the chance to work with the courageous one who told us where the meeting would be and set the plan to destroy the terrorist leadership. Together we may be able to build a new Iran and a new Middle East of hope. Terrorism and hope cannot coexist."

"I can't argue with visionaries," General Hedge responded. "I only hope you are right to trust this unknown one who obviously once was a terrorist himself."

"Tom, when this call ends, I want you to coordinate with General Hedge and Director Hollister to see that all civilian and military forces are advised of this change. Contact the members of the Survival Commission who should arrive in the country later today. Secretary Wisdom, you contact our other representatives who have been sent to carry messages to national leaders. Let's be absolutely sure that we are all on the same page on timing."

"Yes, Mr. President," they answered in unison.

"A change of subject, Mr. President," Senator Besserman said. "Before we all came on the line with you, those of us here at the White House have been talking, and we believe that we need some kind of public diversion to buy a little time before the plan begins to execute. That is even more important since the time may be pushed back by events. I am afraid your long absence from Washington is being questioned, and those of the White House Press Corp that didn't go with Cox are pushing every possible source for information. I have even had informal contact by my old friends in the majority party leadership. If we don't do something to make you appear publicly, we are going to get some leak or disclosure that will endanger everything."

"What do you guys have in mind, Eric?" the president responded.

"Mr. President," he said pausing, "acting with absolutely no authority we have…"

"Well, not exactly," Vice President Marshall interrupted. "I gave them the authority to come up with a plan for your consideration. We really believe we need to do something that will put friends and foes asleep for the next forty-eight hours while the plan is executed."

"What is this magic solution to put me where I am not?" the president asked.

"Sir," Senator Besserman continued, "we have devised a ruse with Mexican President Calderon, who is prepared at this minute to announce a State visit from you to consider a new relationship of cooperation between the United States and Mexico. We have made arrangements for the second Air Force One aircraft to leave very publicly tomorrow morning for Mexico, and have found someone who works with Darrell Reed that looks like you from a distance. He will act the part in a set-up with President Calderon, who will welcome the plane and immediately travel with the other you in a presidential motorcade to his official residence of Los Pinos. There, the other you will remain in consultations until after your speech to the nation Saturday."

"I like it," the president replied. "Not only will it calm the waters here, but it should also enforce the belief among the terrorist leadership that the military exercise is nothing more than that, and we don't have a clue on the real timing of MD. Brilliant, gentlemen and ladies," he said, shaking his head in agreement while still considering the strategy. "Now what is this going to cost me? Nothing is free."

"Not much, really," Secretary of State Wisdom answered. "President Calderon is going way out on a limb in allowing the joint operation against the Oaxaca facility. He really believes that change is possible with you now, and what you are going to hear from him is a speech with his vision for how that change can come about and what it might look like. The speech will also help him prepare his people for the Oaxaca operation. The rest of the price is a real State visit as soon as reasonably possible after this all ends. We will need to have that discussion on a new future. He is serious."

"That makes two of us. I cannot tell you how much that encourages me. If God allows us to survive these days, I believe that is why. Think of it: a new America in the world, not rejecting the past, but focused on a future for everyone. This is our opportunity to make changes in relationships that will truly help oppressed people who were created in God's image just like us. We have always acted to protect our interests and have given resources to those in need in times of disaster, but we have too often closed our eyes to evil in the world with disastrous consequences to the innocent. How did we ignore the slaughter in Rwanda, Somalia, Sudan and on and on? There has to be a better way to work with other nations to stop the slaughter of innocents and give people hope for the future. I have an idea I am going to float with Prime Minister McDonald later tonight. I will then share with Russian President Sorboth if he is still listening Saturday morning after I tell him what I am coming to say."

George Murphy's head was spinning at what he had just heard. "Are we now to become the world's policeman?" he thought. At least he knew something about why they were traveling, even if he didn't know where they were going. He wrote furiously, taking notes, hoping to understand the whole scope of what was playing out before him. This was truly history in the making.

"Mr. President, what is this new idea you are going to float with the Russians? Don't you need military input before you propose something radically new—whatever it may be?" General Hedge responded, obviously frustrated and concerned.

"You know, General, when I was growing up my grandmother used to say when someone got too excited, 'Take a powder.' That was her way of communicating they needed to take something to relax because it wasn't as bad as they imagined. You need to follow my grandmother's advice. We never need to fear an idea."

"Listen up people; I believe that we are not going to survive this unless there is a greater purpose at work here than simply our survival. Three Fridays ago, we learned that we had to choose whose side we were on, and many Americans chose to be on God's side. I am thankful for that, but being on God's side does not simply mean standing with Him until the crisis is over and then returning to the same conduct that probably caused the crisis in the first place. If we survive, there will be more change required, and we need to start thinking that way and praying for the wisdom to know what that change should be. God is not finished with us. He has only just begun, for we have only started to listen."

"Now I'm getting excited," Vice President Marshall responded. "Perhaps I need some of your grandmother's powder. I don't know whether to be terrified or expectant."

"Well after this is over, you and I will get together back at Camp David and try and figure that out. If you are going to run for president, it is important that you know where I am trying to take the country these remaining months so you can be a part of it—or at least criticize it with knowledge."

"Agreed," the vice president answered, "but rest assured I don't go into this wanting to criticize anything you are doing."

"Alright, we all have things to do," the president said, seeking to bring the discussion to a conclusion. "Secretary Wisdom, call President Calderon, accept his offer and thank him. Tell him I will be listening to his speech later with great interest. He has my promise of a State visit and my commitment to seek a new relationship.

"Tom, prepare a press release to confirm the State visit for release after President Calderon's speech. Send the draft here for me to review. I want it to be positive and thankful, looking forward to real change. I remember President Kennedy's Alliance for Progress proposal to change our relationship with Latin America. Unfortunately, it died with him in Dallas that dark day. Perhaps it is time to begin anew and start with Mexico.

"If there is nothing else new to discuss, let's adjourn for now until after I meet with Prime Minister McDonald."

"Yes, Mr. President," the group replied as David Barnes disconnected and turned off the video conference unit.

"George, you understand that nothing you just heard can be shared with anyone on this plane or back home until this is over. We have to keep the circle of knowledge as small as possible to protect against any possible leak."

"Yes, sir, I will not breach your confidence," he replied.

"I sincerely believe that, or you wouldn't be on this plane," the president answered. "Now, I want you and David to go into the conference room and let him take you through the flash drive presentation again and bring you up to speed on how we got to where we are in preparing our response. You need to know it all so that the truth is protected. You are going to be a little like Arthur Schlesinger Jr. was for JFK. You are our historian, and will ultimately have access to everything."

"Thank you, Mr. President," Murphy replied.

"Now if you will excuse me," he said while picking up the phone, "I need to let President Sorboth know that the Mexico trip is not real and that our meeting for Saturday is still on."

The Coming Flood

As Air Force One banked for its approach into the RAF base at Lakenheath, England, the president, and Samuel Evans White had just completed a private time of prayer together in his office. On the ground, Prime Minister McDonald was already waiting in the guest quarters, having earlier secretly been flown by helicopter the 70 miles northeast of London. Lakenheath was a unique base in that it was also the US Air Force's largest operational base in England. Preparations had been made by the American forces on landing to cover the plane as part of a simulated tent city so that it would not be visible from the air. Its landing at night was hoped to shield the plane from discovery.

"Mr. President," the Bookseller spoke somewhat pensively. "I know we only have a few minutes before we touch down wherever we are, but I need to share with you a dream I had this afternoon."

"Please," the president responded with sincere interest.

"While you were in your office, I did what many of us older people do in the afternoon and dozed off. I began to dream, and what I heard and saw was graphic. It was like the scene John saw in Revelation chapter 6 when the fifth seal was opened, and the souls of the martyrs were made visible as they asked when God would avenge their blood on those who dwell on the earth.

"What I saw was not the same group, but it was clearly the souls of millions who had been wrongfully deprived of life. They cried out for revenge, and I saw what appeared to be a flood of their blood washing toward the earth to cover America so that millions would drown in it. But suddenly an enormous hand acting as a dam stopped the flow of blood and held it as a voice spoke with the sound like the roar of many waters. It said, 'Hold your peace for a little longer while we wait to see if they will now value life.' A myriad of angels cried out in grief until they were silenced by a Lamb appearing as though He had been slain, with only a look."

"I don't believe I need an explanation to know what that's about," the president responded soberly. "I remember the comment Ruth Graham shared with her husband Billy when she reviewed one of his books. You probably know it better than me. She said, 'If God doesn't soon bring judgment upon America, He'll have to go back and apologize to Sodom and Gomorrah,'" he paused to take in what he had just heard and said.

"Your dream is about abortion, and the picture is of the over 55 million children never allowed to be born here. I know that grieves God's heart, but it has never captured the heart of the people of America as it should have. If we survive, everything we do going forward has to focus on a culture of life starting with the unborn but carrying forward to the old. Not just in America but throughout the earth. No one made in God's image is unimportant."

"That is certainly part of it," the Bookseller agreed, "but not nearly all of it. That flood also represents lives ruined by so-called 'no-fault' divorce, a living death for millions of children and abandoned spouses who suffer so the covenant breakers can have what they want. It includes the children victimized by the monsters that masquerade as ministers and then abuse them or take advantage of them. It includes those who are deceived and led away from God into the second death by the false teachers and preachers. It includes the victims of 'spiritual abortion.'"

"What is 'spiritual abortion'?" the president asked. "I have never heard that term."

"God cares about children whether they be physical children or spiritual children. A seventy-year-old who is just born again is as much of a child spiritually as a three-week-old baby is physically. Jesus commanded that believers make disciples and teach new believers to obey all He commanded.[101] Unfortunately, what has happened is that American churches today simply want more members, so they never teach or walk with new believers. It is seen as being too difficult and as taking too much time. They just want them to come once a week, give money and invite their friends. God hates that. Most new believers are the most miserable of all—unable to walk with God because they don't know how. They are unhappy, feeling guilty for ending up back in the world because they have nowhere else to go. To God, failing to disciple new believers is like carefully birthing a baby and then throwing them into the street to die. They are unable to care for themselves until they learn and grow into maturity."

"Understand, Mr. President, that America is not done. We have started a long journey, and if we do not complete that journey, the flood pictured in the dream will come somehow in judgment. It takes more than a single day set aside to God for a person or a nation to become one whose God is truly the Lord. Those two questions remain, remember? What in my life or in our nation dishonors the holiness of God's name, and what in my life or in our nation is not God's will being done as it is in Heaven? We are going to have to continue asking, listening and changing if we are to remain on God's side."

"But I can't dictate laws. I can only propose laws, and even then, I can't force a change of behavior," the president responded in obvious frustration.

"You miss the point," the Bookseller continued. "This is not simply about you or any government leader. Christians have gotten lost in their pursuit of politics. God has a very limited place for government. It is like we discussed before, the government is to punish wrongdoers as God defines a wrongdoer.[102] Accordingly, it cannot encourage or embrace what God defines as wrongdoing. It is as simple as that. You may be the president, but you can't change a single heart. That is what God does through Christian leaders in churches. However, principally in the business world, schools and families, Christians simply live like they are to be—a reflection of Jesus Christ. I hate to burst your bubble, but you are not as important to God as you must think you are. If America survives, it will not simply be because of what you have done. It will be because millions of American Christians repented and are now seeking God's ways."

"It may surprise you to know that I'm glad not to be that important," the president responded. "I am only a man, and a very imperfect one at that. I don't want the responsibility.

"Look, I have a request for you; after this is over, would you consider an appointment as a special advisor to the president so that you can continue to help me find those answers and have the right perspective going forward? I still have over twenty months in office."

"Thank you, but no thank you," the Bookseller answered firmly. "That is one I don't need to pray about. I know the answer. The call to teach or preach God's word is the single most important call that exists on the earth, whether it is to teach your own children or to preach to the few who will listen. That is my call, and has been for over fifty years. Your call, for now, is to govern under God, and if you seek the answer to those questions for yourself, God will direct you. You don't need me or anyone else to hear from God."

The Day Ends

Russian President Sorboth was pleased when he hung up the phone with Chinese President Wen Yao. President Strong had already called to assure Yao the American military exercise was not a threat to China. Sorboth had affirmed that the American military positioning appeared to be defensive in nature and that the Russian deployment had been more for domestic consumption than military readiness.

As he considered the discussion, suddenly he wondered why he, a Russian, had called the Chinese to vouch for an American president? "These are strange times," he thought. "I suggested that we reconsider the nature of our relationships with this American. How can that be, based on so little new information? What has changed?"

What had changed was that instructions had been received by angels and Guardians who were dispatched throughout the earth to prepare the way for tomorrow's meetings and to create a climate of trust and curiosity such as was being experienced by President Sorboth at that moment. The forces of darkness were shielded from knowledge of these activities, and thus they continued working with their instruments in preparation for what they believed would be the final day of reckoning for America.

In Iran, the Russian deployment was viewed very differently through dark eyes. The Iranian president saw it as evidence that the Russians were fully committed and would be the shield needed after the attacks of the 11th. "Anyway," he thought, "we cannot fail, for if the crisis we create degenerates into chaos and the nation is endangered. All that will have been done is to speed the return of the Hidden Imam who will come to rescue the nation in the final battle and usher in his perfect government."

A different view of the world was apparent in the Senate majority leader's office, where Howard had just watched the Mexican president's announcement and the White House response. "What new relationship? Is Strong trying to hijack the Together Tomorrow agenda and get that funding for his party?" he screamed at Chairman Crow. "Cox has to succeed. We must destroy this man or he will destroy us!"

The agendas of the forces of light and darkness could be seen most clearly as the sun set across America in the actions of their followers who claimed to be Christians. In the buildings called churches, which were under the control or influence of the forces of darkness, there were loud celebrations of thanksgiving and "prayers" for the success of the Cox mission. "Peace was at hand," Pastor Roy Elkhorn of Faith Church of Joy had loudly and publicly proclaimed. All rejoiced, believing that war and conflict would end soon.

In churches where the forces of light ruled, there were only prayers as the significance of what was happening in the world was felt, if not fully understood. The prayer website had united millions of Christians across the earth who continued in earnest prayer for America and for its president. Emails continued to flood into the website, which kept Darrell Reed's staff hard at work seeking any last-minute intelligence that could require a change of plans.

CHAPTER 23

ENGLAND AND BEYOND

Friday, March 7—MD minus 4 days

THE VIDEO CONFERENCE link was reestablished early in the morning, Washington DC time. Unknown to the public, the White House and Old Executive Office building had assumed somewhat of a bunker status, complete with cots as those who over these next hours would lead the counterattack settled in until it was over. There would be no time to come together for those required to make instantaneous decisions, so they would remain together.

"Prime Minister McDonald reacted about as I expected when he saw the flash drive presentation," the president reported. "The British are on board with the need for a preemptive strike and now understand the risks in the Middle East. They are deploying their nuclear forces over the weekend as a backup should that be necessary, and offered to help us with the rest of the EU when our response is launched."

"What were his concerns?" the vice president asked.

"You can probably state them as well as I can, Wilburn. He is concerned about the attack on Iran's nuclear facility, but he understands. He questions the Israel deployment as an unnecessary risk and believes we need to change our plan as it relates to advising allies about attacks planned in their countries. He wants that done now, rather than waiting for the launch tomorrow. My concern remains discovery. Anything we do has risks, and not everyone on his side of the pond has the same agenda we have."

"Well stated, sir," General Hedge agreed. "We have to have a surprise to be successful."

"Yes, but what about the danger to their citizens and the plans of the terrorists for assassinations in the Middle East? We have so few real friends there. We can't risk the loss of any," Secretary of State Wisdom added.

"Political necessity and the military reality don't always work together, Mr. Secretary," General Hedge responded. "We can't risk American lives here or our troops in the Middle East by advising those governments even one minute before we launch our attack. One leak and our plan fails. The risk is simply too high. Twenty-four hours is not much. Some collateral damage may be required for us to succeed."

"If by collateral damage you mean a Middle East leader assassinated, that is unacceptable if it can be prevented," Secretary Wisdom responded.

"I agree," the president answered, "but the general has a point on the level of acceptable risk. We will advise our European friends today about the transportation risk and provide them the detailed intelligence we have on activities in their countries, but that is it. Tomorrow we will give them detailed information on MD after the attacks commence. The Middle East meetings have to wait until tomorrow. I would really like to act differently, but the risk of disclosure is simply too great. I have no choice."

"Tom, you and Secretary Wisdom contact our European representatives and advise them to go immediately to meet with their assigned leader regarding the transportation threat. Prime Minister McDonald will have already talked with them and prepared the way. Be sure they understand that they are to discuss nothing except the transportation threats—and I mean nothing. Additionally, they need to request that the leaders take no overt action against the people whose identity is provided until after they get a full briefing tomorrow."

"That is going to make the whole process really difficult," Secretary Wisdom replied. "We advise them of an imminent threat, but make them agree not to do anything about it. Is that realistic?"

"It may not seem realistic, but they are just going to have to trust us if they want to be included before the fact," the president responded. "They will understand tomorrow."

"Yes, Mr. President," they replied, and the call ended for now with the line held open on mute.

Time Troubles

Elsewhere, plans had to be changed. The group gathering in Kerman Province was having difficulty traveling because of troop movements. Iranian and Syria forces had tied up transportation arteries as they began their deployment to prepare for MD. The US forces in Israel were also a concern to those who planned their demise because of their expected intelligence gathering capability, which would be ongoing as long as they were in the field. The American military exercise in Iraq created other risks of capture. Everything was moving in slow motion.

A long string of profanities was launched by Ahmad Habid as reports continued to come in by cell phone from field commanders who were needed for the final coordination. "If the Americans had not moved into Israel, we could cancel the meeting, but now it is more important than ever to be sure we coordinate with Hezbollah to kill those fools. They cannot be allowed to stand between us and the destruction of Israel. Perhaps, like Beirut, we can kill them as they sleep," he directed toward Ahmed El-Ahab, who had arrived at the camp late last night.

"How long? How much of a delay?" El-Ahab asked. "We can't risk coordination with what will be happening in America."

"Relax," Habid said, "just a few hours. Rather than early morning, we will go with an early afternoon meeting. We will still have plenty of time to finish and be in position for MD. It's only a half a day."

"I have to get this back to the Sheik right away," El-Ahab answered. "If it's noon here, what time is it in the US?"

"Sit on it," Habid directed. "No calls, no contact with the Sheik until this is over. We cannot risk interception resulting in his discovery. He is too important to the future after MD. We already lost Bin Laden. We cannot afford to lose him too."

Reality struck El-Ahab as he realized that Habid would kill him or anyone else without a thought if he believed they endangered the operation. Their conversation was over as El-Ahab retired to himself, committed to listening in silence.

A Private Conversation

"Wilburn, I want to bring you up to speed on the remainder of my conversation with Prime Minister McDonald," the president began.

"Thank you, sir, I appreciate your call."

"You need to know this in case you must assume the presidency tomorrow. I don't want you to be like Harry Truman after Franklin Roosevelt died, not even knowing there was a Manhattan Project. You need to know as much as you can now that we are underway. At a minimum, you have to hold it together until I get back."

"Well, I sure like that second assignment better than being president in your place."

Ignoring the comment, the president continued, "The prime minister understood the significance of it all—MD, our response and the attempt to keep the Russians out of it. Like I said to the whole group earlier, he questioned the wisdom of a unilateral strike at the nuclear facility but understood why we wouldn't want to leave that for a potential future strike against us or Israel by someone as crazed as the Iranian president. He understands that it is only a matter of time until Europe would be the target, and will stand with us before the UN."

Pausing to smile, he said, "You would have loved to see the look on his face when he saw our detailed intelligence on the cell plotting to attack public transportation in England. He thought we must have infiltrated the cell and was shocked when I told him that the information came from the prayer website. He didn't believe me until I showed him the site, but he wasn't able to read a word! Can you imagine that? But he called in one of his security guards he knew was a Christian, and the man could easily read it all. That may have been the first time in his life he had to consider the possibility of the existence of an all-powerful God."

"Why did you give away our intelligence source?" the vice president asked, surprised.

"I felt it was important that he understand that what is happening across the globe is not simply another international crisis. This event has a clear eternal purpose, and part of that purpose is to begin to open long-closed eyes, like his."

"That led him to ask about that 'religion thing' going on in America, and I had a chance to share what was happening and what I believe about

God. I know most would say that religion has no place in diplomacy, but it is who I am, and I am tired of pretending. We don't want a religious government, and I don't intend to impose my beliefs on anyone, but I am who I am, and that is not something I don't intend to hide anymore, anywhere."

"Boy, isn't that a bit politically incorrect?" the vice president responded. "You will soon be labeled as crazy religious as the Iranian president."

"Crazy religious, yes—at least as some would see it—but I don't want to kill anyone who disagrees."

"One more exciting thing, Wilburn; he liked the idea of a counsel of democracies to act together where possible to address hurt and cruelty in the world. I would really like to be a part of a group willing to act to alleviate suffering and stop genocide quickly. The UN is such a political and bureaucratic malaise that it can't respond. There are so many things that could be done to improve life on this planet if the democracies would work together. It won't always be possible, but more often than not, it could happen. That is what I am going to try and sell to President Sorboth as well. We have military alliances all across the globe, why not a humanitarian alliance that goes beyond politics or the interest of any single country?"

"Sign me up!" the vice president answered excitedly. "If we can get past this and you get it started, I will carry it as an issue into next year's campaign."

"I am really glad to hear that. What is coming out of all this must go far beyond my time as president. Don't forget that, Wilburn. We will not be delivered to continue as we were. I can't because I am not as I was, and I truly believe that America is not either. Something new has been awakened that will change the future for all of us."

"Well, it's for sure that you have been changed. We will have to wait and see if America has changed," the vice president responded. "America has a weird habit of responding to what is before it, but a permanent change is hard to maintain. We react to an emergency and then forget there was ever a threat."

"Historically you are right, but let us continue to live with hope."

Darkness Gathers

Somewhere high over Mexico, there appeared to be an ever-increasing black cloud in the invisible that dominated the sky as Legion, Molech, Chemosh, Baal, Asherah and Ashtoreth gathered to be sure all was prepared for MD. The scene was frantic as thousands of dark wisps from Europe reported that Keepers and Tempters had been blinded and bound by members of the forces of light. Influence had been lost throughout the continent over key leaders, members of the police and military. There were reports of sightings of the American president outside of London in meetings with the British prime minister. The wisps were in panic mode.

"You must look, you must look, something terrible is happening," one cried out to Legion, who had little patience with the small ones.

"I must look for what?" Legion responded, obviously irritated.

"You must look for what the forces of light are doing so we can stop them!" the little one answered in a panic at the tone of Legion's voice. "The effort in Europe; it must have been discovered. Even the American president is there."

"So what?" Legion answered with the false sense of confidence, still in control of his judgment. "It matters not. What would we lose—at the most, the destruction of a few buses and trains? Actually, it is a wonderful development for it means they have totally missed the real attacks. With the Americans trying to crawl out of the ashes, the Europeans are not going to be willing to risk anything for anyone but themselves."

"Don't be so sure," Chemosh joined the discussion. "Why is Strong there?"

"I don't care where he is, as long as it is away from America," Legion continued. "He can't govern America long-distance, and anyway, if he is gone he has to return, and Argon already has his future prepared. He will die in a flash of light before his helicopter can land on the White House lawn. If he comes back before MD, he can still die on national television. It will be glorious!"

"You'd better be right," Baal warned. "I am not going to defend you if we are called to account for a failure of this magnitude before the Dark Master."

"You had better be careful as well, ugly one," Legion answered quickly. "Honesty is not a trait admired in the darkness."

"Enough of these games," Asherah interrupted forcefully. "Why the public relations farce about Strong in Mexico? Are our people here at risk?"

"You are mighty in word and deed, but small in intellect," Legion said with increasing aggression. "Stop looking for the Enemy to defeat us and be real for a moment. Strong is going through this charade to cover his European trip. He will probably go elsewhere tomorrow, which tells us he knows something about the foreign aspect of the plan. However, he still knows nothing about the impending destruction of the US. Who cares where he goes or what cover he uses as long as America remains blind and defenseless? What in this confusion speaks of issues with our forces in the US? There is nothing. We will succeed, and it will be over in less than a week."

"Before the celebration begins, can we review what is happening in all the spheres of attack?" Chemosh asked. "If we find a pattern, we may need to change the plan."

Beginning with Mexico and proceeding around the earth, territorial rulers of the forces of darkness reported on the activities of which they were aware in their area of responsibility. Blinded to the activities of the forces of light anywhere other than in Europe, the reports were limited to the activities of those under their influence.

In Mexico, progress was apparent, and the plan was in place to move the trucks slowly across the border as it opened after midnight. The design had been considered and tested in Iran: a simple detonator box containing plastic explosives was being installed on the tank directly behind the driver. It was wired into the cab rather than taking a chance on remote radio detonation. The driver had to have the truck exactly where required before detonation. There was little room for error if the destruction of the intended target was to be complete. The computer models had shown exactly where the explosion must occur, and that was what the operators continued to rehearse on their laptops throughout the United States and while waiting in Mexico.

The conversation that had been overheard was between Demas Assad and Phygelus Aldar. "This night, the end begins," Assad had said. "The roads open at midnight, and the trucks can cross the border and begin to be positioned for Tuesday."

"Yes, but the border security people on both sides will not be used for the new protocol, and we cannot take a chance that one of our drivers could be stopped and captured," Aldar answered with concern. "Let's be smart and space the trucks out carefully; do not begin until there has been several hours of regular commercial traffic after the border is opened."

And thus, the final plan was put in place. Over 400 trucks would be sent north from Oaxaca, one at a time. They would be sent every ten minutes, timed so that the first truck would cross the border close to 3:00 AM. They would cross at five points—Matamoros into Brownsville, Juarez into El Paso, Nogales toward Tucson, Nuevo Laredo into Laredo, and Tijuana into San Diego. With quick access to the United States interstate highway system at all crossing points, the drivers had ample time to drive their fully loaded and armed vehicles to the point of attack before Tuesday. Every driver would leave Mexico with adequate food and sleeping materials to ensure that the only public stops required would be fuel for the vehicle; and even at that, only if its target location exceeded the capacity of one tank of fuel. Those being sent the furthest would be in the early departures.

Work was only just beginning on the trucks that were arriving at the Brothers Trucking yards across America. The reports from those responsible for the territories where the yards were located were uniformly encouraging. The operators were ready. Those chosen to participate in the assassination squads were focused, ready to kill children. Their passion continued to be inflamed, and there was no evidence of discovery. The major concern was diversion over these next few days before the attacks would commence. Keepers had poured into the minds of those they controlled plans to divert attention and occupy the base nature of these human instruments. This night would be for celebration of what was to come. Alcohol had been obtained in large quantities, along with dark pornographic movies. Strippers and prostitutes experienced in rough sex had been hired so that for this night, their every evil fantasy could be met and they would be ready to die.

"It is good that you leave them without a feeling they have missed anything in this life," Molech observed. "It will cement in their minds the desire for what they believe awaits them once martyred," he said, laughing.

"Yes, but isn't there a risk of bringing others into contact with our operatives several days before the attack begins?" Chemosh worried. "How do you control these women, and how do you assure that these men who know they will die do not go too far and offend these women?"

"The women chosen are of absolute darkness," Legion answered. "You need not fear their response. They are more dangerous than the men. They will take the money and receive pleasure from their ability to manipulate the desires of these men, able to go on their way without thought of who or why. They are all killers; they just use different weapons."

Those over nations in the Middle East reported positively. The cells were prepared to strike at leaders, military units were being positioned to crush Israel, and the terrorist leadership would be gathering in Iran soon to finalize plans for attacks on Western military units, including the American force now in Israel if it remained there on MD.

"And what of Russia?" Chemosh asked. "Are they prepared to stand against whatever remains of America and the West?"

"Oh great ones," the territorial authority answered, "we do not know. Their military has been deployed in response to the American moves, but we cannot read what is happening among the leadership. The two most under our influence are passionate about the Dark Master's plan, but we cannot determine the extent of their ability to control President Sorboth. It is a great concern."

"So kill him," Molech responded.

"Not necessary," Legion replied matter-of-factly. "Russia is not required for the destruction of America. All they were to do was to shore up cowards in Iran and Syria and offset the Europeans if they stumbled across any long-lost courage. Ignore them. This is no more important than today's American activity in Europe. We will deal with Russia later."

Even as this conversation ended and the forces of darkness separated to continue working with their human charges, two B-2 stealth bombers took off from their base in the Philippines. At the same time, Air Force tanker crews were briefed on their station and mission to be sure that the planes remained airborne and available when the signal was received.

Waiting

As those on Air Force One tried to sleep, they wondered why they were still on board without any idea of when they would take off or what their destination was. They all knew that tomorrow was the day… but for what?

Knocking and entering the president's office, David Barnes found him up and on the phone with Janet. When he realized who it was, the president said, "Well here comes my 'speech writer.' I'd better go. I will call you later when we're airborne." Pausing for a moment, he added, "Don't be afraid. I love you."

"I'm not afraid," she responded. "I know I will be with you forever no matter what happens. I'm just not ready for that to be in bodies like angels. I still want to be your wife right here on earth."

"I'll see if I can't cooperate with that desire," the president answered, smiling. He was overwhelmed with thanksgiving at the gift of this precious woman as his wife. "Later," he said as he hung up the phone and turned to David Barnes.

"David, when this is over, you need to stop fooling around and marry Kayla, if she will have you."

"You will get no debate from me on that one," Barnes answered. "I understand what a treasure marriage is. This whole not knowing whether you will survive thing makes life a lot simpler."

"You say that with a lot of emotion. What's up?" the president asked.

"Well, sir, you have to see these final recreations that Defense did on what will happen if MD succeeds. They are terrifying beyond words. I wanted to show them to you as they are included in the video presentation as part of your speech to the nation tomorrow. Assuming we are successful, the American people need to understand the horror we have been delivered from. It will put everything in perspective."

It was all too real seeing the destruction in America. There were horrific scenes including the death of children, assassinations of heads of state, terror attacks in Europe, American forces hit in the Middle East and the move on Israel with the resulting nuclear exchange. The presentation did not end there, as it went forward showing what America would be like after MD: shortages of food, water, and fuel; little electricity, and a basic inability to continue as a nation while the bands of terrorist killers continued to plague the nation with random attacks wherever people gathered.

"It is one thing to be told what will happen, but it is a far different thing to see it," the president said soberly. "I continue to be astounded at the patience and perseverance of these people. They will do anything to kill us. If we stop this one, they will just start planning another one. Somehow this hate has to end. It just seems so hopeless."

"Now you know why you called the nation to prayer," Barnes responded equally soberly. "Without God's intervention, it is impossible to stop this. Cox will soon learn that."

"Yes, but I only hope he survives," the president answered warily.

"Well, you have done everything you can to protect him."

The phone rang, and an exhausted General Hedge appeared on the video screen. "Mr. President, we have been reviewing everything here, and the reality is that we can be successful and stop MD and you are not protected. Please, sir, can we dispatch fighters to escort you to Iceland and back? All we have to do is give the orders. They have been put on standby right where you are. There are adequate forces at Lakenheath."

"Thank you, General, but I don't intend to head for a meeting with the Russian president accompanied by fighters. We are traveling in peace, and we need to appear to be as such."

"But, sir, if the Russians are truly in this with the Iranians, shooting you out of the sky would be easy. Air Force One has some defenses, but it could not defeat a sustained attack from multiple aircraft."

"The Russians are not stupid. They don't want a war with the United States, at least not until after MD. If we are right, that is planned for Tuesday, and this is still Friday—barely."

"But what if we are wrong?"

"Then we are wrong. Get some sleep, General; this all begins in a few hours," the president said as he disconnected the video link.

The phone rang again. This time it was Colonel Phil from the White House, an Air Force One pilot. "Mr. President, it's time. We will be taking off in fifteen minutes."

"Thank you, Colonel. I am grateful that you are the pilot for this mission."

"Thank you, Mr. President."

"David, sorry, but I have to get some sleep. We will look at the speech later."

CHAPTER 24

ICELAND AND BEYOND

Saturday, March 8—MD minus 3 days

IT WAS 4:18 AM when Air Force One made its landing at Keflavik International Airport, thirty-one miles from Reykjavik. The runway lights had been turned on for the landing, and after the plane had taxied to an open hanger, all lights were turned off once again. Air Force One had landed in complete darkness without notice and hopefully were able to get by without any sightings. The Russian president had sent a military convoy to escort the president to the House of Hofoi. Only David Barnes and George Murphy were allowed to accompany him, along with the man who carried the ever-present black briefcase.

"George, for the rest of today your name is Samuel Bolton, special assistant to the president. Got it?"

"Yes, Mr. President, but do we ever get to sleep?" Murphy asked.

"For a while, but not for long," the president answered as they moved through empty streets to the place of meeting.

In Kerman Province, Iran, it was 8:48 AM on Saturday morning. Ahmad Habid had been passionately at work planning the death of Americans. That is how he began every day. Today, however, he rejoiced that he had a way with the help of Hezbollah to create another firestorm of death, as had occurred in Beirut. "If this is not a military exercise and the Americans are going to stay," he said to El-Ahab, unable to hide his excitement, "they will die Tuesday as the attacks in America commence."

"Do as you will to them, but be sure whatever you do starts after MD begins back in the US. Destroying America is far more important than killing some of their troops here."

"What do you care?" Habid answered scornfully. "If we kill them before MD starts, they will merely shift their focus to the Middle East, which opens the door for the attacks in America. Either way, they die, and we never have to face their magic weapons of death. This time they will be the victims."

"Spoken with wisdom as well as hate," the usually silent Arn Au Farrokh said as he left the bunker to walk outside, awaiting other arrivals.

"Even I am frightened by him at times," Habid said turning to El-Ahab. "I cannot read him, and I know that he is always thinking and planning; plotting for the future."

"Yes, and that is why he is the Iranian president's personal representative. Do not fear him. He has a glorious history. He was there with the president as a student revolutionary when the Americans were first taken hostage at their embassy. Remember, for 444 days they were paraded and humiliated before the world. He would have killed them all if it was allowed. He has never flinched at any assignment. He faithfully followed the Ayatollah Khomeini and has been useful to the Sheik on many occasions. He has a ton of blood on his hands but is still only a danger to you if he believes you have become a threat to the plan. Then he would certainly kill you without a second thought."

"I will steer clear of this silent one," Habid replied, "and he had better steer clear of me."

In Oaxaca, Mexico, it was 11:18 PM on Friday night. Final instructions were given to the operatives who would drive into America on their way to their designated target location. Demas Assad was coordinating the release of the vehicles so that the first truck would cross around 3:00 AM, and the others would follow at ten-minute intervals. Phygelus Aldar had handled the final briefing. His instructions were simple. "You may not allow yourself to be captured. If trapped or endangered, pick a target, close in on it and detonate your load. Do as much damage as you can. Others will continue the fight. Remember, your reward awaits you."

Unknown to Assad, Aldar and the others, a combined Mexican/American force had been moved to within thirty miles of the camp with helicopter transportation and gunships awaiting the signal. Tanks had been positioned to be able to quickly cover all roads out of Oaxaca, and Air Force assets were on standby from bases in Texas and Arizona if required.

Military units were now positioned near the five border crossings that led to the United States interstate highway system, although debate continued on just how to employ force and on what side of the border in order to confront the rolling bombs. American commanders were somewhat taken back by the order to allow the Mexican forces to lead and direct anything within ten miles of the border on either side.

In Washington, it was 12:18 AM on Saturday morning. The attorney general and his team hunkered down at the Justice Department with phones and radios connected to team leaders across America. Federal judges known through experience to be willing to move quickly on a showing of probable cause were up and in their chambers, having been alerted that their services may be required throughout the night.

The federal grand jury sitting in Cambridge, Massachusetts was in the grand jury room. They had also having been notified that their presence was required throughout the night. Attorney General Rodriquez hoped that nothing further would be required, but nothing could be left to chance this night. A legal counter-attack was expected at some point.

The geek was feeling more dead than alive, having not slept for days. His fatigue was somewhat muted by an understanding of the significance of what they were about to embark on. His team continued to monitor the prayer website for late email information. A message had been sent from Williams notifying all who monitored the site that reporting on unusual activities this night was essential. Responses were flooding in. He also had to make final preparations for broadcasting the signal that would be heard around the world, as well as the president's speech, which would be transmitted from somewhere after his meeting with the Russian president.

The "sleep in" at the White House and the Old Executive Office building continued as the Joint Chiefs and others carefully coordinated final preparations for the American strike. FBI Director Jackson, Homeland Security Director Hollister, and National Security Advisor Steed were working diligently with teams of police and federal marshals now deployed across the country, waiting for the signal to strike at the believed location of the leaders and the homes where operatives resided while preparing for MD. Those who would be used in these strikes had been carefully chosen. There would be great risk, and the possibility of intelligence errors, so keen judgment and the ability to remain calm under fire would be required. There was also the reality that capture was far more important than simply eliminating the enemy. Information obtained in interrogations could provide what was needed to completely eliminate the threat and deal with all of those responsible—wherever they might be.

CIA Director Crenshaw and Secretary of State Wisdom had very different assignments as they prepared presidential representatives across the world for what message they were to deliver to national leaders when the signal was received. All had a copy of the Iranian flash drive, which would reveal the nature of the attacks planned on America both in the US and at military installations, the strikes against European transportation links and the assassinations planned in the Middle East.

The representatives were only now learning of the attacks Iran and Syria had planned against Israel and the counter strikes to be launched in Iran. Each had a personal message from the president to deliver to their assigned leader. Secretary Wisdom had to finish the briefings and catch a flight to New York to prepare to meet with the secretary general of the United Nations after the signal was given. Similarly, Tom Knight waited for the signal with the same information and a personal note from the president for the Senate majority leadership.

In Williams, it was 11:10 PM on Friday night. With a hand-picked team, Officer Sally Johnson reviewed their assignment in Chicago proper. Intelligence had revealed several possible locations, and because of her proven experience and wisdom under fire, Sally Johnson has been chosen to command one of the units. FBI Special Agent Andy Samuels would command another. This time he did not expect to find the empty house with evidence of murder as he had when commanding the earlier attempt to capture Abdul Farsi. Even Seth Williams was being given another chance in Phoenix. Carl Varvel had volunteered, but had been turned down. Everyone who had been involved and knew what was going on wanted to be a part of striking against those who sought to inflict MD on

America. All who gathered had been provided search warrants and arrest warrants that would authorize their actions.

In Iran, Syria, and Beirut, it was just after 7:00 AM Saturday morning. The trio of Hiram Urbay, Ittai, and Hushai waited separately for the signal, which would send them into the midst of their enemies carrying unknown messages from the American president to those who intended to capitalize on America's destruction. They each prayed in their respective places; separated yet united in spirit and strangely at peace. The closer they came to the danger before them, the more at peace they were.

In Damascus, Leonard Cox still slept. Jet lag had always been a challenge for him, but last night's challenge included a long discussion at the bar with many of his press friends who had joined on this adventure to crush President Strong. Also present at the bar was a group described to him as American graduate students on tour headed by a Professor Travis Austin. "What a dull bunch," Cox mentioned to Rutherford. "Even the secret service group assigned to me loosened up a bit. That bunch didn't do anything but nurse the same drink all night. I guess they stayed around so long because of hero worship. I'm always surprised at what my presence generates."

"Me too," Rutherford chimed in, although the statement carried a very different meaning to him. He swallowed hard to keep from laughing.

Totally missed in the crowd of revelry that night were those who were carefully observing everyone in the room. They were seeking to identify security traveling with Cox while planning an exit strategy as part of a kidnapping or murder. They were prepared to do whatever was required, even as far as killing everyone at the bar.

In Moscow, the sun was just coming up on Saturday morning. President Sorboth, however, was already within two hours of setting down at Keflavik International Airport, still wondering at the unusual meeting request from President Strong. He had slept very little in anticipation and had carefully followed reports from Defense Minister Petrov. Other than the military exercise and the deployment of which he had been advised, the only unusual development that had been detected was activity at British bases. "The drama was intense," he thought, but something seemed to be saying to him that this could all be a signal of a new relationship. He was excited and boldly unafraid.

The forces of light held no meetings, for they were all too busy carrying out instructions that were received one after the other. The time for thinking and wondering had ended. It was time to listen and obey. How God would ultimately allow this day to progress would soon be known.

Waiting in Place

Plans changed again. President Sorboth had arrived at the House of Hofoi a little after 7:00 AM and was anxious to begin. Recognizing the importance of knowing as quickly as possible where the Russians would be in this, President Strong agreed to meet now and dressed quickly, ignoring George Murphy's complaints of fatigue. "History waits on no man, George," the president said. "If you want to be there, you must surrender to the moment." He was surprised at the sense of peace that filled him. He had struggled with how to tell Sorboth, and now he faced a decision on what to tell him and when, since the signal had not yet been received. Should he tell him in advance of the strike and risk a confrontation? Should he demand that the attack be halted, or should he delay in telling him what was to occur until it occurred? He didn't know, so he sought direction in prayer before leaving his room to meet Sorboth.

In Washington, there was a growing sense of anxiety. "It's after 3:00 AM," General Hedge said to the gathered Joint Chiefs who were meeting with Vice President Marshall in the White House Situation Room. "The president is basically out of touch for the moment, and it will soon be daylight in parts of the United States. We need to launch our attacks against the domestic threat before daylight."

"Yes, but we will wait for the signal unless we receive different orders from the president," the vice president responded firmly. "We have a plan, and we will stick to that plan. No one has the authority to act independently. Listen, General, there is an element of faith in all this. You have to wait. Remember, timing is everything."

"Timing is what I am concerned with, sir," General Hedge responded. "You are the commander on the ground for these moments, and you need to authorize action. They are not even going to meet in Iceland until 10:00 AM, which is 6:00 AM here. That is too late. It was a mistake. At 10:00 AM in Iceland, it will be 2:30 PM in Iran. Whatever is going to happen will have happened, or it will be too late. The terrorist leaders there are not going to wait to be killed. You need to order that strike too."

"General, if we don't receive the signal or hear something from the president by 5:00 AM, we will revisit this topic. Until then, I don't care to hear about this again," the vice president answered firmly.

"Yes, Mr. Vice President," the frustrated general replied and returned to his duties.

Others in the field were also wondering about timing and schedules. Throughout the United States, the police, FBI and federal marshal teams were now in place watching the buildings they were to take to search for the operatives and terrorist leadership. Regular military units and National Guard units prepared for assaults on Brothers Trucking yards and Terminal Equipment Leasing facilities where all night activities were obvious.

Teams were also stationed at airports, preparing to seize Kingdom Charter aircraft wherever they may be overnight. The waiting created all kinds of issues as teams sought to be prepared to move on a moment's notice without disclosing their locations. In some places, there were obvious parties and celebrations ongoing with unusually attired women coming and going. "What kind of perverted killers are these?" Sally Johnson wondered as she watched and waited.

Across from the White House, an air defense battery had been set up in the darkness and was now fully operational. Argon's chosen instrument knew what he intended to do, and patiently waited for the opportunity. He had secured a shoulder-fired, anti-aircraft missile, which he placed close to his duty station. One should be sufficient. The plan was simple: down Marine One, and then fire off one shot to the head from his field-issued 45 to end the instrument's miserable little life and stop the pain. Argon was present and confident that this time the victory would be his—and so would dominion over a new territory. Finally, he would receive the command he merited and the forces of darkness would no longer be cursed by having to deal with Joshua Strong as president of the United States.

"I must remember to reward Zaccur," Argon thought. "That curious little one can command a city in my territory."

In the Middle East, American forces were deployed and on full alert, ready to respond to possible retaliatory attacks on their positions, on Israel or any attempt to block the Strait of Hormuz and cut off the flow of oil to the West. The pilots on board the aircraft carrier Abraham Lincoln were ready; their planes armed and prepared for launch on a moment's notice. Cruise missiles on ships and submarines had been targeted for military targets throughout the region and were prepared for launch. The nuclear forces of the United States were on highest alert, ready to respond to the unthinkable. The B-2 stealth bombers flown by Captains Jonathan Adams and Sawyer Yeager had been refueled and were on station waiting for the signal to strike.

In Israel, the cabinet met in a sense of frustration and concern. A vocal minority had the floor and raised a key question. "The one thing we have promised ourselves that we would never do, we have done. Today our security is dependent on another. Never in our history has anyone stood to protect Israel in a time of crisis when the cost could be their nation. Why do we trust the Americans now, Mr. Prime Minister?"

"It is far too late for second-guessing our course," Prime Minister Zimri answered. "I believe that it is a new day and we can trust America under this President Strong. This man is different now, for whatever reason, and the change he seeks to bring about is the only way Israel will ever truly be secure. Look to the East, and you will see American soldiers deployed at great personal risk on our soil to fight with us if we are attacked. What more do you need to see? What more do our enemies need to see? America is prepared to bleed with us and for us, and they have made that declaration to the world. We will allow them to lead, but be prepared to respond in all our strength if needed or required."

"Any news on the Russians?" another asked.

"All we know is that the American president has undertaken that personally. At this moment, he is having a meeting somewhere in the world face to face with Russian President Sorboth, requesting that he stand down and not support Iran and Syria's post MD plan to attack. For now, we wait to hear about that meeting and receive the signal that America has launched its attack. Our intelligence confirms their deployment in accordance with the preemptive strike plan."

The minority was silent as the minister of defense suggested, "Perhaps we should pray." This statement caused great consternation, as that was something never before suggested in this openly secular government.

"Yes," they agreed. "But how?" some of the unashamedly non-religious asked candidly.

"Maybe we should follow the lead of that old man in America and pray what they call the Lord's Prayer," the prime minister suggested. "It is not among our own holy scriptures and texts, but it honors the God of America—this God leading a nation that is ready to bleed for us. I just so happen to have a copy," he said, smiling at the foreign minister. He turned in his borrowed copy of the New Testament to a well-marked, dog-eared page and led the group.

A Change in Reykjavik

"That was not the way it was supposed to begin," the president thought, angry at himself for being so foolish. It seemed innocent enough; he would have George Murphy, the reporter, pretend to be Samuel Bolton, special assistant to the president, but Sorboth saw through that immediately.

"Mr. President," he said in perfect English, "I don't know why you begin with games. We know who this man is. This is George Murphy, a reporter with the *Times Daily*. We read him regularly."

"How stupid of me," President Strong replied. "I thought you would be concerned if a reporter was present at a secret meeting."

"You have much to learn of us, just as we do of you. No one thinks this meeting will remain secret. You have your chosen one to chronicle these events. I have brought my secretary for the same purpose," he said bluntly.

"Let's walk. Just you and me," President Strong asked as he struggled with how to continue after a discouraging beginning.

Once they were alone, President Sorboth did not wait to hear what the American president had to say. He decided to take the measure of the man and the intent of his heart by seizing the initiative.

"We know that you know," Sorboth said, matter-of-fact. "What have you determined to do about it?"

"I have determined to give you the benefit of the doubt and assume Russia will not be part of Syria and Iran's foolishness," President Strong answered, his confidence strangely restored. "I have come to be frank with you and to seek a better future together."

"Together?" Sorboth responded incredulously. "To Americans,

'together' means to do things America's way. That is not together. That is sheep following a shepherd. You are not Russia's shepherd."

"Of course I know that, but I do believe America can be Russia's friend and seek to work together on issues that do not require a different agenda."

"And how would that look?" Sorboth asked.

"Well, for one thing, it would look like an American president coming to speak candidly to a Russian president to reveal military operations in advance—or as they occur—to prevent misunderstanding and unnecessary conflict. We may not agree on what must be done, but a friend understands that individual interests are not always identical and those differences do not need to endanger the friendship."

"Go on; I'm listening," Sorboth replied.

"I am proposing that Russia join with us in a counsel of democracies to do what the United Nations cannot do. The idea is simple; we have alliances for military defense. Why not have alliances that allow us to work together to address natural and human disasters around the world, with resources and force if necessary. Involvement in any individual activity would be voluntary and with the understanding that national interests may differ. This would not, however, be political to advance any nation or political block's interest at the expense of another; it would be intended to deal with human misery caused by natural forces or human cruelty. It would be the world working together to lend a hand without any other agenda, and I would like for us to announce the effort together if Russia decides to be a part of it."

"How would force be employed?"

"Solely to prevent genocide and stop the slaughter of innocents," Strong answered with conviction. "We have both sat and watched the slaughter of innocents with no way to stop it. The United Nations is structurally impotent. Only the world's democracies working together can strike with the necessary force to stop the slaughter and send a message that would strike terror in the hearts of any who contemplate slaughter."

"I want to hear of this," Sorboth responded, "but first you need to know the full extent of the slaughter planned against your nation."

Amazed, President Strong listened as the Russian president laid out MD in detail. Everything from the attacks in America, to the Western European attacks, the Middle East assassinations and the planned attacks on Israel and American forces. He concluded by asking, "What are you doing in defense, and…" he paused solemnly, "how can we help?"

"You can help by not being a part of it, and by making it clear to Iran and Syria that any move against American forces or Israel would not be in their best interest. You can also choose to try to understand why we must move preemptively, even if you do not agree with all we have decided to do."

"I understand preemption. You would be a fool to do nothing, but what are you going to do, and how will it affect Russian interests?"

CHAPTER 25

9/11

Saturday, March 8—MD minus 3 days

IT WAS 12:27 PM in Kerman Province when Ahmad Habid finally turned in frustration to El-Ahab screaming, "Go up and get Farrokh! Everyone is finally present. We must begin. We have lost enough time already. Tell him if he wants to be a part of this, he has to come now!"

Complaining to himself about why he always seemed to draw the unpleasant jobs, El-Ahab climbed the fifty feet of stairs to the surface to find Farrokh walking at the edge of the camp. He delivered the message exactly as spoken, generating an angry response.

"Tell that arrogant fool not to forget that he is a guest in Iran today. I will be down as soon as I report to the president," he said, taking what appeared to be a cell phone from his pocket and walking away from El-Ahab. Shaking his head in frustration, El-Ahab walked back to the entrance and climbed down the stairs to deliver the response.

"To hell with him!" Habid answered as he directed his attention to bringing more than a little hell of his own to the American troops now quartered in Israel.

Signal Sent

The signal was received simultaneously by two agents on the ground, as well as AWAX aircraft circulating high overhead. It was immediately transmitted to Captains Jonathan Adams and Sawyer Yeager, who turned and closed for their target runs. A single red light in their cockpit was all it took to release the two B-2 stealth bombers on their missions of destruction.

Simultaneously, the signal was forwarded through military channels to units throughout the world and Darrell Reed in Washington, who immediately transmitted the 9/11 code throughout the civilian communications network that had been prepared.

Before President Strong had even been able to explain to President Sorboth how the US intended to move preemptively, the code had been transmitted, and his secure cell phone began to vibrate.

The underground bunker in Kerman Providence was already nothing short of an ocean of flames, as was the nuclear facility hidden deep underground beneath the State Security Force headquarters in Hamada. The plan called for the initial attack on the nuclear facility to be followed by coordinated non-nuclear cruise missile strikes every fifteen minutes for the next two hours to assure the complete destruction of the facility and to render any surviving nuclear material unusable. Nothing was to be left to chance. The 9/11 code had reached the Naval vessels involved at the same time it reached the president's cell phone, and the preprogrammed launch sequence was initiated.

It was 7:57 AM in Reykjavik when the president's cell phone alerted him to the commencement of the attacks. He stopped mid-sentence to tell President Sorboth what had just occurred. There was no immediate response; only silence as Sorboth carefully considered his options. Suddenly, a frantic Russian aide sprinted across the field from the House of Hofoi to apprise President Sorboth of what he already knew.

"Wait until we finish our discussion," Sorboth responded, nodding to President Strong. They resumed walking alone; neither of them speaking. Both were aware that what would occur in these next moments would frame both their future and the future of their countries. President Strong prayed silently while waiting for his Russian counterpart to respond, not feeling any need to explain or justify the action taken. That would be for God to do if it was to be done.

Receipt of the 9/11 code resulted in calls to Embassies in Europe and the Middle East as presidential representatives rushed to prearranged meetings with heads of state to deliver the president's individual handwritten messages and review the flash drive presentation. The president's message advised of the actions taken in Iran, as well as the threats to their person or country. The packages delivered also included specific intelligence on the individual threats.

The response varied from thankfulness to relief to anger, but after seeing the flash drive presentation and being advised of the post MD plans, all understood that some preemptive action was required. Secretly, everyone hoped that it was enough and that the threat of a nuclear Iran had been ended for now. The meetings ended with each government moving on the intelligence provided to address their individual threat, contemplating how to publicly deal with the Iranian attacks. Could the Middle East be kept calm and the oil lanes protected? The thought raced through many minds, but those concerns were not immediate priority atop the American agenda. The American focus was on protecting the homeland first. It was "MD then…"

Message for the Enemy

In Israel, it was 10:57 AM when Prime Minister Zimri's secure cell phone began to vibrate. Aircrafts were immediately dispatched for high altitude damage assessment to be sure the nuclear facility had been completely destroyed. They were to watch for any troop movements or missile launches that might threaten Israel. These flights had been pre-approved by US command, who had provided identification codes for the pilots. The Israeli military was on full alert, prepared to launch an immediate counterattack to any threat from any enemy. Nuclear weapons were deployed and ready if required. The promise to the American president had not been forgotten, but Israel would defend itself with whatever it took if attacked.

The commander of US forces on the ground in Israel was ready to respond to any retaliatory attack, as were the carrier-based aircraft which were now waiting hot and ready to fly. The 9/11 code had been received by US forces at the same time it had reached Prime Minister Zimri. For now, radar, satellite observation and spy planes over Iran and Syria revealed nothing threatening. Unmanned drones patrolled the "no man's land" between the American forces in Israel and the border, while air defense assets awaited possible missile or aircraft strikes.

For the Iranian trio, the moments following their receipt of the 9/11 code was strangely similar. Hushai delivered President Strong's handwritten message to Iran's Supreme Leader Ayatollah Ali Alkominian. It read simply:

By the time you receive this message, your underground nuclear weapons facility in Hamada will have been destroyed as well as the training camp in Kerman Province and all those assembled there to plan attacks on American forces. The attacks on the nuclear facility will continue for two hours. Keep everyone away. We have no desire to kill civilians or military, only to be assured that all nuclear capacity has been completely destroyed.

We know about MD and your planned follow-up attacks with Syria, Hezbollah, and Russia on Israel and American interests in the Middle East. Stand down and live. Continue and die. Release the messenger. Your life and his are one.

Joshua Strong

President of the United States of America

Ali Alkominian screamed for confirmation of the American attacks while calling for someone to get the Iranian president on the phone. Turning to the State Security Forces commander on site, he issued two orders. "Bag this scrum messenger for me, and keep him tied in my presence. Then have your forces hold the president in his office until I get there. Use force if necessary. Don't let him do anything!"

Hushai was gagged, his head covered with a bag and his hands tied. He sat imagining the full extent of what must be going on before him, wondering what President Strong had said in his note. He was strangely at peace, and he did not feel alone. He was not alone.

When the Iranian president was reached, Ali Alkominian screamed into the phone, "Do nothing until I arrive!"

"Do nothing about what?" he responded as State Security Forces entered his office and he was told of the attacks. Cursing and grabbing for the phone, he was told to sit and wait for the supreme leader. Strangely, he began to smile. If it were possible to read his mind, the reason for the smile would be obvious. "This is the opportunity we have been waiting for," he was thinking. "There is chaos everywhere. The return of the Hidden Imam is today. The American attack assures it."

Hushai was thrown into a car with the Ayatollah as they headed for the Iranian president's office. Before leaving, Ali Alkominian had confirmed the attacks and issued orders to keep civilians away from the nuclear facility. "How did they even learn of its location?" he wondered. "Dare we torture the truth out of this infidel? Where is Farrokh? He would know what to do."

In Syria and Lebanon, both Ittai and Hiram found themselves similarly gagged, bagged and tied, kept in the presence of the one to whom they had delivered President Strong's message while he scrambled trying to confirm what had happened and decide how to respond. Both leaders were consumed by hate, which made rational thinking impossible. However, the president had correctly understood that this set of leaders were like the commanders of the operatives in America; they were willing to send others to their death as long as it did not put themselves at risk.

Strong's message had made it clear that they were indeed at risk. Unknown to them, unmanned drones armed with "hellfire" missiles were watching their movements, prepared to strike any of the three leaders if necessary. Meanwhile, Captains Adams and Yeager remained on station each with secondary targets already programmed into their weapons for use if required.

Move in Mexico

In Mexico City, it was 2:57 AM when the 9/11 code was received. Decisions had to be made quickly as the first modified fuel truck would cross the border in three minutes, followed by a truck bomb crossing at another of the five locations ten minutes later. This would continue on until some four hundred of the rolling weapons had entered the US headed for their target location for use on MD. "Let the first one pass," General Abrams suggested to his Mexican counterpart, General Garcia. "We will deal with them in the US. Let's focus on stopping the source."

"Agreed," General Garcia responded. "Those units are your problem." He issued orders to US tank commanders in the joint task force on the ground in Oaxaca to block all roads out of the city to stop the movement of any additional trucks that were not already on the way. Contemporaneously, the ground force commanders were ordered to move on the facility. As the tanks came into view, Assad and Alder yelled for all drivers to mount their trucks and charge the tanks.

As the first truck crossed the US border, a helicopter gun ship shadowed his vehicle while elements of the US military began blocking traffic ten miles in front of the vehicle. Soon after, they would set a roadblock a mile from the border so that the interstate would be clear and they could capture or destroy the vehicle without significant risk of collateral damage. Tanks were positioned on the highway to confront and destroy the truck if required. The conflict would take place well within the United States so that the risks on both sides of the border would be obvious to those who would ask questions later.

Domestic Response Teams

In Washington, it was 4:03 AM when Vice President Marshall received the 9/11 code. He immediately called General Hedge to be sure the attacks in Iran were successful, and to find out whether there had been any retaliatory moves against Israel or American forces. Pleased with the report, he dispatched Tom Knight for the "pleasant" task of advising the congressional leadership. Marshall also confirmed the attacks with Secretary of State Wisdom so he could notify the United Nation's secretary general and request an emergency meeting of the Security Council.

He then turned his attention to his most important task: to follow up with FBI Director Jackson, Homeland Security Director Hollister and National Security Advisor Steed on the preemptive strikes in America. For now, all any of them could do was wait for field reports and hope to hear from the president soon about his conversation with the Russians. General Hedge had reported no further movement of Soviet forces, which was encouraging since they had to know of the Iranian attacks by now.

Around the country, the hand-picked teams of federal marshals, FBI field agents, police and National Guard Units all had received the 9/11 code. The geek had done his job well, and God had been gracious.

It remained nighttime in all time zones, and except in the Brothers Trucking yards where the modifications continued around the clock, the targets slept. The delay had actually been helpful in that the evening's entertainment companions had departed all locations so the teams would not have to modify plans to deal with extras. All slept armed, though some slept particularly hard due to the drunken revels of their potential last night on earth.

In suburban Chicago, Officer Sally Johnson positioned her team outside the house they had assigned as the location of potential targets in preparation for their assault. She prayed quietly once more for protection and wisdom, and that no innocents would be hurt. After she was done, she led her team forward exactly as they had rehearsed so often before.

The front door was blown open, and the back door and other possible exits were covered. They entered the house repeatedly shouting, "Police! Don't move or you will be shot!" Equipped with night vision goggles and specially modified gas masks, the advantage was with the team. The hats worn by team members had been coated with a material that glowed bright yellow in the dark when viewed through the night vision goggles, making it easy to distinguish friend from foe.

They moved quickly from room to room, seeking to locate and neutralize all targets. If any responded in a threatening manner, they were shot—not to kill, but to wound if possible. The reality, however, was that the threat had to be eliminated and the targets were all armed killers.

A vicious firefight soon broke out with some members of the assassination squads who were all armed with automatic weapons. CS gas (2-chlorobenzalmalononitrile) canisters were thrown into combat areas, quickly causing the hostiles to become disoriented, unable to see clearly and in pain. The effects, though temporary, were debilitating. As the targets breathed in the gas, it was as if they were inhaling fire and all their exposed skin exploded in pain.

They went racing from the rooms where the gas canisters had been thrown, running into furniture and walls in a panic and firing their weapons indiscriminately. Some team members had also been provided with rapid-fire tranquilizer guns, which were used to neutralize those who had been affected by the gas. The scene was chaotic, but Officer Johnson's team acted coldly professional. They understood the importance of their mission to secure the threat completely while taking as many of the targets alive as possible.

At the exact same moment, this scenario was being repeated in numerous cities across the United States. The teams had been organized into four divisions. There was a raid team, a medical team, an intelligence team, and a prisoner team. Immediate medical care was essential, as was immediate action to secure computers, papers, maps, cell phones and anything else which could provide additional information on the terrorists' plans and network.

The prisoner team also worked quickly to remove the uninjured to a location where they could be immediately questioned. Other members of the police had been dispatched when the attack commenced to handle possible crowd control and traffic issues in the neighborhood. Much of the post-raid activity had to be done in the open because of the CS gas that remained in the building.

Although Sally Johnson had been the first in and the last out of the building, she had not been injured. Unfortunately, that was not true for her whole team. The building they had hit contained a team of assassins and a team of operatives. Despite the advantage of surprise and the hour of the raid, two of her team members had been killed and three wounded in the ensuing firefight. Eight terrorists had been killed and seven wounded, but twelve had been captured. The numbers throughout the country differed, but no fight was lost, none escaped, and all buildings were secured.

Amazingly, there was not a single house raided that did not contain terrorists, and of the seventy leaders previously identified, all but eight were captured. The eight had already left for airports, seeking to leave the country before MD. Police patrols were dispatched to find and arrest them before they could leave the country.

The raids on the Kingdom Charter aircraft at multiple airports in the United States, Canada and Mexico went without incident. Timing was everything, and the timing of the seizures was perfect. None of the terrorist trained pilots were in command of the aircraft, so there was no one to provide armed resistance. Attorney General Rodriquez was advised and had his staff alert Justice Department lawyers in each city that stood ready to immediately respond to any legal challenge to the seizures.

The move on Brothers Trucking yards and Terminal Equipment Leasing facilities preceded with less initial resistance than that encountered in Oaxaca, but they were not without defense. Everyone involved in the preparation process was armed. The decision to block the facilities and contain the vehicles was initially successful, but twenty-seven National Guard troops were killed at three locations when trucks were detonated during attempts to storm the facilities. All guard units were pulled back in containment until a decision could be made on how to neutralize the threat with the least loss of life and property. The terrorists moved quickly to take advantage of the pause in fighting, and used the time to work on modifications to more trucks for use to repulse further attacks.

In Oaxaca, the containment was succeeding for the moment after tanks had been used to destroy a suicide charge of fuel trucks lighting the night sky and littering the roads with dangerous flying debris. An emergency call came into Mexican President Calderon from Secretary of National Defense Ramirez. "Señor Presidente, what do you want us to do? The rebels continue to charge, using their trucks as bombs. We can't stop all of them. The tanks are going to be overrun. There are literally hundreds of trucks that are going to be turned loose in all directions. I need the authority to use more force to stop them now."

"What are my options?" President Calderon asked quickly.

"The Americanos Air Force is about it," he responded.

"Alright, get Vice Presidente Marshall on the line, and I will authorize an air strike from los Estados Unidos. We have to contain this."

Miracle in Reykjavik

Back in Reykjavík, the discussion resumed. "I am glad that Israel was not directly involved in these attacks," President Sorboth responded thoughtfully. "That would have made the situation untenable in the Middle East." He continued to walk, deep in thought as President Strong said nothing.

"The Iranian leadership is stupid and arrogant," Sorboth continued. "They have flaunted their nuclear program before the whole world. They deserve to have it given back to them in pieces. I have never liked the thought of that crowd having nuclear weapons. They don't think rationally. We Russians have learned the hard way that to make a deal with a crazy man is to dig many of our own graves. We remember our peace treaty with Hitler very well. Over 26 and a half million Russians died in the war when he stabbed us in the back. This crowd would ultimately do the same. We must choose our friends more wisely going forward.

"You will need to excuse me as I have some calls to make, and I am sure you have to make some calls as well. I will make it clear to all that need to hear that Russia is out and will support America if asked," he said, smiling. "I want to give this new relationship of which you have spoken a chance."

"Mr. President," President Strong began, but was quickly interrupted.

"My name is Alexi, and yours is Joshua. The time for formality is over. I suggest we begin there."

"Yes, agreed," President Strong replied excitedly as he started over. "Alexi, in my speech to the American people this afternoon and my public statements regarding the crisis and our response, may I credit Russia with its help and send a message to the world that the relationship is changing?"

Before President Sorboth could answer, President Strong continued slowly and deliberately. "Could I even go so far as to refer to Russia publicly as our friend?"

"I would like that," Sorboth responded, "and I want to talk later of this counsel of democracies to address human misery without a political agenda of which you spoke. Russia may want a place at that table."

"One more question, please. Well, really it is a personal favor," President Strong asked. "There are three Iranians who have been critical in providing us information that helped lead to our knowledge of the terrorists' plan. These men were sent on missions at great personal risk. I asked them to deliver personal handwritten messages to the leaders of Iran, Syria, and Hezbollah to advise of the attacks and to caution them to stand down. These men are important to me, and I want their lives protected. I made that clear in messages to the leaders. Perhaps if you could emphasize the importance of that to them when you speak to your contacts, it might help obtain their safe return? If they are harmed in any way, we will retaliate against the person of the leader."

"I am impressed. You really do play—how do you Americans say it—'hardball'?" President Sorboth responded with a small smirk. He then continued, "I will make that point clear. I only hope they are still alive."

"Me too," President Strong said wistfully. "Thank you, friend." He placed his arm around Sorboth and gave him a strong hug as they parted. They were immediately rushed by some very confused aides who were struggling to understand what they had just witnessed.

Into the Valley

The reception Tom Knight encountered when the congressional leadership gathered in the Senate Caucus Room was not exactly like that exchanged between Alexi and Joshua. Senator Howard was livid. "Strong has made us look like fools! He knowingly allowed us to get out on a limb of peace while he knew this crisis was unfolding. Cox is stranded in Syria, about to become a worldwide buffoon. Congress should have been involved with this at every step of the way. We may be in a world war by noon, and all the president cares about is that his opposition looks stupid!"

"Howard, slow down and listen," Chairman Crow interrupted. "That flash drive presentation is frightening. We are at risk here. This is not about politics. He warned us; we just weren't listening.

"Mr. Knight, where are we in dealing with the cells in the United States? Have they been neutralized?"

"All I can tell you right now is that preemptive strikes are ongoing as we speak against every cell we have been able to identify. I came over here to advise you that the action is underway—specifically the strikes in Iran. Coordinated responses with our allies are underway elsewhere in the Middle East and Europe as well."

"So, the massive military deployment we have been witnessing is anything but a field exercise?" the Senate Minority Leader asked.

"You are correct. We had to have a cover for the actual operational deployment," Knight answered.

"Why is the president in Mexico in the midst of this?" the speaker of the House asked.

"He isn't," Knight responded. "That is a cover which we worked out with Mexico where a major operation is also underway. The president is with the Russian president."

"What?!" Crow exclaimed, repeating what others also felt.

"The intelligence we had called for a post MD attack on Israel. That is the reason for the troop deployment there. The president used that deployment and Israel's involvement in our preemptive strike plan to get them to give us a chance to deal with this threat before they dealt with it unilaterally with nuclear weapons. One fact we intentionally eliminated from the flash drive presentation was that Russia was actively considering actions to neutralize our nuclear forces after the country had been devastated by the MD attacks, and to help make an assault on Israel possible by Iran and Syria with Hezbollah's help."

"He is with the Russian president—who is considering attacks on us—while our preemptive strikes are being launched?" the Senate Minority Leader asked in amazement. "What kind of security has been arranged for him? We cannot afford to lose him in the midst of this."

"He ordered that none be provided," Knight answered. "We don't like it either, but the truth is that they are meeting in a secret location with no clear military protection. He wants to try and stop Russia's involvement and eliminate the need to further strike Syria or Iran. He has also acted directly to try and get Hezbollah, Syria, and Iran to stand down."

"Where is the vice president?" the speaker asked.

"He is in the Situation Room holding the military and the civilian components to the approved plan during the time the president may not be accessible or should the unthinkable occur." That statement bought an uncomfortable silence as the reality of what was at stake began to sink in.

"Where are we in all these efforts?" Senator Crow asked.

"I was sent as soon as we had confirmation that the plan had commenced. That is the extent of my knowledge. The vice president will be prepared to meet with you at the White House at 10:00 AM to give you a further update. You are asked not to make any public statements while the operation is still ongoing. The president will hopefully speak to the nation at 2:00 PM."

"What does the president want us to do?" the Senate minority leader asked.

"Pray," he replied candidly. "This is all in God's hands to an extent you can't even imagine."

At that moment, the White House Press Office released a pre-approved statement which simply read:

The United States and many of its friends in North America, Europe, and the Middle East are currently involved in military and police actions to address the greatest terrorist threat ever launched against this nation or the world. The president will speak to the nation at 2:00 PM Washington DC time. Please pray.

"I only hope he gets to deliver that speech," Vice President Marshall thought as he read the release and wondered at the faith it took to approve it so long ago.

The Gift's Time Has Passed

Meanwhile, elsewhere in Washington, a puzzled Darrell Reed struggled with what had occurred the moment he relayed the 9/11 code. It was as if that act somehow signaled the end of the prayer website as a tool for secure communications from believers around the world. The email facility attached to the website had shut down simultaneous with the first code transmission, and nothing he could do would resuscitate that feature. No communications were possible, which had the advantage of shielding unknowing believers from possible interception. The gift's time had passed.

CHAPTER 26

OPERATION BUBBA

Saturday, March 8—MD minus 3 days

IN THE INVISIBLE, there were howls and screams as the forces of darkness responded in hate and fear at what was being played out before them. Was this the end? The return of the Holy One? Or simply a momentary setback in the human creature's ultimate descent into condemnation? With no ability to see into the future and no understanding of the Enemy's purposes in what was happening, their response was to deploy every dark being, seeking to express the Dark Master's desire to "kill, steal and destroy" through the instruments they influenced. Keepers entrusted with the thoughts and purposes of the surviving terrorists all sent the same message—kill, steal and destroy as much and as many as possible.

Only the members of the Counsel of Darkness were able to collect themselves with a view toward the ultimate battle. They understood that the real danger all along was not the failure of MD. Should that occur, they knew there would always be other opportunities. The real danger to the Dark Master was a continuation of the movement to God which began when that old man from Williams stepped to the microphone after the police press conference and asked his question. Nothing had been the same since.

Now, they faced hundreds of thousands of new searchers, believers who were acting like believers, and worst of all, people who were actually praying. Somehow they had to turn emotions back to fear, for a person cannot be afraid and have faith at the same time.

As Keepers, Tempters and dark wisps did their best to resurrect what they could of MD, Chemosh, Legion, Baal, Molech, Asherah, and Tammuz gathered to consider how best to use what remained of MD to damage or stop the movement toward the Enemy and return the people to a life motivated by their emotions and desires. "Remember the Dark Master's encounter with Jesus in the desert?" Chemosh reminded the group. "The three temptations didn't work that time, but the Dark Master never gave up or reacted in despair. Even the writers of the Enemy's Book got it right, 'he departed from Him until an opportune time.'[103] Those times came and went over the next three years. Jesus never surrendered to the temptations, but Jesus was the Son of the Enemy. These humans are anything but God. Now, in the midst of whatever is happening, we have an opportunity."

"But what is happening?!" Molech asked in frustration. "We never seem to know. The Enemy plays with us. We see what He wants us to see and are blinded at His command."

"What do you expect? We are not God," Baal said with anger at the reality of that statement. "We lost the rebellion. Surely you remember."

"Blasphemy, again!" Asherah screamed. "You almost seem to take pleasure in reminding us of our defeat, foul one. Remember whose you are. The Dark Master has not surrendered the throne to the Enemy and His Son, and neither should you. There are battles yet to be fought."

"Yes, we are in one now, and the outcome has yet to be determined," Legion reminded his dark brothers. "Don't become like the humans and let your emotions control you. There are instruments to be used and opportunities to destroy servants of the light. We cannot allow ourselves to be limited by what we don't know."

Even as he spoke, thousands of the dark wisps from all parts of the earth converged with messages from territorial rulers about what was happening that they could see. "Away with all of you," Legion screamed. "We must be more like the Enemy's real followers and not consider what is, but what should be, and then bring it to pass."

"And just what do you suggest?" Molech responded cynically.

"I suggest we get smart and cut through everything to get at the real danger," Legion responded.

"And that might be?" Chemosh asked.

"That might be who it always is," Legion continued. "The only humans that are of any real danger to us are the few that seek to hear and obey the Enemy because they believe in the testimony of Jesus.[104] The rest live in condemnation until they experience physical death, unless their eyes are opened. By simple deception, they live their lives serving us. We have to silence those whose lives and witness endanger our hold on the rest. It is those who heard the old man and followed Strong in his call to choose the Enemy. They must be our target now and in the future."

"And those who lead them," Baal added, "they are the most dangerous of all."

"But what of MD and our terrorist instruments?" Chemosh asked.

"We continue with the Dark Master's plan and attempt to destroy America and Israel, killing all we can; but if we fail, we simply prepare for the next opportunity. We still have Vandenburg, Krenski and others like them who can gain access to nuclear material and weapons. We must protect them and fill them with increasing hate, resentment and a passionate desire to kill Americans and destroy America. The Americans are fools. They may stand with Strong now, but soon they will fall back into their greed and desire for ease, which will make them vulnerable again. They are a people with few of real character, but we must be careful to stop this God movement before there are more."

"Yes, we should kill Strong and try to kill that worthless old piece of junk," declared the previously quiet Argon, who was again present by the invitation of Legion.

"Haven't you heard that the Bookseller is under the Enemy's protection?" Molech reminded.

"*Was* under the Enemy's protection…" Argon answered slowly and deliberately. "One good—if you don't mind me using the word—thing about the Enemy is that He responds to the minute, and a follower like the Bookseller can disobey and find themselves under the judgment of the Enemy. Remember King David, the one the Enemy called a 'man after God's own heart'?[105] We were able to lead even him into adultery and murder, resulting in judgment on him and his whole family throughout history.[106]

| 279

No one is immune from our attacks forever. Perhaps the Bookseller has sinned and is now vulnerable. We should proceed as though he has and try. Perhaps the Enemy is through with him, and he can be killed. We must try to silence him."

"You really are evil. You also never quit," Legion responded with pride. "There is a future for you among us someday."

"Enough backslapping. To work!" Chemosh declared, and they quickly departed to where they believed they would be able to do the most harm. Argon headed to Washington to be sure the instrument of Strong's death was ready. That remained his "big chance" to advance.

Among the Forces of Light, there were no such gatherings, for all were at work as assignments continued to be received moment by moment. One task completed resulted in another assignment. They continued in awe at the workings of God, still wondering what He would ultimately allow and how this would end.

Decisions

As the military convoy made the thirty-one-mile return trip to Keflavik International Airport for the flight home, the president was briefed on a secure phone connection by Vice President Marshall. A slew of emotions flooded the heart of Joshua Strong as he heard of the success of the strikes in Iran, the mixed response of the European and Middle East leaders, the difficulties in Mexico, the result of the assaults in the United States and the still open issues at the Brothers Trucking yards.

"What is President Calderon going to do? His problem is so much larger than ours since the drivers were housed with the trucks. They have the weapons and the people to move them, and most have already been modified," the president asked.

"He just called and asked for the Air Force strike. I authorized it based on your prior instructions," the vice president answered.

"Well, they have to make their own decision, but I sure hate to see that have to happen. What are we doing to bring those yards in America under control since the assaults failed?"

"No one has an answer to that, Mr. President."

"Is General Hedge there?"

"Yes, sir, he is."

"Put him on please."

"Yes, Mr. President."

"General, what are the military's plans for securing those truck yards and protecting civilians in the area?"

"We are scrambling for that right now, sir. The Mexican option is probably the most favored response. We can't let those vehicles out into the country."

"Not a chance, General. I want a different plan right away, and if you don't have one, consider this. Every one of those units should have sharpshooters. Keep people away from the trucks. Shoot them if necessary. Wound them if you can, but no one gets to the trucks and those already in the trucks are the primary targets. While you are at it, shoot out their tires so they can't be moved."

"That just might work," General Hedge acknowledged, surprised that it took a non-military man to find the obvious solution.

"Great. Issue the orders and begin immediately," the president answered. "Add to that the use of sound equipment repeatedly telling the terrorists to surrender or die. They may not all be as willing to die for their believed virgin reward if they know they now have an option to live."

"Yes, Mr. President," General Hedge responded, handing the phone to the vice president and leaving to issue the orders.

"When we get to Air Force One, let's reconvene the video conference phone hook-up, and I will fill everyone in on the details regarding the Russians," the president said. "Suffice it to say it went so much better than expected that you might even call it a miracle. Not only are they not going to be a problem; they are allied with us to stop Syria and Iran if needed."

"How did that happen?" the vice president asked incredulously.

"I can tell you what happened, but not how. There is a lot about this that no one will ever be able to explain."

Speechless at Last

In Damascus, two calls arrived close to the same time. One was for the leader of the cell charged with dealing with former President Cox, and the other was for Cox himself. One was a complaint; the other was instructions. One was received soberly; the other received angrily.

Elsewhere in the same hotel, Commander Travis Austin had received the 9/11 code when transmitted. With that, Seal Team 4 was prepared to respond as required. Some team members were again deployed throughout the bar, and the remainder waited in a warehouse just down the street. Seal Team 10 was also on alert and prepared to move to the site quickly with heavy weapons and transportation as needed. The USS Kamehameha sat offshore in the Mediterranean Sea, awaiting the package. "Operation Bubba" was about to be launched.

"You will not believe how stupid we look right now," Majority Leader Howard exclaimed to Cox. "Have you seen the press release?"

"I did. Is it real? Is this political or is there a real threat?" Cox replied nervously.

"How can you ask that?" Howard answered in anger and disbelief. "You are sitting in what may at any minute become a war zone, and you are worried about politics and whether this is real? Our country is under attack, and the president is out there somewhere trying to talk down conspirators, and you think this isn't real? Turn on the television and take a look! What planet are you from?"

"Well then get me out of here, now! I signed on for a peace conference, not to be a casualty in a war."

"It's not that simple. You are sitting in a hotel in the capital of a city where the government was planning a joint action with Iran and Hezbollah against Israel after the United States had been rendered incapable of responding militarily. I saw the plan and the Pentagon projections of what would be left after the attacks if they were successful. You would not believe what we let grow under our own eyes right here in America," Howard continued.

"What should I do?" Cox said, now with paralyzing fear entering his voice. "I could be a target. I need to get out of here. Send the Marines!"

"We can't send anybody right now until we know what we face and if the preemptive strikes succeeded. You'd better hunker down with your Secret Service protection and wait for instructions. Strong won't leave you there unprotected. You are a former president, and he can't allow you to be a casualty if it can be prevented."

"If it can be prevented?!" Cox roared. "Call the White House. I want to talk to the president."

"The Secret Service is already communicating with the White House, but here is reality: you are behind enemy lines. They can't protect you. They can't immediately get you out unless Syria allows. I suggest that you wait in a public place so that nothing can happen without Washington knowing immediately so they can respond."

When he hung up the phone, Cox gathered his Secret Service details and headed for the bar. "What better place to hide out? Not only is it a public place, but I'll be able to enjoy a liquid painkiller," he thought to himself.

As he entered, the bar looked strangely like it did last night. The college bunch was there in blazers with ties, and so were his media friends. A group of locals was disbursed through the room with several standing at the bar. Cox sat down by Rutherford and the others who gathered around a television, watching the fires in Mexico and the United States, brutal killing scenes and photos of the injured on lawns of homes in literally every major city. There were no reports of the attacks in Iran, and all the White House would say was in the short press release. All were waiting for the president's coming speech, which was still hours away.

"What is this all about?" Rutherford asked Cox, as if he should somehow know because he had once been the president.

Seizing the opportunity to spin his situation, Cox replied, "All I know at this point is that it is real and we have been the pawns of the Sheik who talked peace while his people prepared to kill. The State Department should have warned us of what they knew."

As he spoke, locals had slowly moved about the bar until one was sitting next to every Secret Service agent that had been identified the night before. Four of them had gathered near Cox, seemingly interested in the conversation, but also wanting to see the television news. From where they sat throughout the bar, "Professor" Thompson and his "graduate students" observed every movement carefully as locals entered their assigned sectors of responsibility. Silently, assignments were made as they awaited orders to move.

It all happened in a split second: every Secret Service agent was shot in the head at close range. A bag was placed over Cox's head and his hands tied behind his back as he screamed. Automatic weapons appeared from behind the bar in the hand of the three locals who sought to cover the remaining patrons. "No one moves, or they die," the leader said coldly. "This is not about any of you. We only want Cox. Sit, look and remember. If you give us no trouble, you will live."

Rutherford was grabbed and dragged to the terrorist leader. "Reporter, you are to get your cameras here now to record this."

"They are in his room," he said, pointing to one of his camera crew. "We don't have them here."

"Faisal," the leader said to one of the three with automatic weapons, "go with him and bring the cameras now."

They left and returned quickly with a single camera unit as preparations were made to clear a place to film Cox alone. There was panic in the room among the reporters, not sure what they were about to witness until from behind the bar, a long knife was passed to the leader who walked to where Cox was being held by the four.

"Turn on your camera and film everything I say and do. Show this to your American audience," he said, taking the bag off Cox's head. As soon as he saw the knife, he screamed and immediately began begging for his life. As the leader's hands slowly approached Cox's throat with the knife, he turned for a moment to the camera and said with hate dripping from his lips, "This is Muslim justice. Die America…"

Those were the last words he ever spoke as a single hole appeared in the center of his head, and the back of his skull exploded all over the still screaming Cox. The others fell simultaneously without a sound as the members of Seal Team 4 fired while remaining seated, each making their kills with silencers on their weapons.

Cox was freed, untied and forced out of the bar. He was pushed into the street still covered with the leader's gore, unsure of what was happening and who had him. The street had been cleared by the remainder of Seal Team 4, who had secured the area for helicopters manned by members of Seal Team 10 to land. Before leaving the bar, Commander Travis—who was the first in and last out—turned to the shocked media representatives and said calmly but firmly, "The president has asked us to make your escape possible. We leave from the street in five minutes. The area is secured. Leave all your stuff now and come if you want to go with us. We wait for no one."

As quickly as it started, it was over. Cox and his protectors, along with some of the traveling White House Press Corp, headed across Lebanon and over the Mediterranean Sea to the awaiting USS Kamehameha, now on the surface with fighter aircraft high overhead for security. Assigned team members had changed into wetsuits and helped Cox into one after they had cleaned him up. For once in his life, he had nothing to say as they coaxed him out of the helicopter and down a rope ladder for a short jump into the sea. There, a rescue team waited to pull him into a raft for the short trip to the sub. The helicopters left to return to Israel from where the other team members would be flown to base and the press representatives would be offered immediate Air Force transport back to the US. Cox, now in the raft, sat silent. He was still in shock, simply grateful to be alive.

Heading Home

Aboard Air Force One, now in flight back to Washington, the video conference link had been reestablished, and the president had completed his report on his discussions with the Russian president Sorboth. "I am really hopeful that this is a new beginning and that his intervention will assure that Syria, Iran, and Hezbollah stand down. Is there any evidence apparent on the ground one way or another?"

"None as of yet, Mr. President. We see no signs of preparation to retaliate on any front," General Hedge responded. "It is as if they are waiting to decide what to do."

"Good, we will wait too, but don't stand down any of our forces or reduce the threat level. I want us ready to respond quickly and decisively to the slightest perceived threat."

"Yes, Mr. President."

"For the Russians to turn and support us is nothing short of amazing," Vice President Marshall added, reflecting on what he had heard.

"That would be one word for it," the president said in agreement as he quickly changed the subject. "Any news on Cox? They are bound to move on him if only to protect their pride."

"We just got a report from the USS Kamehameha. Cox is on board," General Hedge reported. "He had to be extricated from Damascus. A terror cell sought to cut his head off and televise the event. We lost his security detail and would have lost him completely if it wasn't for the Seal teams you authorized. We got most of the traveling press out with him."

"Are you sure that was a terrorist cell and not a planned Syrian military action?"

"Believe me, it was a terrorist cell on orders from the Sheik," General

Hedge answered. "As soon as the helicopters were airborne, our embassy was contacted by the Syrian government to deny any involvement and assure they would not interfere."

"I would expect that Cox will not be so generous with his tolerance after nearly losing his head," the vice president observed.

"Tough way to learn a lesson," the president responded. "Be sure someone contacts his wife and the congressional leadership to assure them he is safe."

"Yes, Mr. President," Troy Steed acknowledged.

"Tom, put out a press release to confirm that the former president is safe. Don't go into any details. Leave that to him and the people who were with him. Let them have the first opportunity to explain. I will refer to it in my speech only briefly."

"Yes, Mr. President."

"How has the sharpshooter approach worked on the Brothers Trucking yards?"

"It appears to have worked to keep them away from the trucks. They have been able to explode several by gunfire, but the damage has been limited to the individual site," the vice president reported. "We have captured a number of the operatives who tried to escape."

"What is the plan to bring closure to this?" the president asked.

"We believe that as night falls, what we should do is cover the yards with intense bright lights to enable us to control the field and keep them away from the trucks with the sharpshooters. At 2:00 AM Washington time, the lights will be cut off and troops equipped with night vision equipment will storm the yards. The bright light should have made the terrorists even more night blind than usual, so our forces will be able to move quickly and take the yards before those still present can effectively oppose them or get to the trucks. At least that is the theory," General Hedge detailed.

"Good, that would seem to offer the best opportunity for success with the least possible causalities on either side," the president responded. "Be sure you have backup so that no truck gets out of those yards."

"Believe me, sir; we have whatever firepower is required available for every site, as well as an Air Force backup option."

"Is Darrell in the room?" the president asked.

"Here, sir," he replied.

"I wanted to thank you for the hook-up to pass the code. It seemingly worked well everywhere,"

"Thank you, sir, and wait until you see some of the intelligence that the police and federal marshal raids found. We have names, contact information, bank information, phone numbers, email addresses and more. It is a treasure trove of information, much of which leads back to a small group in Saudi Arabia."

"I guess you know what you will be doing for a while," the president responded, smiling. "Make sure the FBI and CIA coordinate the follow-up with Justice so we make the maximum use of the information. If any of it seems to have military value, get it to General Hedge and Tom Knight. Particularly if it reveals any other locations or people in the US we might have missed."

"Yes, Mr. President."

"Wilburn, is there anything new on the Iranian trio?"

"Nothing yet, sir," he responded.

"I have an idea. Darrell, can you get me an additional secured line directly to me and no one else?"

"Certainly, sir."

"Good, set it up and get me the number as soon as you can. I want to be able to receive calls here aboard Air Force One immediately after the speech, and I will need State and CIA to coordinate delivery of the number to our contacts in Hezbollah and the Syrian and Iranian governments. I want it delivered to the same people who received my message from the Iranians. I know we have eyes on them. Take it to them, wherever they are. The speech will tell you when."

"Yes, Mr. President."

"Ladies and gentlemen, I'm signing off for now. David and I have a speech to polish. Call me with any news of significance, or if there is any evidence anywhere of preparations to retaliate." The picture went blank as David and the president began to work through the most recent draft. The Bookseller excused himself with Paul Phillips to find a quiet place to pray, while George Murphy left to write.

CHAPTER 27

THE FINAL THREAT

Saturday, March 8—MD minus 3

THE ANNOUNCER SPOKE, and masses of people around the world stopped to watch and listen, not knowing from where the broadcast initiated and having little understanding of the extent of the crisis.

"Ladies and gentlemen, we present to you the president of the United States."

"I come to you this afternoon in the midst of what we have learned to be the greatest terrorist threat ever launched against our nation and around the world. Some five years ago, a plot was hatched to take advantage of our porous southern border and our generous admission standards for foreign students to send an army of terrorists into our country for an assault they code-named 'MD.' This stands for Memorial Day—the initial planned date of execution.

"The plan was simple; first, send terrorist leaders as graduate students to some of our most prestigious universities where they would obtain master's degrees in education and then spread throughout the nation as teachers in school systems in every major city. They would then prepare and coordinate the operatives who would actually carry out the attacks.

"The operatives were trained in Iran with the knowledge and participation of their government, and in secret in Mexico. Since commercial aircraft would be much more difficult to hijack after 9/11, a new primary weapon of choice was selected. The rolling bombs would be gasoline tank trucks along with rental vehicles which would be equipped with explosives such as those which destroyed the Alfred P. Murrah federal building in Oklahoma City. Private aircraft would also be flown into particular targets that could not be accessed with trucks.

"To make the necessary equipment easily available, foreign investors acquired a United States trucking company, an equipment company, and a private aircraft leasing company. Similar acquisitions were made in Mexico. The regular employees of these companies are currently on furlough so that the trucks, equipment, and aircraft would be available to the operatives who have been in the country waiting to attack."

"The operatives have crossed our border with Mexico one by one over the past few years, then traveled to a gathering point in Southern Arizona where the trucking company diverted vehicles to pick them up and deliver them to their assigned city to wait for MD. There were two groups of operatives, the first consisting of suicide truck drivers and pilots. The second group contained assassination squads, much like the ones we have witnessed in Williams over these past weeks.

"The suicide operatives were part of a carefully coordinated series of simultaneous attacks on key infrastructure, which if successful, would have rendered America incapable of even supporting its own people for decades. In our investigation, we captured a terrorist presentation of the plan that was presented to the leaders in Iran. What you will now see is that terrorist presentation followed by a Defense Department assessment of what America would be like had the planned attacks been successful."

The screen went to the video presentation that had been shown to the leaders of affected countries by the president's representatives earlier in the day. There were audible gasps and shock throughout the nation at the reality of what had been planned against the country. As the video presentation ended, the president continued.

"Over the intervening weeks since we discovered the plot, MD was moved up and rescheduled to commence next Tuesday, March 11th. Along with the attacks portrayed in their training video, the assassination squads were set to attack and kill children in kindergartens across the country as they sought to do in Williams.

"But America was not to be the sole target. Attacks were also planned in Europe, as well as assassinations of Middle East leaders who had stood with us against terrorists. Iran, Syria, and Hezbollah mobilized forces intending to attack Israel once American was neutralized. Terrorist groups organized and prepared to attack American forces in the Middle East. Attempts were made to recruit other world powers to join in the effort.

"Over these past several weeks, I have been reminded often of the dark days of Valley Forge when the Continental Army had little hope of surviving the continuing campaign of the British. They were unsure of what they would face, when or where, but understood that along with what they knew and had, they could not win. What I remember most about Valley Forge is a remarkable picture of George Washington on his knees praying in the snow. God obviously heard his prayer (and that of many others) and delivered the Continental Army, ultimately bringing victory in the revolution and a new nation with a new form of government.

"That victory was not accomplished, however, without help from friends. The French stepped forward and lent their support, helping make the victory possible. Those same two elements—prayer and the help of our friends—have allowed us this day to strike preemptively against those who sought to destroy our way of life.

"I can report to you that last night as you slept, strikes were launched against enemies here, in Mexico and in the Middle East. In Iran at a terrorist training camp, a meeting of terrorist leaders planning the last stages of the assaults against the United States military forces in the Middle East was struck and destroyed. Similarly, the facility where Iran was assembling a nuclear device for use in the post MD attacks was destroyed. Our Mexican friends under the bold leadership of their president, Felix Calderon led an assault on a major facility from which over 400 of the truck bombs were to be driven across our border for use in the MD attacks.

In our country, special units of local police departments, along with federal marshals and the FBI, assaulted locations where the operatives were living in hiding waiting to attack, and their leaders. Regular military units along with units of the National Guard acted to seize the leased aircraft, trucks and equipment that were intended to be used as weapons. Those actions continue now, and will until all of the potential weapons have been secured. We expect that to be accomplished within the next twenty-four hours, but you can be assured that the vehicles will not be allowed to leave their current location. You do not need to be afraid.

"In Europe and the Middle East, our friends are acting to prevent the attacks planned there. We expect that they will be successful and arrests will be made shortly. We have issued warnings to Iran, Syria, and Hezbollah to stand down from their planned attacks on Israel and American interests in the Middle East. We have positioned US forces in Israel in the hope that their presence will deter any foolish military action by any party in that region. All of our military forces are deployed and on full alert, ready to move against any threat anywhere. We are prepared to launch whatever level of response is necessary, and I again ask the leaders of Syria, Iran, and Hezbollah to publicly declare their intention to stand down. I invite them to accept my invitation to receive Secretary Wisdom, who will be prepared to travel and meet with them over the next few weeks to explore a new relationship if they are prepared to disavow terrorism and past animosities and turn their attention to making life better for all in the Middle East.

"I know that many of you will be wondering about the fate of former President Cox, who was unknowingly in the middle of all this in Syria. He sought peace from a people who intended only death and destruction. The supposed peace initiative was nothing but deception to draw attention away from preparations for MD. An attempt was made on his life, but he now sits safely aboard a US Navy vessel, having been extracted in the midst of the attempt by brave men and women of our Armed Forces. I will leave the details for him to reveal when he is ready.

"Much of what has occurred over these past few days will seem impossible when viewed through the objective lens of history. How could we find out about this plan? How could we locate the leaders and operatives hiding in this country and Mexico? How could we find their intended weapons and learn of the plans for Europe and the Middle East? How did we get our enemy's training information?

"All I can tell you is that when millions here and around the world answered the Bookseller's call to choose God, it was as if blinders were lifted from our eyes and information began to be made known. There is no other explanation.

"Some will wonder how I can call for Syria, Iran, and Hezbollah to stand down under the threat of military action and then offer the hope of a new relationship. Well, as you wonder on what might be possible as we move forward, consider this: one friend who stepped forward to help us against any possible military strike in the Middle East was an old enemy, Russia. I have chosen my words carefully, and I repeat, Russia is now our friend. President Sorboth has been a great encouragement and help to me personally. I have steadfast hope for a new partnership going forward.

"Our friends in the Middle East are both Arabs and Israelites. We stand for the security of Israel, but in so doing we do not stand against our Arab friends. Looking to the future, we have hope for new relationships and partnerships there too. Perhaps when the historians seek to tell future generations of this time, they will write that out of threats and conflict came a new beginning. That is my sincere hope, and that hope is what we offer to all who have chosen to participate in this effort to destroy us.

"A new beginning requires a first step be taken. To the leaders of Syria, Iran, and Hezbollah: please hear me. While I have been speaking, State Department personnel have sought an audience to provide you with a phone number to a secured phone which I am carrying at this moment. I want to hear from you with my own ears that you will stand down; that you will release unharmed my personal representatives whom you are holding, and that you will receive Secretary Wisdom in the next few weeks. Then we want to see on-the-ground action which evidences that your military is standing down. I hope you will call and that you will stand down, but if not, have no doubt that the message I sent to you earlier today will be carried out and we will use whatever force level is necessary to defeat any movement made toward increased conflict.

"Let me close for now with this—our actions have not been without casualties. Brave men and women have died and suffered extensive wounds. Other nations who have stood with us have similarly suffered casualties as have those who chose to join in the attempt to destroy America. We do not yet know the extent of the losses, and since our operations are not complete, more are probable. Many more will occur if Syria, Iran, and Hezbollah do not stand down. Please continue to pray, as I know so many of you have been doing. We want this to end quickly and with a minimum additional loss of life. We want a new beginning to rise from this violence; for enemies to become friends, but those decisions are in other hands.

"As I said, MD was to have been launched Tuesday. Believing that my phone will soon ring, when I return to the White House I am declaring Tuesday to be a day of Thanksgiving for all Americans. It will be a day to thank God for His deliverance; a day to recommit this nation to His care that we become truly one nation under God, even as it says on our money and in many hearts.

"It is with sincere thankfulness and hope for the future that I bid you good afternoon."

Seeking a Crutch

The response in the invisible was nothing less than uproar. Members of the Counsel of Darkness decided on their own to use their power and influence over leaders in Syria and Iran, along with Hezbollah to urge them to ignore the president and push forward the attack on Israel and American interests in the Middle East. Lesser beings sought to cause the remaining operatives to rush the vehicles and detonate their explosive cargoes. It was a picture much like the large herd of pigs Legion had driven down a steep bank and into a lake where they all drowned.[107] None survived, and none were able to detonate their vehicles. It was over in fifteen minutes. The truck yards were quickly secured.

Argon had his marching orders, and he was off with enthusiasm. The president had made it clear he was returning to the White House, and he would be there across the park waiting for him with a final farewell.

The phone calls came in, despite the influence and power of the Counsel of Darkness. Fear is a greater motivator than hate or anger, and the three leaders to whom the president had spoken understood that it was over. Strangely, as the calls were made, there was a mutual sense of hope in some kind of new future. Even Hezbollah looked forward to the promised conference with the secretary of state.

In Iran, actions were taken to ensure a new future. As Hushai was released, the Iranian president was bagged and tied. When the call came into the president, Ali Alkominian reported sadly that the Iranian president had died in the raid on the facility in Hamada. Arn Au Farrokh was now the new leader.

"What do you see on the ground?" the president asked General Hedge.

"There appears to be movement back to bases. I think it may be over; they are standing down," he replied.

"Well, General, there is still too much of the Gipper in me, remember—trust, but verify. Continue to monitor every movement, every radio transmission; anything that would tell us what their real intentions are. Leave our forces on full alert until we are absolutely sure this is over."

"Yes, Mr. President."

"Wilburn," the president said, now directing his conversation to the vice president. "We can't take any chances at home or abroad on Tuesday. We think we got all of the operatives, but we still can't be sure. We have the truck bombs and aircraft under control, but we don't know about the assassination squads. I want you to get with Director Jackson, Director Hollister, and Troy to be sure that every kindergarten and elementary school in the country is protected. Use local police and citizen's militia groups first, but where necessary use federal marshals or troops. We want an armed presence visible to deter anyone we may have missed, and to encourage parents that it is safe for their children."

"I understand," Wilburn responded.

"When we announce that to assure parents later today, I want you to make the announcement. The people need to begin to understand your importance in this operation."

"Mr. President, that is something you should do as president, not me," Wilburn responded.

"Perhaps that is the way it has been in the past, but it's a new world out there after all this. Frankly, I am tired of the cult of the presidency. We get either too much credit or too much blame for what happens. The very idea that one person can solve all of America's problems is stupid," the president answered. "When I get out of office, there will be no presidential library or any other memorial. Don't need it; don't want it. I just want to be found faithful in the job while I'm in it."

"I am not sure America is ready for the 'new' edition of Joshua Strong, a.k.a. the president," Wilburn responded with sincere wonder.

"I won't be around long enough for them to have to get used to it," he answered, smiling. "That may be your problem shortly."

"I had really hoped so until the last few days, Mr. President, but I may rethink that now. This is over my head."

"Mine too," the president answered.

"One last thing, Wilburn, and I then need to go. Could you have someone contact Carl Varvel and get him to the White House? I have one more project for him."

"Will do, sir," and with that, the video link was disconnected.

After a few minutes, the president turned to the Bookseller—who had been sitting with him—and asked, "What now?"

"Why do you ask me?" he responded.

"Well, you're the one God used to get this all started. I figure that you are the one He will use to lead us forward wherever He wants us to go," the president answered. "What has God revealed to you for me?"

"Wait a minute. Have you missed what happened these past days? God leads. We follow. It is not about following a man—any man, for that matter—it is about men following God," the Bookseller said in a fatherly tone. "One of America's greatest problems is in following men, even well-intentioned men or women. The most anyone can do is lead by following Jesus,[108] and that is your assignment as president."

"But how do I know? There are so many voices and so many who claim to speak for God," the president answered with a sense of urgency and frustration.

"Do you think that God has lost your 'phone number'?" the Bookseller replied with a twinkle in his eye.

"What do you mean?"

"I mean, who told you what to do in the crisis through which we just passed? You have done things that would be seen as foolish in the world's eyes if they were known, yet they were exactly the right thing to do at the exact right moment. How did you know what to do?"

"I don't know. I just knew deep within what I should do and felt a compulsion to do it," the president answered.

"And where do you think that came from?"

"I guess it must have been God directing me."

"Ah, now you see," the Bookseller said. He paused for emphasis, then asked, "And why would God have spoken to you at the exact moment you needed to hear?"

"I guess I don't know the answer to that question," the president responded, deep in thought.

"That is the most important question of all," the Bookseller replied. "God spoke to you because He knew you were listening and would obey. You made the obedience choice before He spoke, so He could trust you with His will. Had you only decided to consider what God might say, you would have never heard from him."

Pausing again to gather the words God wanted him to share, the Bookseller sighed and took on, for the moment, the mantle of a prophet. "Listen closely, Mr. President. What has happened will not be repeated based on your obedience and that of the believers in America who chose God at the moment they were confronted with the decision. God's own people Israel shut their ears to God after great victories and returned to the path of declination into judgment and rejection by God. They rejected God, so God rejected them. He will do the same to America, and He will do the same to you if you stop listening and remaining ready to obey Him.

"There is nothing special about you or me or America. God created everyone and everything. No nation exists apart from the fact that He allows it to exist, and should He lift His hand against a nation, it is soon gone. Consider the great empires of history. None have survived. Why should we believe that America will? Its future will depend on the choices of its people and leaders. When America rejects God, God will reject America."[109]

"I will never knowingly reject God," the president answered passionately.

"Yes, but you are not America. It is God's people in America, not simply the leaders who must choose and then live within their choice. You can point the way by example, but they must choose for themselves to follow God, and it is not for a single day. It is every day. Remember what Jesus said, 'If anyone would come after me, he must deny himself and take up his cross daily and follow Me.'[110] Your cross is your office and all you must deal with in a cruel and hateful world."

"This is not easy," the president observed.

"No, but then Jesus said, 'I have told you these things so that in Me you may have peace. In this world you will have trouble. But take heart! I have overcome the world.'"[111]

"He certainly proved that these last days," the president agreed. "I have not been afraid or confused."

"And so it can be as long as you are to carry this burden, if you continue to choose wisely and follow Him."

Argon's Instrument Strikes

Suddenly, Major Seth Edwards understood what he must do. He rushed to set a parameter of sufficient size around the White House to deal immediately with any apparent threat against the president. He included troops on the ground, in cars and in helicopters watching for anything that would reveal an attempt to attack the president's transportation into the White House. The anti-aircraft batteries were already placed to deal with aircraft, but what about some kind of rocket attempt to bring down Marine One?

The park was secure because of the presence of the anti-aircraft batteries, but not the surrounding area of the city. The unthinkable had been ignored until he realized after the president's speech that the president would soon be returning and no provision had been made for a direct assault on Marine One from surrounding neighborhoods or businesses.

It had been Barnabas who, after receiving instructions from the Spirit, awoke Major Edwards to the president's danger. Watching amused was Argon, who was busying himself with preparations for that very danger. "The fools," thought Argon. "Let them busy themselves with the surrounding neighborhoods and businesses. This attack will come from one of their own, directly in the center of the mall across from the White House."

The assigned Keeper dug his long fingers deep into the brain of the chosen instrument while Tempters continued their influence to drive this man to total despair and a desire to die. They cared not who he was, only that he was available to do their bidding. The man had a name. It was Sigmund, and he was known by those in his platoon as 'Siggy."

Siggy had placed the shoulder-fired missile near his feet at his assigned position. When questioned why he had this weapon too, his response was, "I am taking no chance with the life of this president."

Three Marine One helicopters left Andrews Air Force Base together. The president, David Barnes, Paul Phillips, George Murphy, and the Bookseller in one; Jim Hunt and the ITN crew in the second, and the third was empty, being used solely as a decoy. As they rose for the trip to the White House, they began to shift in formation like a presidential shell game so that no one would know which of the helicopters carried the president. Jim Hunt had argued for position behind the president so they could film the landing. After the president insisted, the request was granted for the final approach to the White House lawn, but they traveled in a different order for now.

"I have asked for no cameras or formal greeting," the president announced to those aboard. "I just want to hug Janet for a long time and finish up what we must do so this day can finally end."

"You sound tired, sir," Barnes observed.

"I am, but it is a thankful kind of tired," he said as the familiar buildings and monuments of Washington began to take shape below them.

The sound of the helicopters generated immediate activity throughout the now presumed secure zone. Another of the presidential shell games commenced as Siggy reached down, prepared to pick up the weapon. As they came out of the shift, the helicopter carrying the president led, followed by the ITN crew filming the homecoming and the empty helicopter.

Those on the ground had not been told which of the three carried the president, but Siggy knew because Argon knew. He had slipped into each craft as they made their approach and influenced Siggy to target the first in line.

For a reason he could not explain, Major Edwards felt a compulsion to head for the White House and his vehicle raced toward the far side of the mall as the helicopters came into view. He ran toward the anti-aircraft battery, expecting to find an airborne threat because the compulsion had been so strong. Yelling for the battery commander who seemed to be nowhere in sight, suddenly he saw Siggy as he raised the shoulder-fired weapon and prepared to shoot. Screaming but not knowing what to do as he ran across the mall, he fired one shot from his pistol toward the area of the shooter almost at the same instant as the rocket fired and began to leave the cylinder toward the target. It was over in a moment as the rocket exploded below the helicopters, hitting a parked security vehicle.

Siggy was taken into custody before he could kill himself or further endanger the president.

As the pilots struggled to understand what had just happened, they landed safely in succession. The president got his long hug with Janet, and they entered the White House together. At the mall, Major Edwards

298 |

found the empty cylinder and saw the impression the bullet had made an inch from the end of the barrel at the exact moment necessary to change the rocket's trajectory and save the president's life. He sat there for a long time, knowing he could never have made that shot running across a field and firing in the dark. And he was right.

CHAPTER 28

MD

Tuesday, March 11 - MD

TUESDAY, THE DAY that was intended to be MD, ended. As the sun went down across the earth, there was no violence or military confrontation anywhere—just a sense of relief as people gathered in response to the president's call for a day to thank God for His deliverance.

The Counsel of Darkness gathered, still stinging from the scorching rebuke they suffered from the Dark Master. He was in one of his volcanic rages at another catastrophic defeat. They knew he would have killed them all except for the fact that they were eternal beings just like him and could not die. They feared loss of position or eternal punishment from the one who sat on the throne, but it was not the end, so they began to move in preparation for their next assault on those created in the image of the Enemy.[112]

"What now?" Chemosh asked. "The Enemy found a few, and that was enough. How can we destroy them all?"

"I'll let you think about that," Legion answered. "I am off to a cave where a faithful servant waits, buried in anger and hate. He is always available, and his heart for death has no limits. Right now he needs another visit from me, his perceived god, and that can be arranged. He and his servants will never stop as long as there is life in their bodies. They are my flock of pigs that will carry millions with them in death."

"Well I hope some of those who die are of the light," Baal sneered cynically. "For all your minions' passion, there have been relatively few deaths among those who are our enemies."

"What do you call relative?" Legion responded angrily.

"Shut up," Molech said rebuking both. "Go and try as you will. I will return to what always works. My name became known by all as the god to whom children were sacrificed. Even the leadership of the Jews were led to burn their own children in my honor.[113] This crowd is no different. They will burn their children on my altar."

"Right, you are going to take this crowd back two thousand years and get them to burn their children? I don't think so," Legion responded with contempt.

"I don't have to kill them to take their life," Molech answered quickly. "We have the tool of abortion that kills many, but then they are the lucky ones. The others must live in this world we control; time without meaning, and life without purpose. As long as we can continue to advance divorce and same-sex equality, home will just be a place, not a way of life. If we maintain control over the school systems, media, music and fashions, we cause parents to turn children into mere things, useful to the darkness but without joy or life. Watch how they run around always plugged into something or on something because they have no true life. That is our victory. Parents sacrifice their children every day. It is my crowning glory—a living death followed by the second death."

"That doesn't help us with the few who believe," Baal responded. "They are the danger. They are the ones who did us in this time. You know who I mean, the few who actually believe what is written in the Enemy's Book."

"Well, I am going to continue with the angel of light bit and go for the church crowd," Chemosh answered. "They are still ready to believe in anything that excites them, and we can certainly excite. Look at what we have already been able to do with what they call 'worship.' Look at the fools who think God makes them writhe on the floor in laughter or bark like a dog. All of them like the feel-good gospel. It is really not much of a challenge."

"You say that, but look what just happened. That will keep the bunch headed for the second death while believing they are 'glory bound' under control, but what about those who really believe?" Asherah asked.

"That is my assignment," said Argon, now the same size as the others and a member of the Counsel. He had been advanced by the Dark Master because his hate of the believing humans was unmatched; he was willing to try anything to destroy them, even in the face of a declared prohibition by the Enemy. Having been increased in size and authority, he had exercised his newly-found powers to similarly advance the ever-present Zaccur, who was waiting for his assigned city.

"Hold on, little one," Chemosh interrupted. "You may have been promoted, but you are no equal here. No one ever worshipped you as a god," he said as derisively as he could while staring in contempt.

"Clearly that status is no longer necessary, you failure," Argon responded with equal contempt. "If you had been able to accomplish the Dark Master's purposes, I would still be carrying messages for the likes of you. My assignment is clear. I get the politicians and judges. Those are the ones we can use to attack the real believers. We are already back on the right track. Soon it will be illegal to believe what is written in the Enemy's book. We will shut the mouths of the real ones. It will be as effective as in China or Russia where only 'official' churches are allowed. The gospel according to the government will stop the real ones either by threat or imprisonment."

"Maybe, but you forget that hasn't worked historically. The real ones endure persecution well," Chemosh reminded him. "I like that they die, but their joy in death takes all the fun out of it."

"Perhaps, but dead is dead and then they are silenced," Argon answered.

"Go forth, little one, but my focus will be to kill them all," Tammuz replied with determined calmness. "Our Russian friends still have access to nuclear weapons and materials. Placed in the right hands, America will be uninhabitable for thousands of years. Believers or unbelievers, they will all die together, and we already have a willing servant among the Sheik's crowd. His name is Adnan el-Gulstare. Remember that name, for he will accomplish what the last group could not. He will truly be the butcher of all history."

"Enough talking; let's get to our tasks," Legion said. "You are quick to brag about what you say you are going to do. Brag afterward when there is proof of something to brag about."

Angry and resentful, the Counsel separated, each to their chosen assignment.

Another Perspective

Barnabas and Lucius had observed the exchange with interest. "Nothing new," Barnabas exclaimed.

"True, but I am always surprised that there is no sadness among any of them after all that happened. Many who served them faithfully died doing their bidding, and they feel nothing for them. There is hate and fear and anger at their failure, but no sadness," Lucius observed.

"How different it is for us," Barnabas answered. "We lost some faithful ones who are now with the Father, and there is great rejoicing over their eternal presence. However, there is also great sadness at the many who even now endure the second death. I know they deserve what they are receiving. It is justice on those who rejected the great sacrifice,[114] but the Father does not want to lose even one."

"Well, it is over for them. Death ends every opportunity to be born again,[115] but the battle continues for the hearts of those who remain."

They left together to join the others who were waiting at the place of prayer in Iran. It was here that the Father began to move in response to the prayer to end the MD threat, and it had become for them a holy place. It seemed right that here was where they should come this night to begin a new journey; to be with those all around the world who had chosen to be faithful.

"Why am I feeling such joy?" Hiram asked as the three dried their tears and ended their time of singing and prayer together. "We have no idea what is next for us or for our country, and yet I am overwhelmed by a sense of joy like I have never experienced before. What does it mean?"

"Do you remember the experience of the seventy-two that Jesus had sent out empowered to confront Satan and his demons to prepare the way for Him in the cities where He was about to go?"[116] Hushai asked.

"I do," Hiram replied.

"Then you have the answer to your question," Hushai answered.

"When they returned, they encountered Jesus 'full of joy through the Holy Spirit'[117] and so have we. I'll bet that before this night ends, many believers who proved faithful in the crisis will experience the same joy."

"Yes," Ittai affirmed, "it is the 'joy of the Lord' which is our strength."[118]

Tears again came to Hiram's eyes as he thought about the reality of bringing joy to Jesus. They were silent for a time, and then Hushai continued. "I don't know about you guys, but I still believe my place is here. I know the authorities are well aware of who we are and what we did. There is great risk in staying, but there is a nation and people here who need to hear the truth."

Hushai's comments were followed by a chorus of "Amen." They would all stay because that is where they believed they were meant to be. As they pondered what this could mean, they heard the racing of an engine as another cab appeared and headed directly for their location. Surprised at the intrusion, they watched and waited, wondering if the site was no longer under God's protection. The cab stopped, and a familiar face emerged. It was Carl Varvel with another note from President Strong—an invitation to a private weekend together at Camp David with wives for those who were married.

They smiled and quickly agreed. Hushai wrote an acceptance knowing that if this were God's plan, they would be able to get out of the country and come back in later. The note had a request, "Please invite the Bookseller too. We have to meet him on this side of eternity."

Varvel was off, and the Iranian brothers began to thank God again.

"They have no idea what God has planned for them here or for their country," Niger said, turning to the forces of light gathered there. "The Spirit has already been issuing instructions. I would expect cell phones to ring soon, but we need to be off." They left to do exactly what Hushai had discerned. Tonight's assignment was to share in the joy of the Lord with faithful groups gathered all around the earth in response to President Strong's call for thanksgiving.

Joy and Thanksgiving

In Williams, the scene of so many of the events preceding the past few days, many groups gathered to express their thanks. The change in people was obvious. The largest group was at College Church, where the blood-stained carpet remained as did the memory of that day and the funeral of Susan Stafford. The Bookseller and Margaret were present with Paul and Samantha, Sally Johnson and the still recovering Tom Campy. Saul Greenfield came, as did Sam Will, still in a wheelchair, with a group of his trucking buddies. The gathering was presided over by Pastor Scribes, who understood that this night was a night for everyone to share thanksgiving, not for him to speak. So, once again, he was silent.

Across the street and up several blocks, Chaplain Forrest marveled as the students filled the Williams College chapel, flooding the night with prayers of thanksgiving. Like those gathered in College Church, there was an overwhelming sense of joy and hope which filled the buildings as if a blanket of clouds had descended. Chaplain Forrest was actually the most thankful for the change that he knew had taken place in his own heart. Now he would truly be able to shepherd these kids who would one day lead others.

Down the road and across the railroad tracks, parents gathered with teachers and kids at Kingdom Daycare to remember their day of deliverance and be thankful. Parents still wondered how one who had killed and terrorized the community for all that time had been transformed into someone who would give her life for a child.

Pastor Wilson and his congregation rejoiced that they had been able to be useful in the review of the prayer website emails and in how God had directed them to pray. They too experienced the joy of which Hushai had spoken on the other side of the world.

In Washington, it was also a joyful moment as the president and Janet gathered in the East Room with those who had walked together through these difficult times. He had chosen the East Room, for this was the place where his own choice had been made. It had become special—holy, even— as the place of prayer in Iran.

Those who gathered with him understood better than any how much they had to be thankful for this night, and how much had occurred that could not be explained in the physical. Present by invitation were Vice President Marshall, David Barnes and Kayla Walker, Darrell Reed a.k.a "the geek," Tom Knight, Troy Steed, Director Jackson, Attorney General Rodriquez, Senator Besserman, Director Hollister, Secretary of State

Wisdom, Director Crenshaw, George Murphy, General Hedge, and the other members of the Survival Commission.

Also present, but this time without cameras, were ITN Producer Carl Stern and the film crew that accompanied the president on the journey to Iceland.

It was a time of remembrance in prayer as thanksgiving was raised by each in attendance for the impossible which God had obviously made possible. No one doubted the obvious; God had chosen to deliver America from an event which would have crippled the nation for decades.

The unseen gathering rejoiced with those in the flesh, and the joy of the Lord was present in all its fullness. The light in that room could be seen from the throne in Heaven.

Later in the privacy of their personal quarters, the president asked Janet, "Did you notice that everyone seemed to have the same question? 'What next?'"

"I did," she replied. "Why didn't you open the floor to talk about that after we finished praying? Frankly, I was surprised."

"Because no one really knows beyond what God has already revealed," he answered. "I think I have learned from this that if I truly want to be within God's will for myself and the nation, I can't think too far down the road. I have to wait for God to reveal what it is I am to do, and that will be when He wants me to do it.

"I remember a story Corrie Ten Boom used to tell about when she was a little girl. She asked her father how God would help her to deal with what would be impossible for her in the future. Her father wisely reminded her of what happened when they took a trip into town on the train. 'When do I give you the ticket?' he asked the child, Corrie.

"'Right before we get on the train,' she answered.

"'That's right,' her father responded, 'and that is when God will give you what you need, right when you need it.'

"I expect that is when we will know, and not a moment sooner."

Unexpected

Elsewhere, others who had been involved in these events had also made their way into churches to express their thanks. Some were expected, such as Juan Martinez in Carmen, Arizona or Jason Wilson who stopped in Tulsa, Oklahoma on a cross-country trip to Los Angeles. Others surprisingly slipped into churches, compelled but embarrassed. Two such people were Harkins Professor Larry Trice in Cambridge, Massachusetts, and former President Leonard Cox, who sat for a long time alone on the back row of the National Cathedral in Washington, simply thankful to be alive.

Later having observed the unexpected duo, Barnabas asked, "New searchers?"

"Perhaps," Lucius answered. "Nothing is impossible with God," and they smiled knowingly, waiting for their next assignment.

Simultaneously, back in Williams, having just completed dinner in their warehouse apartment, the Bookseller smiled at Paul and Samantha as he reached for his Bible and removed the carefully folded sheet of paper which contained the questions they had given him when their journey began. "I believe it's time," he said, and together they commenced to work through the list.

ENDNOTES

1. John 5:18
2. Matthew 10:34-36
3. Matthew 4:1-11
4. Acts 2:1-12
5. Numbers 12:3
6. 1 Samuel 16:1-13
7. Acts 13:22
8. John 10:27
9. Romans 6:23
10. Acts 22:4, 1 Timothy 1:15-16, Acts 9:10-16
11. Romans 10:9-10
12. Daniel 9:4-6
13. Daniel 9:17-19
14. 2 Corinthians 5:17
15. Luke 23:36
16. John 15:18-21
17. John 16:2b-4
18. John 17:14, 18
19. 2 Timothy 3:12
20. Revelation 12:17
21. John 14:1-3
22. Luke 22:17-20
23. Luke 1:37
24. 2 Kings 22:8-20
25. 2 Kings 23:25-27
26. Exodus 21:23-25

27	Matthew 7:3-5
28	Matthew 24:3, 36
29	Matthew 24:44
30	Luke 21:36
31	Matthew 24:45-51
32	John 10:27; Luke 6:46
33	Luke 12:48b
34	Philippians 4:6-7
35	1 John 5:14-15
36	Mark 10:27; Luke 1:37
37	Matthew 26:36-38
38	Genesis 2:5-8
39	Jeremiah 23:18, 22
40	Deuteronomy 28:1
41	Deuteronomy 28:7
42	Deuteronomy 28:15
43	Deuteronomy 28:66-67
44	Daniel 9:10-11
45	Daniel 9:14-15
46	Ezra 1:1-4
47	Nehemiah 2:1-8
48	Isaiah 6:5
49	Isaiah 6:6-8
50	Matthew 6:9-13
51	James 4:8
52	Matthew 7:7
53	Revelation 3:20
54	Matthew 10:34-39
55	Jeremiah 29:13
56	Acts 2:1-11
57	Isaiah 6:8
58	Nehemiah 8:10
59	John 8:44
60	John 4:1-11
61	2 Corinthians 11:14
62	Matthew 1:20-25; Matthew 2:13-15, 19-23

63	Matthew 24:24
64	Numbers 22:22-35
65	Joshua 5:13 – 6:5
66	Revelation 19:11-16
67	Revelation 1:12-16
68	Matthew 26:36-38; Mark 14:32-34
69	Acts 9:31
70	Ester 4:9-17
71	2 Chronicles 18:1 – 19:3
72	Ephesians 6:10-12
73	Revelation 12:7-9
74	Matthew 25:41; Matthew 8:29
75	Revelation 20:14-15; Romans 5:9
76	Luke 19:41-44
77	2 Peter 3:9
78	John 3:16
79	Luke 4:1-13
80	Romans 11:25-29
81	Acts 9:1-19
82	Matthew 5:21-22
83	Matthew 15:19
84	Jeremiah 23:18, 21-22
85	Luke 24:44-49; Acts 1:8
86	Romans 13:1-4
87	1 Peter 1:18-20; Revelation 13:8
88	Isaiah 53:5-12; Matthew 27:1-61; Luke 23; John 19
89	1 John 1:7
90	John 3:18; John 8:24; Mark 16:16
91	Acts 22:1-5
92	Acts 22:6-21
93	Acts 4:18-20
94	John 10:27
95	Luke 6:42
96	Romans 1:26-32; Galatians 5:19-21; Revelation 21:8 (for sins not forgiven)
97	Ephesians 5:11

98	Matthew 18:6
99	Revelation 20:11-15
100	Acts 4:18-20
101	Matthew 28:19-20
102	Romans 13:1-4
103	Luke 4:13
104	Revelation 12:17
105	Acts 13:22
106	2 Samuel 12:7-14
107	Mark 5:1-13
108	John 10:27
109	2 Chronicles 15:1-2
110	Luke 9:23
111	John 16:33
112	Genesis 1:26-27
113	2 Kings 16:1-3
114	Hebrews 10:10-18
115	Hebrews 9:27; Revelation 20:11-15
116	Luke 10:1-12
117	Luke 10:17-21
118	Nehemiah 8:10

www.ingramcontent.com/pod-product-compliance
Lightning Source LLC
LaVergne TN
LVHW091530060526
838200LV00036B/553